PENGUIN 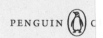 C

T0201048

RUSSIAN MAGIC TALES FROM PUSHKIN TO PLATONOV

ROBERT CHANDLER has translated Sappho and Guillaume Apollinaire for Everyman's Poetry. His translations from Russian include Aleksandr Pushkin's *Dubrovsky* and *The Captain's Daughter*, Nikolay Leskov's *Lady Macbeth of Mtsensk* and Vasily Grossman's *Life and Fate* and *The Road*. With his wife Elizabeth and other colleagues he has co-translated numerous works by Andrey Platonov; *Soul* won the 2004 American Association of Teachers of Slavic and East European Languages award for best translation from a Slavonic language, as did his translation of *The Railway* by the contemporary Uzbek novelist Hamid Ismailov. His *Russian Short Stories from Pushkin to Buida* is published in Penguin Classics.

ELIZABETH CHANDLER is a co-translator, with her husband, of Pushkin's *The Captain's Daughter* and of several titles by Andrey Platonov and Vasily Grossman.

PROFESSOR SIBELAN FORRESTER teaches at Swarthmore College, Pennsylvania. Her broad range of interests include Russian folklore, the poetry of Marina Tsvetaeva and Russian Women's Writing. She has translated many books – both poetry and prose – from Croatian, Russian and Serbian. Wayne State University Press will soon be publishing her translation of Vladimir Propp's *The Russian Folktale*.

ANNA GUNIN has translated *I am a Chechen!* by German Sadulaev and *The Sky Wept Fire* by Mikail Eldin. She is now translating a complete edition of Varlam Shalamov's *Kolyma Tales* for Penguin Classics.

PROFESSOR OLGA MEERSON teaches at Georgetown University and is the author of books about Dostoevsky, Platonov and Russian poetry. She is a co-translator, with Robert and Elizabeth Chandler, of Andrey Platonov's *Soul* and *The Foundation Pit*.

Russian Magic Tales from Pushkin to Platonov

Translated by ROBERT CHANDLER
and ELIZABETH CHANDLER
with SIBELAN FORRESTER, ANNA GUNIN
and OLGA MEERSON

Introduced by
ROBERT CHANDLER
with an Appendix by
SIBELAN FORRESTER

PENGUIN BOOKS

PENGUIN CLASSICS

Published by the Penguin Group
Penguin Books Ltd, 80 Strand, London WC2R 0RL, England
Penguin Group (USA) Inc., 375 Hudson Street, New York, New York 10014, USA
Penguin Group (Canada), 90 Eglinton Avenue East, Suite 700, Toronto, Ontario, Canada M4P 2Y3
(a division of Pearson Penguin Canada Inc.)
Penguin Ireland, 25 St Stephen's Green, Dublin 2, Ireland (a division of Penguin Books Ltd)
Penguin Group (Australia), 707 Collins Street, Melbourne, Victoria 3008, Australia
(a division of Pearson Australia Group Pty Ltd)
Penguin Books India Pvt Ltd, 11 Community Centre, Panchsheel Park, New Delhi – 110 017, India
Penguin Group (NZ), 67 Apollo Drive, Rosedale, Auckland 0632, New Zealand
(a division of Pearson New Zealand Ltd)
Penguin Books (South Africa) (Pty) Ltd, Block D, Rosebank Office Park,
181 Jan Smuts Avenue, Parktown North, Gauteng 2193, South Africa

Penguin Books Ltd, Registered Offices: 80 Strand, London WC2R 0RL, England

www.penguin.com

This collection first published in Penguin Classics 2012

020

Copyright for stories by Bazhov © The Bazhov estate, 2012
Copyright for stories by Platonov © The Platonov estate, 2012
Copyright for stories by Teffi © Mme Szyòlowski, 2012
Appendix and translation of stories by Khudyakov © Sibelan Forrester, 2012
Translation of stories by Bazhov © Anna Gunin, 2012
Translation of all other stories and editorial material © Robert Chandler, 2012

The Acknowledgements (pp. 439–40) constitute an extension of this copyright page

Set in 10.25/12.25pt PostScript Adobe Sabon
Typeset by Jouve (UK), Milton Keynes
Printed in Great Britain by Clays Ltd, Elcograf S.p.A

ISBN: 978-0-141-44223-5

www.greenpenguin.co.uk

Contents

PART THREE

EARLY TWENTIETH-CENTURY

COLLECTIONS

PART FOUR

PART FIVE

PART SIX

FOLKTALE COLLECTIONS FROM
THE SOVIET PERIOD

PART SEVEN

Introduction

The hero has one clear, linear task. At the end of it lies his reward, usually a princess. While accomplishing the task, he encounters various helpers, whose gifts or services are all palpably material. Helpers and obstacles appear from nowhere and disappear without a trace; a dark void opens up on either side of the narrow path of the plot. Whatever is on that path, however, is lit up in brilliant primary colours: metallic reds, golds, blues. Throughout his travails the hero expresses no astonishment, curiosity, longing, or fear, and apparently does not experience pain. He never reassesses his goal or his reward.

Caryl Emerson, *The Cambridge Introduction to Russian Literature*

Off he went towards the blue sea.
(The blue sea was blacker than black.)
He called out to the golden fish . . .

Aleksandr Pushkin, from 'A Tale about a Fisherman and a Fish'

I used to be Snow White, but I drifted . . .

Mae West

The magic tale – also often called the 'wonder tale' or 'fairy tale' – is remarkably adaptable. Transformation is its central theme, and the tales themselves seem capable of almost infinite transformation. In one Russian version of the Cinderella story the heroine is helped by a doll; in another Russian version she is helped by a cow; and in a written version from seventh-century China she is helped by a fish. In different versions of 'Beauty and the Beast', the heroine marries a serpent, a white bear, a falcon and – in an English version recorded in the 1890s – 'a great, foul, small-tooth dog'. And what is essentially the same tale can find a home for itself in a Walt Disney film, in a Russian peasant hut, within the sophisticated framework of *The Arabian Nights*, or in the nurseries of well-brought-up Victorian children.

This adaptability, however, has obscured our understanding of these tales. What have become by far the best-known versions are those derived from Charles Perrault's *Tales of Mother Goose*, which was first published in 1697. It was Perrault who established the fairy tale as a literary genre and he intended his versions for the children of the French upper and middle classes. And in 1812 the Brothers Grimm chose to follow Perrault, entitling their famous collection *Children's and Household Tales*. The oral magic tale, however, is often violent, scatological and sexually explicit. It is probable that its origin lies in archaic rituals, that it was seen as endowed with occult power and that there were strict conditions as to when, where, how and by whom it could be told. Such taboos survived longer in Russia than in most European countries; according to the American scholar Jack Haney, many storytellers in the far north of European Russia observed strict taboos as late as the 1930s; tales could be told only by men, to male audiences, after dark, and never during the main Orthodox fasts. The underlying reason for these taboos was the belief that spirits of all kinds enjoyed listening to tales. At night and in winter, when a peasant's animals were safely shut up, spirits presented less of a danger. When the animals were out in the fields, however, spirits might come and steal them – and in spring and early summer they might steal the animals' young.[1] Haney's view is that women storytellers first appeared in Russia only in the early nineteenth century.[2] This is impossible to establish with certainty, but Haney's broader point remains incontrovertible: the tales were not to be told lightly.

Magic tales are perhaps easier to recognize than to define. Most involve some kind of quest – often into the underground realm of a dangerous witch; this may be like a vestige of some shamanic initiation rite. Often the hero is able to achieve his goal only thanks to the wisdom and practical help provided by birds, fish or other creatures whom he has helped earlier in the tale; this, too, is reminiscent of a shaman calling on his spirit helpers. Sometimes the hero is transformed from bird or animal to human, or vice versa; sometimes he is cut to pieces, then put together again. Just as all initiation rites involve some kind of transformation and/or symbolic dismemberment, so do all magic tales.

One of the first scholars to articulate these understandings was the Soviet folklorist Vladimir Propp, in his *Historical Roots of the Wonder Tale* (first published as long ago as 1946 but still not translated into English in full).[3] Propp's view was that participants were prepared for an initiation ritual by being given some indication of what they were about to undergo. The rituals eventually ceased to be practised, but the accounts – or metaphorical accounts – of their content went on being told and eventually took on a life of their own, as 'magic tales'.[4] Propp's theories may, of course, be too absolute, and there is no reason to suppose that all magic tales have the same origin.[5] Nevertheless, it is not difficult to see that many magic tales do indeed reflect traditional rites of passage. A clear example from the present volume is 'Mishka the Bear and Myshka the Mouse'. A girl is sent out into the forest by a cruel stepmother. She is required to play blindman's bluff with a murderous bear; a mouse, however, takes the girl's place, leaping around the hut from bench to floor and back up onto the bench again. Eventually the bear admits defeat and rewards the girl. This motif is reminiscent of the 'search for the bride' that, in some regions of Russia, still remains a part of peasant weddings. It closely parallels an anonymous account of a mid nineteenth-century peasant wedding: 'The guests began to chant to the bride, "Do not go, our child; do not go, our dear Annushka, along your father's benches; do not leap, do not leap; don't play about [. . .]; jump, jump into your [wedding] tunic." To which the bride replied, "If I want to, I'll jump; if I don't, I won't." [6] And in some parts of Russia the groom and bride were known as 'the he-bear' and 'the she-bear'.

'The Tsarevna who would not Laugh' affords a still more striking example of the link between the magic tale and archaic rituals. Afanasyev's version (p. 70) begins with the tsarevna sitting miserably in her room, unable to laugh or take any joy in life. Her father promises her in marriage to whoever first makes her laugh. A peasant has been working hard for three years, making his master's crops grow and his animals multiply even in the most unpropitious conditions. While on his way to the city, this peasant shows kindness to a mouse, a beetle and a catfish. He then falls down in the mud outside the tsar's palace. The three creatures appear and express their gratitude to him by cleaning him up. The tsarevna sees all this from her window and laughs. A rival tries to take the credit for her laughter, but the tsarevna points to the peasant and says that it was he who made her laugh. The tsarevna then marries the peasant. Propp relates this tale to the Eleusinian mysteries and the myth of Demeter, one of whose titles was 'the unlaughing one' (*agelastos*). Citing evidence from many different cultures, he establishes that laughter was once credited with the power to evoke life and – after the beginning of agriculture – with the power to bring fertility to crops. Then he summarizes the story of how Demeter, in mourning for her lost daughter, subjected the earth to months of famine. The famine ended only when an old woman by the name of Baubo lifted her skirt and exposed herself to Demeter; this made Demeter laugh – and the earth then regained her fertility. Demeter and Afanasyev's tsarevna are evidently one and the same figure; the tsarevna must be made to laugh in order for the crops to grow.

In the same context, Propp discusses another tale (not included here) in which the tsar promises his daughter not to whoever can make her laugh, but to whoever can say what birthmarks she has on her body. A peasant with miraculous power over animals (in a version published in 1915 by Dmitry Zelenin he is accompanied by dancing pigs,[7] while in 'The Herder of Hares' (p. 304) he has power over hares) sells her three of his animals on condition she expose herself to him. He then tells the tsar that his daughter has a golden hair to the right of her groin and a birthmark under her right breast. The peasant discredits an aristocratic rival by tricking him into smearing himself with his own shit, then marries the tsarevna. The Demeter myth and the two Russian tales are evidently different arrangements of the same constituent elements. The association of hares with fertility is universal and, since Baubo was married to a swineherd, the dancing pigs are no less closely linked to the theme of Demeter and the earth's fertility.[8] And there is, of course, no fertility without manure. In Afanasyev's tale it is the hero who falls into the mud, while in Zelenin's it is the hero's rival who ends up smeared with shit. As so often, what is important in a magic tale is the presence of a particular motif; which character is associated with it seems to be of only secondary importance.

In Russia, Propp is best known for his *Historical Roots of the Wonder Tale*. In the English-speaking world, however, he is best known for an earlier study, *The Morphology of the Folktale*. At first glance, this almost-mathematical analysis of the structure of magic tales may seem like the work of a different writer. These two studies, however, were originally conceived as a single book, and there is a clear link between them. In *The Morphology of the Folktale*, Propp establishes that all magic tales share a common structure; only then can he go on, in *Historical Roots of the Wonder Tale*, to show how this common structure mirrors the structure of initiation rites. Propp himself has provided the best summary of his understandings and how he first came to them:

In a series of wonder tales about the persecuted stepdaughter I noted an interesting fact: in 'Jack Frost' [p. 300] the old woman sends her stepdaughter into the forest to Jack Frost. He tries to freeze her to death, but she speaks to him so sweetly and so humbly that he spares her, gives her a reward, and lets her go. The old woman's daughter, however, fails the test and perishes. In another tale the stepdaughter encounters not Jack Frost but a forest spirit, in still another, a bear. But surely it is the same tale! Jack Frost, the forest spirit and the bear test the stepdaughter and reward her each in his own way, but the plot does not change. [...] To Afanasyev, these were different tales because they contained different characters. To me they were identical because the actions of the characters were the same. [...] I devised a very simple method of analyzing wonder tales in accordance with the characters' actions – regardless of the shape these actions took. To designate these actions I adopted the term 'functions'. [...] It turned out [...] that all wonder tale plots consisted of identical functions and had identical structures.[9]

Soviet folklorists collected a vast number of tales and made a still undervalued contribution to our historical understanding of them, but they said little about why these tales should still hold our interest. In Europe and the United States, however, a great deal has been written about the psychological and moral truths concealed in these seemingly primitive tales. Carl Jung and his colleague Marie-Louise von Franz look on magic tales as illustrations of universal patterns of psychological maturation and the obstacles that stand in its way. Often they see these tales as expressing values, or giving a place to images, that are compensatory to the dominant values and images of a particular culture; they see the image of the folktale witch, for example, as a necessary balance to the image of the Virgin Mary. The Freudian analyst Bruno Bettelheim, in *The Uses of Enchantment*, also sees magic tales as illustrating universal patterns, though he focuses more exclusively on the transitions of childhood and adolescence. These psychological approaches to the magic tale complement – but do not in any way contradict – Propp's historical and structural analyses. Jung did not have the opportunity to read Propp, but he would have valued Propp's elaboration of the parallels between magic tales and archaic rituals; he himself saw both tales and rituals – along with dreams, alchemical texts and accounts of religious practices of every kind – as a guide to the innermost structure of the psyche.

The magic tale usually says little or nothing about the emotions experienced by a hero or heroine; situations and actions are left to speak for themselves. It is, no doubt, frightening to be approached in the forest by Jack Frost, but the storyteller's reticence leaves the listener or reader free to sense this fear as much or as little as they choose. This is part of what lends these tales so universal an appeal. Every transition in life – from childhood to adolescence, from adolescence to adulthood, from being single to being married – is frightening. The magic tale speaks of these transitions succinctly, vividly and in a language that can be understood by all of us.

It is generally thought that the magic tale did not fully acquire its present shape until the early medieval period. Nevertheless, something similar to the European oral magic tale can be found in many of the earliest works of written literature, and in many different parts of the world. Versions of several of the tales in this collection can be found in the *Mahabharata*, the Sanskrit epic from ancient India. The earliest written version of 'Beauty and the Beast' – the story of Amor and Psyche – is included in Apuleius's *The Golden Ass*, written in Latin in the second century of the Common Era. In these and similar instances, there is little doubt that the written text draws on an earlier oral version. It is equally clear, however, that the written text then influenced subsequent oral versions. Since literature was first written down, there has always been interplay between written and oral texts.

The magic tale, as we have seen, is remarkable both for its stability and for its fluidity. The central plots of most tales – what folklorists refer to as 'the tale-type' – vary little from country to country. What changes are the surface details, the ways in which the tales reflect different social, climatic and geographical realities. There are also differences of emphasis. The magic tales of all European countries, for example, include dangerous witches, but the image of Baba Yaga – the archetypal Russian witch – is especially vivid and well developed. Baba Yaga appears in many of the stories in this collection, and the American scholar Sibelan Forrester discusses her at length in an article we have included as an appendix.[10]

The Russian magic tale stands out in at least one other respect.

Russia's vastness, and her backwardness compared with other European countries, meant that there was a much longer period during which it was possible for folklorists to study a relatively intact peasant culture. In many European countries, scholars began recording folklore only after industrialization was well under way; in Russia, by contrast, an entire century passed between Pushkin's first transcriptions of folktales and the assault on the peasantry constituted by Stalin's collectivization of agriculture. We cannot be certain how folktales were told four or five hundred years ago, but we do know that they were enjoyed by members of *all* social classes until the late eighteenth century. And we have reliable and detailed accounts of the social setting in which tales were told in the north of European Russia in the late nineteenth and early twentieth centuries. Here, for example, is an account by the brothers Boris and Yury Sokolov of what they call 'the local conditions of the life of the tale' in the Belozersk region in 1908–9:

Here the tale lives a full life. [...] The development and life of the tale in the places where we were collecting is greatly influenced by the nature of the peasants' work. First, there is tree felling: often an entire village – men, women and children – is gathered together deep in the forest, in winter and far from any habitation. The day is taken up by heavy work but, as soon as it turns dark, everyone enjoys a well-earned rest by a blazing hearth. There in the forest they have constructed a 'camp'; that is, a spacious hut dug into the earth with a hearth in the middle. Everyone crowds inside. And once they have warmed their frozen limbs and satisfied their hunger and thirst, they begin to while away the long winter evening. How glad they are then to see the storyteller! Deep in the forest, amid trees letting out loud cracks in the extreme cold, to the accompaniment of the howls of wolves and beside a blazing fire – what more appropriate setting, what richer soil could there be for a magic tale filled with every possible terror! [...] Then comes the jester, the teller of funny stories. Witticisms and mocking jibes pour out as if from a horn of plenty. The entire audience is attuned to joy and merriment. An unbroken stream of enthusiastic exclamations encourages the jester in his

merry wit. Had it been possible to write down the tales with absolute stenographic exactitude, recording on paper every exclamation from the public, there is no doubt that our transcripts would
create a far livelier and fresher impression. [...]

Just as 'collective' life in the forest camp creates supportive
conditions for the life of the folktale, so does fishing in the
region's lakes. The fishermen go out onto these lakes for long
periods of time. After they have cast their nets, or while they are
waiting for a following wind, they often have to sit through long
hours of forced inactivity – and this makes them particularly well
disposed towards storytellers. There was an occasion when the
fishermen took advantage of our presence. They joined us in the
hut where we were recording tales, listened to the different storytellers and then concluded a kind of bargain with the teller they
liked most, promising him a certain proportion of the catch if he
would go out onto the lake with them.

Yet another supportive environment for stories of every kind
is the mill – a peculiar kind of rural club. Large numbers of peasants gather there and sometimes they have to spend several days
there as they wait for their turn. Here too there is no better way
to while away the time than telling tales. The diffusion of tales is
also greatly helped by people who have to travel from place to
place in the course of their work, people who have the opportunity to see a great deal and to listen a great deal – people like 'icon
daubers', tailors, soldiers, beggars and other wanderers.[11]

Russian high culture, at least from the late eighteenth century,
has been as sophisticated as that of any country in Europe.
Until recently, however, most of the inhabitants of Russia were
peasants – and until the emancipation of the serfs in 1861 the
government's intermittent moves towards modernization had
barely affected their way of life. The imperial capital, St Petersburg, was an island of avowedly Western culture surrounded
by a world as Asian as it was European. Even the most Western-
oriented of nineteenth-century Russian writers could not help
but be more familiar with folk ways and folk literature than
their contemporaries in other parts of Europe. It is, indeed,
often difficult to understand much of Russian literature without

some knowledge of folklore.[12] Because, in Russia, there has always been such a close link between the written and oral traditions, we have included in this volume not only translations of anonymous magic tales, as recorded by a number of nineteenth- and twentieth-century folklorists, but also versions of these magic tales by four great Russian writers: Aleksandr Pushkin, Nadezhda Teffi, Pavel Bazhov and Andrey Platonov.

Andrey Platonov once described Aleksandr Pushkin as being one of a very few writers endowed with the ability 'to enrich and inform a popular folktale with the power of [his] own creativity and endow it with the definitive, ideal combination of meaning and form that will allow this tale to continue to exist for a long time or forever'. My aim has been to include only those literary retellings to which these words seem applicable. Lev Tolstoy's versions are omitted because they are moral fables rather than magic tales. I have omitted Aleksey Tolstoy's well-known versions from the mid 1940s because they are no more than competent paraphrases of Afanasyev; Aleksey Tolstoy has not informed them 'with the power of his own creativity'. I hesitated for longer over Boris Shergin. The baroque energy of his language is attractive, but in the end I came to feel that it is a surface overlay; he has not, like Platonov, entered deep into the heart of a tradition and then created afresh. I have omitted Pyotr Yershov and Marina Tsvetaeva for a different reason; their verse tales are so brilliant that they seem all-but impossible to translate.[13] Lastly, I have excluded literary fairy tales with little relation to the folk tradition; this meant omitting Pogorelsky from the nineteenth century and many important representatives of Russia's Silver Age.

As for the oral tales, reading all the published Russian collections might take five years, and reading all the archival material – a lifetime. And the more one reads, the harder the task of selection. An element of randomness seems inescapable. All I can say is that I have listened out for the vivid image, the flash of wit, or the compelling rhythmic structure that can make one version of a well-known story more memorable than another. I have tried to give a sense both of the variety of different tale-types and of the no less remarkable variety that can often be found within a single tale-type. And I have included as much material as possible that allows us a glimpse of the individuality of the storytellers.

To the best of our ability, my co-translators and I have translated accurately. When we have taken liberties with the meaning in order to reproduce a rhyme, we have included a literal translation in the notes. We have kept the language clear, colloquial and energetic, but we have not tried to reproduce the peasant dialect of many of the originals; contemporary English is too far removed from any peasant culture for this to be possible. We have not ironed out the logical hiccups or sudden jumps that are typical of oral storytelling. Nor have we imposed any false stylistic consistency; the tales were told by many different tellers to several different collectors, each of whom tried in his or her own way to reproduce their tone and rhythms. And the tales were recorded over a long period – from the early nineteenth century to the middle of the twentieth century – during which two somewhat contradictory tendencies were at work; folk traditions were dying out, but folklorists were being ever more precise in their ways of recording them.

I am grateful to Sibelan Forrester for allowing me to include an abridged version of her article about Baba Yaga. The complete version is included in *Baba Yaga: The Wild Witch of the East in Russian Folklore*. And I am especially grateful to Jack Haney for his generous help and enlightening correspondence. Readers in search of a more comprehensive collection of Russian oral folktales should turn at once to his seven-volume *Complete Russian Folktale*.

Robert Chandler, July 2011

NOTES

The A-T numbers refer to the comprehensive index of folktales begun by the Finnish folklorist Antti Aarne and further developed by Stith Thompson. The standard Russian index, the *Comparative Index of Types: The East Slavic Tale* (Barag *et al.*, 1979), often referred to as SUS after the initial letters of its Russian title, uses the same numbers.

The A-T index has recently been further revised. See Hans-Jörg Uther, *The Types of International Folktales: A Classification and Bibliography*, 3 vols. (FF Communications No. 284. Helsinki: Suomalainen Tiedeakatemia, 2004). Intimidating as these indices may seem, they are indispensable to anyone wishing to compare variants of a particular tale-type from different cultures.

The most comprehensive collection of Russian folktales in English is the seven-volume *The Complete Russian Folktale* by Jack Haney. In these notes I refer to this collection in two different ways. A parenthesis, as in '(Haney 290)', indicates that Haney, too, has translated the tale in question and that it appears in his collection as no. 290; where I have used the words 'see also', as in 'see also Haney 270', this indicates that Haney has translated a different variant of this tale-type.

I have used the following abbreviations: 'Af.' for Afanasyev, *Narodnye russkiye skazki*; 'Zelenin, *Vyat.*' for D. K. Zelenin, *Veliko-russkiye skazki Vyatskoy gubernii*; 'Haney, *Complete*' for Haney, *The Complete Russian Folktale*; 'Haney, *Intro.*' for Haney, *An Introduction to the Russian Folktale*. I give chapter, rather than page, references to Sibelan Forrester's translation of Propp's *The Russian Folktale*, since this is only now being prepared for publication. In any cases where further publication details are needed, the reader should refer to the Bibliography.

1. See D. K. Zelenin, 'Religiozno-magicheskaya funktsiya fol'k-lornykh skazok' in Yu. Krachkovsky, *Sergeyu Ol'denburgu. Sbornik statey* (Leningrad, 1934), pp. 215–40.

2. Haney, *Complete*, vol. 3, p. xxxviii. The Hungarian scholar Linda Degh also sees men 'as the storytellers among European peoples' (*Folktales and Society*, pp. 91–3). Propp has written, 'According to Irina Karnaukhova's observations, almost every woman tells folktales, while among men not everyone tells them. However, if a man does know folktales, he knows more of them than women do, and men's repertoire is richer, since they leave home in the wandering trades, enriching their repertoire, while women rarely leave the boundaries of their home areas' (*The Russian Folktale*, chapter 7). According to Jack Zipes, the nineteenth-century Sicilian folklorist Salvatore Salomone-Marino 'reports that there were specific occasions like sowing and harvesting when men would also tell the stories. Within the family, however, the prominent storytellers were women, which is why women also figure predominantly as the narrators in the dialect collections of Pitrè and Salomone-Marino and in Gonzenbach's book' (*Beautiful*

Angiola, Routledge, 2003), pp. xvii–xviii. Most of the main Russian collections were recorded from male narrators, but this may simply reflect the fact that most early Russian folklorists were male and it was hard for them to win the trust of peasant women.

3. Propp's understandings were anticipated by the Belgian folklorist Arnold van Gennep, in his *Les rites de passage* (1909).

4. See Anatoly Liberman's introduction to Vladimir Propp, *Theory and History of Folklore*, p. lxvii.

5. The most important of the criticisms made of Propp is that he seems to assume that all cultures, throughout the world, pass through identical stages.

6. This discussion is summarized from Haney, *Intro.*, pp. 58–9 and p. 117, note 7.

7. 'Ivanushko-durachok', Zelenin, *Vyat.*, p. 91.

8. And in Zelenin's tale, the peasant buys the pigs from a ploughman; the pigs were following him down the furrow he was ploughing.

9. Propp, *ibid.*, p. 69 (translation adapted by R.C.).

10. A longer version of this serves as an introduction to a forthcoming collection of tales about Baba Yaga: Sibelan Forrester, Helena Goscilo and Martin Skoro, *Baba Yaga: The Wild Witch of the East in Russian Folklore*.

11. Sokolov, *Russky fol'klor*, pp. 306–7.

12. The American Slavist Linda Ivanits writes in the preface to her excellent *Russian Folk Belief* that this mini-encyclopaedia of Russian folklore began as a set of background notes for the students on her Dostoevsky course.

13. Though Angela Livingstone's translation of *The Ratcatcher* (Tsvetaeva's retelling of the Pied Piper legend) is one of the finest translations into English of any Russian poetry.

Russian Magic Tales
from Pushkin to Platonov

PART ONE

ALEKSANDR SERGEYEVICH PUSHKIN

(1799–1837)

Aleksandr Pushkin composed the first significant works in a great variety of literary genres. He was also the first Russian poet to pay serious attention to the folktale or skazka.

Our first clear evidence of Pushkin's interest in folklore is from his period in exile in Mikhailovskoye, his mother's family estate in northern Russia. The person he saw most during these two years of isolation was Arina Rodionovna, a household serf who had once been his nurse and who always remained something of a mother to him. In 1824, in a letter to his brother Lev, Pushkin described how in the evenings he would listen to Arina Rodionovna telling folktales: 'I thus compensate for the short-comings in my cursed upbringing. How charming these tales are! Each one is a whole poem . . .'[1] According to Jack Haney, the versions of these tales that Pushkin recorded are 'the oldest surviving versions of tales in Russian taken down from popular storytellers in something akin to the popular language'.[2] These versions are concise summaries rather than transcripts, but Pushkin reproduces both the tales' rhythmic structure and the vividness of the language. Pushkin's grasp of the language of folk poetry and folktale seems to have been nearly perfect; he once gave Pyotr Kireyevsky (Vasily Zhukovsky's great-nephew) a file containing his own imitations of folksongs together with genuine folksongs that he had transcribed, challenging Kireyevsky to figure out which were which. Kireyevsky – an acknowledged authority in this field – was unable to do this.

Pushkin's attitude towards folk literature was respectful. He did not see it merely as a source of raw material to exploit, but he seems to have understood that a verbatim transcription is not always enough to convey its power and vitality. As if to compensate for the loss of the immediacy of living speech, he composed all his own skazki *in verse, and their rhythmic energy is one of their most striking features. Pushkin's* skazki *(the Russian word can be applied both to true folktales and to literary adaptations) have always been popular with children, and illustrated editions continue to be published in large print-runs. They have also inspired paintings and provided librettos for operas. Rimsky-Korsakov composed operas based on 'The Tale of Tsar Saltan' and 'The Golden Cockerel', and Shostakovich wrote the music for a never-completed cartoon film based on 'A Tale about a Priest and his Servant Balda'.*

Pushkin seldom, if ever, repeats himself, and his six skazki *differ greatly from one another. For this collection I have chosen the two that are most obviously Russian in both style and content. 'A Tale about a Priest and his Servant Balda' is based on one of the tales Pushkin recorded from Arina Rodionovna. The deftness with which he reproduces folktale rhythms, images and turns of phrase is remarkable; many of his most brilliant inventions are now often taken for genuine traditional sayings. Pushkin wrote this* skazka *in September 1830, during the first of his astonishingly creative 'Boldino autumns', when he was confined – because of quarantine restrictions due to a cholera epidemic – to his father's remote estate in southeastern Russia. Only the previous day he had written the short poem 'Demons' – the vision of evil from which Dostoevsky took the title of one of his greatest novels. It is clear from Pushkin's manuscript that 'Demons' was first conceived as something lighter and more comic; a darker vision – of swarms of snowflakes as swarms of demons – seems to have imposed itself on him almost against his will. 'A Tale about a Priest and his Servant Balda' seems to have been Pushkin's counterspell, an attempt to laugh off this dark vision, to ridicule these terrifying demons. Some lines from the manuscript of 'Demons' (e.g. the description of the 'devillet' as mewing like a hungry kitten) ended up almost unchanged in the* skazka.[3]

'A Tale about a Fisherman and a Fish' was written three years later, in October 1833, during the second of Pushkin's 'Boldino autumns'. Pushkin's immediate source was the Brothers

Grimm, but this would be hard to guess. Not only do the rhythms and images seem completely Russian, but the tale also reflects Pushkin's concern with Russian history. Pushkin's greatest achievement of these months was the narrative poem 'The Bronze Horseman', which is devoted to the figure of Peter the Great; but he also wrote several works relating to Catherine the Great. As well as composing the whole of his short story 'The Queen of Spades', which includes reminiscences of her reign, he completed the final draft of 'A History of Pugachov', a historical account of a peasant and Cossack rebellion that Catherine managed to suppress only with great difficulty. 'A Tale about a Fisherman and a Fish' also – though less obviously – belongs to this cycle of works about Catherine the Great.

The tale's hidden meaning is revealed by what appears at first to be no more than a careless slip. It seems odd that Pushkin's old woman should consider ruling over the sea as a higher destiny than that of being 'a mighty tsaritsa'. Catherine the Great, however, was eager to rule over the Black Sea; between 1768 and 1792 she fought two wars against Turkey in order to achieve this ambition. And Catherine, like Pushkin's old woman, had usurped her husband's place, having deposed her husband Peter III in 1762, before these wars. In reality Catherine was generous to her favourite Prince Potyomkin and her subsequent lovers, but Pushkin evidently saw her as having treated her male favourites abusively – as the old woman does in this skazka. *In* The Captain's Daughter *(most of which was written two to three years later) Pushkin presents a positive picture of Catherine, but in his historical works he is extremely critical.[4]*

It seems likely that folktales and folk poetry were important to Pushkin above all for their language. In his 'Refutations of Criticism', for example, Pushkin wrote, 'The study of old songs, tales, etc., is essential for a complete knowledge of the particular qualities of the Russian language. Our critics are wrong to despise these works.'[5] Pushkin's very greatest creation was that of a literary language capable of giving expression to all realms of human thought and experience. Establishing a free and easy relationship with the language of the peasantry was an important step towards this achievement.

A Tale about a Priest and his Servant Balda

A priest, thick
as a brick,
was wandering about the fair
when he met Balda.
'Father, what's brought *you* here
so bright and early?'
'I need a servant, a burly
carpenter, a sterling
cook, an able
stable-boy.
I can't offer much
in the way
of pay.
Where should I look?'
'No further, Father!
I'll do all you ask,
whatever you wish,
in return for a daily dish
of wheaten porridge
and three flicks,
when the year's up,
on your priestly forehead.'
The priest was worried;
he scratched his forehead.
There was danger,
he knew,
in the flick of a finger;
but payment day

was a year away
and he placed his faith,
as Russians do,
in the ways of fate.

'All right!' said the priest.
'Move in right now!
This will suit both of us
down to the ground!
Show me your zeal –
and it's a done deal!'

Balda slept on straw;
he ate as much as four men
and worked like seven.
By dawn's first glow
he was on the go.
He cleaned the stable,
harnessed the mare
and ploughed the field;
he went to the fair;
he lit the stove
and laid the table;
he boiled a hen's egg
and even peeled it.
Everything went
without a stumble or stutter –
like a knife through butter.
Our priest's good wife
sang Balda's praises
all day and all night.
Our priest's dear daughter
sighed for him
all night and all day.
And to the little boy-priestlet
he cared for and dandled
Balda
was 'Da-Da'.

Only the priest
was not entranced,
nor the least inclined
to be lovey-dovey.
A threat
hung over his forehead.
He was in debt
and pay day
was not far away.
He couldn't eat, sleep or drink.
A furrow – a crack or a chink? –
lay on his brow.
He spoke, at last, to his wife,
who came straight out
with a wily ruse:
'I'll tell you what you can do!
Set him a task he can never fulfil,
something well and truly
impossible!
That's the charm
that will shield your forehead
from harm.
That's the way
to escape having to pay!'

Emboldened,
the priest said to Balda,
'Listen to me, my trusty servant:
a band of devils are meant
to be paying me quit-rent
for the rest of my life.
Once it was a splendid income,
but now the devils
are years in arrears.
Go and have a word with them,
talk some sense into them
when you've eaten your porridge.
Call the wretches to account –

and mind you collect
not a kopek less
than the full amount.'

Obedient,
without argument,
off Balda went
to the sea shore.
There he began whirling
and twirling a rope, dipping
one end in the deep, rippling
the water, whipping up waves
where the sea,
only a moment before,
had been
flat, calm and on the level.
Up crawled an old devil:
'What's brought you here, Balda?'
'I'm just starting a few ripples,
roughing up the sea a little,
twisting the sand,
making a few waves break.
We've had all we can take,
you see,
of you and your wretched clan!'[1]

'What have we done?'
the devil asked gravely.
'Why, all of a sudden,
have we fallen
from favour?'
'You're in debt,' said Balda,
'years behind with your rent.
So I'm going to let rip
with this rope
and teach you curs a lesson
you won't forget.'
'My dear Balda, my good friend,

don't do anything rash!
You shall have all your cash –
my own grandson will deliver it.'
In less than a moment
a young devillet
slipped out of the water.
'Should be a pushover!'
laughed Balda.
'I can twist this mewling kitten
of a devil-imp
round my little finger!'

'Good day, dear Balda!
What's this I've just heard
about quit-rent?
That's a delight we devils
have always been spared.
Still, have it your own way!
I don't want you to have hard feelings
or think us unfair.
Let it never be held
we devils
are mean in our dealings.
We'll fill you a bag full of gold.
Only let's just agree
to race round the sea –
and whoever outruns the other,
whoever's the winner,
takes all!'

Balda laughed slyly:
'*You* against *me*?
A devillet chase *Balda*?
Not likely!'
Balda disappeared into the trees,
plucked two young hares
from a forest glade,
tucked them into his knapsack

and strolled slowly back.
He took one little leveret
by the tip of his ear,
lifted him
up in the air,
then addressed the devillet:
'Look here,
little devil-imp,
you must do as I say,
you must dance as I play.
You haven't the strength yet
to compete
against the likes of me.
That simply wouldn't be fair.
First you must race my baby brother.
Get set, ready – quick as you can!'
Away they ran –
the devillet along the sea shore
while the hare,
winged by fear,
fled back to his glade.
All the way around the sea
sped the devillet
and there he was again –
pink tongue hanging out,
panting, gasping,
all in a lather,
wiping the sweat off his snout
with a little paw,
but pleased, at least,
not to have to run any more
and to have put an end to this bother
with Balda.
But then what did the devillet see?
He saw Balda hugging his baby brother,
patting him on the head
and saying,
'Well done, well done indeed!

That poor wretch
was outclassed –
he didn't stand a chance!
But you're tired out, you poor thing!
Now you must put your little feet up
and have a good rest!'
The devillet was astounded.
Frowning, dumbfounded,
droop-tailed,
with a sidelong glance
at Balda's slip of a sibling,
he said
he would go fetch the rent.
Back to grandad he went.
'I've been trounced,'
he announced,
'outstripped by a stripling,
by Balda's young brother.'
The old devil, vexed,
racked his brains,
wondering what to do next –
while Balda whipped up
such a racket
that the whole sea went crazy,
flinging waves right up to the sky.

Back to Balda went
the devillet:
'All right, you peasant,
We're sorting the rent.
Only – see this stick?
Choose any mark you like.
Whoever hurls this stick beyond it –
let's say
the money's his for the taking!
What's up, Balda?
Why so despondent?
Afraid you might strain your shoulder?'

'See that storm cloud over the bay?'
answered Balda.
'When it's blown this way,
I'll throw your stick
right into the thick of it
and bring a storm down onto our heads.'
Scared out of his wits,
the devillet returned to his grandad
to tell him of Balda's strange gifts
while Balda went back
to making his racket.

Back once more came the devillet.
'What's all this fuss?
Why all these threats?
Be patient a moment –
we're sorting the rent.
Only first of all,
why don't you and I just—'
'No!' said Balda. 'This time it's my turn
to name
the rules of the game –
a trifling trial
that will show us
what fibre you're made of.
See that grey mare over there?
Just carry her up to those trees.
It's no distance at all –
just a third of a mile.
Carry her all the way –
the rent's yours!
But if you drop her –
it's mine!'
The silly devillet
crept under the mare's belly,
struggled and strained
with might and main,
strove for all he was worth –

and raised her just off the earth.
He took a step,
and a second,
and a third –
and came a cropper.
'Silly devillet!' said Balda.
'When will you understand?
When will you grasp
that you're outclassed?
You can't even grip her between your hands
while I can lift her between my two legs!'
Balda mounted the mare
and galloped a mile.
Dust clouds
climbed high in the air.
The devillet took fright
and crept back
to admit his defeat.
His clan gathered around him –
but what could they do?
They collected their quit-rent
and threw the sack at Balda.
It was a heavy sack
and Balda grunted grunt
after heavy grunt
as he plodded back.

The priest feared for his life
and cowered behind his wife,
but there was no escaping Balda,
who proffered the gold to him
and reminded him
of what in his greed
he'd agreed.

The poor priest
presented his forehead
for three quick flicks of a finger.

The first
flung him up to the ceiling.
The second
cost him his tongue.
The third
plastered the wall with his brain.[2]
And Balda said,
with disdain,
'A cheapskate, Father, often gets more
than he bargained for.'

A Tale about a Fisherman and a Fish

By the very edge of the blue sea
lived an old man and his old woman.
For three and thirty years they had lived
in a tumbledown hut made of mud.
The old man caught fish in his fishing net;
the old woman span with her spinning wheel.
One day the old man cast his net
and all he caught in his net was slime.
The old man cast his net a second time
and all he found in his net was weed.
A third time the old man cast his net
and what he found in his net was a fish –
no ordinary fish, but a golden fish.
The fish begged, the fish begged and implored;
the fish prayed in a human voice:
'Release me, set me free in the sea –
and in return you'll receive a grand ransom,
I'll grant you whatever you wish.'
The old man was amazed and frightened.
Three and thirty years he had fished –
and not once had he heard a fish talk.
He returned the fish to the water,
saying gently as he let her go free,
'God be with you, golden fish!
I don't need your grand ransom.
Off you go – into the deep blue sea!
Swim free, swim where you wish!'

The old man went back to his old woman
and told her of this great wonder:
'Today I caught a fish in my net –
no ordinary fish, but a golden fish.
The fish spoke, she spoke in our tongue;
she begged to go home, into the blue sea.
She promised me a splendid ransom;
she said she would grant whatever I wished.
But I didn't dare take this ransom.
I set her free in the deep blue sea.'
The old woman scolded her old man:
'Simple fool, fool of a simpleton!
What stopped you taking this ransom?
A mere fish – and you were too frightened!
You could at least have got a new washtub.
Ours is cracked right down the middle.'

Off he went towards the blue sea.
(The blue sea looked a little troubled.)
He called out to the golden fish
and the fish swam up and asked him,
'What is it, old man, what do you want?'
The old man bowed to the fish and said,
'Have mercy on me, Sovereign Fish.
My old woman is cursing and scolding me.
Though I am old, she gives me no peace.
She needs a new washtub, she says.
Ours is cracked right down the middle.'
The golden fish replied straight away,
'Take heart – and God be with you!
Outside your hut you'll find a new washtub!'
The old man went back to his old woman.
His old woman now had a new washtub,
but she was cursing more fiercely than ever:
'Simple fool, fool of a simpleton,
all you got from the fish was a washtub.
What wealth can be found in a washtub?

Get on back, you fool, to the fish.
Bow down to the fish and say
you want a handsome house built of wood.'

Off he went towards the blue sea.
(The blue sea was a little rough.)
He called out to the golden fish
and the fish swam up and asked him,
'What is it, old man, what do you want?'
The old man bowed to the fish and said,
'Have mercy on me, Sovereign Fish.
My old woman is cursing and raging.
Though I am old, she gives me no peace.
She wants a handsome house built of wood.'
The golden fish replied straight away,
'Take heart – and God be with you!
You shall have your house built of wood.'
The old man set off for his hut,
but not a trace of his hut could he find.
In its place stood a house built of wood
with a whitewashed brick chimney
and two strong gates hewn from oak.
Sitting by the window was his old woman,
swearing at him for all she was worth:
'Simple fool, fool of a simpleton,
all you got from the fish was a house.
Get on back, you fool, to the fish.
I don't want to be a lowly peasant.
I want to be a noble lady.'

Off he went towards the blue sea.
(The blue sea was not calm.)
He called out to the golden fish
and the fish swam up and asked him,
'What is it, old man, what do you want?'
The old man bowed to the fish and said,
'Have mercy on me, Sovereign Fish.
My old woman is shouting and swearing,

cursing me for all she is worth.
Though I am old, she gives me no peace.
She doesn't want to be a lowly peasant.
She wants to be a noble lady.'
The golden fish replied straight away,
'Take heart – and God be with you!'

Back went the old man to his old woman –
And what did he see? He saw a tall mansion.
His old woman was standing there in the porch.
She was wearing a splendid 'soul-warmer' –
a precious waistcoat trimmed with sable.
On her head was a brocade head-dress;
round her neck hung heavy pearls
and gold rings encircled her fingers.
On her feet were fine red boots
and before her stood zealous servants;
she was slapping them and pulling their hair.
The old man said to his old woman,
'Good day, Lady Countess Baroness!
I hope you've got all you want now!'
The old woman flew at her husband
and packed him off to work in the stables.

A week passed, and another week.
The old woman grew madder than ever.
She sent her old man back to the fish:
'Go back to the fish, bow low – and say
I don't want to be a fine lady.
I want to be a mighty tsaritsa.'
The old man took fright. He implored her:
'What's got into you, woman? Are you crazy?
Have you been eating black henbane?
You don't know how to walk like a tsaritsa.
You don't know how to talk like a tsaritsa.
You'll be the laughing stock of your tsardom.'
The old woman flew into a fury.
She struck her husband across the cheek:

'How dare you, peasant, answer me back?
How dare you talk like that to a lady?
Back you go again to the sea – or, upon my word,
You'll be dragged there against your will.'

Off he went towards the blue sea.
(The blue sea was blacker than black.)
He called out to the golden fish
and the fish swam up and asked him,
'What is it, old man, what do you want?'
The old man bowed to the fish and said,
'Have mercy on me, Sovereign Fish.
My old woman is raging again.
She doesn't want to be a fine lady.
She wants to be a mighty tsaritsa.'
The golden fish replied straight away,
'Take heart – and God be with you!
Your old woman shall be a tsaritsa.'

The old man went back to his old woman.
Before him stands a splendid palace
and his old woman is there in the hall.
She is a tsaritsa sitting at table.
Nobles are standing and waiting on her,
pouring her wines from across the seas
while she nibbles on honeycakes.
All around stand fierce-looking guards
with sharp axes poised on their shoulders . . .
The old man was frightened. He bowed to the ground
and said, 'Greetings, O dread Tsaritsa –
and I hope you've got all you want now!'
The old woman didn't look at him;
she just ordered him out of her sight,
and her nobles and courtiers came running
and shoved him out through the door;
and the guards ran up with their axes
and all but hacked him to pieces,

and everyone laughed at the old man:
'Serves you right, you ignorant lout!
Let this be a lesson to you, bumpkin!
Don't get too big for your boots
or sit in another man's sleigh!'

A week passed, and another week.
The old woman grew madder than ever.
She sent her courtiers to fetch her husband.
They found him and brought him before her
and the old woman said to her old man,
'Go back, bow down to the fish.
I don't want to be a mighty tsaritsa,
I want to be a Sea Empress;
I want to live in the Ocean-Sea
with the golden fish as my servant
to bring me whatever I ask for.'

The old man did not dare say a word;
he was too frightened to open his mouth.
Off he went towards the blue sea.
Raging there was a black storm!
Waves were flinging up spray;
angry waves were crashing and howling.
He called out to the golden fish
and the fish swam up and asked him,
'What is it, old man, what do you need?'
The old man bowed to the fish and said,
'Have mercy on me, Sovereign Fish!
What am I to do with the wretched woman?
She no longer wants to be a tsaritsa,
she wants to be a Sea Empress.
She wants to live in the Ocean-Sea
with you as her faithful servant
to bring her whatever she asks for.'
Not a word did the fish reply.
She just slapped her tail on the water

and dived deep into the blue sea.
The old man waited and waited
but that was all the answer he got.
He went back – to a hut made of mud.
His old woman was sitting outside it;
and before her lay a broken washtub.

PART TWO

THE FIRST FOLKTALE
COLLECTIONS

ALEKSANDR AFANASYEV

(1826–71)

The Brothers Grimm published their famous collection of German tales in 1812. The first person to suggest that Russian folktales might also be worth recording was the poet Vasily Zhukovsky; in 1816 he wrote to his three nieces Anna, Avdotiya and Yekaterina, asking, 'Could you not collect for me Russian tales and Russian legends, which is to say, get our village storytellers to tell stories to you and write down their tales. Don't laugh! This is our national poetry . . . I would like for you . . . each to take two notebooks and in one write down the tales (and with as many of the exact words of the storytellers as is possible) and in the other write down miscellaneous things: superstitions, legends, and the like.'¹ Anna, at least, appears to have acted on her uncle's suggestion, but her notebooks have been lost. Over two decades later, Zhukovsky returned to this idea, suggesting that Anna and Avdotiya compile a collection to be titled 'A Library of Folktales'. The prospective publisher went bankrupt, but the tales recorded by Avdotiya's son Pyotr Kireyevsky were included in the collection of Russian Folktales *published by Aleksandr Afanasyev – the most famous of all Russian folklorists – between 1855 and 1863. This collection, published in eight small books or 'fascicles', is usually seen as the Russian counterpart to the work of the Brothers Grimm.*

Aleksandr Afanasyev was born in 1826 in a small town in the province of Voronezh, the 'Black Earth' region between Moscow and Ukraine. His mother died when he was very small; his father worked as a scrivener. Afanasyev first became interested in folktales as a child, and his interest seems to have remained constant. He went to school in the city of Voronezh and then studied law at Moscow University. After completing his studies, he worked briefly as a schoolteacher, but is said to have been unable to enforce discipline. From 1849 until 1862 he worked as an archivist in the Ministry of Foreign Affairs. This allowed him enough leisure to write numerous articles about Russian history and literature and – above all – Russian folklore. He was evidently determined and energetic, and he had an excellent knowledge of a large number of European languages.[2]

Although Afanasyev himself collected only about ten tales first-hand, he gradually built up a collection of well over a thousand Russian folktales. Around a third of these were passed on to him by the Russian Geographical Society, which had been collecting folktales since 1847. Other tales were contributed by the ethnologist and lexicographer Vladimir Dal', and still more – as we have seen – were given to him by Pyotr Kireyevsky, the chief authority on Russian folklore during the years when Afanasyev was first beginning to publish. Kireyevsky had collected a large number of songs and tales but had published little himself.

Like many subsequent Russian folklorists, Afanasyev suffered at the hands of the authorities. The repressive nature of Russian public life lent a particular urgency and even danger to what in other countries might have been an apolitical enterprise. The main problem for Afanasyev was that most folktales portray the clergy critically or even mockingly. Afanasyev was relatively fortunate with his Russian Folk Legends (1859), *which was banned only in 1860, after it had already sold out, but the page proofs of the fifth and sixth fascicles of his* Russian Folktales, *which he received in 1861, were – in his words – 'slashed and crimsoned with red ink'. Afanasyev was combative in his defence of his work. When Filaret, the Moscow Metropolitan, denounced his* Russian Folk Legends *as 'thoroughly blasphemous and immoral', Afanasyev replied publicly, 'There is a million times more morality, truth and human love in my folk legends than in the sanctimonious sermons delivered by Your Holiness.'*

In 1858, Afanasyev founded the literary and historical journal

Bibliographical Notes. *When articles intended for this journal fell foul of the censor, Afanasyev sent them abroad to be published in the* Free Russian Press, *a journal published by the exiled writer and political thinker Aleksandr Herzen, whom Afanasyev later met while on a visit to London, and with whom he corresponded. His links with Herzen were probably the reason why, in 1862, Afanasyev's apartment was subjected to a police search and he was forced to leave his post as an archivist. This may also have been connected to his completion, that year, of the collection of tales known in manuscript as* Russian Folk Tales – Not for Print; *some of these tales were unpublishable because of their obscenity, others because they were seen as anti-clerical. A selection from* Russian Folk Tales – Not for Print *was first published two years after Afanasyev's death – anonymously and in Geneva. It was not until 1997 that the collection was published in full.*

The last years of Afanasyev's life were difficult. For four years he was unable to find work, and was reduced to selling most of his huge library. In an attempt to exclude draughts from his cold apartment, he used to tear up copies of his Bibliographical Notes *and lay them in thick layers on the floor. Eventually he managed to make a living and support his family through poorly paid secretarial jobs. In spite of these hardships he continued with his work as a folklorist; between 1865 and 1869 he published the three volumes of what he himself saw as his most important work,* The Poetic Outlook of the Slavs on Nature.

Serious folktale collecting had begun with the Romantic Movement, and both the Brothers Grimm and Aleksandr Afanasyev belonged to the then dominant 'mythological school' of folklorists. They tended to see folktales essentially as the remnants of ancient myths – often about the changing seasons, the movements of the sun and moon or other celestial phenomena. Although Afanasyev is now remembered primarily for his collection of folktales, his real ambition was to use these tales as a basis for the reconstruction of an archaic Slavic mythology, few written records of which had survived. The mysterious Balda, for example, appears in a large number of oral tales as well as in Pushkin's well-known version; Afanasyev makes a convincing case for Balda being an incarnation of an ancient thunder god – a god half-preserved and half-forgotten in the memory of the people.

In 1870 Afanasyev published a collection of sixty-one of his folktales, omitting dialect words and material he thought unsuitable for children, under the title Russian Children's Tales. *Though even this collection was criticized because of the supposed immorality of the tales' many trickster heroes, it has always been popular. Many of the finest nineteenth- and twentieth-century Russian artists have illustrated it, and it has been reprinted many times. Afanasyev was also working at this time on a second, annotated edition of his* Russian Folktales, *but this was published only posthumously.*

In 1870 Afanasyev was diagnosed with tuberculosis – poverty had undermined his health – and he died in 1871. In a letter to the poet Afanasy Fet, the novelist Ivan Turgenev wrote, 'Afanasyev died recently, from hunger, but his literary merits, my dear friend, will be remembered long after both yours and mine are covered by the dark of oblivion.'[3]

Afanasyev was a pioneer, and an editor of genius. Many important collections of Russian folktales were published during the hundred years after his death, but none has won such popularity. Afanasyev's particular gift was his blend of pragmatic good sense and an intuitive sympathy with his material, a kind of literary tact. Little of his archive has survived, but it is clear that, for the main part, he followed some kind of middle path. It would, in any case, have been difficult for Afanasyev to adhere to any more rigorous methodology, since the texts he received came from a variety of different sources and had been transcribed with varying degrees of fidelity. He also appears to have recognized that much of the charm of folktales lies in their variety; unlike the Brothers Grimm, he did not attempt to combine different variants into a single 'ideal' version. Often he includes up to six or seven versions of a single tale. Sometimes the differences between these versions are a matter of plot details, sometimes more a matter of language – Afanasyev

*often includes not only Russian but also Ukrainian and/or
Belarusian versions of a single tale.*

*Afanasyev was working in the first decades of folklore studies,
before any consensus had been reached as to how best to record
tales. Some scholars looked on the language of the peasantry
with contempt; others insisted on the need for verbatim transcription. Some critics attacked Afanasyev for including too
many vulgarisms, too many dialect words and too many repetitions; others attacked him for over-polishing his texts. And he
himself criticized his younger contemporary Ivan Khudyakov
both for using too many bookish words – i.e. over-editing –
and for failing to clarify obscure passages – i.e. under-editing.
This is interesting not so much for what it tells us about Khudyakov, who was very gifted, as for the light it casts on Afanasyev
himself; a scrupulous scholar but a still more scrupulous artist.*

The Crane and the Heron

There was an owl, a merry fowl. She flew and flew, then sat a while. She span her tail, she looked around, she flew and flew, then sat a while. She span her tail, she looked around, then flew and flew ... I've rhymed my rhyme – so now it's time, high time indeed, to tell my tale.

The crane and the heron both lived in a bog. They built themselves huts at opposite ends of this bog. The crane began to find it lonely on his own. He decided to marry. 'I'll ask for the hand of the heron,' he said. 'She's like me. She's got a long nose and long legs.'

The crane set off. He waded five miles through the bog. He waded and waded all the way to the heron's hut. 'Heron,' he called, 'are you at home?' 'Yes,' said the heron, 'I am.' 'Marry me.' 'No, crane, I won't marry you. You have long legs and your coat is too short. You fly badly and you won't be able to provide for me. Go away, spindleshanks!'

Hanging his head, the crane went off back home. Then the heron thought better of it, 'It's lonely being on my own,' she thought. 'I'd do better to marry the crane!' She went to the crane and said, 'Crane, take me to wife!' 'No, heron, you're no good to me. I don't want to marry you. I won't take you to wife. Be off with you!' The heron wept with shame and went back home. Then the crane thought better of it and said to himself, 'I did wrong not to marry the heron. I feel lonely all on my own. I'll go and marry her now.' He went back to the heron and said, 'Heron! I've made up my mind to marry you. Be my wife.' 'No, crane, I won't be your wife!' And the crane went back home.

And now the heron thought better of it. 'Why did I refuse him?' she said to herself. 'It's no fun living alone. I'd do better to marry the crane!' She went off to ask him, but the crane refused. And to this day each goes on proposing marriage – but they're not married yet.

The Little Brown Cow

In a certain land, in a certain tsardom, there lived a tsar and tsaritsa, and they had one daughter, Marya Tsarevna.[1] When the tsaritsa died, the tsar took another wife, Yagishna.[2] This Yagishna gave birth to two daughters; one had two eyes, the other three. And she took against her stepdaughter, Marya Tsarevna.[3] One day she sent her out to take Buryonushka, the little brown cow, to pasture. For her dinner she gave the girl a crust of dry bread.

The tsarevna went out into open steppe, bowed to Buryonushka's right leg – and found food and drink and fine attire, all a lady could require. All day long, dressed as a lady, she followed Buryonushka. When the day was over, she bowed a second time to the little cow's right leg, took off her fine clothes, went back home and put her crust of bread on the table. 'How does the bitch stay alive?' wondered Yagishna. The next day she gave Marya Tsarevna the very same crust of bread and sent her out together with her elder daughter. She said to her daughter, 'Keep an eye on Marya Tsarevna. See what she's finding to eat.'

They reached open steppe, and Marya Tsarevna said to her sister, 'Let me look through your hair for you' (See Appendix, p. 424). She began to look and as she looked, she said, 'Sleep, sleep, little sister. Sleep, sleep, my dear one. Sleep, sleep, little eye. Sleep, sleep, other eye.' Her sister fell fast asleep. Marya Tsarevna got to her feet, went up to Buryonushka, bowed to her right leg, ate and drank her fill, put on her fine attire and walked about all day like a lady. When it was evening, Marya Tsarevna took off her fine clothes and said, 'Wake up, little sister.

Get up, my dear one. It's time to go home.' 'Dear, oh dear,' thought the sister. 'I've slept through the whole day. I haven't seen anything at all. Mother will be angry with me.'

They got back home. 'So what did Marya Tsarevna find to eat and drink?' asked the mother. 'I don't know,' said her daughter. 'I didn't see anything.' Yagishna swore at her. The following morning she sent her three-eyed daughter out with Marya Tsarevna. 'Keep an eye on her,' she said. 'See what the bitch eats and drinks.' The girls reached Buryonushka's pasture and Marya Tsarevna said to her sister, 'Sister, let me look through your hair for you.' 'Please do, sister! Please do, my dear!' Marya Tsarevna began to look through her sister's hair for her. And as she looked, she said, 'Sleep, sleep, little sister. Sleep, sleep, my dear one. Sleep, sleep, little eye. Sleep, sleep, other eye.' But she forgot about the third little eye – and that third little eye watched and watched. It saw everything; it saw Marya Tsarevna run up to Buryonushka, bow to her right leg, eat and drink her fill, put on her fine attire and walk about all day like a lady. And as the sun began to set, Marya Tsarevna bowed to Buryonushka a second time, took off her fine clothes and said to her three-eyed sister, 'Wake up, little sister. Get up, my dear one. It's time to go home.'

Marya Tsarevna got back home and put her crust of bread on the table. The mother began asking her daughter, 'What does she eat and drink?' The girl with three eyes told her everything. Yagishna said to her husband, 'Old man, slaughter the little brown cow!' And her husband slaughtered the little brown cow. Marya Tsarevna begged him, 'Dearest Father, please at least give me some of the gut!' And so he threw her the lower gut. She took it and planted it by a gatepost. And where she planted it, there very soon appeared a bush. And on the bush grew beautiful berries, and all kinds of little birds perched there and sang all kinds of songs – the songs peasants sing and the songs tsars sing.

Ivan Tsarevich[4] heard about Marya Tsarevna. He went to her stepmother, put a dish on the table and said, 'Whichever maiden picks me a dish full of berries, her I will take as my wife.' Yagishna sent her elder daughter to pick berries, but the little birds wouldn't even let her come close. They very nearly pecked out her eyes. Then Yagishna sent her other daughter, but the birds didn't let her come close either. At last she let Marya Tsarevna go. Off the girl went to pick berries – and the little birds put twice as many berries on her dish as she was able to pick herself. Marya Tsarevna came back, put the dish full of berries on the table and bowed to the tsarevich. There was a merry feast and a wedding. Ivan Tsarevich took Marya Tsarevna away to be his wife, and the two of them began to live and prosper.

After some time – maybe a long time, maybe a short time – Marya Tsarevna gave birth to a little son. Then she wanted to see her father, and she went to visit him with her husband. Her stepmother straight away turned her into a goose and disguised her elder daughter as Ivan Tsarevich's wife. Ivan Tsarevich returned home. The old man who had been Ivan's tutor got up early in the morning, had a good wash, took the baby boy in his arms and went out into the open steppe till he came to a little bush. Some geese, some grey geese came flying by. 'My dear geese, my grey geese, where have you seen the mother of this baby?' 'In the next flock,' they answered. Another flock appeared. 'My dear geese, my grey geese, where have you seen the mother of this baby?' The baby's mother jumped down to the ground, cast off her skin, cast off a second skin, took the baby in her arms and began feeding it at her breast, crying, 'Today I shall feed you and tomorrow I shall feed you, but the day after tomorrow I shall fly away beyond dark forests, beyond high mountains!'

The old man went back home. The baby boy slept all through the night without waking, though the false wife was complaining bitterly: why had the old man taken her son off into the open steppe and nearly starved him there? In the morning the old man got up early, had a good wash and went out into the open steppe with the baby boy. Ivan Tsarevich got up too, crept after the old man and hid away in the bush. Some geese, some grey geese came flying by. The old man called out, 'My dear geese, my grey geese, where have you seen this baby's mother?' 'In the next flock,' they answered. Another flock appeared. 'My dear geese, my grey geese, where have you seen the mother of this baby?' The baby's mother jumped down onto the ground, cast off her skin, cast off a second skin and began feeding the baby at her breast. As she fed the baby, she was saying her farewells: 'Tomorrow I shall fly away beyond dark forests, beyond high mountains!'

She gave the baby back to the old man. 'What is that awful smell?' she asked. She wanted to put her skins back on. She reached out, but they weren't there. Ivan Tsarevich had burned them. He seized hold of Marya Tsarevna. She turned into a frog, into a lizard, into all kinds of other reptiles and then into a spindle. Ivan Tsarevich broke the spindle in two, threw the bottom behind him and the top in front of him – and before him, as a beautiful young maiden, stood Marya Tsarevna. Together they set off back home. Yagishna's daughter kept shouting and yelling, 'The killer is coming! The destroyer is on her way!' Ivan Tsarevich called together his princes and boyars and asked them, 'With which wife will you give me freedom to live?' 'With the first!' 'Well, gentlemen, whichever wife is first to leap to the top of the gate, with her will I live.' Yagishna's daughter climbed straight to the top of the gate, but Marya Tsarevna merely clutched the gate and didn't climb up. Then Ivan Tsarevich took his rifle and shot the false wife, and he and Marya Tsarevna began once again to live well, as I've heard tell, and to know all that was good, as I've understood.

Vasilisa the Fair

In a certain tsardom there once lived a merchant. Although he had been married for twelve years, he had only one child, a girl called Vasilisa the Fair. When Vasilisa was eight years old, her mother fell ill. She called Vasilisa to her side, took out a doll from under her pillow and said, 'Listen, Vasilisa. Remember these last words of mine and do as I say. I'm dying now and together with my parental blessing I give you this doll. Keep the doll with you wherever you go, but never show her to anyone. When you meet trouble, just give her some food and ask her advice. First she'll have something to eat. Then she'll tell you how to help your unhappiness.' And the mother kissed her daughter and died.

When the merchant had finished mourning his wife, he decided to marry again. He was a good, kind man, and there were plenty of young women who'd have been only too glad to marry him. Instead, however, he chose a widow. She was no longer young, and she had two daughters who were almost the same age as Vasilisa. He thought she'd make a good house-keeper and mother, but he was mistaken. Vasilisa was the most beautiful girl in the village, and her stepmother and stepsisters were jealous of her. They thought she'd grow ugly if she were outside all day in the sun and wind, so they gave her all the work they could find. The girl had a hard life.

But Vasilisa did as she was told and never complained. And with every day she grew plumper and more beautiful. Her step-mother and stepsisters could see this, and their envy made them grow thinner and uglier – even though they just sat around the whole time like ladies, with their arms folded.

So how did all this come about? But for the doll, things would have been very different indeed. Some days Vasilisa ate nothing at all. She'd wait until everyone was in bed in the evening and then go up to her attic with some special titbit for the doll. 'Here, doll! I've brought you some food. Listen to me now. This stepmother of mine's going to be the death of me. Tell me how I can live and what I must do!' First the doll would eat. Then she would talk to Vasilisa and comfort her in her grief. And in the morning she would do all her work for her. Vasilisa would lie down in the shade, or perhaps pick flowers, while the doll weeded the beds, watered the cabbages, went to the well and lit the stove. The doll even gave Vasilisa herbs against sunburn. Life went well for her with the doll.

The years passed. Vasilisa grew up. All the young men in the village wanted to marry her, while no one would so much as look at her stepsisters. The stepmother grew to hate Vasilisa even more. 'No,' she would repeat, 'I'm not giving the youngest away before her elder sisters.' Then she would send the young men on their way and take it out on Vasilisa by beating her.

Then one day, Vasilisa's father had to go on a long journey. Her stepmother moved to a hut on the edge of the forest. In this forest was a glade, and in the glade was a hut where a baba yaga lived. This baba yaga lived on her own and she ate men and women as if they were chickens. Every now and then the stepmother would think of a reason to send Vasilisa into the forest, but Vasilisa always came back safe and sound. Her doll showed her the way and did not let her go anywhere near this baba yaga's hut.

Autumn set in. One evening the stepmother set each of the girls a task. She told Vasilisa to spin yarn, one of her daughters to make lace and the other to knit stockings. Then she snuffed out all the candles except where the girls were working. She went up to bed. For a while the girls kept on with their work. Then the candle began to gutter. One of the girls took the tweezers. And then, as if by mistake, instead of trimming the wick, she extinguished the candle – just as her mother had told her to. 'What can we do now?' said the girls. 'There isn't a light in the house and we haven't nearly finished our work. Someone will have to go round to the baba yaga's.' 'I'm not going,' said the one who was making lace. 'I can see by the light of my pins.' 'I'm not going,' said the one who was knitting stockings. 'I can see by the light of my knitting needles.' 'Then it will have to be you!' the two girls shouted at Vasilisa. 'Go on. Go and see Baba Yaga!' And they pushed her out of the room.

Vasilisa went up to her attic, laid out the supper she'd prepared for her doll and said, 'Here, doll! I've brought you some food. Listen to me now. They want me to go to the baba yaga to ask for a light. She'll eat me alive!' The doll ate her food. Her two eyes shone bright as candles. 'Have no fear, O Vasilisa the Fair! Do as they say, but be sure to take me with you. Baba Yaga can do you no harm as long as I'm there.'

So Vasilisa put on her coat, put her doll in her pocket, crossed herself and set off into the deep forest.

Vasilisa walked on, trembling and trembling. Then a horseman swept by. His face was white, he was dressed in white and he was riding a white horse with white trappings. Day began to dawn.

She walked on further. Another horseman came by. His face was red, he was dressed in red and he was riding a red horse. Then the sun rose.

Vasilisa had walked all through the night, and now she walked all through the day. Late in the evening she came to the baba yaga's hut. Round the hut was a fence made of bones. Skulls with empty eyeholes looked down from the stakes. The gate was made from the bones of people's legs, the bolts were thumbs and fingers, and the lock was a mouth with sharp teeth. Vasilisa was too scared to move. Then another horseman galloped up. His face was black, he was dressed in black and he was riding a black horse. He rode through the gate and vanished, as if the earth had swallowed him up. Night fell. But the darkness did not last long. All the eyes in the skulls on the fence began to glow and the glade grew bright as day. Vasilisa trembled in terror but, not knowing which way to run, she stood there without moving.

Then the forest was filled with a terrible noise. The trees creaked and cracked, the dead leaves crackled and crunched – and there was the baba yaga. She was riding on her mortar, spurring it on with her pestle, sweeping away her tracks with a broom. She rode up to the gate, sniffed all around her and called out, 'Foo, foo! I smell the blood of a Russian! Who is it?' Trembling with fear, Vasilisa went up to the old woman, gave a deep bow and said, 'Grandmother, it's me. My stepsisters sent me to ask for a light.' 'Very well,' said the baba yaga. 'I know those sisters of yours. But first you must stay and work for me. If you do as I say, then I'll give you a light. But if you don't, then I'll eat you for dinner.' Then she turned to the gate and shouted, 'Slide back, strong bolts! Open up, broad gate!' The gate opened. The baba yaga whistled as she rode in. Vasilisa walked in after her. The gate swung to and bolted itself behind her.

The baba yaga stretched herself out on a bench and said to Vasilisa. 'I'm hungry. Bring me whatever you find in the stove.' Vasilisa lit a taper from the skulls on the fence and began taking out the baba yaga's dinner. There was enough to feed ten strong men. Then she went down to the cellar to fetch kvas,[1] mead, beer and wine. The old woman ate and drank everything Vasilisa put in front of her. All she left the girl was a half-bowl of cabbage soup, a crust of bread and a scrap of pork. The baba yaga lay down in her bed and said, 'Tomorrow morning, after I go, you must clean the yard, sweep the hut, cook the supper and wash the linen. Then you must go to the corn bin and sort through a bushel of wheat. And if you're not finished by the time I get back, I'll eat you.' After giving these orders, the baba yaga began to snore. Vasilisa took her doll out of her pocket, placed the baba yaga's leftovers before her, burst out crying and said, 'There, doll, I've brought you some food. Listen to me now. The baba yaga's set me a hard task. And she says that, if I don't finish it in time, she'll eat me. What can I do?' 'Have no fear, O Vasilisa the Fair. Eat your supper, pray and have a good sleep. Mornings are wiser than evenings.'

Vasilisa woke early, but the baba yaga had already risen. Vasilisa looked outside: the light in the skulls' eyes was already fading. The white horseman swept by and day began to dawn. The baba yaga went out into the yard. She whistled – and there were her pestle, mortar and broom. The red horseman flashed by – and the sun rose. The baba yaga sat in her mortar and rode off, spurring it on with her pestle and sweeping away her tracks with her broom. Vasilisa was left on her own. She went slowly round the baba yaga's hut. Never in her life had she seen such abundance. Then she stopped, wondering where to begin with her work. She looked around – and realized there was nothing left to do. The doll was standing by the corn bin, picking out the last grain of chaff from the wheat. 'My saviour!' said Vasilisa. 'You've delivered me from death.' 'All you have to do now is prepare the supper,' said the doll as she climbed back into Vasilisa's pocket. 'Cook it with God's help – and then you can have a good rest.'

Towards evening Vasilisa put everything ready on the table and sat down to wait for the baba yaga. It began to get darker. The black horseman flashed past the gate – and it was night. The only light was from the skulls on the fence. The trees creaked and cracked, the dead leaves crackled and crunched, and there was the baba yaga. Vasilisa went out to meet her. 'Is everything ready?' asked the baba yaga. 'See for yourself, grandmother,' said Vasilisa. The baba yaga looked round the hut. She could see there was nothing for her to get cross about – and this made her crosser than ever. 'Very good,' she said, and then called out, 'My friends, my faithful servants, grind my wheat.' Three pairs of hands appeared. They took the wheat and carried it out of sight. The baba yaga ate her fill, lay down in her bed and said to Vasilisa, 'Tomorrow you must do the same as today. But then you must go to the storeroom and sort through the poppy seeds. I want them perfectly clean. Someone threw dirt in the bin to spite me.' The old woman turned towards the wall and began to snore. Vasilisa fed her doll. The doll ate her supper and said, 'Pray to God and then go to sleep. Mornings are wiser than evenings. Everything will be done, my dear Vasilisa!'

In the morning the baba yaga rode off again in her mortar. Vasilisa and the doll finished the housework in no time at all. The old woman came back in the evening, had a good look round and called out, 'My friends, my faithful servants, press the oil from these poppy seeds.' Three pairs of hands appeared.

They took the poppy seeds and carried them out of sight. The baba yaga sat down to eat. Vasilisa stood there without saying a word. 'Why don't you say anything?' asked the baba yaga. 'Anyone would think you were mute.' 'I didn't dare,' answered Vasilisa. 'But if you'll allow me, there are a few things I'd like to ask about.' 'Ask away!' said the baba yaga. 'But take care. Not every question has a good answer. The more you know, the sooner you grow old.' 'Grandmother, I only want to ask about what I saw on the way here. First a man rode past on a white horse. He had a white face and he was dressed all in white. Who was he?' 'That was my Bright Day,' answered the baba yaga. 'Then I was overtaken by a man on a red horse. He had a red face and he was dressed all in red. Who was he?' 'That was my Red Sun,' answered the baba yaga. 'And then who was the black horseman who came past while I was standing outside your gate?' 'That was my Black Night. The three of them are my faithful servants.'

Vasilisa remembered the three pairs of hands and kept her mouth shut. 'Don't you want to ask about anything else?' asked the baba yaga. 'No, grandmother, that's enough. You said yourself that the more one knows, the sooner one grows old.' 'Very good,' said the baba yaga. 'I'm glad you only asked about what you saw on the way. I don't like my dirty linen being washed in public and if people are too inquisitive, I eat them. And now I've got a question for you. How did you manage to get all the work done so quickly?' 'It's my mother's blessing that helps me. I could never have done it all on my own.' 'Oh, so it's like that, is it?' said the baba yaga. 'You'd better be off then, O blessed daughter. We don't want anyone blessed round here.' She dragged Vasilisa out of the room and pushed her outside the gate. Then she took one of the skulls with blazing eyes, stuck it on the end of a stick and gave it to the girl, saying, 'Here's a light for your stepsisters. That's what you came here for, isn't it?'

Vasilisa ran off as fast as her legs could carry her. The skull's eyes lit up the path, and they didn't go out until dawn. She walked all through the next day, and by evening she was nearly home. She was about to throw the skull into some bushes – after all, her sisters couldn't be needing a light any longer, could they? – when she heard a muffled voice from inside the skull. 'No, don't throw me away. Take me to your stepmother.'

She looked up at the house. Not in a single window was there any light to be seen: maybe they did need the skull after all. For the very first time, her stepmother and stepsisters greeted Vasilisa kindly. They said they hadn't had a light or a fire in the house since Vasilisa had left. None of them had been able to strike a light herself and, whenever they had tried to bring one back from a neighbour, it had gone out as they crossed the threshold. Vasilisa carried the skull in. The skull began to stare at the stepmother and the two stepsisters. Its eyes burned and burned. The three of them tried to hide, but the eyes followed them wherever they went. By morning they were burned to cinders. Vasilisa was left on her own.

Vasilisa buried the skull in the garden, locked up the house, went to the town and began to live with an old woman who had no family. She was hoping her father would come back soon. One day she said to the old woman, 'Grandmother, it's boring with nothing to do. Go and get me the best flax you can find. I want to do some spinning.' The old woman bought some good flax. Vasilisa was quick-fingered, and the yarn she spun was fine and even. It was soon time to start weaving the yarn, but there were no spools fine enough for Vasilisa's yarn. She couldn't find anyone who could make one, so she asked her doll. The doll replied, 'Just bring me any old reed, an old shuttle and a horse's mane. I'll make everything in no time at all.'

Vasilisa did as her doll said, went to sleep and found a splendid loom waiting for her the next morning.

By the end of the winter she had finished weaving her cloth, a cloth so fine you could draw it through the eye of a needle. When spring came, they bleached the cloth and Vasilisa said to the old woman, 'Grandmother, take this cloth and sell it. Keep the money yourself.' The old woman looked at the cloth and gasped. 'No, my child. No one can wear cloth like this except the tsar. I'm going straight to his palace.' The old woman went to the palace and began walking up and down outside the tsar's window. The tsar saw her and called out, 'What is it, grandmother? What do you want?' 'your Majesty, I've brought you some wonderful merchandise. But I don't want to show it to anyone except you.' The tsar had the old woman let in. She showed him her cloth. He gazed at it in amazement. 'How much do you want for it?' he asked. 'I can't put a price on it, your Highness. I've brought it to you as a gift.' The tsar thanked her, had her given some presents and sent her back home.

He wanted to have some shirts made from this cloth. He had them cut out, but nowhere could anyone find a seamstress who was able to sew them. In the end he called the old woman and said, 'It was you who span the yarn and made the cloth. You must be able to sew it into shirts for me.' 'No, your Majesty, I didn't do the work myself. It's the work of an orphan girl who lives with me.' 'Well then, ask her to sew the shirts.' The old woman went back home and told Vasilisa what the tsar had said. Vasilisa smiled. 'I knew all along,' she said, 'that I'd end up having to do this myself.' She shut herself up in her room and began sewing. She didn't stop till she'd made a dozen shirts.

The old woman took the shirts to the tsar. Vasilisa washed, did her hair, put on her best clothes and sat down by the window. Soon one of the tsar's servants came by. He knocked on the door, entered and said, 'The tsar wishes to see the seamstress who sewed his wonderful shirts. She must go to the palace to receive her reward from his royal hands.' Vasilisa went to the palace. As soon as the tsar saw Vasilisa the Fair, he fell head over heels in love with her. 'No, my beauty, I shall never part with you. You must be my wife.' The tsar took Vasilisa by her fair hands and sat her down beside him. They were married then and there. Soon Vasilisa's father came back and was overjoyed to hear of her good fortune. He and the old woman both came to live at the palace. As for the doll, Vasilisa carried her around in her pocket until the day she died.

Marya Morevna

In a certain land, in a certain tsardom, lived Ivan Tsarevich. He had three sisters: Marya Tsarevna, Olga Tsarevna and Anna Tsarevna. Their father and mother both died. On their death-bed they said to their son, 'You must give your sisters to the first suitors who ask for their hands. Don't keep them at home long.' The tsarevich buried his parents. In his grief he went out to walk with his sisters in their green garden. Suddenly up in the sky appeared a black cloud. A terrible storm came up. 'Quick, sisters! We must get back inside!' said Ivan Tsarevich. The moment they were back in the palace, there was a clap of thunder, the ceiling split open and a bright falcon flew into the room. He struck against the floor, turned into a handsome young warrior and said, 'Greetings, Ivan Tsarevich! I came before as a guest. Now I come as a suitor. I want the hand of your sister, Marya Tsarevna.' 'If my sister loves you,' said Ivan Tsarevich, 'I won't stand in her way. May God be with her!' Marya Tsarevna agreed. The falcon married her and carried her off to his tsardom.

Hours followed hours. Days followed days. A whole year went by as quick as if it had never been. Ivan Tsarevich and his two sisters went out for a walk in their green garden. A black cloud appeared. A whirlwind. Then lightning. 'Quick, sisters! We must get back inside!' said Ivan Tsarevich. The moment they were back in the palace, there was a clap of thunder, the roof fell apart, the ceiling split open and an eagle flew in. He struck against the floor, turned into a handsome young warrior and said, 'Greetings, Ivan Tsarevich! I came before as a guest. Now I come as a suitor.' And he asked for the hand of Olga

Tsarevna. 'If my sister loves you,' said Ivan Tsarevich, 'I won't stand in her way. May God be with her!' Olga Tsarevna agreed. The eagle married her and carried her off to his tsardom.

A second year went by. Ivan Tsarevich said to his youngest sister, 'Come on. Let's go for a walk in our green garden!' They walked about for a while. A black cloud appeared. A whirlwind. Then lightning. 'Quick, Anna! We must get back inside!' They rushed back. Before they had time to sit down, there was a clap of thunder, the ceiling split open and in flew a raven. He struck against the floor and turned into a handsome young warrior. The first two had been handsome enough, but he was more handsome still. 'Greetings, Ivan Tsarevich! I came before as a guest. Now I come as a suitor. Give me the hand of Anna Tsarevna.' 'My sister's will is as she wills. If she loves you, my sister can marry you.' Anna Tsarevna married the raven, and he carried her off to his tsardom.

Ivan Tsarevich lived on his own for a whole year and he began to feel bored and lonely. 'I'll go and look for my sisters,' he decided. He made ready and set off. He rode and rode. One day he came to a field covered by a whole army of dead. He called out, 'If there is one of you left alive, answer me! Who was it defeated this great army?' The one man still alive replied, 'We were defeated by Marya Morevna, the beautiful tsarevna.' Ivan Tsarevich went on until he came to a camp of white tents. Marya Morevna walked out to meet him: 'Good day, Ivan Tsarevich! Where is God taking you? Is it your will that you travel, or is your will not free?' 'A young warrior,' replied Ivan Tsarevich, 'journeys only as he wills.' 'Well then,' said Marya Morevna, 'if you're in no hurry, be my guest for a while.' Ivan Tsarevich gladly agreed. He stayed two nights, and Marya Morevna found him pleasing. They married.

Marya Morevna, the beautiful tsarevna, took him with her to her own land. They lived together for some time, but then the tsarevna took it into her head to go to war. She left everything in the hands of Ivan Tsarevich. All she said to him was, 'Go wherever you like. Look at whatever you like. Only mind you never look into this storeroom.' This was more than Ivan Tsarevich could bear. As soon as Marya Morevna was gone, he rushed straight into the storeroom, opened the door and looked in. There hung Koshchey the Deathless. He was bound by twelve iron chains. 'Have pity on me!' Koshchey begged. 'Give me something to drink. I've been in torment here for ten years. I've had no food and no water. My throat is parched.' Ivan Tsarevich gave him a whole bucket of water. Koshchey drank it down and said, 'My thirst needs more than one bucket. Bring me another.' Ivan Tsarevich gave him a second bucket. Koshchey drank it down and asked for a third. As he swallowed the last drop, all his old strength came back to him. With one shake he snapped the twelve iron chains. 'Thank you, Ivan Tsarevich!' said Koshchey the Deathless. 'But you won't be seeing Marya Morevna again. No, you're as likely to see her again as you are to see your own ears!' He turned into a terrible whirlwind and flew out of the window. He overtook Marya Morevna, the beautiful tsarevna, snatched her up and carried her back to his home.

Ivan Tsarevich wept bitter tears. Then he made ready and set off on his way. 'Come what may,' he said to himself, 'I shall find Marya Morevna.' He walked for a day. He walked for a second day. On the dawn of the third day he saw a wonderful palace. Beside it stood an oak, and perched on the oak was a bright falcon. The falcon flew down from the tree, struck against the ground, turned into a handsome young warrior and called out, 'Ah, my dear brother-in-law! How is God treating you?' Marya Tsarevna ran out, threw her arms round Ivan Tsarevich, and asked him how was he keeping and how had he been living. Ivan stayed for three days as their guest and then said, 'I cannot stay as your guest for long. I'm looking for my wife, Marya Morevna, the beautiful tsarevna.' 'She'll be hard to find,' said the falcon. 'You must at least leave us a keepsake. Leave us your silver spoon.' So Ivan Tsarevich left his silver spoon with the falcon and set off.

He walked for a day. He walked for a second day. On the dawn of the third day he saw a second palace. It was even finer than the first. Nearby stood an oak, and perched on the oak was an eagle. The eagle flew down from the tree, struck against the ground, turned into a handsome young warrior and called

out, 'Olga Tsarevna! Quick! It's our dear brother!' Olga
Tsarevna ran out to meet him. She embraced him and kissed
him. She asked him how was he keeping and how had he been
living. Ivan stayed for three days as their guest and then said, 'I
cannot stay as your guest any longer. I'm looking for my wife,
Marya Morevna, the beautiful tsarevna.' 'She'll be hard to
find,' said the eagle. 'You must at least leave us a keepsake.
Leave us your silver fork.' So Ivan Tsarevich left his silver fork
with the eagle and set off.

He walked for a day. He walked for a second day. On the
dawn of the third day he saw a palace that was still finer than
either of the first two. Nearby stood an oak, and perched on
the oak was a raven. The raven flew down from the tree, struck
against the ground, turned into a handsome young warrior and
called out, 'Anna Tsarevna! Come out at once! Our brother's
come!' Anna Tsarevna ran out to meet him. She greeted him
joyfully. She embraced him and kissed him and asked him how
was he keeping and how had he been living. Ivan stayed for
three days as their guest and then said, 'Goodbye. I'm going to
look for my wife, Marya Morevna, the beautiful tsarevna.'
'She'll be hard to find,' said the raven. 'You must at least leave
us a keepsake. Leave us your silver snuffbox.' So Ivan Tsarevich left his silver snuffbox with the raven and set off.

He walked for a day. He walked for a second day. On the
third day he found Marya Morevna. The moment she saw him,
she threw herself into his arms, burst into tears and said, 'Ivan
Tsarevich! Why, why didn't you listen to me? Why did you
look into the storeroom and let out Koshchey the Deathless?'
'Forgive me, Marya Morevna. But let's not talk of the past. We
must set off at once! Quick – otherwise Koshchey will catch up
with us!' They made ready and set off. As for Koshchey, he was
out hunting. In the evening, as he made his way back, his fine
steed stumbled beneath him. 'Why are you stumbling, you old
nag? Is something the matter at home?' 'Ivan Tsarevich has
come and taken Marya Morevna away with him,' answered
the horse. 'Can we catch up with them?' 'If you were to sow a
field of wheat, wait for it to grow, reap it and thresh it, winnow
it, grind it into flour, bake five ovenfuls of bread and not set out

until you had eaten the last crumb of that bread – even then we could catch up with them!' Koshchey galloped off. He caught up with Ivan Tsarevich. 'Well,' he said. 'I'll pardon you once for your kindness in giving me water. I'll even pardon you a second time. But after that, take care – or I'll cut you to pieces.' He took Marya Morevna and carried her back. Ivan Tsarevich sat on a stone and began to weep.

He wept and wept. Then he went back again for Marya Morevna. Koshchey the Deathless was out. 'Let's go, Marya Morevna!' 'But Ivan Tsarevich, he'll catch up with us!' 'Let him. At least we'll have a little while together.' In the evening, as Koshchey made his way back, his fine steed stumbled beneath him. 'Why are you stumbling, you old nag? Is something the matter at home?' 'Ivan Tsarevich has come and taken Marya Morevna away with him.' 'Can we catch up with them?' 'If you were to sow a field of barley, wait for it to grow, reap it and thresh it, winnow it, make beer from it, get dead drunk on it, and not set out till you've slept it off – even then we could catch up with them!' Koshchey galloped off. He caught up with Ivan Tsarevich. 'I told you before. You're as likely to see Marya Morevna again as you are to see your own ears!' He took Marya Morevna and carried her back.

Ivan Tsarevich was left on his own again. He wept and wept. Once more he went back for Marya Morevna. Once more Koshchey was out hunting. 'Let's go, Marya Morevna!' 'But he'll catch up with us, Ivan Tsarevich! And this time he'll cut you to pieces!' 'Let him cut me to pieces. I can't live without you.' They made ready and set off. In the evening, as Koshchey made his way back, his fine steed stumbled beneath him. 'Why are you stumbling, you old nag? Is something the matter at home?' 'Ivan Tsarevich has come and taken Marya Morevna away with him.' Koshchey the Deathless galloped off, caught up with Ivan Tsarevich, hacked him into tiny pieces, stuffed the pieces into a barrel, sealed the barrel with pitch, bound it with iron hoops and threw it into the blue sea. And he took Marya Morevna back home with him.

Just then the pieces of silver Ivan Tsarevich had left with his three brothers-in-law all went black. 'Oh!' they all cried.

'Something bad must have happened!' The eagle flew straight to the blue sea, snatched up the barrel and carried it back to the shore. The falcon flew off to fetch the water of life. The raven flew off to fetch the water of death. The three birds met together, smashed open the barrel, took out the pieces of Ivan Tsarevich, gave them a good wash and put them in the right order. The raven sprinkled the pieces with the water of death, and they all joined together. The falcon sprinkled the body with the water of life – Ivan Tsarevich gasped, got to his feet and said, 'Goodness me! I must have been sleeping for days!' 'You'd have slept even longer if it weren't for us,' answered the brothers. 'Now you must come and stay with us for a while.' 'No, brothers, I must go and look for Marya Morevna.'

He found Marya Morevna and said, 'Get Koshchey the Deathless to tell you where he found such a fine steed.' Marya Morevna waited till the time was right and asked Koshchey. He replied, 'Beyond thrice-nine lands, in the thrice-tenth tsardom, on the other side of a river of fire, lives a baba yaga. She has a mare on which she flies once round the world every day. And she has many other fine horses. I worked for her for three days as a herdsman. I didn't lose a single mare, so she paid me with one of her foals.' 'But how did you cross the river of fire?' 'I have a handkerchief. I only have to wave it three times over my right shoulder and it becomes a high bridge – too high for any fire to reach.' Marya Morevna remembered all he said and repeated it to Ivan Tsarevich. And she took the handkerchief and gave it to him too.

Ivan Tsarevich crossed the river of fire and set off to find the baba yaga. He walked a long way with nothing to eat and nothing to drink. Then he saw a strange bird from over the seas. With her was a family of chicks. 'I'll have one of those chicks to eat,' he said. 'No, Ivan Tsarevich! Don't!' said the bird from over the seas. 'Don't eat him. One day I'll do you a service.' He went on further. Deep in a forest he saw a hive of bees. 'Well,' he said. 'I'll help myself to a little honey.' 'No, Ivan Tsarevich!' answered the queen bee. 'Don't touch my honey! One day I'll do you a service.' So he left the honey alone. Further on he saw a lioness with a cub. 'Well,' he said. 'At least I can eat that little cub. Otherwise I'll die of hunger.' 'No, Ivan Tsarevich!' answered the lioness. 'Don't touch him. One day I'll do you a service.' 'All right then. I'll do as you say.'

He walked hungrily on. He walked and walked. After a long time he came to the baba yaga's hut. Around it was a circle of twelve stakes. Eleven of them were topped with a human head; only one stake was empty. 'Good day, grandmother.' 'Good day, Ivan Tsarevich. Why have you come? Is it of your own free will or from need?' 'I've come to work for you. I've come to earn a steed fit for a warrior.' 'As you wish, Ivan Tsarevich. You won't have to work for a year, only for three days. If you look after my mares well, I'll give you a steed fit for a warrior. But if you fail – don't be angry. Your head will go on that last stake.' Ivan Tsarevich agreed. The baba yaga gave him some food and drink and set him to work. Ivan let the mares out of the stable. They flicked up their tails and galloped far away over the meadows. Before he could even look round, they were out of sight. He wept and wept. Then he sat on a stone and fell asleep. The sun was already setting when the bird from over the seas awoke him: 'Get up, Ivan Tsarevich. The mares have all gone back home now.' Ivan Tsarevich got to his feet and walked back. The baba yaga was cursing and yelling at her mares: 'Why did you all come back?' 'What else could we do? Flocks of birds flew down from every corner of the world. They nearly pecked out our eyes.' 'All right, don't run about the meadows tomorrow. Scatter deep into the forest instead.'

Ivan Tsarevich slept all night. In the morning the baba yaga said to him, 'Take care, Ivan Tsarevich. If you don't look after my mares well, if you lose even one mare, then tomorrow your bold head will be stuck up on that stake.' Ivan let the mares out of the stables. They flicked up their tails and ran deep into the forest. Once again Ivan Tsarevich sat on a stone. He wept and wept. And then he fell asleep. The sun set beyond the forest. Then the lion came up to him and said, 'Get up, Ivan Tsarevich. The mares have all been rounded up now.' Ivan Tsarevich got to his feet and walked back. The baba yaga was cursing and yelling at her mares more wildly than ever: 'Why did you all come home?' 'What else could we do? Wild beasts came after us from every corner of the world. They nearly tore us to pieces.' 'All right. Tomorrow you must go to the blue sea.'

Once again Ivan Tsarevich slept all through the night. In the morning the baba yaga sent him out again with her mares. 'Remember,' she said. 'If you lose even one mare, then tomorrow your bold head will be stuck up on that stake.' Ivan let the mares out of the stables. They flicked up their tails and vanished from sight into the blue sea. And there they stood up to their necks in the water. Ivan Tsarevich sat on a stone, wept and fell asleep. He slept all day. At sunset a bee flew up to him and said, 'Get up, Tsarevich. The mares have all been rounded up. Go back now, but don't let the baba yaga see you. Hide in the stables behind the manger. You'll see a sickly colt that lies about all day in the dung. That's the one you must steal. Wait until midnight – and then go!'

Ivan Tsarevich stole into the stables and hid behind the manger. The baba yaga was cursing and swearing at her mares again: 'Why did you all come back?' 'What else could we do? There were more bees than you've ever seen in your life. They must have come from every corner of the world. They flew at us from all sides and began stinging us right to the bone.'

The baba yaga fell asleep. At midnight Ivan Tsarevich took the sickly colt, saddled it and galloped off towards the river of fire. He waved the handkerchief three times in the air to his right – and there stood a tall, splendid bridge. Ivan Tsarevich crossed the bridge and waved the handkerchief to his left, but only twice. The bridge was still there over the river, but it was now thin and narrow. The baba yaga awoke in the morning and found that her colt had gone. She galloped off furiously on her iron mortar, spurring it on with her pestle, sweeping away her tracks with a broom. Up she galloped to the river of fire. 'What a fine bridge!' she said to herself. But when the baba yaga was halfway across, the bridge broke in half. She was flung headfirst into the river – and there she died a terrible death. Ivan Tsarevich pastured his colt in green meadows, and it grew into a handsome steed.

Ivan Tsarevich made his way to Marya Morevna. She ran out and threw herself into his arms. 'How did God bring you back to life?' she cried out. He told her all that had happened and then said, 'Let's go now!' 'But I'm frightened, Ivan Tsarevich! What if Koshchey catches up with us and hacks you to pieces again?' 'He won't catch up with us this time. I have a steed that flies like a bird – a steed fit for a warrior.' They mounted and set off. As Koshchey the Deathless made his way back in the evening, his steed stumbled beneath him. 'Why are you stumbling, you old nag? Is something the matter at home?' 'Ivan Tsarevich has come and taken Marya Morevna away with him.' 'Can we catch up with them?' 'I don't know. Ivan Tsarevich has a steed fit for a warrior. It gallops faster than I do.' 'No,' said Koshchey the Deathless. 'I won't stand for it.' After a long time, or maybe a short time, he caught up with Ivan Tsarevich, leapt to the ground and was about to slash at Ivan with his sharp sabre when Ivan's steed kicked him with all his might and smashed his skull into splinters. The tsarevich then finished him off with his cudgel. After that Ivan Tsarevich gathered a great heap of wood, lit a bonfire, burned the body of Koshchey the Deathless and scattered the ashes to the four winds.

Marya Morevna mounted Koshchey's steed, Ivan Tsarevich mounted his own, and off they rode. They went first to the raven, then to the eagle, then to the falcon. In each palace they were greeted with joy: 'Ivan Tsarevich! We thought we'd never set eyes on you again. Well, now we know why you had to go on all those journeys. There can't be another such beauty as your wife in the whole world.'

They stayed for a while in each palace, enjoyed many feasts, then set off for their own tsardom. And there they lived, in health and good cheer and free of all fear. There they lived for many a year, free of need and drinking good mead.

The Little White Duck

Once there lived a prince who married a beautiful princess. But before he had had time to feast his eyes on her, before he had had time to talk and listen to her to his heart's content, he had to part from her. He had to go on a journey and leave his wife in the hands of people who barely knew her. What else could he do? As they say, a man and woman can't spend their whole life in embraces. The princess cried and cried. The prince gave her wise advice. He told her not to come down from her tower, not to talk with strangers and not to listen to evil words. The princess promised to do as he said. The prince left. The princess locked herself up in her chamber and never came out.

After a long time, or maybe only a short time, an old woman appeared down below. No one could have looked kinder or more honest. 'It must be boring and lonely for you up there,' she said to the princess. 'Why don't you come down and have a look at God's world? At least you could go for a walk in the garden. A breath of fresh air blows away every care!'

For a long time the princess made excuses. She really didn't want to go down. But then she thought again: what harm, after all, could come to her in the garden? And so down she went – and there in the garden was a crystal spring. 'It's a hot day,' said the woman. 'The sun's blazing down and the water's cool and fresh. Look at it splashing. Why don't we bathe in it?' 'No, no,' said the princess, 'I don't want to!' But then she thought again: what harm, after all, could come to her in the water? She took off her dress and jumped in. Once she was in the water, the woman struck her on the back. 'Swim on,' she said, 'as a little white duck.' And the princess swam on as a little white duck.

The witch put on the princess's dress and jewels, painted her face and sat down to wait for the prince. As soon as the little dog barked and the little bell tinkled, there she was – running towards the prince, throwing herself into his arms, kissing him and saying all kinds of tender words to him. The prince was overjoyed. He embraced the witch and never saw her for who she was.

As for the little white duck, she laid three eggs and hatched out three little children. Two were strong and healthy, but the third was weak and sickly. The little white duck took good care of all three of them. Soon they had learned how to catch gold fish, how to gather up little scraps of cloth and sew themselves fine kaftans, how to swim through the tall reeds, how to climb up onto the green meads. 'No, no, children, not so far!' the mother kept telling them. 'Not *that* way!' The children did not listen. One day they played about on the bank; the next day they were in the garden. One day they were on the green sward; the next day they were in the great yard. The witch knew them; she sensed who they were and gnashed her teeth. Then she called them after her. She gave them food and drink and put them to bed. Then she went and told her servants to light the fire, to boil the water and sharpen their knives.

The two strong brothers went straight to sleep. But the little sickly one felt too cold. Usually his brothers did as their mother said and kept him warm in their bosoms – but this time they had forgotten. Towards midnight the witch crept up to the door. 'Little ones, are you asleep yet?' she called. She heard a little voice answer:

> We're asleep yet not asleep.
> We are thinking a strange thought,
> Thinking we are to be slaughtered,
> That cranberry branches are burning,
> That cauldrons are steaming,
> That steel knives are being sharpened.

'Not asleep yet,' the witch said to herself. She went away, walked about for a while, then asked again, 'Little ones, are you asleep yet?' The little sickly one gave the same answer:

> *We're asleep yet not asleep.*
> *We are thinking a strange thought,*
> *Thinking we are to be slaughtered,*
> *That cranberry branches are burning,*
> *That cauldrons are steaming,*
> *That steel knives are being sharpened.*

'Why's there only one voice?' thought the witch. She gently opened the door and looked in. The two strong brothers were fast asleep. She touched them with a dead hand and they died.[1] In the morning the little white duck called for her ducklings, but no one came. Her heart guessed what had happened, and she flew straight to the courtyard.

There side by side lay her children, white as handkerchiefs and cold as stones. She rushed towards them, stretched out her wings and wrapped them over her children. In the voice of a mother, she began to lament:

> *Krya-krya-krya, little children!*
> *Quack-quack, my little doves!*
> *Though we lived in need, I gave you my all.*
> *I gave you my own tears to drink;*
> *I lay awake through the darkest nights;*
> *All that was sweet was yours to eat.*

'Listen, wife! Who'd have believed it? There's a duck out here that can talk.'

'What's the matter with you, husband? You must be dreaming. Anyway, what's the duck doing in the yard? Tell someone to drive it away.'

The prince had the duck driven away. She flew straight back again and began to sing to her children:

> *Krya-krya-krya, little children!*
> *Quack-quack, my little doves!*
> *A cruel snake has destroyed you,*
> *An evil witch has been the death of you.*
> *She took you away from your father,*

She took you from my dear husband,
She drowned us in a swift stream,
She turned us into white ducks
So she can strut, strut, strut about the palace.

'What's all this?' thought the prince. And then he shouted out, 'Catch me the little white duck!' Everyone rushed about, but the little white duck always kept just out of their reach. Then the prince tried himself – and she flew straight into his hands.

He held her by one wing and said, 'Be a silver birch behind me! Be a fair maiden before me!' A silver birch sprang up behind him and a fair maiden appeared before him – and this fair maiden was his young princess. Then they caught a magpie, tied two little vials to her legs and told her to fetch life-giving water in one and talking water in the other. The magpie flew off and brought back the water. The parents sprinkled their little ones with life-giving water – and the children gave a start. They sprinkled them with talking water – and the children began to talk.

And so the prince now had a whole family, and together they began to live and prosper and forget past evil. As for the witch, they tied her to a horse's tail and dragged her across the open steppe. Where her legs snapped off, there appeared two shovels. Where her arms snapped off, there appeared two rakes. Where her head snapped off, there appeared a bush and a log. Birds flew down and pecked at her flesh. Winds got up and swept away her bones. Not a trace, not a memory was left of her.

The Frog Princess

In a certain land, in a certain tsardom, there lived a tsar and tsaritsa. They had three young sons, all of them braver and more handsome than storyteller can say or pen can portray. The youngest was called Ivan Tsarevich. One day the tsar said to his sons, 'It's time you were married, sons. You must each take one arrow, draw your stout bows and loose your arrows. Where your three arrows land will be where your three brides stand.'

The eldest brother's arrow landed in the courtyard of a nobleman; the daughter of the house picked it up and handed it back to him. The second brother's arrow landed in the fine porch of a merchant's house; the merchant's daughter picked it up and handed it back to him. The youngest brother's arrow landed in a foul bog – and was found by a croaking frog.

Ivan went back to his father and said, 'How can I marry a frog? A frog's no equal of mine!' 'Marry her,' said his father. 'Your fate is your fate – it can't be escaped.'

The three brothers married. The eldest brother married the nobleman's daughter; the second brother married the merchant's daughter; and Ivan married the croaking frog. After a while the tsar called his three sons together and said, 'For tomorrow I want each of your wives to bake me a loaf of soft white bread.' Ivan walked gloomily back, his bold head below his broad shoulders. 'Kva, kva, Ivan Tsarevich! What are you looking so sad about?' asked the frog. 'Has your father said something unkind?' 'How can I not look sad? My father commands you to bake him a loaf of soft white bread for tomorrow.' 'Don't grieve, Ivan Tsarevich,' said the frog. 'Go to bed and have a good sleep. Mornings are wiser than evenings.' She put the tsarevich to bed, shook off her frog skin and turned into a fair maiden – Vasilisa the Wise. She stepped out onto the fine porch, clapped her hands and called out in a loud voice, 'Women! Servants! Bakers! Bake me a loaf of soft white bread by tomorrow morning – one like we used to eat on holidays in the home of my dear father!'

Ivan Tsarevich got up next morning and found that the frog's loaf was already baked. It was a loaf to take your breath away, more beautiful than pen can portray or anyone but a storyteller can say. It was embellished in many ways, and on each side of the loaf could be seen a gated city. Ivan was overjoyed. He took the loaf to his father. And along came his two brothers with the loaves that their own wives had baked.

First the tsar looked at the loaf brought by his eldest son. He turned it over, looked at it from all sides – and had it sent down to the kitchen. Then he did the same with the loaf brought by his second son. Then he looked at Ivan's loaf and said, 'Now this is bread. This is what I call bread. This is the kind of bread you eat on a holiday.' He ordered it to be served at his own table.

Then he said to his sons, 'Now I want each of your wives to weave me a carpet. And I want the carpets ready by tomorrow morning.' Ivan walked gloomily back, his bold head below his broad shoulders. 'Kva, kva, Ivan Tsarevich! What are you looking so sad about? Did your father not like the loaf I baked him? Has he said something cross or cruel?' 'How can I not look sad? My father thanks you for the bread and commands you to sew him a silk carpet by tomorrow morning.' 'Don't grieve, Ivan Tsarevich. Go to bed and have a good sleep. Mornings are wiser than evenings.'

She put the tsarevich to bed, shook off her frog skin and turned into a fair maiden – Vasilisa the Wise. She stepped out onto the fine porch, clapped her hands and called out in a loud voice, 'Women! Servants! Weavers! Make me a silk carpet by tomorrow morning – one like I used to sit on in the home of my dear father!'

Ivan Tsarevich awoke in the morning and found the carpet already finished. It was the most sumptuous carpet you've ever set eyes on, more beautiful than in any dream, more beautiful than pen can portray or anyone but a storyteller can say. It was flecked with silver and gold and on it could be seen the entire tsardom – every city and village, every mountain and forest, every river and lake. Ivan Tsarevich was overjoyed. He took the carpet to his father. And along came his two brothers with the carpets that their own wives had woven.

First the tsar looked at the carpet brought by his eldest son. He had it spread out on the floor, looked at it carefully and said, 'Thank you! This is a carpet to lay on the threshold.' Then he looked at the carpet brought by his second son. He felt it between his fingers and said, 'Thank you! This is a carpet to wipe one's boots on.'

Then he had Ivan's carpet spread out on the floor. Everyone gasped. The tsar took it in his hands and gazed at it. He turned to his servants and said, 'And I want this carpet beneath my royal throne.' And then the tsar ordered his three sons to bring their wives to a banquet that evening.

Ivan walked gloomily back, his bold head below his broad shoulders. 'Kva, kva, Ivan Tsarevich! Why are you looking so sad? Has your father said something cross or cruel?' 'How can I not look sad? My father's asked me to bring you to a banquet this evening. What can I do? How can I show you to so many people?'

'Don't grieve, Ivan Tsarevich. You go first and I'll follow. When you hear loud cracks of thunder, say, "That's my little frog, riding along in her little box".'

Ivan went to the palace. And along came his two brothers; their wives were arrayed in all their finest clothes and jewels. The brothers looked at Ivan and began to laugh. 'Why haven't you brought your own wife along then?' they asked. 'You could have wrapped her up in a silk handkerchief and carried her here in your hands. Where did you find such a beauty anyway? You must have had to search every bog in the tsardom.'

Suddenly there were cracks of thunder. The palace shook. Everyone jumped to their feet in fear, but Ivan said, 'Don't be afraid, honest guests. That's my little frog, riding along in her little box.'

Drawn by six white horses, a gilded carriage drew up to the palace gate – and out stepped Vasilisa the Wise, more beautiful than pen can portray or anyone but a storyteller can say. She took Ivan Tsarevich by the hand and sat down with him at the oak table.

The guests began to eat, drink and be merry. Vasilisa drank her glass of wine and poured the dregs into her left sleeve. She ate some roast swan and dropped the bones into her right sleeve. The elder brothers' wives watched what she did, then did the same themselves.[1]

When everyone had eaten and drunk, it was time to dance. Vasilisa the Wise took Ivan Tsarevich by the hand and got up. As she danced, she waved her left arm in the air – and out of nowhere appeared a beautiful lake. She waved her right arm in the air – and there, swimming across this lake, were seven white swans. The tsar and his guests were filled with wonder. Then the wives of the two elder brothers began to dance. They waved their left arms in the air – and sprayed wine over the guests. They waved their right arms in the air – and the bone of a swan flew into the tsar's eye. The tsar was furious, and he had the two women thrown out of the palace.

After that Ivan Tsarevich slipped out and rode back home. He found the frog skin and threw it onto the fire. Then Vasilisa the Wise came back. She looked round but couldn't see her frog skin anywhere. 'Ivan Tsarevich! Ivan Tsarevich!' she lamented. 'What have you done? If you'd only waited, if you'd only waited, I could have been yours forever. But now – farewell! If you want me, you must seek me beyond thrice-nine lands, in the thrice-tenth tsardom. I'll be with Koshchey the Deathless.'

She turned into a white swan and flew out of the window.

Ivan Tsarevich wept bitterly, then made ready, said farewell to his mother and father and set off where his eyes looked. He walked a long way, or maybe a short way; he walked for many a day, or maybe less than a day. Then he met an old, old man.

'Greetings, young warrior!' said the old man. 'Where are you going? What are you looking for?'

Ivan told him his story.

'Ivan Tsarevich!' said the old man. 'What made you burn the

frog's skin? It wasn't your own attire – nor was it yours to throw in the fire. Vasilisa the Wise was born smarter and wiser than her own father. Her father didn't like this, so he turned her into a frog for three years. Well, I'll do what I can for you. Here, take this ball! Follow boldly wherever it rolls.'

Ivan Tsarevich thanked the old man and set off after the ball. As he was walking through open steppe, he caught sight of a bear. He was about to shoot the beast when it said, in a human voice, 'Don't kill me, Ivan Tsarevich. One day I'll be of service to you.'

He walked on further. He saw a drake flying overhead. He had taken aim with his bow, he was about to shoot the drake, when it cried out in a human voice, 'Don't kill me, Ivan Tsarevich. One day I'll be of service to you.'

He walked on further. A hare ran past. He raised his bow and was taking aim when it said in a human voice, 'Don't kill me, Ivan Tsarevich. One day I'll be of service to you.'

Ivan took pity on the hare too. He walked on till he came to the sea. There on the shore lay a pike. It was dying. 'Ivan Tsarevich!' it gasped. 'Take pity on me. Throw me back into the sea.' Ivan picked up the pike and threw it into the water.

After a long time, or maybe a short time, the ball rolled up to a little hut by the very edge of the sea. It was built on chicken legs and it was turning round and round in circles.

'Stand still, little hut!' said Ivan. 'Stay as your mother made you. Stay with your back towards the sea and your door towards me.'

The hut turned round and came to a stop with its back towards the sea. Ivan walked in. There on the stove, on the ninth brick, lay a bony-legged baba yaga. Her nose had grown into the ceiling and the snot from it was hanging across the threshold. She had slung her tits up over a hook and was sharpening her teeth.[2] 'What's brought you here, my fine fellow?' she asked.

'What a slut you are! First you should give me something to eat and drink. You should take me to the bathhouse for a good steam. After that you can ask me again.'

The baba yaga gave him food and drink and took him to the

bathhouse. Then the traveller told her he was looking for his wife, Vasilisa the Wise.

'Oh yes,' said the baba yaga, 'I know all about her. She's with Koshchey the Deathless. You won't find it easy to get her away from him. His death lies in the tip of a needle. This needle lies inside an egg. This egg lies inside a duck. This duck lies inside the belly of a hare. And this hare lies inside a chest hidden at the top of a tall oak that Koshchey watches over like the apple of his eye.'

The yaga told Ivan Tsarevich where this oak grew, and there he went – but he had no idea how to get his hands on the chest.

Just then a bear came along and uprooted the tree. The chest fell to the ground and smashed to pieces. A hare leaped out and shot into the bushes.

A second hare shot after it, caught it and tore it apart.

A duck leaped out of the hare's belly and flew high into the sky. A drake swooped down and gave it such a blow that it dropped the egg it was carrying straight into the blue sea. This was more than Ivan Tsarevich could bear – he sat down by the shore and began to weep tear after bitter tear.

All of a sudden a pike swam up to the shore. In its mouth it was holding an egg. Ivan took the egg and went straight to where Koshchey lived. Seeing the egg in Ivan's hands, Koshchey began to tremble. Ivan Tsarevich began playing with the egg, tossing it from one hand to the other. Koshchey writhed and struggled and swayed from side to side. Then Ivan cracked the egg, took out the needle and snapped off the tip – and that was the end of Koshchey. Ivan went into Koshchey's stone house. There he found Vasilisa the Wise, and he took her back with him to his own land.

When they got back, Ivan's father invited the whole country to a banquet in their honour. After that they lived happily together for many years.

Pig Skin

A great prince had a beautiful wife and he loved her with all his heart. His wife died and he had only his daughter, who was as like her mother as one drop of water is like another drop of water. The prince said to his daughter, 'Dear daughter, I shall marry you!' The girl went to the cemetery, to her mother's grave, and began to weep bitterly. The mother said, 'Order a dress to be bought for you – a dress covered in stars!' The prince bought the girl just such a dress and fell in love with her more than ever. The girl went to talk to her mother again. The mother said, 'Order a dress to be bought for you – a dress with the silver moon sewn on its back and the golden sun on its front.' The father bought the dress and fell still more deeply in love. The girl went to her mother again and wept bitterly: 'Mother, my father now loves me more than ever.' 'Well, my child,' said the mother, 'now you must order a pig skin to be made for you.' The father had that made too; and, as soon as the skin was ready, the daughter put it on. The father spat on her and threw her out of their home. He didn't allow her any maids, nor did he even give her any bread to take with her. The girl crossed herself and walked out through the gate. 'I'll go,' she said, 'wherever God wills.' She walked for a day, and for a second day, and for a third day; she entered unknown lands.

Storm clouds appeared and it began to rain. Where could she shelter? The princess saw a huge oak tree; she climbed up and sat in its branches. Just then a tsarevich came past; he was going hunting. His dogs rushed at the oak; they leaped at the tree and barked at it. The tsarevich was curious; why, he wondered, were his dogs barking at a tree? He sent his servant to look. The servant came back and said, 'your Highness! There's a beast sitting up in the oak tree – only it's not a beast but a marvellous wonder, a wondrous marvel!' The tsarevich went to the foot of the tree and asked, 'What kind of a marvel are you? Can you or can you not speak?' The princess replied, 'I am Pig Skin.' Instead of going on with his hunting, the tsarevich sat Pig Skin in his carriage and said, 'I shall show my mother and father this marvellous wonder, this wondrous marvel.' His mother and father marvelled at Pig Skin and had her put in a special room.

Soon afterwards the tsar gave a ball; everyone at court went to make merry. Pig Skin asked one of the servants, 'May I stand by the door and watch the ball?' 'Don't even think of it, Pig Skin!' She went out into open steppe and put on a dress that was scattered with glittering stars. She let out something between a shout and a whistle – and there beside her was a carriage. Off she drove to the ball. She arrived, went in and began to dance. Everyone marvelled: where had such a beauty appeared from? She danced and danced, and then she disappeared; she put on her pig skin and ran back to her room. The tsarevich went to her room and asked, 'Wasn't that you, Pig Skin? Weren't you that beauty?' 'Me with this skin of mine!' she replied. 'How could I have been at the ball? I just stood by the door.'

The tsar gave another ball. Pig Skin asked to be allowed to go and watch. 'Don't even think of it!' She went out into open steppe and let out something between a shout and a whistle – and a carriage appeared. She cast off her pig skin and put on a dress; the moon shone on her back, and the golden sun from her breast. She arrived at the ball and began to dance. There she was, dancing at the ball. Everyone watched. She danced for a while, and then she disappeared; she put on her pig skin and ran back to her room. 'What am I to do?' thought the tsarevich. 'Who can that beauty have been? How am I to find out?' Then he had an idea: he would smear the first of the steps with pitch. Then her shoe would stick and be left behind.

At the third ball the princess seemed more beautiful still. But when she left the palace, her little shoe stuck to the pitch. The tsarevich took this little shoe and began to search everywhere in the tsardom: whose foot would the little shoe fit? He travelled through all his lands and found no one whom the shoe fitted. He got back home, went straight to Pig Skin and said, 'Show me your foot.' She showed him her foot; the little shoe proved a perfect fit. Then the tsarevich slit open the pig skin and took it off the princess. Then he took her by her white hand, led her to his mother and father and asked their permission to marry her. The tsar and tsaritsa gave the young couple their blessing. When they were married, the tsarevich asked his wife, 'Why were you wearing a pig skin?' 'It was because I looked like my late mother,' she replied, 'and my father wanted to marry me.'

The Tsarevna in an Underground Tsardom

Once there were a tsar and tsaritsa who had a son and a daughter. They told their son that when they both died, he must marry his sister. And after a while – maybe a long while or maybe only a short while – the tsar and tsaritsa died. The brother ordered his sister to prepare for their wedding, and he himself went to the priest, to ask him to marry them.

The sister began to dress herself and she made three dolls. She put the dolls on the windowsill, stood in the middle of the hut and said, 'Dolls, wake up!' 'What is it?' asked the first doll. 'The brother is marrying the sister,' said the second doll. 'Earth, open up! Sister, fall down!' said the third doll. And the three dolls said all this a second time and a third time. The brother came and asked his sister, 'Have you finished dressing yet?' The sister replied, 'No, not quite.' So he went to his chambers and waited for his sister to get ready. But the sister said once again, 'Dolls, wake up!' And the first doll asked 'What is it?' And the second doll said, 'The brother is marrying the sister.' And the third doll said, 'Earth, open up! Sister, fall down!' And the sister fell down into the other world. When the brother came back, he could not find his sister anywhere. He was left on his own.

After falling into the other world, the sister walked and walked until she saw an oak tree. She went up to the oak and took off her clothes. The oak opened up. She put her clothes in the hollow, made herself into an old woman and walked on. She walked and walked until she came to a tsar's palace. There she asked if she could work as a maid. They said she could stoke the stoves. Now the tsar had a son who had not yet married. When Sunday came, this son was dressing, getting ready to go to church. He asked the old woman to give him a comb. The old woman was rather slow, and he lost his temper and hit her with this comb on the cheek. Then he finished dressing and went off to church. The old woman went to the oak where she had hidden her clothes; the oak opened up for her. She dressed, made herself into a very beautiful tsarevna, then went to the church. The tsarevich saw her there and asked one of his servants where she was from. The servant knew she was the old woman who stoked the stoves and that the tsarevich had hit her with his comb, and so he answered, 'She comes from the town of Combblow.' The tsarevich went back home. He asked everyone where he could find this town, but no one could tell him.

Somehow it happened a second time that the tsarevich got angry, hit the old-woman-tsarevna with a boot and then went off to church. The unknown beauty was there again, wearing the clothes she had hidden in the oak tree. Seeing her, the tsarevich once again asked his servant where she was from. The servant answered, 'From Bootblow.' The tsarevich searched and searched for this town but couldn't find it anywhere in his tsardom. And he began to wonder what he could do: how could he get to know this beautiful stranger? He had fallen in love with her and he wanted her for his wife. In the end he came up with a ruse. He ordered pitch to be smeared on the floor of the church, in the place where she always stood – just a little, so that she wouldn't see it.

On Sunday the tsarevna came in her fine clothes to the church and stood in her usual place. The service came to an end; it was time for her to go back. She took a step, but her slipper stuck to the pitch. She went back home with only one slipper. The tsarevich had the other slipper brought to him. He took it back home and then began trying it on all the young girls in the tsardom. The slipper didn't fit anyone; it only fitted the old woman who stoked the stoves. The tsarevich questioned her; she told him who she was and where she was from. And so he married her. I was at the wedding feast – yes, I drank mead and wine there. No drop passed my lips; it all flowed down my beard.

The Tsarevna
who would not Laugh

How great – if we think about it – is God's world! In it live rich and poor. There is space for all and the Lord watches and judges all. The wealthy live in idleness; the wretched toil. To each his lot is given.

In the tsar's palace, high above the world in her royal chambers, lived a beautiful tsarevna who wouldn't laugh. What a life she had! What freedom! What luxury! She had everything, all her heart could wish for. Yet not once did she smile or laugh; it seemed her heart took no joy in anything.

It was painful for the tsar to look on his sad daughter. He welcomed to his royal palace anyone who wished to be his guest. 'Let them try to entertain the tsarevna who will not laugh!' he said. 'Whoever brings her joy may take her for his wife!' No sooner had he spoken than the palace was surrounded by a dense crowd. From all sides – in carriages, on horseback, on foot – came tsareviches and princes, boyars and noblemen, important generals and simple people. Great feasts were eaten and much mead was drunk – but not once did the tsarevna laugh or smile.

Meanwhile, just outside the city, in a little corner of his own, there lived an honest worker. Every morning he swept his yard; every evening he pastured his livestock; he laboured constantly. His master, who was as just as he was wealthy, wanted to pay the worker his due. At the end of the year the master put a bag of money on the table, said, 'Take as much as you want', and left the room. The man went up to the table. 'How can I avoid sin?' he wondered. 'How can I avoid taking too much for my labour?' In the end he took a single coin. Holding the coin in his fist, he went to the well for some water. He bent down. The coin fell out of his hand and dropped to the very bottom of the well.

The poor worker was left with nothing. Another man would have wept and grieved and thrown up his hands in despair – but not him. 'Everything comes from the Lord,' he thought. 'The Lord knows to whom to give. Some he rewards generously; from others he takes away their last kopek. I must have been lazy and worked little. From now I shall be more zealous.' He returned to work. And whatever task he turned his hand to, it was done well – and done in a flash.

Another year passed by, and his master again put a bag of money on the table. 'Take as much as you want,' he said, and left the room. The worker thought again about how not to anger God by taking too much for his labour. He took a single coin. Holding it in his fist, he went to the well for some water. He bent down – and somehow he let the coin slip. It fell into the well and dropped down to the very bottom. After that he began working still more zealously, sleeping only a little and eating only a little. And his work bore fruit. While other men's grain was fading and withering, his master's filled out and ripened. While other folk's cattle could barely put one foot in front of the other, his master's would be capering down the street. While other people's horses, fearful of slipping, had to be dragged down a steep hill, his master's could hardly be held back. His master was no fool and he knew whom to thank for all this. At the end of the year he placed a heap of money on the table. 'Take as much as your soul desires,' he said. 'It was your labour and it's your money.' And he left the room.

Once again the man took only one coin. Once again he went to the well for a drink of water. But this time his coin stayed safe in his hand and the two coins from before floated up to the surface. He took them, understanding that the Lord had rewarded him for his labours. Full of joy, he said to himself, 'It's time I saw more of the wide world. It's time I learned more about the people who live in it.' He thought for a little, then set off where his eyes looked. He walked through a field – and a mouse ran up to him and said, 'Give me a coin, brother. One day I'll do you a service!' So he gave the mouse a coin. He walked through a wood – and a beetle crept up to him and said, 'Give me a coin, brother. One day I'll do you a service!' So he gave the beetle a coin too. He swam across a river – and he met a catfish. The catfish said, 'Give me a coin, brother. One day I'll do you a service!' He did not refuse the catfish either; he gave him his last coin.

The man made his way into the city. So many people! So many doors! He gazed about him; he turned in one direction after another, but he didn't know which way to go. In front of him stood the tsar's palace, decked with silver and gold. And sitting at her window, looking straight at him, was the tsarevna who wouldn't laugh. What should he do with himself? Where could he hide? His eyes clouded over, sleep dropped down on him, and he fell flat on his face in the mud. And straight away, as if out of nowhere, appeared the big-whiskered catfish, the beetling beetle and little Miss Mouse. There they all were, and they quickly got down to work. The mouse took the man's coat off; the beetle cleaned his boots; and the catfish drove the flies away with his big whiskers. The tsarevna who wouldn't laugh couldn't take her eyes off all this. She burst out laughing.

'Who has brought joy to my daughter?' asked the tsar. 'I did!' said one man. '*I* did!' said another. 'No!' said the tsarevna who wouldn't laugh. 'It was him!' And she pointed to the worker down below. He was led into the palace at once, and there before the tsar he became a handsome young fellow. And the tsar kept his royal oath; the young couple were betrothed that very evening.

'Didn't the worker just dream all this?' I sometimes say. But people tell me this is the honest truth – and so we must believe it.

Misery

In a certain village there once lived two brothers. One was poor, the other rich. The rich brother went to live in the city, built himself a fine house and became a merchant. But the poor brother often didn't have so much as a crust of bread in the house; his little children, each littler than the next, were always weeping and begging for something to put in their mouths. From morning till night the man struggled to keep his head above water – but all in vain. One day he said to his wife, 'I'm going to the city to see my brother. Maybe he'll help us out.' He found his rich brother and said, 'Dear brother, help me a little in my misery. My wife and children are without bread. They're going hungry for days on end.' 'Do a week's work for me – then I'll help you.' What could the poor brother do? He set to work. He swept the yard; he groomed the horses; he fetched water and he chopped wood. At the end of the week the rich brother gave him a loaf of bread. 'Here you are!' he said. 'This is for the work you've done.' 'For this,' said the poor brother, 'I thank you.' He bowed low and was about to set off back home. 'Wait a moment,' said the rich brother. 'Come back tomorrow. Be my guest. And bring your wife too. Tomorrow's my name day.' 'What do you mean, brother? How can I? Your other guests will be merchants. They'll be wearing boots and fur coats. But I've only got my bast sandals and my old grey kaftan.' 'That doesn't matter. Come along anyway. There'll be a place for you too.' 'All right, brother, I'll come.' The poor brother went back home, gave the loaf of bread to his wife and said, 'Listen, wife! We've been invited to a feast tomorrow.' 'What do you mean? Who by?' 'By my brother. Tomorrow's his name day.' 'All right then, let's go.' The following morning they went straight to the city. They went to the house of the rich brother, gave him their congratulations and sat down on a bench. Sitting at the table were many distinguished guests, and the rich brother was feasting them all splendidly. But he completely forgot about the poor brother and his wife. He didn't give them anything to eat at all. Their only entertainment was to sit and watch everyone else eating and drinking. When the dinner was over, the guests rose from the table and began to thank their host and hostess. The poor brother got to his feet too, then bowed to the ground before his brother. And the guests went off in their carriages, drunken and merry, singing at the tops of their voices.

The poor brother had to walk home on foot, and with an empty stomach. But he said to his wife, 'We must sing a song too!' 'What do you mean, you fool? People sing because they've eaten and drunk their fill. But what have we got to sing about?' 'I've just been at a feast – the name day of my own brother. I'm ashamed to walk home without singing. If I sing, people will think I've had a good time.' 'All right then, you sing if you must – but I won't!' The peasant began to sing. What he heard, though, was not one voice but two. He stopped and said to his wife, 'Was it you just then, singing along with me in a high voice?' 'What do you mean? I wasn't doing anything of the kind.' 'Who was it then?' 'I don't know,' said the wife. 'But try singing again. I'll listen.' The husband began to sing a second time. He was singing alone, but there were two voices. 'Is that you, Misery, singing along with me?' And Misery replied, 'Yes, Master, it was me.' 'Well, Misery, come back home with us then!' 'Yes, Master, I'm not going to leave you now.'

The peasant got back home. Misery invited him along to the tavern with him. The peasant said, 'But I haven't got any money!' 'Who cares about that? What do you need money for? You're wearing a sheepskin, but it'll be summer soon and you won't need it then. Let's go to the tavern – and off with that sheepskin!' The peasant and Misery went to the tavern and drank away the sheepskin. The next morning Misery was moaning and groaning. Misery had a hangover from the night before and he wanted the peasant to go back to the tavern with him for some more vodka. 'But I haven't got any money!' 'Who cares about that? What do you need money for? Take your sleigh and your cart – that'll be more than enough.' What could the peasant do? There's no getting away from Misery. He took his sleigh and his cart and dragged them along to the tavern; then he and Misery drank them away too. The morning after, Misery was moaning and groaning more than ever. He had to drink away his hangover; he got the peasant to go back to the tavern yet again. This time the peasant drank away his harrow and plough. Before a month had gone by, the peasant had squandered everything he possessed. He had even pawned his hut to a neighbour and drunk away all the money the neighbour had given him for it. But there's no getting away from Misery. 'Come on, friend, let's go to the tavern!' 'No, Misery, I'll do what you will – but there's nothing more I can sell.' 'What do you mean? Your wife has two dresses. You can leave your wife one of them – but we must drink away the other.' The peasant took one of the dresses, drank it away and said to himself, 'Now I truly am cleaned out. Neither house nor home. Neither my wife nor I have anything left.'

Misery woke up the next morning, saw there was nothing more he could take from the peasant and said, 'Master!' 'What is it, Misery?' 'Listen now. You must go round to your neighbour and ask if you can borrow a cart and a pair of oxen.' The peasant did as Misery told him. He said to his neighbour, 'Let me borrow your cart and a pair of oxen, just for a little while. In return I'll do a week's work for you.' 'What do you want them for?' 'To go to the forest for firewood.' 'All right then, but mind you don't overload the cart.' 'Certainly not, my friend!' The peasant took the oxen, sat down with Misery in the cart and drove out into the steppe. 'Master,' said Misery, 'do you know the big stone over there?' 'How could I not know it?' 'Well then, drive right up to it.' They came to the stone, stopped and got down from the cart. Misery told the peasant to lift up the stone. The peasant lifted the stone, and Misery helped too. Beneath the stone lay a pit filled with gold. 'Come on then,' said Misery. 'Don't just stand and stare. Load it into the cart.'

The peasant got to work. He filled the cart with gold. He completely emptied the pit, down to the very last gold rouble. When he was quite sure there was nothing left, he said to Misery, 'Have a look, Misery. Are you sure there isn't anything left there?' Misery leaned down over the pit. 'Where? I can't see anything myself.' 'There – in the corner! I can see a coin glittering.' 'I can't see anything at all.' Misery crawled down. As soon as he was safely in the pit, the peasant laid the stone back on top of him. 'It'll be better like this,' said the peasant. 'If I were to take you back with me, O miserable Misery, you'd drink our way through all this too. Yes, sooner or later you'd drink away every last piece of gold.' The peasant went back home, stored the money in his cellar, returned the oxen to his neighbour and began to think about how best to establish himself in the world. First, he bought plenty of wood and built himself a fine house – and soon he was living twice as wealthily as his brother the merchant.

Time passed – maybe a long time, maybe a short time. One day he rode to the city to invite his rich brother to his name-day party. 'What do you mean?' asked the brother. 'You've got nothing to eat yourself. How can you be celebrating your name day?' 'There was a time when I had nothing to eat. But now – thanks are to God – I have no less than you. Come along and you'll see!' 'Very well then, I'll come.' The following day the rich brother and his wife set off to the feast. They could hardly believe their eyes: this wretched pauper now had a grand new house – grander than many a merchant's. And he was treating them to one delicacy after another – and to every kind of mead and wine. 'Tell me,' said the rich brother, 'what turn of fate has brought you these riches!' The poor brother told him the honest truth, how Misery had fastened on him; how he and this miserable miserybags had gone to the tavern and drunk away all he owned, down to his last thread of clothing, until there was nothing left to him but the soul in his body; how Misery had taken him to a store of buried treasure out in the steppe; how he had taken the treasure for himself and said goodbye forever to Misery.

The rich brother felt envious. 'I'll go out into the steppe myself,' he thought. 'I'll lift the stone up and set Misery free.

Let him ruin my brother completely. How dare my brother boast to me of his riches?' And so he sent his wife home and drove out into the steppe. He drove up to the big stone, moved it to one side, then bent down to see what was there. But barely had he looked down before Misery had jumped out of the pit and onto his shoulders. 'Ah!' he yelled. 'You thought you could starve me to death, did you? Well, I won't leave you now for anything in the world!' 'No, Misery, it wasn't me! It wasn't me who imprisoned you beneath the stone!' 'Who was it then? Who else could it have been?' 'It was my brother. It was my brother imprisoned you, and now I've come to set you free.' 'You're lying. You tricked me once, but you're not going to trick me a second time.' Misery sat fast on the rich man's neck. The rich man took Misery back home with him, and everything in his life began to go wrong. Every morning Misery was hard at it, doing the work he did best. Every morning he took the merchant along to the tavern with him, so the two of them could drink away their hangovers. Very soon, the merchant was a great deal poorer and the tavern-keeper a great deal richer. In the end, though, the merchant understood that this was no way to live. 'I've been giving Misery too good a time,' he said to himself. 'I really must send him on his way now – but how?'

The merchant thought and thought. In the end he thought his way to an answer. He went out into his yard, made himself two oak wedges, took a new wheel and knocked one of the wedges into the hub. Then he went up to Misery. 'What's up, Misery? Why are you just lying about all the time?' 'What else have I got to do?' 'What else? Let's go out into the yard together and play hide-and-seek.' Misery was only too glad. Out they went into the yard. The merchant hid first. Misery found him at once, and then it was his turn to hide. 'Well,' he said. 'You're going to find this difficult. I can hide myself inside the very tiniest of cracks.' 'Nonsense!' said the merchant. 'You couldn't get inside this wheel, let alone into a crack.' 'What do you mean? Just watch me!' Misery crept into the wheel. The merchant took the other oak wedge and drove it into the hub from the other side. Then he threw the wheel into the river, along with Misery. Misery drowned, and the merchant returned to his former life.

The Wise Girl

Two brothers were travelling together. One was poor, and the other rich. Each had a horse. The poor brother had a mare; the rich brother a gelding. They stopped somewhere for the night. During that night the poor man's mare bore a foal, and this foal rolled under the rich man's cart. In the morning the rich man woke his poor brother with the words, 'Get up, brother! My cart's foaled during the night!' The poor brother got up and said, 'How can a cart bear a foal? The foal belongs to my mare!' The rich man said, 'If it were your mare's foal, it would be lying there beside her!' They argued and argued, then went to the authorities. The rich man gave the judges money; the poor man made his case with words.

The tsar himself got to hear of this lawsuit. He summoned both brothers before him and asked them four riddles: 'What is the strongest and swiftest thing in the world? What is richer and fatter than anything in the world? What is the softest thing in the world? And what is the sweetest thing?' He gave them three days: on the fourth day they were to return to him with their answers.

The rich man thought and thought, remembered his god-mother and went to ask her advice. She sat him down at her table, gave him something to eat and drink and asked, 'Why are you so sad, my godson?' 'Because the sovereign has asked me four riddles and I have only three days to answer them.' 'What are the riddles? Tell me!' 'Well, godmother, this is the first riddle: "What is the strongest and swiftest thing in the world?"' 'Call that a riddle? My husband has a dark bay mare. There's nothing swifter than her in the world. You only have to show her the whip and she can outrun a hare!' 'And this is the second riddle: "What is richer and fatter than anything in the world?"' 'We've been feeding a spotted boar for over two years now. He's grown so fat he can barely stand.' 'And this is the third riddle: "What is the softest thing in the world?"' 'Everyone knows the answer to that. Nothing in the world is softer than down.' 'And this is the fourth riddle: "What is the sweetest thing in the world?"' 'The sweetest thing in the world is my grandson Ivanushka.' 'Thank you, godmother! You have spoken good sense. I shan't forget it.'

As for the poor brother, he wept bitter tears and then set off back home. He was met by his seven-year-old daughter; this daughter was all the family he had. 'Why are you sighing and shedding tears, father?' 'How can I not sigh and shed tears? The tsar has asked me four riddles and I wouldn't be able to answer them even if I had a million years.' 'Tell me – what are these riddles?' 'These are the riddles, my daughter: what is the strongest and swiftest thing in the world? What is richer and fatter than anything in the world? What is the softest thing in the world? And what is the sweetest thing?' 'Go to the tsar, father, and tell him that the strongest and swiftest thing in the world is the wind. The richest and fattest thing is the earth – there's nothing that lives and grows that the earth doesn't feed. The softest thing in the world is a hand – no matter what a man sleeps on, he will put his hand under his head. And the sweetest thing in the world is sleep!'

The poor brother and the rich brother went to the tsar. The tsar heard their answers, then asked the poor brother, 'Did you guess the riddles yourself? Or did someone teach you?' The poor brother answered, 'your Majesty, I have a seven-year-old daughter. It was she who taught me.' 'If your daughter is so wise, then here is a silken thread for her. Let her weave me a patterned towel by tomorrow morning.' The brother took the silken thread and went back home, sad and grieving. 'We're in trouble,' he said to his daughter. 'The tsar orders you to weave a towel out of this little thread.' 'Don't be sad, father,' said the seven-year-old girl. She broke off a little twig from a broom, gave it to her father and said, 'Go to the tsar and tell him to find a master craftsman who can make a loom from this little twig. Then I'll be able to weave him his towel!' Her father did as she said. The tsar gave him 150 eggs. 'Give these eggs to your daughter,' he said. 'Let her hatch 150 chicks for me by tomorrow.'

The father went back home, now sadder than ever. 'Oh my daughter,' he said, 'barely do we see off one trouble before another is upon us.' 'Don't be sad, father,' said the seven-year-old girl. She baked the eggs, put them aside for their lunch and their supper and sent her father back to the tsar. 'Tell him,' she said, 'that the chickens need one-day grain. Let a field be ploughed, and the millet sown, harvested and milled in a single day. That's the only grain our chickens will eat!' The tsar heard this answer and said, 'If your daughter's so wise, let her appear before me tomorrow morning. Let her come neither on foot nor on horseback, neither naked nor clothed, and let her come neither gifted nor giftless.' 'Now we're well and truly undone,' thought the father. 'Not even my daughter can unriddle this.' 'Don't be sad, father,' said the seven-year-old girl. 'Go to the hunters and buy me a live hare and a live quail.' And so the father bought her a hare and a quail.

The following morning the seven-year-old girl took off her clothes and put on a net. She took the quail in her hands, mounted the hare and rode to the palace. The tsar met her at the gate. She bowed to the tsar and said, 'Here's a little gift for you, your Majesty!' – and held out the quail to him. The tsar reached out his hand but – flap, flap, went the quail, and away it flew. 'Very good,' said the tsar. 'You have done as I said. Tell me now. Your father is very poor – what do you live on?' 'My father goes fishing on a dry bank. He never puts his traps in the water. And I make fish soup in the hem of my skirt.' 'Don't be so stupid! When did fish ever live on a dry bank? Fish swim about in the water.' 'And are you so very clever yourself? Whoever heard of a cart bearing a foal? Foals come from mares, not from carts!'

The tsar awarded the foal to the poor brother. As for the seven-year-old daughter, he took her into his palace. And when she had grown up, he married her and she became the tsaritsa.

IVAN ALEKSANDROVICH KHUDYAKOV

(1842–76)

The life of Ivan Khudyakov, Afanasyev's brilliant younger contemporary, is still more tragic than that of Afanasyev himself. For Khudyakov, learning from the people (by collecting and studying their folklore) and educating them (by teaching them both basic literacy and revolutionary ideas) were inseparable parts of a single social and artistic enterprise.

In 1860, while still only an eighteen-year-old student at Moscow University, Khudyakov published a collection of historical folksongs and the first volume of a collection of folktales; he published the second and third volumes in 1861 and 1862. He also published a collection of riddles, the first volume in 1861 and the second in 1864.

In 1861, however, Khudyakov was one of several students excluded from Moscow University after lodging a complaint about one of the teachers. This pushed Khudyakov towards the revolutionary opposition, and in 1866 he was arrested (members of the commission that searched his apartment were apparently amused by his manuscript collection of obscene and anti-clerical folktales – a collection later lost in a fire).[1] Convicted of complicity in a plot to assassinate Tsar Alexander II, Khudyakov was exiled to eastern Siberia – to Verkhoyansk, which is probably the coldest town on Earth. Initially undaunted, he studied the language and folklore of the native Yakut people, compiled a Yakut–Russian dictionary and wrote a number of articles, but in 1869 he began to suffer from what was probably clinical depression and by 1874, when he was transferred to a psychiatric hospital in Irkutsk, he had lost his reason. He died a year later.

Khudyakov's contribution to the study of Russian folklore was, of course, far smaller than it might have been. In two respects, however, his collection marks an advance on Afanasyev's; all his transcripts are verbatim, and he included information about individual storytellers. He may also have been the first of many exiled revolutionaries to study the languages and culture of the native peoples of Siberia. His Verkhoyansk Anthology *was finally published by the Eastern Siberian Section of the Geographical Society in 1899, and his* Brief Description of the Verkhoyansk Region, *long considered lost, was published in Leningrad in 1969. Khudyakov evidently came to a deep understanding of the nature of oral poetry. After only a few years in Verkhoyansk, and in spite of the terrible conditions of his exile, he was reaching conclusions that Western scholars reached only a century later. 'During my student days,' he writes, 'I thought it improbable that a single popular singer could have known and sung by heart such a long tale as the* Iliad *or the* Odyssey, *remembering a large number of proper names and not omitting even such details as a nail in a ship. Yakut storytellers sing and tell stories of no less a length and go into still finer details.'*[2]

The Brother

Once there lived a lady. She had three daughters and a little son. She took very great care of her son and wouldn't let him out of the house. One splendid summer day the daughters came to their mother and asked her to let them take their brother to walk in the garden. For a long time the mother wouldn't agree, then finally she let him go. They walked for a long time in the garden. Suddenly a strong wind came up. The sand and dust rose up in a cloud, and the child was torn out of the nanny's arms and carried off to who knows where. They looked and looked for him in the garden, but they couldn't find him. They cried a bit, then went and told their mother that their little brother had disappeared.

The mother sent the oldest daughter to look for him. She went out into a meadow, where three paths were in front of her. She set off along the one that went straight ahead. She walked and walked, until she came to a birch tree. 'Birch tree, birch tree! Tell me, where's my little brother?'

'Pick leaves from me, take half of them for yourself, and leave half for me. I'll come in handy to you in time!'

The girl didn't listen. She said, 'I don't have time!' and she went on further. She came to an apple tree. 'Apple tree, apple tree! Did you happen to see my little brother?'

'Pick all the apples off me; take half for yourself, and leave half for me. I'll come in handy to you in time.'

She said, 'No, I don't have time! How can I pick fruit? I'm going to look for my very own blood brother!' She walked and walked. She came to a stove. And the stove had been lit; it was very hot. 'Stove, stove! Did you happen to see my own little brother?'

'Fair maiden! Sweep out the stove, bake a wafer, take half for yourself, and leave half for me. I'll come in handy to you in time.'

'How can I sweep and bake? I'm on my way to take care of my brother!'

She went on further. A house was standing on chicken legs, on spindle heels; it stood there and spun around. She said, 'Little house, little house! Stand with your back to the woods, your front to me!' The house turned around, and she went up into it. She said a prayer to God and bowed in all four directions.

A baba yaga was lying on the bench, with her head in the wall, her legs sticking up into the ceiling, and with her teeth on the shelf. The baba yaga said, 'Fie, fie, fie! Until now there was no smell or sight of a Russian soul. You, maiden, are you doing a deed or fleeing a deed?'

She said, 'Granny! I've walked over mosses and over swamps. I got all soaked through, and I've come to you to warm up.'

'Sit down, fair maiden! Look for things on my head!'

She sat down to look and saw her brother sitting on a chair, while the tomcat Yeremey told him stories and sang songs. The old woman, the baba yaga, fell asleep. The girl took her brother and ran off to take him home.

She came to the stove. 'Stove, stove! Hide me!'

'No, fair maiden, I won't hide you.'

She came to the apple tree. 'Apple tree, apple tree! Hide me!'

'No, fair maiden, I won't hide you.'

She came to the birch tree. 'Birch tree, birch tree! Hide me!'

'No, fair maiden, I won't hide you!' She walked on further.

But then the cat started to purr, and the baba yaga woke up and saw the boy was missing. She shouted, 'Grey eagle! Fly off at once. The sister's been here, and she's taken the boy!' (This eagle was the one who had carried the boy away from his mother.)

The grey eagle flew off. 'Stove, stove! Did you happen to see, did a girl pass by here with a little boy?'

'Yes, she did.'

The eagle flew further. 'Apple tree, apple tree! Did you happen to see, did a girl pass by here with a little boy?'

'She just went by!'

The eagle flew on to the birch tree. It caught up with the girl, took away her brother, and scratched her all up, scratched her all over with its claws.

She came home to her mother. 'No, mother, I didn't find my own dear brother!'

Then the middle sister asked, 'Will you let me go search for our brother?' They let her go. She set off and everything happened just the same way. She came home all tattered, scratched all over.

The youngest sister started asking to go. They told her, 'Your two sisters went out and didn't find him, and you won't find him either!'

'God knows, maybe I will find him!' She set off. She came to the birch tree. 'Birch tree, birch tree! Tell me where my little brother is!'

'Pick leaves off me. Take half for yourself and leave half for me. I'll come in handy to you some time!'

She picked the little leaves, and she took half for herself and left half for the tree. She went on further, and she came to the apple tree. 'Apple tree, apple tree! Did you happen to see my own little brother?'

'Fair maiden, pick apples from me. Take half for yourself, leave half for me. I'll come in handy to you some time!' She picked the apples. She took half for herself and left half for the tree, and she went on further. She came to the stove. 'Stove, stove! Did you happen to see my own little brother?'

'Fair maiden! Sweep me out and bake a wafer. Take half for yourself, leave half for me!' So she swept out the stove, baked a wafer, took half for herself, and left half for the stove.

She went along further. She came close and saw a little house standing on chicken legs, on spindle heels, spinning around. She said, 'Little house, little house! Stand with your back to the forest, with your front to me!' The house turned. She went inside and said a prayer to God. (And she had brought along from home: a piece of butter, some pretzels, some of everything.)

The baba yaga said, 'Until now there was no smell or sight of a Russian soul, but now a Russian soul appears before my eyes! What are you doing here, fair maiden, doing a deed or fleeing a deed?'

'No, granny! I was walking through the forest, through the swamps, and I got soaked through, chilled through. I've called in on you so I can warm up!'

'Sit down, fair maiden!' said the baba yaga. 'Look for things on my head!'

The girl began to look and kept saying, 'Fall asleep one eye, fall asleep other eye. If you don't fall asleep I'll pour pitch over you, I'll stop you up with balls of cotton!' The baba yaga fell asleep. The girl took some cotton and dipped it in pitch, and smeared the baba yaga's eyes with pitch. Right away she gave the cat Yeremey a piece of butter, and a doughnut, and some pretzels, and some apples, some of everything. And she took her brother. The cat ate his fill, lay down, and took a nap.

She left with her brother. She came to the stove and said, 'Stove, stove! Hide me!'

'Sit down, fair maiden!' Right away the stove spread out, it got much wider. She sat down in it. And the baba yaga woke up, but she couldn't pull her eyes open, so she crawled to the door and shouted, 'Tomcat Yeremey! Claw my eyes open!'

But he answered her, 'Purr, purr! I've lived with you so long, and I never saw so much as a burnt crust. But the fair maiden came for only an hour, and she gave me a lump of butter!'

Then the baba yaga crawled to the threshold. She shouted, 'Grey eagle! Fly at once, the sister's been here, she's taken her brother away!'

The eagle flew off. It flew up to the stove. 'Stove, stove! Did you happen to see, did a girl happen to pass here with a little boy?'

'No, I haven't seen anything.'

'And why, stove, have you become so wide?'

The stove said, 'It's just for a time. I was stoked not long ago!'

Then the eagle went back again, scratched and scratched at the baba yaga's eyes, scratched her all over. The sister and brother came to the apple tree. 'Apple tree, apple tree! Hide me!'

'Sit down, fair maiden!'

The apple tree made itself fluffy, curly.

She sat right down in a crevice in the trunk. Then the grey eagle came flying again and flew to the apple tree. 'Apple tree, apple tree! Did you happen to see, did a girl happen to pass here with a little boy?'

It answered, 'No.'

'Why, apple tree, have you become so curly, lowered your branches right down to the ground?'

'The time has come,' it said. 'I'm standing here all curly.'

The eagle went back to the baba yaga. It clawed and clawed, but it couldn't scratch her eyes open.

And the girl came to the birch tree. 'Birch tree, birch tree! Hide me!'

'Sit down, little mother!' it said. It made itself fluffy, curly, like the apple tree.

The grey eagle came flying again. 'Birch tree, birch tree! Did you happen to see, did a girl happen to pass by here with a little boy?'

'No, I didn't.'

The eagle went back again. The girl came home, and she brought the little boy with her. Everyone rejoiced.

I was there, and I drank mead and beer. It dripped down my moustache, but none got into my mouth.

The Stepdaughter and the Stepmother's Daughter

There lived an old man and an old woman. They had only one daughter. The old woman died, and the old man married another woman. He had a daughter with the second wife as well. The old woman didn't like her stepdaughter and was always trying to hurt her. Once the old woman sent her to the river to wash yarn and told her, 'Watch out! If you let the yarn sink to the bottom, then don't bother coming home!'

The girl went to the river and laid the yarn on the water. The yarn floated along the river, and she walked slowly along the bank after it. The yarn floated all the way to the forest and sank.

She went into the forest and saw a little house on chicken legs. She said, 'Little house, little house! Stand with your back to the woods, your front to me!' The little house obeyed.

The stepdaughter went into it and saw a yaga baba. Her head lay in one corner of the house, her feet in another. The yaga baba saw her and said, 'Fie, fie, fie! I can smell a Russian soul. What are you up to, girl, doing a deed or fleeing a deed?'

The girl told her that her mother had sent her to wash thread and said that if she let it sink, she shouldn't come home.

The yaga baba made her heat up the bathhouse. The girl asked the yaga baba, 'Where's your firewood?'

And the yaga baba answered, 'My firewood is behind the bathhouse!' But the fuel stacked there was really human bones.

The girl went to heat up the bathhouse, hauled in lots of bones and put them in the stove, but no matter how she tried she couldn't make them catch fire. The bones only smouldered. Then she sat on the ground and cried, and she saw a sparrow come flying up to her. The sparrow said, 'Don't cry, girl! Go into the woods, gather firewood there and use it to stoke the stove!'

The girl did just that. Then she went and told the yaga baba that she'd heated the bathhouse. But the yaga baba said, 'Now go and bring water in a sieve!'

She went and thought, 'How am I going to bring water in a sieve?'

The sparrow flew up again and said to her, 'Why are you crying? Smear the sieve with clay!'

The girl did just that. She brought plenty of water and went to call the yaga baba to the bathhouse, but the yaga baba answered, 'You go to the bathhouse! I'll send you my children now!' The girl went into the bathhouse.

Suddenly she saw worms, frogs, rats and all sorts of insects come crawling up to her in the bathhouse. She washed all of them and gave them a good steaming. Then she went to get the yaga baba and washed her too. Then she washed herself. She came out of the bathhouse, and the yaga baba told her to heat up the samovar. She did this, and they drank tea.

The yaga baba sent her into the cellar too.

'There are two trunks in my cellar,' she said. 'A red one and a blue one. Take the red one for yourself!' So the girl took the red trunk and went home to her father. Her father was glad to see her. He opened the trunk, and the trunk was full of money.

The stepmother started to envy her and sent her own daughter to the yaga baba, who told the girl to stoke the bathhouse with bones. The sparrow flew down to her and said, 'Go into the woods and gather firewood!'

But the girl swatted the bird with her hand. 'Go away,' she said. 'I don't need you to tell me that.' Yet she herself couldn't get the bathhouse heated. Then the yaga baba told her to bring water in a sieve.

The sparrow flew up to her again and said, 'You could smear the sieve with clay.'

She hit it again. 'Go away,' she said. 'I don't need you to tell me that.' But then she saw that rats and frogs and all sorts of vermin were coming into the bathhouse. She squashed half of them, but the others ran home and complained about her to their mother. The stepmother's daughter went back to the yaga baba too. The yaga baba told her to heat up the samovar, and she did. After tea the yaga baba sent her to the cellar and told her to take the blue trunk. The girl was very happy. She ran into the cellar, grabbed the trunk, and ran off home. Her father and mother were waiting for her at the front gate. She and her mother went into the shed and opened the lid of the trunk. But there was fire in it, and they were both burned up.

PART THREE

EARLY TWENTIETH-CENTURY COLLECTIONS

The third important period for Russian folklore was the last decade of the nineteenth century and the first two decades of the twentieth. This was a time when many European artists, composers and writers were turning to folklore as a source of images and motifs, but nowhere did folklore seem as important as it did in Russia. Russian native traditions were as significant to the Russian modernists as African and Oceanic art to Picasso and Matisse. Vasily Kandinsky's move to abstraction arose directly from his encounter with the art of the Komi, one of the indigenous peoples of northern Russia. Leon Bakst, Pavel Filonov, Natalya Goncharova, Mikhail Larionov, Kazimir Malevich, Kuzma Petrov-Vodkin, Nikolay Roerich, Valentin Serov, Viktor Vasnetsov, Mikhail Vrubel – almost every important artist of the period found inspiration in Russian icon painting and Russian folk art. Many of these artists illustrated scenes from folktales; several drew on folk art for the sets or costumes they designed for Diaghilev's Ballets Russes. The finest of all Russian folktale illustrations – Ivan Bilibin's illustrations of tales from Afanasyev – were first published between 1899 and 1902. The image of the firebird, above all, was extraordinarily popular.

The composers of the period were no less interested in folklore. Mussorgsky, Rimsky-Korsakov and the other Romantic nationalist composers known collectively as 'The Mighty Handful' all incorporated themes from Russian folklore in their compositions; Rimsky-Korsakov, in particular, was greatly influenced by Afanasyev's The Poetic Outlook of the Slavs on Nature. And Stravinsky's most famous works for the Ballets

Russes – The Firebird *and* The Rite of Spring – *draw heavily on folk rhythms and motifs.*

Russian writers of this period seem, however, to have been less successful in their attempts to use material from folklore. Sologub, Remizov and others wrote works they called skazki, but these bear only a distant relationship to the traditional magic tale and most of them, in any case, now seem false or precious. I have therefore limited this section to examples of the oral folktales collected during the thirty years before the Revolution. Several fine collections were published then, and Afanasyev's pre-eminence has led to their being neglected, especially by translators.

In Russia, perhaps even more than in other European countries, the early twentieth century was a period not only of artistic and political upheaval but also of spiritual ferment. There was intense interest in paganism, in eastern religions and – above all – in the potent brew that Madame Blavatsky had concocted from a variety of religions and philosophies and labelled Theosophy. Folktale collectors must have felt that, rather than researching a remote past, they were engaging with the most pressing questions of the day. The nature writer Mikhail Prishvin, for example, wrote in 1907, 'I doubt if there is any place where the heathen world is in such close contact with the Christian world as in the area around Lake Vygozero. To this day there are hermits living in this region who try to recreate the life of the first Christian ascetes. And sometimes, into the huts of these hermits wander hunters like Philipp – people who throughout their lives have had dealings only with forest spirits, sorcerers and bears.'[1]

The first two stories in this section are taken from an important ethnographic journal, Zhivaya starina ('Living Antiquity') that was established in 1890.

The Tsar Maiden

Once there was a tsar who had three sons: Fyodor Tsarevich, Dmitry Tsarevich and Ivan Tsarevich.

This tsar gave a great feast.

And he asked his assembled generals and counts, 'Sirs! I have three sons. Which of them is able to gather my flowers and follow my footsteps?'

The eldest son, Fyodor Tsarevich, stepped forward and said, 'Give me your blessing, father, to gather your flowers and follow your footsteps.'

This gladdened the tsar. He ordered his son to be given the best horse in the stables. The horse was saddled and bridled, and the brave lad rode off into open steppe.

He rode till he came to a pillar, and on the pillar was written:

'He who takes the road to the right will eat well, but his horse will go hungry. He who takes the road to the left, he himself will go hungry, but his horse will eat well. And he who takes the middle road will lay his head on the executioner's block.'

Fyodor Tsarevich thought for a while, then took the road to the right.

And he came to a copper mountain. He dismounted, left his horse at the foot of the mountain and climbed up. He wandered about the mountain but he could find nothing there except a copper snake, a most beautiful snake made of copper. And he put it in his pocket and returned to his own country.

And he returned to his father. He went into his father's private chambers and showed him this copper snake.

But his father was very angry, and he said only, 'What filth have you brought? It could destroy our tsardom!'

And the tsar remained angry for a long time.

But then, as he was walking about the garden, the tsar began to feel merry again. He gave orders for a feast to be prepared, and for there to be dancing.

And everyone at the feast got drunk.

Amid this merriment the tsar stood up and said, 'My counts and generals! Although my children are now all fully grown, none of them has yet proved able to gather my flowers and follow my footsteps!'

Dmitry Tsarevich stepped forward, bowed to his father and said, 'Give me your blessing, father, to gather your flowers and follow your footsteps.'

This gladdened the tsar. He ordered his son to be given the best horse in the stables.

The son mounted the horse and rode off into open steppe.

And he rode through open steppe and rode till he came to a pillar, and on the pillar was written:

'He who takes the road to the right will eat well, but his horse will go hungry. He who takes the road to the left, he himself will go hungry, but his horse will eat well. And he who takes the middle road will lay his head on the executioner's block.'

The young man thought, then wept: 'Where shall I go? I shall take the road to the left. My horse will eat well, and he will carry me out of trouble.'

He rode on – maybe a short way, maybe a long way. He rode until he came to a great mansion. He rode around the mansion and through the gates into the courtyard. There he saw finely turned columns and gilded bridle rings. He tethered his horse, gave him some millet and went up some stairs to the upper rooms. A woman came out to meet him. She hurried towards him and greeted him warmly. The table was covered with all kinds of good food. She told the young man to eat and drink. When he had eaten his fill, she took him to a bed so he could rest. But no sooner had he lain down than the bed tipped over and he flew straight down into a cellar.

The tsar waited a long time for his son to return; he sorrowed for a long time.

Then the tsar ordered a feast to be prepared. He felt merry again, and he said to his counts and generals, 'My counts and generals! I have brought up three sons. But however diligent they have been, however zealous in the service of our tsardom, not one has yet gathered my flowers and followed my footsteps!'

Then Ivan Tsarevich stepped forward and asked for his father's blessing.

'O Ivan Tsarevich, Ivan son of the Tsar! Your brothers were better men than you – and what have they achieved? You'd do better to lie by the stove. Why attempt what you can never achieve?'

This angered Ivan Tsarevich. He said, 'Father, great lord! If you grant me your blessing and forgiveness, I shall ride away. And if you do not grant me your blessing and forgiveness, away I shall ride.'

And the tsar ordered him to be given the best horse – so he might ride wherever he wished.

The grooms offered him the very best horse of all. But Ivan Tsarevich went and chose the very worst horse of all, the horse that was used only for carrying water. And the brave young prince mounted this horse with his face towards the horse's tail. All the lords laughed: how could the son of a tsar ride so badly?

Ivan Tsarevich rode into open steppe. Then he seized his horse by the tail, tore off its hide and hung this hide up on a nail.

'Fly down, magpies and crows! Enjoy the dinner the Lord bestows!'

He roared like a wild beast, then whistled like a dragon. Up galloped a steed whose hooves made our damp Mother Earth tremble. It was breathing flames from its mouth and sparks from its nostrils. Pillars of smoke and fumes rose from its ears and from its arse it was shitting smouldering logs.[1]

But Ivan Tsarevich took hold of this fine steed and stroked it – and the steed went so quiet that a child of three could have ridden it.

Then Ivan Tsarevich went down into the great deep cellar that his grandfather had given him. He ate and drank his fill and took his best plaited bridle and Circassian saddle. He harnessed his fine steed and took a sharp sword. Then he sat on his fine steed and rode out into open steppe.

And he rode through open steppe till he came to a pillar, and on the pillar was written:

'He who takes the road to the right will eat well, but his horse will go hungry. He who takes the road to the left, he himself will go hungry, but his horse will eat well. And he who takes the middle road will lay his head on the executioner's block.'

The brave young tsarevich wept and thought, 'Is it not an honour for a fighting man to ride to his fate, though he lay his head on the executioner's block?'

And off he galloped through open steppe. He had only to raise his hand – and his fine steed left rivers and lakes far beneath its hooves. Its mane whirled in the wind and its tail spread over the earth.

Ivan Tsarevich came to green meadows. There he saw a hut on a spindle heel – its porch towards him and its back to the trees. He leaped down from his fine steed and said, 'I don't mean to stay a long stay – I mean to stay for one night. I shall go inside you and come out again too.'

And the young man went inside. As is right and as is written, he crossed himself; as is right and as is written, he bowed.

An old woman was sitting there. With her nose she was poking the fire; with her eyes she was watching her geese outside; with her hands she was spinning silk.

'Foo, foo, foo! Till now not even the black raven has brought me a Russian bone, but now a living Russian stands before my eyes. What brings you here, my child? Is it your will? Or is your will not free?'

The young man leaped towards the old woman and cried out, 'I'll knock you about the lughole so air comes out of your cunt-hole. I'll smash you across the ears so sand flies out of your arse. Old woman, you should learn not to ask too many questions. A fighting man needs his food and drink!'

The old woman laid the table, gave Ivan Tsarevich his food and drink, then asked, 'Child, what brings you here? Is it your will? Or is your will not free?'

And he replied, 'My own free will – but three times more, my unfree will. There were three of us, three brothers. The first rode out from home – and brought back only a copper snake from the copper mountain. And our father threw him in prison. The second brother rode out no one knows where – and no more is known of him. And then it was my turn to serve, my turn to gather my father's flowers and follow his footsteps. Tell me, grandmother, did our Papa ride far in his day?'

'Lie down to sleep, my child. Morning is wiser than evening, and the light of day brings rewards!'

In the morning the old woman woke the brave young fellow. She gave him food and drink, gave him a fine steed of her own, led him out onto the road and said, 'My sister lives further on and she knows of you and your task.'

And off he galloped again through open steppe – from mountain to mountain and from hill to hill. He had only to raise his hand – and his fine steed left rivers and lakes far beneath its hooves. The steed's mane span as it streamed in the wind and its tail spread over the earth.

And Ivan came to green meadows. Evening was drawing in. There at the edge of a field he saw a hut standing on a goat's leg, on a spindle heel. 'Stand still, little hut!' he called. 'I don't mean to stay a long stay – I mean to stay for one night. I shall go inside you and come out again too.'

The little hut stood its ground, its back to the trees, its porch towards the tsarevich.

And he leaped down from his fine steed and went inside. A woman still older than her sister was sitting there. With her hands she was spinning silk; with her nose she was poking the fire; with her eyes she was watching her geese outside.

'Foo, foo, foo! Till now not even the black raven has brought me a Russian bone, but now a living Russian stands before my eyes. What brings you here, my child? Is it your will? Or is your will not free?'

Ivan Tsarevich had been feeling tired and hungry. These words angered him and he leaped at the old woman and threatened her: 'I'll knock you about the lughole till air comes out of your cunt-hole. I'll smash you across the ears so sand flies out of your arse. Old woman, you should learn not to ask too many questions. You should learn to give a fighting man food and drink and give him a feather bed to lie on!'

The old woman laid the table, gave him his food and drink, let him lie and rest for a while then asked, 'Child, what brings you here? Is it your will? Or is your will not free?'

'Oh, grandmother,' he replied. 'Twice more, my unfree will. Our Papa ordered us to gather his flowers and follow his footsteps. Tell me, grandmother, did our Papa ride far in his day?'

'Lie down to sleep, my child. Morning is wise, and the light of day brings rewards. Morning is wiser than evening, my child. Come morning I'll tell you!'

The old woman woke him early the next morning. She gave the young fellow food and drink, gave him a fine steed of her own, keeping the other steed with her, and led him out into open steppe.

And off he galloped again through open steppe – from mountain to mountain and from hill to hill. He had only to raise his hand – and his fine steed left rivers and lakes beneath its hooves. Its mane whirled in the wind and its tail spread over the earth.

And he came to green meadows. The day was drawing to an end, the sun sinking towards evening. And there in the green meadows he saw a hut.

'Stand still, little hut!' he called. 'Stand still on your goat's leg, on your spindle heel! I don't mean to stay a long stay – I mean to stay for one night. I shall go inside you and come out again too.'

And he rode up on his fine steed to the porch. And he leaped down from his fine steed and went inside. A very old woman was sitting there. She was spinning silk and poking the fire with her nose; and with her eyes she was watching her geese in the field outside.

'What brings you here, my child? Is it your will? Or is your will not free?'

Ivan Tsarevich had been feeling tired and hungry. These words angered him and he leaped at the old woman and threatened her: 'I'll knock you about the lughole till air comes out of your cunt-hole. I'll smash you across the ears so sand flies out of your arse.'

No longer did the old woman feel like sitting there. She gave him food and drink, let him rest for a while and only then began to ask questions.

'Oh, grandmother,' he replied, 'let me tell you of my deeds. There were three of us brothers, three sons to the tsar. The first brother was Fyodor Tsarevich. Our father sent him off to gather his flowers and follow his footsteps – but he rode only as far as the copper mountain and he brought back from there only a copper snake. And this angered our father, and our father threw him in prison. The second brother was Dmitry Tsarevich. Our father sent him out too, but he disappeared no one knows where. He has never returned. And then it was my turn to serve, to gather my father's flowers and follow his footsteps. My father said, "Where do you think you're going, Ivan? Your brothers were better men than you are. You'd do better to sit at home on the stove and not play the hero. Your brothers were older than you are, but they have still not come back to me!" What could I do but step forward and ask for my father's blessing? "Father," I said, "if you grant me your blessing and forgiveness, I shall ride away. And if you do not grant me your blessing and forgiveness, away I shall ride." This pleased the tsar, and he let me go. And so my turn came to gather his flowers and follow his footsteps. Tell me, grandmother, did Papa ride far in his day?'

'Morning is wise, child, and the light of day brings its rewards. Morning is wiser than evening. I'll tell you in the morning.'

The old woman woke him early the next morning. She gave him her own fine steed, led him out onto the road and said to him, 'At the very middle of the day, child, you will come to the tsardom under the sun. A maiden rules there as tsaritsa, and her name is Marya the Fair, Marya of the Long Tress of Hair. Her bed stands on nine pillars and she sleeps on it at the very middle of the day. But you must hurry – you must leap straight over the city wall. In the garden stands a young apple tree, and there too is the water of life and the water of death. This is why your father rode to the city. You must fill two phials with these waters, but first you must tear a young raven in half and test which of these waters is which. To your right should be the water of life; to your left the water of death.'

Ivan Tsarevich rode into the tsardom under the sun, went on foot into the garden and caught a young raven and tore it in half. He sprinkled the raven with the water of death and its body grew together again. Then he sprinkled the raven with the water of life – and away it flew.

And then the young fellow wanted to go inside, into the rooms of the palace. He wanted to look at the Tsar Maiden. He wanted to see how she slept at noon – Marya the Fair, Marya of the Long Tress of Hair. He walked through the rooms and chambers, and all the maidens were sleeping on their beds. And he came to the chamber of Marya the Fair, Marya of the Long Tress of Hair. She was beautiful beyond all measure. And as she breathed in, doors closed, and as she breathed out, doors opened. And – the young man's ardent heart caught fire.

'Is this not an honour?' he thought. 'At this well I shall water my horse.'

Through Marya's shift he could see her body, and through her body he could see the very marrow of her bone.

And he was on fire, and he wanted to do his wish. And the maiden sensed nothing of his wish and pleasure . . .

And then he went quietly out of the room, and quietly out of the palace.

And he went out into the broad courtyard, and he found his steed standing very tired. He led his steed to a spring and he doused his steed with fresh water, and then he gathered the apples of youth and filled his knapsack with them, and he filled two phials with the water of life and the water of death and he then wanted to leave the tsardom with all haste.

And he mounted his fine steed and, eager to ride away, he struck the steed on its broad quarters. And the steed leaped straight over the city wall – and with its left hoof it struck a copper wire. All around the city copper wires and bells rang out, and the Tsar Maiden awoke, and she awoke all her maids. And she made them all winged – and she flew off in pursuit of Ivan Tsarevich.

'A thief has been in our realm and he has watered his horse at my well. He has stolen our apples of youth and the waters of life and death!'[2]

Ivan Tsarevich rode on till he came to the old woman, and she led out a fine steed for him. And the tsarevich leaped from steed to steed, and on he galloped.

And then the old woman invited her niece, the Tsar Maiden, to drink tea with her and to drink coffee with her.

'What are you saying, woman? I have no time or leisure. Have you not seen some fool ride by?'

'Oh, my child!' said the old woman. 'He won't escape you. His horse is tired now. He's beating the poor horse with a stick, urging it on. Be my guest for a while!'

While the Tsar Maiden was being entertained, Ivan Tsarevich spurred his steed on. He came to the second old woman.

Meanwhile, the Tsar Maiden arose and she too sped on to the second old woman.

'Woman, have you seen a fool pass by, on foot or on horseback?'

'My child,' said the old woman. 'Some fool did pass by. He was beating his horse, and it stumbled. He won't get much further!'

And she insisted the Tsar Maiden be her guest, for tea and for coffee.

And the Maiden went in.

While she was being entertained, Ivan Tsarevich came to the third old woman. She returned his own fine steed to him and sent him straight on his way.

And the Tsar Maiden got up, left the second old woman and went in pursuit. She flew on to the third old woman and asked, 'Woman, have you seen a fool pass by, on foot or on horseback?'

'Come in as my guest! Some fool did pass by, but he is already flaying the skin off his horse.'

And the old woman begged her to come in. 'It's hot,' she said. 'You must rest!'

The Tsar Maiden rested. She ate and drank. Then she set off in pursuit.

But Ivan Tsarevich had already reached Holy Russia, and his pursuer was unable to catch him!

And he rode through open steppe till he came to the pillar with the inscription.

Here Ivan Tsarevich thought, 'Is not this an honour? I have travelled down unknown roads. I have fulfilled my father's wishes. Now I shall search for my brother, Dmitry Tsarevich!'

And so, in search of his brother, he set off down the road where his horse would eat well but he himself would go hungry.

And he came to green meadows. And he saw a huge house there, and he rode up to it. He rode through the gate, stabled his horse and gave it fresh white barley. His brother's horse from the tsar's stables recognized the new guest and neighed for all it was worth. Ivan Tsarevich walked up to the fine-turned columns and climbed the gilded staircase. A beautiful woman came down to meet him. She invited him to her chamber and seated him at her table.

She gave him food and drink and all kinds of delicacies. After he had eaten, she showed the young man where he could rest. She wanted him to lie next to the wall, but he wanted her to lie there herself. They argued long. In the end Ivan Tsarevich seized her round her belly and threw her against the wall. The self-turning bed turned right over – and down into a deep dungeon flew the beautiful woman.

'A new companion!' called out those already imprisoned in this dungeon. 'God has granted us a new companion!'

'Tear her limb from limb!' called out Ivan Tsarevich. 'This woman was your undoing!'

The prisoners seized her. One tore off an arm; another a leg; another her head.

Then Ivan Tsarevich let down a rope, and he gave the young men their freedom. When he saw his brother Dmitry, he took him by his white hands and his golden breast. He kissed him on his sweet lips and called him his dear brother Dmitry

Tsarevich. He gave him food and drink, then rode off with him towards their city.

They came into open steppe. Ivan Tsarevich was overwhelmed by a deep and irresistible sleep. For nine days and nine nights he had ridden without sleeping, eating or drinking. And so he and his brother put up their white tents and rested.

Ivan Tsarevich slept without waking.

On the third day Dmitry Tsarevich stole the apples of youth, the water of life and his brother's knapsack. And off he rode to their father's realm.

Ivan Tsarevich awoke. There was nothing to be seen. He mounted his fine horse and rode to the border of his father's realm. Then he took off the Circassian saddle and the plaited bridle and said, 'Run out into the fields, Sivka-Burka! Rest in the fields, my grey-brown one! Rest until I need you again!'

Ivan Tsarevich went back on foot to his city. There he passed his time in the taverns, drinking with whoever he found there.

In the meantime the tsar received Dmitry Tsarevich with great honour, with dancing and revelry.

Three years passed, but what's quick to say takes many a day. And then the Tsar Maiden sailed up to the city. In the middle of the night, in the hour after midnight, she began to fire on the city with guns and cannons. She demanded the surrender of whoever was guilty.

The tsar didn't know what to do. Which criminal should he surrender?

The tsar gathered his counsellors. 'Counsellors and boyars, let us think! Do we have here some criminal we should surrender?'

'Merciful sovereign, if it please you, we can give counsel. Has Fyodor Tsarevich not perhaps made mischief in foreign lands? Has he not perhaps committed a crime in some other realm?'

And so Fyodor Tsarevich was delivered to the ship. Marya the Fair, Marya of the Long Tress of Hair saw him coming. She ordered a gangplank to be lowered, and for it be spread with red cloth. And there were two beautiful little boys running about the ship, and they called out, 'Mama! Mama! Our Papa's coming!'

'No, children,' she answered. 'It's not your father; it's your eldest uncle.'

Then she gave orders to her men: 'Seize this fellow and stretch him out on the deck. Hack three strips from his back and strip three strips from below his hips. Let him learn not to plough another man's ground! And then – throw him back on shore!'

Once again she began to bombard the city day and night, with guns and cannons. She demanded the surrender of whoever was guilty.

And the tsar gathered his counsellors. 'Is there some criminal here in our realm? Is there someone we should surrender?'

'If it please you, your Highness, send Dmitry Tsarevich. Perhaps *he* is the guilty man!'

And so the tsar sent his second son to the ship. A gangplank was lowered, and it was spread with red cloth. The two little boys ran up to their mother and said, 'Mama! Mama! Our Papa's coming!'

'No, children,' she answered. 'It's not your father; it's your second uncle.'

Then she gave orders to her men: 'Seize this fellow by his white hands and stretch him out on the deck. Hack three strips from his back and strip three strips from below his hips. Let him learn not to plough another man's ground! And then – throw him back on shore!'

Once again she began to fire on the city, with guns and cannons, and to demand the surrender of whoever was guilty.

And once again the tsar gathered his counsellors. 'Well, counsellors, who among us has done wrong? Give me advice and counsel.'

And one of them was bold enough to answer, 'Your Imperial Highness, it is your Majesty who is at fault.' And he went on to say, 'Ivan the Layabout is also a tsarevich. He too is your son. It does not befit me to say this, but he hangs about the inns and taverns and tells all kinds of lies and tall stories and passes them off as high wisdom.'

'Search for him straight away,' commanded the tsar, 'and bring him to me. Perhaps it is *he* who has committed a crime!'

They searched all over the city for him. They searched for him in the inns and taverns, and they searched for him outside the city walls. In the end they found the layabout tsarevich and summoned him to his father's presence. And he appeared before his father in a ragged uniform, and this greatly angered his father.

'Are you trying to escape the blame, Ivan Tsarevich? Is this not your crime? Answer for your deeds – so we may live once more in peace!'

Ivan answered boldly, 'What is this trifle for which no one but me can answer?'

No one could answer him.

Ivan set off towards the ship. He did not take the cleanest path. Instead, he walked through mud and dirt. But no one on the ship asked why. A gangplank was lowered, and it was covered with red cloth. And the two little boys ran up to their mother: 'Mama! Mama! Isn't this our very own dear Papa?'

And the Tsar Maiden replied, 'Children, take him by his white hands! Take him by his gold breast! This is your own dear Papa, your own true father!'

And Marya the Fair, Marya of the Long Tress of Hair, took him by his white hands and called him her betrothed husband.

'By your own seed, by the seed you have sown, I wish to enter into lawful marriage with you!'

And they began to celebrate. His father invited Ivan Tsarevich to a feast and paid him great honour. And Ivan Tsarevich recounted all his deeds and all that had happened to him. And he also asked for his father's blessing, his father's eternal blessing, on his lawful marriage with the Tsar Maiden.

'My thoughts and my powers were enough, and I obtained both the water of life and the water of death, in order that you, our father, should become still younger – and may God grant you many years of health! And I also ask you to release me so I can go with the Tsar Maiden to the tsardom under the sun – for I will not reign here!'

And he rode away into the tsardom under the sun, and he lives well and happily there, and he wishes long-lasting peace for both himself and his children.

As I have heard this tale, so I have told this tale.

Ivan Mareson

It began with an old man and an old woman. They grew more and more poor, till they had neither bread nor flour. All they had left was their mare. And so the old woman said to her old man, 'We must slaughter our mare!'

'How will we fetch firewood then?'

'God willing, we'll fetch it ourselves.'

And so they agreed to slaughter their mare.

Just then some crows happened to be flying by. And the old couple's hut was hardly a hut at all. It was all too like this hut of our own – roofed by the sky, fenced by the stars.

The first crow said, 'Krr! Your master wants to kill you, mare!'

The middle crow said, 'Mare! If you have any sense at all, escape!'

The last crow said, 'Don't waste time. They're going to kill you. Jump out of the yard. Run where your eyes look!'

The mare did not think for long. She jumped out of the yard and ran off into the dark forest.

She ran and she ran till she came to a glade. There she ate a little, then went on further.

She saw a large cloth. A man, a dead Tungus,[1] was lying on it. The mare took a bite from the knee of this Tungus. She took a bite from his right knee and fell pregnant by him.

She wandered about till her time came. Then she gave birth to a son. And she gave him a name – Ivan Mareson. And she gave him her blessing: 'Make yourself a bow and arrow, my child. Go hunting – but when night comes, stand your arrow in

the ground. Then I'll know that you're alive. But if your arrow
is not standing, then I will go and search for your bones.'

Ivan said farewell to the mare. He made himself a bow and
arrow and went off hunting, to fill his belly. He walked and
walked until he came to a glade. There in the glade was a tree
stump, and a man was walking around it.

He went up to the man and said, 'God save you, young
warrior!'

'I thank you.'

'What are you looking for?'

'I've lost an arrow.'

Ivan looked around. Standing in the ground, not far away,
was an arrow.

'What's your name?' asked Ivan Mareson.

'Ivan Sunson.'

'Allow me to be your comrade,' said Ivan Mareson.

'I'll be glad of a comrade. You be the elder brother, Ivan
Mareson, and I'll be the younger brother.'

They went off hunting together. They wandered and wandered until they came to a glade. There in the glade was a tree
stump, and a man was walking around it.

Ivan Mareson went up to the man and, just as he had done
before, he said, 'God save you, young warrior!'

'I thank you for your kind words.'

'What are you looking for, young warrior?'

'I've lost an arrow.'

Ivan Mareson looked and looked.

'Here you are,' he said. 'Here's your arrow. And what is
your name, young warrior?'

'I'm Ivan Moonson.'

'Will you join us and be our comrade?'

'I'll be glad of comrades.'

And Ivan Moonson went on to say, 'You be the eldest
brother, Ivan Mareson. Let Ivan Sunson be the middle brother,
and I, Moonson, will be the youngest.'

They decided to make their home where they were. They
built a yurt for themselves there in the glade.

Then they began hunting birds and beasts of all kinds, heaping up furs and feathers. Before nightfall they all three stood their arrows in the ground. Come morning, they found that someone had decorated their arrows.

Ivan Mareson got to his feet and said, 'Well, brothers, we're in trouble. Someone's making fun of us.' And he said to his youngest brother, 'Well, Ivan Moonson, you stay on guard tonight. Find out who's coming to our yurt.'

Night fell. Ivan Moonson was on guard. The others lay down in the yurt to sleep. Ivan Moonson sat there on the floor until midnight. Then he wanted to sleep. He hadn't seen anyone. At midnight he lay down under the furs and fell fast asleep – and so he didn't see anything at all.

In the morning the eldest brother got up and saw that the arrows had been decorated again.

'Well, brother, well, Ivan Moonson, did you see anyone in the night?'

'I saw no one at all.'

'Well, you're certainly not much use as a guard, Ivan Moonson! Well, brother, well, Ivan Sunson, it's your turn next. You stay on guard this coming night!'

Come evening, they stood their bare arrows in the ground.

Ivan Sunson was on guard. He sat there on the floor. He sat and sat, but he didn't see anyone. At midnight he got under the heap of feathers, quickly warmed up and fell fast asleep – and so he didn't see anyone at all.

In the morning the other two brothers got up. Ivan Mareson checked the arrows. They had been decorated in many colours, more beautifully than ever.

'Well, brother, well, Ivan Sunson, did you see anyone in the night?'

'I saw no one at all.'

'You're certainly not much of a guard, Ivan Sunson!'

The third night set in. 'Well, brothers,' said Ivan Mareson, 'you two are certainly no use as guards. Go into the yurt and lie down to sleep. Tonight it's my turn to be on guard. How much longer can we be made to look like fools?'

He sat there, and he sat there. It was close to midnight. Ivan

Mareson lay down under the furs. He heard a noise. In flew three spoonbills.

They struck against the ground and turned into fair maidens. Each bent over her arrow, and they began to laugh. 'This,' said one, 'is the arrow of *my* sweetheart.' 'And this,' said the second, 'is *my* sweetheart's arrow.' 'And this arrow,' said the third, 'belongs to *my* sweetheart.'

Then Ivan Mareson quietly crept up to their birdskins and wings and hid them away in his pocket. The maidens all went on laughing and embroidering until morning, until it was time for them to fly away.

They leaped to their feet and hurried to put on their birdskins and wings. But there was nothing there.

'Oh sisters,' they said in the Russian tongue. 'We're done for. Yes, it seems we were led here by fate.'

'Who is guilty of this?' asked Marfida Tsarevna. 'If you are older than us, be our father. If you are younger than us, be a brother to us. If you are our own age, be my betrothed.'

From the heap of furs, Ivan Mareson asked, 'Is your word spoken in good faith?'

'A royal word is not spoken three times. It is spoken but once.'

Ivan climbed out from under the furs.

Well, he was very handsome, but she was more handsome still. She fell in love with him, and he fell still more in love with her. In only a moment they were holding hands. Then they exchanged golden rings, and then they kissed. He said, 'Love me, and I shall love you!' And she replied, 'But don't you have comrades here? I have sisters.'

Ivan woke his brothers: 'Hey, brothers! Get up, you sleepy grouse!'

The brothers got up and went outside.

'Well, brothers, when you were on guard, you never saw our visitors. But I've found myself a betrothed, and I've found comrades for you too.'

And just as Ivan had done, so did his two brothers each take a betrothed and exchange rings with her. And they all went on living in the same yurt.

They all slept in the yurt, and then, come morning, the men

would leave their women to look after the household while they themselves went out hunting.

All of a sudden Ivan Mareson realized that something was the matter with the women – and, above all, with his own woman: she was fading and withering. He said to his brothers, 'Brothers, someone must be visiting our women. They're looking all sad.'

And then he noticed some burrows dug under the yurt. He had no trust in his brothers, so he sent them out hunting. 'You go out hunting today,' he said to them. 'I'll stay on guard here at home.'

At noon the brothers set off.

Ivan Mareson stayed on guard.

Out crept a fiery serpent. He went into the yurt and began sucking the women's breasts. That was how the serpent was tormenting the women and drying them up. Ivan drew his stout bow, loosed a tipped arrow and shot the serpent right in his chest.

The serpent fell from Ivan's betrothed. From the breast of Ivan's betrothed he fell straight back into his burrow. But first, in the Russian tongue, he said 'Wait for me, Ivan Mareson. In three days' time I'll be back with a fiery cloud.'[2]

The brothers returned from their hunting. Ivan Mareson said, 'Brothers, for three days and nights we must make bows and arrows. I have found our adversary. But I failed to kill him properly – I only wounded him. He's promised to come back in three days' time with a fiery cloud.'

And so for three days and nights they made bows and arrows. They went on working until the last moment. Then Ivan Mareson said, 'Ivan Moonson, go and see if there's a storm cloud coming this way.'

Ivan Moonson went outside. He said, 'Oh, brothers! There's a black cloud rising up from the earth.'

Not long after this, Ivan Mareson sent out Ivan Sunson.

Ivan Sunson went outside. He said, 'Oh, brothers! There's a huge cloud. It's drawing closer and closer.'

Not long after this Ivan Mareson went outside. There overhead stood the black cloud.

And so the battle began. The brothers battled and battled – and felled one third of the cloud. And Ivan Moonson also lay felled. Two-thirds of the cloud remained. The brothers battled and battled – and felled one half of the cloud. And Ivan Sunson also lay felled. But there remained one half of the cloud – a host of unclean spirits. Ivan Mareson battled and battled. He felled a third of the cloud – and then he too lay felled. And then the women were seized and taken away by what still remained of the cloud.

The mare was wandering about the forest. She remembered her son and ran to look for his arrow. She galloped headlong to the place of the battle. She found the arrow. It had fallen over.

'My son must have died,' she thought. And she made her way between the dead heads. She walked on and on, and then she found her son's head and his body. She gave them a lick, turned round and gave them a kick – and they grew together. She gave her son another lick, turned round and gave him another kick – and her son gave a sudden start. She gave him a third lick, a third kick – and her son got to his feet.

'Oh, Mama!' he said. 'I've been sleeping a long time. Now quicken my comrades, Mamasha. Quicken Ivan Sunson and Ivan Moonson.'

The mare found the heads of Ivan Sunson and Ivan Moonson, together with their bodies. And with three licks and three kicks she quickened them – just as she had quickened her son. Then the son said to his mother, 'But where are our women, Mamasha?'

'I don't know.'

Then he said to his brothers, 'They must have been seized by that heathen power.'

And the mother said, 'You must stand your arrow in the ground again. Then I shall know you're still alive.'

And away she galloped to a broad valley.

'Well, brothers,' said Ivan Mareson. 'Now we must hunt for three days and nights. We need skins so we can stitch a long rope.'

For three days and nights they hunted wild beasts and stitched a long rope from their skins.

'Well, brothers,' said Ivan Mareson. 'Now you must lower

me into this burrow. If the rope isn't long enough, then you must tie your belts to the end of it. And if I don't tug on the rope within twelve days, you must leave the burrow and go where your eyes look.'

They lowered him down in a cradle. Down and down he went. Then the cradle came to a stop. They had only needed to tie one belt to the end of the rope.

Ivan Mareson got out of the cradle and set off along a path. He walked maybe a long way, maybe a short way, until he came to a lake. He walked all the way round this lake. He saw three women coming towards him. He hid in the undergrowth. As the women drew level with him, he shot an arrow across the path. The three women were going to the lake; they were carrying buckets and were on their way to fetch water. And the first of them was his betrothed. As the arrow flew past, she gave a start and a little scream: 'Oh!'

'Sister, why did you scream?' asked her two sisters.

'It was just a little mouse. It ran across the path in front of me.'

And that was all she said.

The three sisters filled their pails. Then the first sister began to dawdle.

'Sister, why are you hanging back?' asked her sisters.

'I feel like staying out in the fresh air. You go on your way. I'll come back later.'

Once her sisters were out of sight, she said in the Russian tongue, 'Is it you, my betrothed? Are you here?'

'Yes, it's me.'

She was overjoyed. They began talking. Ivan asked her, 'What about the serpent? Where is he? Is he lying wounded?'

'He's lying wounded – stretched out in a cradle.'

'What shall I do? Shall I go and fight him now? Or shall I wait?'

'Wait till noon. Wait till the cradle goes still. That'll mean he's fallen asleep.'

Ivan Mareson went up to the cradle. It was still rocking. But at noon it went still. The serpent had fallen asleep. Ivan took hold of the serpent and squeezed the life out of him. And that was the end of the last of the fiery cloud.

And off Ivan went to find his women. He took all they needed from the storeroom, and he led his women to the foot of the burrow.

Ivan Mareson tied the stores to the rope. He tugged on the rope, and his brothers hauled the stores up. The brothers let the rope down again, and he tied Ivan Moonson's woman to the rope. He tugged on the rope, and his brothers hauled her up. The brothers let the rope down again. He tied Ivan Sunson's woman to the rope. He tugged on the rope, and they hauled her up too. The brothers let the rope down once again. Then Ivan Mareson and his betrothed began to argue. Yes, deep in her heart she had a sense . . .

'Let's tie *you* to the rope!' said his betrothed.

'No, let's tie *you* to the rope!' said Ivan Mareson. 'You've been badly frightened down here.'

Ivan Mareson won the argument. He tied his betrothed to the rope. But when it came to his turn, they pulled him half-way up and then cut the rope. He fell to his death. His brothers seized his betrothed and led her away from the mouth of the burrow.

The brothers began to assault his betrothed; they tried to force themselves on her. She did not give in. They punished her. Whenever they took their yurt down, it was she who had to move it. She would have to drag it along on a sled; she would wash herself in her own tears. She began to fade and wither. Yes, she was withering like a blade of grass; she could barely even drag her own two legs any further.

The mare remembered her son. She ran to look for his arrow. It had fallen over. She began running about. Nowhere could she find the mouth of the burrow. She turned the yurt upside down. Now she could see the burrow. She sniffed inside it: yes, she could smell her son. She made her way down. She reached the bottom: there he was, lying dead on the ground. Just as she had done before, she quickened him. When she had finished, Ivan Mareson leaped to his feet and shook himself.

'Oh, Mama!' he said. 'Oh Mamasha, I've been sleeping a long time.'

'Yes, indeed,' she replied. 'And if I hadn't come, you would never have got to your feet again.'

'Mamasha,' he said, 'how are we going to get up to the upper world again?'[3]

'My child,' she replied. 'For three days and nights you must kill wild beasts. You must stitch two bags from their skins. You must chop up their meat. Then you must fill the bags with the meat.'

Ivan Mareson worked for three days and nights. Then he filled two bags and hung them over his mother the mare. Then she said, 'Sit on my back, child. I'll start to climb up. Each time I look round, you must give me a piece of meat. That way, I'll get to the upper world again.'

Each time the mare looked round, he gave her a piece of flesh.

But he ran out of flesh. She looked round – and he had nothing to give her. He cut off a toe from his right foot and gave it to her. She looked round again – and he had nothing to give her. He cut off a piece of his right calf and gave it to her. She looked round a third time – and he had nothing to give her. He cut off a piece of his right ear and gave it to her.

Now they had come to the light of the upper world. Ivan Mareson dismounted from his mother the mare.

'Oh, my child,' she said. 'I'm tired. But what was the sweet piece of gristle you gave me last of all?'

'My ear,' he replied.

She coughed it up and licked it back into place.

'And what was it you gave me the second time that was so sweet?'

'That was from my right calf,' he replied.

She coughed it up and licked it back into place.

'And what was the hard bit you gave me the first time?'

'One of my right toes,' he replied.

She coughed it up and licked it back into place.

Then Ivan Mareson fell down at her feet, before her right hoof.

'Farewell, my dear mother,' he said. 'Farewell forever. I don't think we'll be meeting again.'

'Where are you going now, my dear son?' she asked.

'I'm going to catch up with my brothers, Mamasha!' he replied. 'And with my betrothed.'

Ivan Mareson said farewell – and off he ran. His mother remained behind. Ivan ran and ran. He came to the site of a fire – but no one was there. He came to the site of a second fire – but no one was there. He came to the site of a third fire – his brothers had left only just before him.

Not far away he could see a woman. She was pulling something – a Tungus sled. And on this sled were stacked all the poles from a yurt – this was how his betrothed was being punished. His betrothed was alone with her burden. There was no one else to be seen. On she walked, washing herself with her tears. Ivan Mareson began pulling the poles off the sled. At first she sensed nothing, but when he removed the last pole, she sensed that the load behind her had grown lighter. She stopped, looked round and saw a young warrior. With her eyes full of tears, she could not see who it was.

'A fine young warrior you are!' she said. 'My end was drawing near, but you've added more tears and more grief.'

'What's happened to you, Marfida Tsarevna?' replied Ivan Mareson. 'How can you not know your own betrothed?'

Her heart leaped within her. She wiped away her tears. She knew him.

'Oh my betrothed and beloved! See how near I was to my end! See what they've done to me!'[4]

Ivan Mareson got rid of the sled, sat his woman on his shoulders and set off after his brothers. Very soon he caught up with them. They were making a fire for the night. He lost no time. In the fury of his heart, he squeezed the life out of them.

Then he took from his pocket the spoonbills' birdskins and wings. He pulled out some of the feathers from these six wings and made wings for himself too. Then the sisters put on their birdskins and they all four of them – Ivan and the three sisters – flew away to the Mountains of Zion and their silken grasses. Then Ivan and his betrothed were married. And her two sisters became her servants. And so Ivan lived and grew old – and now this tale is told.

IVAN YAKOVLEVICH
BILIBIN

(1876–1942)

Other than Pushkin and Afanasyev themselves, there are few figures more closely associated with the Russian magic tale than the illustrator and stage designer Ivan Bilibin.

While still studying under the painter and sculptor Ilya Repin, Bilibin was commissioned to illustrate seven Russian folktales; the resulting series of slim paperbacks (1899–1902) brought him to the attention of the 'World of Art' group headed by Serge Diaghilev and Alexander Benois. Bilibin went on to work for the Ballets Russes.

Just as Diaghilev had a uniquely holistic vision of the potential of opera, so Bilibin had a unique vision of the potential of the illustrated book. The art historian David Jackson has written that 'Bilibin pioneered the modern notion of the book as a total design entity, a work of art, rather than an object that merely contained works of art. [. . .] His ability to conceive the overall vision of the completed object, rather than place images alongside appropriate sections of text as "illustrations" was unrivalled. Interlinking motifs, border decorations, integrated and stylized typography, vignettes and "split screen" techniques based on the forms of indigenous architectural styles reveal an artist–designer in a class of his own.'[1]

In 1920, Bilibin left Russia for Cairo, and in 1925 he settled in Paris, where he earned his living by decorating private mansions and Orthodox churches. In 1936, however, he decorated the Soviet Embassy; soon after this he returned to Soviet Russia. From then until 1941 he lectured in Leningrad, in the Soviet Academy of Arts. He died in February 1942, during the Siege.

Though not widespread as an oral tale, 'The Tale of Ivan Tsarevich, the Grey Wolf and the Firebird' was versified by two important Romantic poets, Nikolay Yazykov and Vasily Zhukovsky. It was the first of the tales that Bilibin illustrated and during the last hundred years it has been republished countless times, usually together with Bilibin's illustrations. Bilibin's other illustrations from this period were published with texts taken from Afanasyev. 'The Tale of Ivan Tsarevich, the Grey Wolf and the Firebird', however, was published in a version different from Afanasyev's. It is this more succinct and dramatic version that follows.

Ivan Tsarevich, the Grey Wolf and the Firebird

In a certain land, in a certain tsardom, lived Tsar Demyan. He had three sons: Pyotr Tsarevich, Vasily Tsarevich and Ivan Tsarevich. And he had a fine orchard; no tsar in the world had a finer orchard. In it grew many precious trees, and there was an apple tree that bore golden apples. The tsar treasured these apples and he counted them every morning. But then he realized that someone was robbing his orchard. In the evening he would see a beautiful apple, ripening on his beloved tree – and in the morning that apple would be gone. And there were no guards who could catch the thief. Every morning the tsar counted one less apple on his beloved tree. His grief stopped him from eating, drinking or sleeping. In the end he called his three sons and said, 'Listen, sons! You must each stand guard in my orchard. Whoever of you catches the thief shall reign over half of my tsardom while I'm alive and inherit the whole of it when I die.'

The three sons promised to do as he said. First it was the turn of Pyotr Tsarevich. All evening he walked up and down the garden, but he saw nothing. Then he sat down on the soft grass beneath the tree – and what did he do but fall fast asleep! In the morning some apples were missing.

'Well, my son?' asked his father. 'Will you bring joy to my heart? Did you see the thief?'

'No, Father and Tsar. I was awake all night, but I saw nothing. I don't know how the apples can have disappeared.'

It seemed impossible to catch the thief. The tsar felt still sadder. But he hoped his second son would do better.

Next it was the turn of Vasily Tsarevich. He went out in the evening and sat beneath the tree. He began watching the bushes:

was someone hidden there? But as the night grew darker, he fell fast asleep. And by the morning there were several fewer apples left on the tree.

'Well, my son?' asked his father. 'Will you bring joy to my heart? Did you see the thief?'

'No, Father and Tsar. I didn't close my eyes once all night. I watched and watched, but I saw no one. I don't understand how the golden apples can have disappeared.'

The tsar felt still sadder. On the third evening it was the turn of Ivan Tsarevich. He began walking about by the tree. He was afraid of falling asleep and he didn't dare sit down for even a minute. He kept watch for an hour, and he kept watch for a second hour. He kept watch for a third hour. When he felt sleep creeping up on him, he washed his eyes with dew.

In the small hours something glimmered in the distance. A light was flying through the air, straight towards him. The whole garden grew bright as day. It was the Firebird. She perched on the tree and began to peck at the golden apples. Ivan Tsarevich crept along the ground, leapt into the air and grabbed her by the tail. But, no matter how hard he gripped, it was not enough. The Firebird pulled and pulled – and away she flew, leaving one tail feather behind in his hand.

That morning, as soon as the tsar awoke, Ivan Tsarevich went to show him the feather and tell him who had been stealing the apples. The tsar was delighted that his youngest son had something to show him, even if it was only a feather. He took this feather and hid it away in his room. After that the Firebird never came back and the tsar began eating, drinking and sleeping again. But he would gaze and gaze at the feather and he could not stop thinking about the Firebird. In the end he decided he'd send his sons to go and catch the Firebird. He called them to him and said, 'Listen, my dear sons! I want you to saddle your fine steeds, ride out into the wide world and catch me the Firebird. Otherwise she might come back and start stealing my apples again.'

The two eldest sons bowed to him, saddled their steeds, put on their fine armour and rode off. As for Ivan Tsarevich, he was the youngest son and the tsar wanted to keep him at home.

But Ivan implored his father with tears in his eyes, and in the end the tsar gave him leave to go.

Ivan Tsarevich mounted his fine steed – and off he rode. He rode a short way, or maybe a long way – what's quick to say can take many a day. At last, however, Ivan Tsarevich came to a stone pillar where three roads met. On it was written:

If you ride straight on, you will grow cold and hungry;
If you turn to the right, you will live but your horse will die.
If you turn to the left, you will be killed but your horse will live.

Ivan Tsarevich read these words and thought for a long time: which road should he follow? In the end he turned to the right, in order to stay alive.[1]

He rode all that day and all through the next day. On the third day Ivan Tsarevich came to a deep forest. It turned dark and all of a sudden a big grey wolf sprang out of the bushes and leapt at Ivan Tsarevich's horse. Before the tsarevich could draw his sword, the wolf had torn his horse in half and vanished into the bushes.

Ivan Tsarevich felt very sad: how could he keep going without his good steed? But he walked on. He walked all that day and all through the next day. On the third day he sat down on an old tree stump to rest. He was tired to death, and he was hungry. And then, as if from nowhere, the grey wolf sprang out and said, 'Why do you grieve, Ivan Tsarevich? Why are you hanging your head like that?'

'How can I not grieve, Grey Wolf? Where can I go without my good steed?'

'It was you who chose this road. Still, I feel sorry for you. Where is it you're going?'

'My father the tsar sent me to catch the Firebird who was stealing his golden apples.'

'Well,' said the wolf, 'you wouldn't have found your way to her on your good steed in a thousand years. I'm the only one who knows where the Firebird lives. You'd do best to ride on my back and hold tight. It was I who killed your steed – now I shall serve you in word and in deed.'

Ivan Tsarevich mounted the grey wolf. The wolf leapt forward and raced off. With each stride the wolf cleared a mountain or vale, and he swept his tracks clean with his tail. After a long time, or maybe a short time, they came to a high wall. The wolf stopped and said to Ivan Tsarevich, 'Here you are, Ivan Tsarevich. Climb over the wall and you'll come to a garden. In the garden you'll find the Firebird in a golden cage. The guards are all asleep. Take the Firebird, but whatever you do, don't try to steal the cage. If you do, you're in trouble.'

Ivan Tsarevich listened to the wolf's words, climbed over the wall and saw the Firebird. He opened the cage door and took her out. He was about to climb back when he thought, 'Why have I taken the Firebird out of her cage? I'll never be able to carry her all the way in my bosom. And it's a precious cage – all studded with diamonds!' He forgot what the grey wolf had said to him and turned back. The moment he touched the cage, there was a knocking and ringing that went all through the garden. Attached to the cage were hidden strings with all kinds of little bells and rattles.

The guards awoke, rushed into the garden, seized Ivan Tsarevich, bound his hands and took him straight to their master, Tsar Afron. Tsar Afron was furious. 'Who are you and where are you from?' he asked. 'Who is your father and what is your name?'

'My name is Ivan Tsarevich and I'm the son of Tsar Demyan. Your Firebird kept visiting our garden. Every night she was stealing the golden apples from my father's beloved tree. In the end my father sent me to catch the Firebird and bring her back to him.'

'Ivan Tsarevich!' said Tsar Afron. 'You could have come honourably and asked me for the Firebird. Then I'd have given her to you honourably or maybe exchanged her for something. Now, though, I shall send my messengers to every land and to every tsardom, till everyone knows that the son of a tsar has turned out a thief.' After a pause, Tsar Afron went on, 'But listen now. If you do me a service, I shall pardon you in your guilt. I'll even give you the Firebird of my own free will. You must ride far, far away, beyond thrice-nine lands to the thrice-tenth tsardom and fetch me Tsar Kusman's horse with the golden mane.'

Ivan Tsarevich bowed his head in sorrow, walked back to the grey wolf and told him what Tsar Afron had said.

'Ivan Tsarevich,' said the wolf. 'Why didn't you listen to me? I told you not to take the cage. I said it would only bring trouble.'

'I'm sorry,' Ivan answered. 'Forgive me, Grey Wolf.'

'Very well,' said the grey wolf. 'Sit on my back and hold tight. The grey wolf will take you where you must go.'

Ivan Tsarevich mounted the grey wolf. The wolf leapt forward and raced off. With each stride the wolf cleared a mountain or vale, and he swept his tracks clean with his tail. After a long time, or maybe a short time, they came to Tsar Kusman's tsardom. The wolf stopped in front of the white stone walls of the tsar's stables and said to Ivan Tsarevich, 'Here you are. Climb over the wall, take the horse with the golden mane and be off. But take care. And whatever you do, don't touch the golden bridle. If you do, you'll be in trouble again.'

Ivan Tsarevich climbed over the stone wall and crept into the stable. The guards were all asleep. He took the horse by the mane. But as he was leading him out he caught sight of the golden bridle. 'It's not right to take the horse without the bridle,' he said to himself. 'I can't leave it behind.' He went back for it – and the moment he touched it, the whole stable began to ring and thunder. The guards woke up, seized Ivan Tsarevich and took him straight to Tsar Kusman.

'Who are you and where are you from?' asked Tsar Kusman. 'Who is your father and what is your name?'

'My name is Ivan Tsarevich and I'm the son of Tsar Demyan.'

'Ivan Tsarevich!' said Tsar Kusman. 'Is this how an honourable knight behaves? You could have come and asked me for the horse with the golden mane. Out of respect for your father, I'd have given him to you. Now, though, I shall send my messengers to every tsardom, to tell everyone that the son of a tsar has turned out a thief.' After a pause, Tsar Kusman went on, 'But listen now. If you do me a service, I shall pardon you. I shall even give you the horse with the golden mane as a gift. Ride far,

far away, beyond thrice-nine lands to the thrice-tenth tsardom and fetch me Yelena the Beautiful, the daughter of Tsar Dalmat.'

Ivan Tsarevich left the tsar's palace and wept bitter tears. He went back to the grey wolf and told him all that had happened.

'Ivan Tsarevich,' said the wolf. 'Why didn't you listen to me? Why did you have to touch the golden bridle? It's me, Grey Wolf, who has to do all the work. All you do is make trouble.'

'Once again I am guilty before you,' said Ivan Tsarevich. 'Please forgive me once more.'

'Very well,' said the grey wolf. 'Once a task is begun, never leave it half done. Sit on my back, hold tight and we'll try to find Yelena the Beautiful.'

Ivan Tsarevich mounted the grey wolf. The wolf ran like the wind. With each stride the wolf cleared a mountain or vale, and he swept his tracks clean with his tail. After a long time, or maybe a short time, they came to Tsar Dalmat's tsardom. The grey wolf stopped by the golden fence that ran round his garden and said, 'Ivan Tsarevich. This time I'm going into the garden myself. Jump down and walk back the way we've just come. Wait for me in the open steppe, under the green oak.'

Ivan Tsarevich did as the wolf said. The grey wolf waited till the dark of night, leapt over the fence and hid in the bushes. All through the next day he sat waiting for Princess Yelena the Beautiful. Only in the evening did she come out into the green garden for a stroll and a breath of fresh air. With her were all her maids and nurses and ladies-in-waiting. Yelena the Beautiful wandered along picking flowers till she came to the bush where the grey wolf lay hidden. The grey wolf leapt out, threw Yelena the Beautiful across his back, leapt over the fence and galloped away with her. He was gone like a flash. He found Ivan Tsarevich under the oak tree and said, 'Quick! Get on my back with Yelena the Beautiful! They'll be after us.'

Ivan Tsarevich took Yelena the Beautiful in his arms and mounted the grey wolf. The wolf galloped off as fast as his legs could carry him. Back in the palace gardens all the maids and nurses and ladies-in-waiting were screaming at the tops of their voices. The tsar couldn't make out what on earth had happened. When he at last understood, he called all his huntsmen and galloped off after the wolf. But no matter how swiftly they galloped, the grey wolf galloped more swiftly, and the tsar returned empty handed.

After a while, Yelena the Beautiful opened her eyes and found she was in the arms of a handsome young warrior. Riding on the back of the grey wolf, they could hardly have torn themselves apart if they'd wished to. They fell deep in love.

When the grey wolf reached the tsardom of Tsar Kusman, the tsarevich began to weep bitter tears.

'Why do you grieve, Ivan Tsarevich?' asked the grey wolf. 'Why are you weeping?'

'How, Grey Wolf, can I help weeping? I love Princess Yelena. How can I part with such a beauty?'

The grey wolf looked at them both and said, 'I've done you many services, Ivan Tsarevich, and I can serve you once more. You'll have to pass me off as Yelena the Beautiful. I'll strike against the ground and turn myself into a princess. Then you must take me to Tsar Kusman while Yelena waits under that oak over there. Tsar Kusman will give you the horse with the golden mane and the two of you can ride off. In no time at all I'll catch up with you.'

They put Yelena the Beautiful down by the oak. The grey wolf struck against the ground and turned into her spitting image. Ivan Tsarevich led him into Tsar Kusman's palace. The tsar was delighted. He had his grooms fetch the horse with the golden mane. He even gave Ivan the golden bridle as well. Ivan Tsarevich mounted the horse and set off. He found Yelena the Beautiful, lifted her up in his arms – and off they rode towards the tsardom of Tsar Afron.

Meanwhile Tsar Kusman prepared to celebrate a splendid wedding. His oak tables were laden with flagons of mead and the sweetest delicacies. The guests sat down and began toasting the bride and groom, shouting, 'Bitter! Bitter!' This was the moment for Tsar Kusman to kiss his sweet bride.[2] He leant over towards her, but instead of the soft lips of Yelena the Beautiful he found he was kissing the bristly muzzle of the grey wolf. He jumped back and let out a terrible scream. The grey wolf jumped out of the window, and that was the last any of them saw of him.

The grey wolf caught up with Ivan Tsarevich and Yelena the Beautiful and said, 'You sit on my back, Ivan Tsarevich. Let the princess ride on the horse with the golden mane.'

Ivan Tsarevich mounted the grey wolf – and off they rode. Just before they came to the tsardom of Tsar Afron, Ivan began looking sad again.

'What's the matter, Ivan Tsarevich?' asked the grey wolf. 'What are you thinking about?'

'About the horse with the golden mane. I don't want to give him away in exchange for the Firebird. But if I don't, Tsar Afron will spread slanders about me in every land.'

'Don't worry, Ivan Tsarevich. Didn't I promise to serve you in word and in deed? I'll turn myself into a horse with a golden mane and you can give me away to the tsar.'

They hid both Princess Yelena and the horse with the golden mane in the forest. The grey wolf struck against the damp earth and became a horse with a golden mane. Ivan Tsarevich jumped onto his back and rode to Tsar Afron's palace. The tsar came out to meet Ivan Tsarevich in his great courtyard, took him by the right hand and led him into his fine chambers of white stone. He wanted him to stay and eat bread and salt, but Ivan was in a hurry to return to Yelena the Beautiful. The tsar handed him the Firebird in her golden cage. Ivan walked into the forest, sat himself behind Princess Yelena on the back of the horse with the golden mane, picked up the cage again and set off.

Next morning Tsar Afron wanted to ride his new horse in the open steppe. He rode out with his huntsmen. They came to a forest and began to chase different beasts. A fox leapt out of the bushes. The huntsmen all galloped after this fox, but only Tsar Afron could keep up with it. The huntsmen were left far behind.

Suddenly the huntsmen saw the horse with the golden mane stumble and vanish into thin air while a grey wolf leapt out from under the tsar's legs. The tsar was thrown right up to his shoulders into the mud. The huntsmen galloped up. Somehow or other they dragged the tsar back onto his feet. They wanted to give chase to the wolf, but they couldn't even find his tracks.

Soon the grey wolf caught up with Ivan Tsarevich and Yelena the Beautiful. Ivan got on his back, and they rode on. When they came to where the wolf had torn Ivan's horse apart, the wolf stopped and said, 'Ivan Tsarevich. This is where I killed your horse, and this is as far as I'll take you. Now I am no longer your servant.'

Ivan Tsarevich bowed to the ground three times before the grey wolf. The wolf said, 'That's enough. We're not saying goodbye forever. You'll need me again.'

'Why's he saying that?' wondered Ivan Tsarevich. 'I won't be needing any more help now.' He mounted the horse with the golden mane, sat Yelena the Beautiful before him, took the Firebird's golden cage in one hand and rode on. After some time – maybe a long time, maybe a short time – he reached his father's tsardom. When he was nearly home, he stopped for a while to rest. Just then his two brothers came past. They had travelled through one country after another, searching for the Firebird. Now they were on their way back, empty handed. And there was Ivan – sleeping on the ground, with the Firebird, Yelena the Beautiful and the horse with the golden mane all lying there beside him. They both had the same thought: 'Ivan's already made fools of us once. He plucked the feather from the Firebird's tail when we couldn't even stay awake. Now look at what he's gone and done. I think we should teach him a lesson.'

They drew their swords and slashed off Ivan Tsarevich's head. Yelena the Beautiful awoke. Seeing that Ivan Tsarevich was dead, she began weeping bitterly. 'You're in *our* hands now,' said Pyotr Tsarevich, holding the tip of his sword to her breast. 'And you must tell the tsar that *we* won you, and that *we* found the Firebird and the horse with the golden mane. Or shall I put you to death straight away?'

The beautiful princess nearly died of fright then and there. She promised to do as they said. Then Pyotr and Vasily drew lots. Vasily Tsarevich won the horse with the golden mane and Pyotr Tsarevich won Yelena the Beautiful. They sat Yelena the Beautiful on the horse with the golden mane, took the Firebird and set off back home.

Ivan Tsarevich was left in the field. Ravens were circling

overhead, ready to pick at his flesh. And then, as if out of nowhere, the grey wolf appeared. He saw Ivan Tsarevich, sat down to one side and waited. A raven flew down and began to peck at Ivan's breast. With it was a family of young. The wolf sprang forward and seized one of the young ravens in his jaws. The parent begged him to let it go.

'Very well,' said the grey wolf. 'But first your child must stay with me for a while. I want you to fly far away, beyond thrice-nine lands to the thrice-tenth tsardom and fetch me the water of life and the water of death. Then I'll give you your child back.'

The raven flew off. He flew for a long time, or maybe a short time, and in the end he came back with two little phials. One was filled with the water of life, the other with the water of death. The grey wolf took the phials, tore the young raven in two, put the two halves next to each other and sprinkled them with the water of death; the two halves grew together. He sprinkled the body with the water of life; the little raven gave a start and shot into the air.

After that the grey wolf placed Ivan's head on his neck and sprinkled it with the water of death; it grew onto his body. He sprinkled Ivan with the water of life. Ivan came to life and said, 'Goodness! I must have been sleeping for ages!'

'Yes, Ivan Tsarevich. And without me you'd have slept forever. Your brothers chopped off your head. Then they took Yelena the Beautiful, the Firebird and the horse with the golden mane and rode back home. Get on my back now. We must gallop fast. Today's the wedding of Yelena the Beautiful and Pyotr Tsarevich.'

Ivan Tsarevich mounted the grey wolf. The wolf leapt forward and was off. Outside the city gates he stopped and said, 'Farewell, Ivan Tsarevich – this time, forever. Quick! There's no time to lose!'

Ivan Tsarevich walked through the city. Outside the palace was a huge crowd of brightly dressed people. He asked what was happening.[3]

'Today the eldest tsarevich is marrying Yelena the Beautiful,' they told him.

Ivan Tsarevich ran into the palace. The servants recognized him and ran to tell the tsar. Ivan followed. Pyotr Tsarevich fainted with terror. Yelena the Beautiful rushed up to Ivan Tsarevich and took him by the hand. Then she turned to the tsar and said, 'This is the man who won me. He is my bridegroom.'

And Yelena told the tsar all that had happened. The tsar was furious with his two elder sons. He banished them from his tsardom and proclaimed Ivan Tsarevich his heir. The wedding was celebrated soon afterwards and there was a feast for the whole world. And Ivan and Yelena lived well, as I've heard tell, and they knew every good, as I've understood.

NIKOLAY YEVGENEVICH ONCHUKOV

(1872–1942)

Several major folktale collections were published shortly before and after the outbreak of the First World War. The most important collector from this period was Nikolay Onchukov. Like Afanasyev and Khudyakov before him, he is a tragic figure.

Onchukov's mother, his father and his maternal grandmother all died before he was twelve. He trained as a field doctor and worked for several years in the north of European Russia, where he grew increasingly interested in folklore, publishing articles in journals and newspapers and then obtaining sponsorship from the Russian Geographical Society to collect heroic epics and folktales in the far north. In 1908 he published Northern Tales (Severnye skazki), *a large volume that included not only tales he had collected himself but also tales collected by three other linguists and folklorists. This was the first Russian collection in which the stories were arranged by location, collector and teller, and it served as a model for later collections. In his introduction Onchukov wrote, 'The bards and storytellers are exceptional people. Though often not even literate, they are the village intelligentsia. They have no school diplomas, but they stand out for their intellectual abilities and often very great artistic gifts [. . .] These poets and artists of the word inspire in anyone who has had real contact with them a deep respect for the intellectual powers of the Russian village and the variety of artistic talent concealed in its depths – for a potential that can only be fully developed through education.'[1]*

Between 1900 and 1908 Onchukov spent a great deal of time in the far north; these were the most fruitful years of his life. Even then, however, he was contending with difficulties that are hard for a modern reader to imagine. In the preface to one of his first publications he writes, 'I left Petersburg on 2 April and was in Arkhangelsk on the 5th. I left for Pechora the following day [. . .] I had to cover five hundred miles by sleigh, and it was the worst possible time for this. This was the far north and it was still only early spring, but the sun was blazing mercilessly, the snow was melting quickly and the tracks were quickly deteriorating. [. . .] Since a good half of the winter route to Pechora lay along frozen rivers, this was not without danger. The ice cover over the river was now free of snow and shone blue in the sun. Large areas free of ice had begun to appear by the banks and there were sinister patches of open water right by the edge of the sleigh track. Badly worn out, I arrived on 12 April, after covering five hundred miles in six days.'[2] In the course of two months, Onchukov covered 3,500 miles on foot, by boat, on horseback or in carts and sleighs. He does not explain the reason for his extreme haste; probably it was simply a matter of such journeys being easier to make by sleigh, while the ground was still frozen.

After the 1917 Revolution, Onchukov continued to work as a folklorist, a historian and a journalist, but he encountered many obstacles. During the 1920s and 1930s he compiled three more collections of folktales, but none was published until more than fifty years after his death. At some point in the 1920s he wrote, 'In other countries the study of folklore is treated with due seriousness. It is deeply unfortunate and to our great discredit that Russia, the country with the very richest inheritance of oral folklore, treats this rich inheritance with particular carelessness. Every year ethnographers and folklorists go on excursions to far-flung parts of Russia, make notes, prepare material for publication – and then everything is salted away. When the materials will see the light of day, whether they will ever see the light of day, is uncertain.'[3]

In 1931 Onchukov was arrested, on a trumped-up charge of counter-revolutionary activity, and exiled to a town near Vologda. Thanks to Maksim Gorky's intervention, however, he was allowed to return to Leningrad, where he worked on a

Dictionary of the Russian Language. *In 1934 he moved to Penza, 400 miles to the southeast of Moscow; there he earned his living through clerical work and occasional journalism. In 1939 he was arrested for a second time, again accused of counter-revolutionary activity, and in 1942 he died in a labour camp.*

The Black Magician Tsar

Once there was a tsar, a tsar who always did as he pleased and who lived in a country as flat as a tablecloth. He had a wife and a daughter and many servants, and he was a black magician. One day he had a feast prepared for all his people – for all his nobles, all his peasants and all his townspeople. When everyone was present and the feast had begun, the tsar said, 'Whoever can hide from my sight, to him I will give the hand of my daughter. I will give him half my tsardom, and after my death he shall sit on my throne.' The guests fell silent; they were all rather scared. But after a while, some daring young fellow said, 'Tsar, master of us all, I can hide from your Highness.' 'Very well, young man, you go away and hide. Tomorrow I'll look for you. And if I find you, it's off with your head.' The young man left the palace and walked all through the town. He walked and walked until he came to the bathhouse that belonged to the priest. 'I know where I can go and hide,' the young man said to himself. 'I'll hide in the priest's bathhouse. I'll go and hide in the corner, under the bench. The tsar will never be able to find me there.'

The black magician tsar got up early the following morning. He lit the stove, sat in his wicker chair, took out his magic book and began to read, to divine where this young man had gone: 'The young man left my palace of white stone and walked all through the town. He walked and walked until he came to the bathhouse that belongs to the priest. "I know where I can go and hide," the young man said to himself. "I'll hide in the priest's bathhouse. I'll go and hide in the corner, under the bench. The tsar will never be able to find me there."' And so the tsar told his servants to go and fetch the young man from the priest's bathhouse. The servants hurried along, went into the bathhouse, looked in the corner – and there under the bench was the young man. 'Good day, young man!' 'Good day, royal servants!' 'You must come with us, young man. Our father the tsar has called for you.' The servants led the young man into the tsar's presence. 'Why didn't you hide from me?' 'I was unable to hide from your Highness.' 'Well then, it's off with your head.' And the tsar drew his sharp sword and, just like that, cut off the young man's bold head.

To this tsar, cruelty was sport. The following day he gave another feast and another ball. He summoned all his nobles, all his peasants and all his townspeople. When the tables were set with food and the feast had begun, the tsar got to his feet and said, 'Whoever can hide from my sight, to him I will give the hand of my daughter. I will give him half my tsardom, and after my death he shall sit on my throne.' The guests fell silent; they were all rather scared. But after a while, some daring young fellow said, 'Tsar, master of us all, I know how to hide from you.' 'Very well, young man, you go away and hide. Tomorrow I'll look for you. And if I find you, it's off with your head.' The young man left the tsar's white palace and walked all through the town. He walked and walked. He walked far and wide; he walked high and low. In the end he came to a huge barn. 'I'll go and hide in here,' the young man said to himself. 'The tsar will never be able to find me in all this chaff and straw.'

The black magician tsar slept all night, then got up early in the morning. He washed with water from the spring, dried himself with his towel, lit his stove, took out his book of magic, sat on his wicker chair and began to read, to divine where this young man had gone: 'The young man left my palace of white stone and walked all the way through the town. He walked and walked. He walked far and wide; he walked high and low. In the end he came to a huge barn. "I'll go and hide in here," the young man said to himself. "The tsar will never be able to find me in all this chaff and straw." ' And so the tsar told his servants to go and fetch the young man from the barn. The servants hurried along, found the barn, searched through the straw – and there was the young man. 'Good day, young man!' 'Good day, royal servants!' 'You must come with us, young man. Our father the tsar has called for you.' The servants led the young man into the tsar's presence. 'Why didn't you hide from me?' 'I was unable to hide from your Highness.' 'Well then, it's off with your head.' And the tsar drew his sharp sword and, just like that, cut off the young man's bold head.

To such tsars, cruelty is sport. The following day the tsar gave another great feast. Once again a bold young man took up the tsar's challenge and said he would hide from him. The tsar agreed. The young man left the white palace and walked down the street. He walked and walked. Then he turned himself into a stoat with a black tail and began to run along the ground. He crept under tree roots and fallen trees and went on running about the earth. He ran and he ran until he came back to the tsar's palace. He turned into a twisting gimlet, a little golden tool,[1] and began dancing about outside the palace windows. He danced and danced. Then he turned into a falcon and flew to the window of the tsar's daughter's bedroom. The tsarevna saw the falcon, opened her window and called the falcon inside: 'Come in, my fine falcon, come in, my handsome little falcon!' The falcon perched on the window ledge, leaped onto the floor and turned into a handsome young man. The tsarevna greeted him and sat him at her oak table. They drank and feasted and did what was good. Then the young man turned himself into a gold ring, and the tsarevna put this ring on her finger.

The black magician tsar slept all night, then got up early in the morning. He washed with water from the spring, dried himself with his towel, lit the stove, took out his magic book, sat on his wicker chair and began to read, to divine where this young man had gone. He called his servants and said, 'Go and fetch my daughter or else bring me the ring she has on her finger!' The servants went to the tsarevna's room and said, 'The tsar has summoned you to his presence.' 'Why? Why does he need me?' 'If you don't want to go yourself, then just give us the ring from your finger.' The tsarevna took off her ring and handed it to the servants. The servants took the ring to the tsar, the tsar threw the ring over his left shoulder, and the ring turned into a handsome young man. 'Greetings, young man!' 'Greetings, your Highness!' 'Well then, I've found you – so it's off with your head.' 'No, my lord, I can hide twice more. That's what we agreed.' 'All right then, go away and hide!'

The young man left the tsar's palace, went out into open steppe and turned himself into a grey wolf. He ran and ran. He roamed over all of the earth, then turned himself into a bear. He lumbered through dark forests, then turned into a stoat with a black tail. He ran and ran. He squeezed under tree roots and fallen trees. He came back to the tsar's palace and turned into a gimlet. He danced about outside the palace windows. Then he turned into a falcon and flew to the tsarevna's window. The tsarevna saw the falcon and opened her window. 'Come in, my fine falcon!' she called out. The falcon perched on the window ledge, leaped onto the floor and turned into a handsome young man. The tsarevna greeted him and sat him at her oak table. They drank and feasted and did what was good. Then they thought hard and long: how was the young man to hide from the tsar? They decided he should turn into a bright falcon and fly far, far away into open steppe. The young man turned into a bright falcon. The tsarevna opened her window, placed the falcon on the ledge and said, 'Fly, falcon, fly far into open steppe and turn into one of seventy-seven blades of grass that all look the same!'

The black magician tsar slept all night, then got up early in the morning. He washed with water from the spring, dried himself with his towel, lit the stove, took out his magic book, sat on his wicker chair and began to read, to divine where this young man had gone. He called his servants and said, 'Go out into the open steppe. When you come to this grass, tear up a whole armful and bring it all back to me!' The servants went and found the grass, tore it out of the ground and brought it back to the tsar. The tsar sat in his chair, went through the blades of grass, found the blade he was looking for and threw it over his left shoulder. It turned into a handsome young man. 'Greetings, young man!' 'Greetings, your Highness!' 'Well then, I've found you again – so it's off with your head.' 'No, my lord, I can hide one last time.' 'All right then, go away and hide – tomorrow I'll look for you!'

The young man left the tsar's palace, walked down the street, went out into open steppe, turned himself into a grey wolf – and off he ran. He ran and ran. He ran till he came to the blue sea. There he turned into a pike – and off he swam. He swam across the blue sea. He came to land. There he turned into a bright falcon. He soared high into the sky and flew far away. He flew and flew over open steppe. In a green oak he saw the woven nest of the Magovey bird.[2] Down he dropped into this nest. The Magovey bird was not there at that moment, but after a while she came back. There in her nest she saw a young man. 'What a way to behave!' said the Magovey bird. 'Flying into someone else's nest, dropping down and then just lying there!' She seized the young man in her claws and took him out of her nest; then she carried him over the blue sea and laid him outside the window of the black magician tsar.[3] The young man turned into a fly, flew into the tsar's fine hall, then turned into a flint and lay down in the tinder bag.

The black magician tsar slept all night, then got up early in the morning. He washed with water from the spring, dried himself with his towel, lit the stove, took out his magic book, sat on his wicker chair and began to read, to divine where this young man had gone. In his book of magic he read everything the young man had done until the Magovey bird took him out of her nest. 'Go, servants,' he said, 'into the open steppe. Cross the open steppe, sail across the blue sea in a boat and search for the green oak. Then cut the oak down, find the nest and bring the young man back to me.' Off went the servants. They cut down the oak and found the nest. They searched and searched, but there was no sign of the young man. They went back and said to the tsar, 'We found the green oak. The nest was there, but the young man was not.' The tsar looked in his book, and the book said that the young man was indeed in the nest. The tsar put on his robes and went off to see for himself. He looked and looked, he searched and searched – but he could find nothing. He had the green oak chopped into bits and burned on a fire till not a splinter was left. The tsar said to himself, 'Well, I may not have found the young man, but I've made sure he's not alive anywhere on this earth.'

The tsar returned to his tsardom. A day went by, and then a second day and a third day. In the morning a maid came to make fire. She took a flint and the steel from the tinder bag, laid out the tinder and struck the steel against the flint. The flint flew out of her hands and over her left shoulder and turned into a handsome young man. 'Greetings, your Highness!' 'Greetings, young man – but now it's off with your head!' 'No, your Highness, you searched for me for three days and then you gave up. Now I've appeared of my own accord. Now you must give me half of your tsardom and your daughter in marriage.' And there was nothing the tsar could do. Straight away there was a merry feast and a wedding. The young man married the tsar's daughter and received half of his tsardom. And when the tsar died, the young man would sit on his throne.

Bronze Brow

Once upon a time there lived a tsar, a sovereign tsar in his sovereign tsardom. He married a beautiful woman, and in less than a year his wife gave birth to a son. The midwife took the tsar's son to the bathhouse, brought him back again and said to the tsar, 'Your son is strong and he will be agile, but there is one misfortune. It is inscribed on his head that he will kill his father.' This saddened the tsar, but he pitied the child. While he was still little, the tsar decided, he could live together with them. Then they would see what kind of man he was turning out to be.

The son began to grow up, and the tsar assigned a man to keep a sharp eye on him. And he and the tsaritsa kept an eye on him too. One day the boy was out in the garden with his tutor when all of a sudden he caught sight of a man with a bronze brow and a tin belly sitting beneath a bush. The tsarevich rushed to his father and told him: out there in the garden was a man with a bronze brow and a tin belly! The tsar ordered his soldiers to surround the garden and catch whoever they found there. The garden was surrounded and the man was brought to the tsar: yes, he really did have a bronze brow and a tin belly. The tsar ordered him to be imprisoned in the fortress. Some time passed and the tsar let it be known throughout his lands, and in foreign lands too, that whoever wished to see a man with a bronze brow and a tin belly should come to visit for three days. And he announced the hour when he would exhibit this man.

Meanwhile the son was learning to use a bow and arrow. Every day he went into the garden with his tutor and practised, and he became very skilled indeed; and he had a favourite arrow with which he could hit any target he chose. Now the wall of the fortress where Bronze Brow was imprisoned was just by the garden. One day the tsarevich shot his arrow and it went in through Bronze Brow's window. The tsarevich went to look for his arrow and found it lying beside the wall. He picked it up and checked to see whether or not the tip had been blunted. Written on the shaft of his favourite arrow were the words, 'Let me out and you will receive whatever you want!' The tsarevich realized that it was Bronze Brow who had written this, and he and his tutor decided to let Bronze Brow out of the fortress that night.

Then all the tsars and all kinds of other people gathered together to look at Bronze Brow, but he was not to be found. The tsar sternly ordered his men to find out how Bronze Brow had been able to get out of the fortress. When the tsar discovered that it was thanks to the tsarevich and his tutor, he ordered the tutor to be imprisoned in the fortress and the tsarevich to be sent to the border, under guard, and banished from the tsardom forever.

And so the tutor remained in the fortress and the tsarevich wandered off where his eyes looked. He began to feel bored and sad, and so he made a horn for himself and learned to play. He came to a city and found lodgings there with an old man who was a herder, in charge of the royal horses and cattle. For a modest wage, the tsarevich began to work for the old man, going with him into the forest and playing on his horn. The old herder played well, but his new assistant played still better. And after a while he was playing so beautifully that people would gather together to listen to him and the tsar's daughter even asked her father to make sure that this young herder continued to come and play on his horn every morning. She and her mother used to sit together and listen.

The old herder died and the tsarevich took over his work. He took the horses into the forest on his own for the first time and said to himself, 'Look at me now – a mere herder! Bronze Brow must be around somewhere. If only he'd help me a little and tell me what to do!' Deep in the forest he saw the horses tossing their heads about. 'What's up with the horses?' he said to himself, but he had no idea what it could be. And then one day, when he was playing on his horn with great feeling, the horses all lay down on the ground. And that very evening, when he set off back home, he saw a marvellous wonder: the horses had all grown silver manes. Everyone was amazed and the tsar wondered, 'What does this mean? What kind of man is this herder of mine?'

The tsar ordered his new herder to pasture his cattle: 'You've done a splendid job with the horses. Now look after the cows!' And the tsar ordered his wages to be doubled. The herder pastured the cows and kept thinking about Bronze Brow. The cows grew fatter and fatter, and then one evening he noticed that they were growing bronze hooves and horns. He brought the cows back with their bronze hooves and horns and everyone was amazed.

The tsar ordered his new herder to look after the swine and ordered him to be paid three times his former wages. 'Now they're making me herd swine,' the tsarevich said to himself. 'What will it be next?' He remembered Bronze Brow. He went on herding the swine. And then one day everyone was filled with wonder. He brought the swine back – and each of them had grown a pearl on every bristle, and the bristles had turned to gold. Everyone was amazed, and the tsar wondered more and more. He called the herder and asked, 'What kind of man are you?' The herder replied, 'I'm the son of a tsar, but my father banished me from his tsardom when I let Bronze Brow out of the fortress.' 'I've heard tell of that,' said the tsar. The tsar told his wife and daughter, and he guessed that his daughter loved the herder. To test this, he suggested she marry him – and she agreed with joy. The tsar realized this was a dangerous business and, secretly from his wife and daughter, he ordered the herder to be taken under strict guard to the border and for guards to be posted there to make sure he never came back. His orders were carried out, but as soon as the herder crossed the border, the horses, cows and swine all became ordinary once more, just as before. When they were brought back in the evening, the tsar felt sad, and he told his wife and daughter that he had banished the herder because he was the son of a tsar and his father might declare war on him if he kept him at court.

The tsarevich walked on further. The path led through a forest. He walked on through the forest until he came to a large house. He went inside, but the house was empty. Night fell. At midnight the tsarevich heard someone at the door. He felt frightened, but what could he do? In came a young devillet. 'You're young,' he said to the tsarevich. 'And I'm young too. Together we can have a good time!' The tsarevich remembered about Bronze Brow and at once felt something appear in his pocket. He felt it with his fingers and thought it might be a snuffbox. He took it out: yes, it was a snuffbox – and it was full of tobacco. The devillet looked at it and asked what it was. 'Tobacco,' said the tsarevich. 'That's something I've never tried,' said the devillet. 'Have a sniff then!' The devillet had a sniff and began to sneeze. 'That's splendid stuff!' he said. 'Let's play cards. We'll play three hands. If I win the third hand, you can give me your snuffbox. But if you win, I'll give you whatever you want.' And he offered the tsarevich a great many wonderful things, but the tsarevich said he would take a purse that had nothing in it at all – but when you opened it, the purse was full of gold. You could give away all the gold you liked – there would always be more in the purse. The devillet dealt. They played one hand; the tsarevich lost. They played a second hand; the tsarevich lost. The devillet dealt a third hand. This time the tsarevich thought about Bronze Brow and asked him to help. The devillet led; the tsarevich played a higher card. Twice more the tsarevich played higher cards. Then the tsarevich began playing clubs, and he won several more tricks. And so he defeated the devillet and won the purse. He let the devillet have another sniff of tobacco. Then the devillet left.

The tsarevich continued on his way. He came to a city. He went to a market and bought something. He took gold coins from his purse, but there were always more left. He decided to stay in this city. He played cards with the merchants and lords, and after a while found himself playing cards with the tsar. The tsar liked playing cards and his daughter often played, too. In the end the tsarevich was playing cards with the tsar's daughter every evening – and every time he played with her, he lost. The tsarevna began to wonder where all his money was coming from, and she realized he must have a purse that never grew empty. And then one day she gave the tsarevich a sleeping potion and took his purse. The tsarevich was left with nothing at all. And when the tsarevna told her father the tsar what she had done, he ordered the tsarevich to be taken under strict guard to the border and banished forever from his tsardom.

The tsarevich was taken to the border, and he went on his way. 'Well now,' he said to himself, 'it seems I've been left with nothing at all. Help me, Bronze Brow, to get out of this trouble. Then I shall make my home in one place and make no more mistakes.' He walked straight on and he came to a sea. There on the shore were some apple trees, and the apples on them were already ripe. He picked some. He ate one apple; a horn grew on his brow, but he didn't notice it. He ate another apple – and another horn grew on his brow. He ate a third apple and saw something moving by his feet. He grabbed at it and realized that he had grown a tail. Then he wanted to rub his eyes, but his hand caught on one of his horns. Then he felt the other: yes, he really did have two horns on his brow. The tsarevich took fright. He remembered Bronze Brow, but the horns and the tail remained where they were. He wandered about the shore, then went on further. He walked on for several more days, looking at himself in the water and seeing his horns. Then he came to a place where there was a thicket of thorns, and in between the thorns were some small trees, and on them were some red fruits that looked quite like apples. He picked one of these fruits and thought, 'Well, it was apples that made the horns and the tail grow. Maybe these fruits will make something else grow. Then I can be a real marvel – maybe that's the way it has to be!' He ate one fruit and felt one horn fall off him. He ate a second fruit – and his second horn disappeared. Then he ate a third fruit – and his tail fell off too. He looked at himself in the water and saw it was true: his horns and his tail really had disappeared now. The tsarevich was overjoyed and he picked more of these fruits, thinking, 'I'll eat some more.

Maybe it will end up even better.' He ate one more fruit, looked in the water and no longer knew himself at all; he had become more beautiful than pen can portray or storyteller can say. 'Well,' he said to himself, 'I can go back home now. I've become another man and no one will know who I am.'

He set off. On the way he picked some of the apples that had made him grow horns and a tail. He reached the border. No one stopped him. He went on till he came to the royal palace. There he began selling apples. Two servant girls slipped out of the palace and he sold them some of the other fruits. They ate these fruits and became so beautiful that they could no longer recognize each other. They talked for a moment, then went to the tsar's daughter. She didn't recognize them either; but when they told her their story, she gave them some money and told them to go and buy some more apples. One of the servant girls ran after the tsarevich and asked to buy three more apples, for the tsar's daughter. The tsarevich took the money and gave her three apples. The servant girl ran back with the apples; the tsarevna went to her room and ate all three of them. She got up to go to the mirror and felt something trailing along behind her; then she looked at herself in the mirror and saw horns growing from her brow. The tsarevna was horrified, and she sent at once for the apple-seller. Along he came. She asked him to cure her. The apple-seller waited there till evening, and the tsarevna strictly forbade her servant girls to say anything to anyone about what had happened. When everyone had gone to bed, the apple-seller took a hammer and struck one of the horns. This hurt the tsarevna, but she endured the pain: anything to remedy her misfortune! Then the apple-seller gave her one of his fruits; she ate it and the horn fell off. Then he gave her another of his fruits, and the other horn fell off too. 'Well, tsarevna, now we must settle up – and then, tomorrow night your tail will fall off too.' 'What shall I give you?' 'I love gold. You can pay me in gold.' The tsarevna took out her purse and took out some gold coins, but the apple-seller saw that it was his own purse and he asked if he could keep it till the following night, since he had nowhere to put all the gold. For a long time the tsarevna refused, but then she gave in; she was thinking he wouldn't realize it was a magic purse. She handed it to him and asked him to be sure to bring it back the next evening. The apple-seller left the city that night, taking his purse with him and leaving the tsarevna her tail. After a while, he came to the city where he had herded the tsar's livestock; there he sat down by the palace and began selling apples. The tsarevna came out, bought one of his fruits, ate it and became a great beauty. She invited him into the palace and he told her everything: where he had gone after being banished and all that had befallen him. He went on living at the palace, and the tsarevna asked her father the tsar to make him the palace steward. The steward was open-handed with his gold and he made friends with everyone. The tsar died and the steward became tsar in his place. He and the tsarevna were married. And so he ruled the tsardom, and nowhere was there anyone richer.

OLGA ERASTOVNA OZAROVSKAYA

(1874–1931)

Olga Ozarovskaya was the daughter of an artillery officer. Endowed with a love of travel and a gift for storytelling, she lived a rich and varied life. She herself compared her fate to the 'diligent' ball of thread that serves as both guide and path to many folktale heroes and heroines: 'the ball rolled tirelessly along the ground, tormented by curiosity. It chose unexpected little paths. It rolled safely up to aristocratic mansions. It would rest, curling up into a little grey ball, and then it would unwind again, rolling away, its thread glittering, towards the home of a peasant.'[1]

In 1898, a year after completing a degree in mathematics, Ozarovskaya started work in the Chamber of Weights and Measures; the director was Dmitry Mendeleyev, the discoverer of the Periodic Table. Ozarovskaya was the first woman in Petersburg to be offered work in a major scientific institution.

Ozarovskaya had long been admired as an amateur actress and reciter. After Mendeleyev's death in 1907, she began to work in this field as a professional, giving public recitals of poems and stories. Her repertoire included humorous stories by Chekhov and Averchenko, Kipling's Just-So Stories, poems by Balmont and Tyutchev, scenes from novels by Dostoevsky and Hamsun – and folktales. In 1911 she moved to Moscow, where she taught acting and declamation in her Studio of the Living Word.

She especially loved the folktales and heroic epics of the Russian north and between 1915 and 1925 she visited the region four times. She herself played the role of fairy god-mother to Mariya Dmitrevna Krivopolyonova, a gifted singer

*and storyteller whom Ozarovskaya met during the first of
these trips. Krivopolyonova, then aged seventy-one, had been
orphaned at the age of ten and had lived much of her life as a
beggar. Ozarovskaya not only transcribed Krivopolyonova's
songs and stories but also arranged for her to perform, to great
acclaim, in most of the main cities of European Russia. In 1921
Anatoly Lunacharsky, the first Bolshevik Commissar of
Enlightenment, invited Krivopolyonova to his Kremlin apartment and went to fetch her in his own car. Krivopolyonova,
however, was unimpressed. What moved her, it seems, was not
the wonders of a modern city but the spirit of the legendary
past that she could still sense in Moscow – a past that had been
a living present to her in the songs she had been singing
throughout her life.*

In 1916 Ozarovskaya published A Grandmother's Past
(Babushkiny stariny), *a collection of some of the folksongs and
tales that Ozarovskaya had recorded from Krivopolyonova,
together with an account of their meetings. During the Soviet
period Ozarovskaya continued to work both as a performer
and as a teacher. In 1929 she published a memoir about Mendeleyev, and in 1931 she published* Five Rivers (Pyatirechiye), *a
collection of folktales, one of which is included here. She died
that same year.*

*Ozarovskaya's tact and sensitivity in her dealings with peas-
ant singers and storytellers enabled her to win their trust. 'I
never ask for a particular tale,' she wrote. 'I wait for the storyteller himself to choose the first story. An artist always begins
with something he can perform with confidence. Later he will
tell the story that means most to his soul, and this will be clear
from a particular excitement in his voice.'[2]*

The Luck of a Tsarevna

Here is what I once heard – from people of all kinds, from old maids, from old bitches.

In a certain land, in a certain tsardom, in a place as flat as a tablecloth, there lived a tsar and his wife; they had no children. A daughter was born to them. The daughter was christened. The godfather and godmother held her in their arms and said that when the girl grew up, she would be led through the market place and whipped with a knout. The tsar said, 'How on earth! No, I'll never let her out of my sight.'

Tales are told quickly; lives are lived slowly. The girl grew up and began begging her father to let her go out and about.

'Papenka,' she said, 'let me go out for a walk. Let me go out with the mothers and nannies and the old ladies. Let me go out into the fields, let me go to the steep shore of the deep blue sea.'

Her father let her go. Off went the tsarevna with the mothers and nannies and the old ladies. Off she went into the fields, to the steep shore of the deep blue sea. There by the shore stood a little ship with sails. The tsarevna climbed into the ship and a fair wind began to blow. The ship took her across the blue sea – far, far away. The tsar searched and searched, but she was gone, quite gone. And the tsarevna stepped out of the ship onto another steep shore. There on the shore was a well. By the well grew a tall, tall tree. The maiden climbed up into the tree and sat on a branch. Now in that tsardom there was a yega baba (that's a bad word, isn't it?),[1] and this yega baba had a daughter. And the yega baba sent this daughter off to the well, saying, 'Off with you, you ugly creature. Go and fetch me some water.'

Her daughter went to the well and began drawing out water.

There in the well she saw the beautiful tsarevna. She went back to her mother and said, 'Why do you call me ugly, mother? There's no one in the world more beautiful than I am.'

Her mother jumped up: 'What on earth's got into you?'

'Come to the well with me and you'll see what a beauty I am!'

Off they went. They looked in the well and the yega baba saw the beautiful maiden.

'Don't be such a fool!' she said to her daughter. And she looked up into the tree and saw the tsarevna.

'Climb down from that bush, girl!'

The tsarevna climbed down.

'You can come and live with me, girl. What skills do you know? Do you know how to embroider a towel?'

'Yes,' said the tsarevna. She was very skilled indeed, more than words can say. She began embroidering, and the yega baba took the towels and sold them.

Around that time the tsar made a proclamation: 'Whoever can set pearls in my crown, him or her I will take to my heart. Be it an old woman, she will become a grandmother to me. Be it an old man – a grandfather. Be it a woman of middle years – an auntie. Be it a man of middle years – an uncle. Be it a man of my age – he shall be my brother. Be it a woman of my age – she shall be my betrothed wife.'

The yega baba heard about all this. 'My daughter will be able to set the pearls,' she said. She went back home and said to the tsarevna, 'Set the tsar's pearls, daughter.'

The tsarevna laid out all the pearls on the windowsill and set to work. She sewed and sewed and soon there was only one pearl left to be set. It was the central pearl, the one that would lie above the tsar's nose. There it was, lying on the windowsill. And down flew a raven. The raven pecked the pearl up in its beak – the pearl, after all, was very shiny – and away it flew. Soon the time came to return the crown to the tsar. The yega baba brought it along and said, 'It's not the fault of my own daughter. It's a girl I adopted who was doing the work.'

'Bring her here at once. She must be put on trial.'

It was decreed that the girl be led through the market place and whipped with a knout.

A poor old woman and her husband appeared. They lived in somebody's back yard, along with the cattle. The old woman said, 'Don't harm the girl's body, don't put her to shame. Give her to me as a daughter. We've got no one at all.'

And so the old woman took the girl in. She turned out to be a good and obedient daughter. After a while it was the old man's name day, the day of his angel.

'We're going, daughter, to the holy liturgy, to pray to God. You stay behind and prepare the food. There's cooking to be done, and baking. When everything's ready, you must lay the table, put out the food and then go out onto the porch. There you must bow to all four sides and say, "Luck of my Grandfather, please eat and drink with me – eat bread and salt with me, and all kinds of dishes."'

And so the girl did. She went out onto the porch, bowed and said:

> *Luck of my Grandfather,*
> *Please eat and drink with me –*
> *Eat bread and salt with me,*
> *And all kinds of dishes.*

Along came Grandfather's Luck. She was splendidly dressed; she looked truly magnificent. She sat down at the table. She ate and drank, but there was still as much food and drink on the table as ever. She poured a heap of silver coins onto the table, thanked the girl and went on her way. The old people came back from the church and asked, 'Well, daughter, who came?'

'Grandfather's Luck came. She ate and drank, but there was still as much food and drink on the table as ever. She poured out a heap of silver.'

The following day was the name day of the old woman.

'You must cook and bake,' she said to the girl, 'and then invite my Luck to the table.'

The girl cooked and baked. She laid the table, put out the food and went out onto the porch. She bowed to all four sides and said:

> Luck of my Grandmother,
> Please eat and drink with me –
> Eat bread and salt with me,
> And all kinds of dishes.

Grandmother's Luck was no less finely dressed. She ate and drank, but there was still as much food and drink on the table as ever. She poured out a heap of gold coins and thanked the girl. The old people came back from the church and the girl told them everything.

'Well, daughter,' they said to her. 'Tomorrow's your own name day. You must cook and bake. Then you must invite your own Luck to the table. But don't let her go without paying something for her dinner – even if you have to demand it of her!'

The girl cooked and baked. She laid the table, put out the food and went out onto the porch. She bowed to all four sides and said:

> Bitter Luck, bitter lot of my own,
> Please eat and drink with me –
> Eat bread and salt with me,
> And all kinds of dishes.

Along came her Luck. She was ugly as ugly can be, and all in rags. She looked well and truly horrible. She sat down at the table and gobbled everything up. Not a scrap of food was left. And off she went without so much as a word of thanks. The girl chased after her. 'Bitter Luck, bitter lot of my own,' she said, 'you must pay me something for your dinner. You've eaten and drunk everything I put out. Now you must give me something in return.'

Her Luck tried to creep away into a pit, but the girl grabbed hold of her rags and did not let go. 'No!' she repeated, 'you have to give me at least something.'

Her Luck tore off a little bundle and threw it to the girl. She did the same with a second bundle, and a third bundle. The girl picked up the three bundles and set off back home.

She felt sad. 'What will Grandfather and Grandmother say?' she was thinking.

The old people came back from the church: 'Well, daughter, did your Luck come and eat her meal?'

'Yes, she did. She was ugly as ugly can be, and all in rags. She looked truly horrible. She gobbled up everything I gave her.'

'Did she give you anything?'

'She gave me three bundles of rags.'

'Let's have a look at them.'

The girl showed them the three bundles. The first bundle was simply a bundle of rags. The second bundle was simply a bundle of rags. But in the third bundle were a golden hook and a golden eye.

'Well, daughter, these are worth keeping. One day they'll come in useful.'

Soon afterwards the tsar made another proclamation. He was sewing a kaftan; he was sewing himself a royal garment. But he did not have enough gold for the last hook and eye. He had asked everywhere, but there was none in his kingdom. 'Who,' he asked, 'can bring me a golden hook and a golden eye to match the ones I already have?'

'Go along, daughter,' said the old people. 'Maybe your hook and eye will be just what he needs!'

Off she went. She showed her hook and eye to the tsar. Her own hook and eye were just like the tsar's hook and eye. They could have been cast from the same mould. The tsar said then and there, 'You shall be my betrothed wife!'

They celebrated their wedding with a merry feast. They lived and prospered. Good things came their way, and they kept evil at bay. One day they went for a walk in their garden. All of a sudden a raven flew over their heads.

'Why's it croaking like that?' asked the tsar.

The tsaritsa raised her arm and held her hand out above her. The raven flew down and spat a pearl out onto her hand. And the tsaritsa said, 'Once I was sewing pearls onto your crown and a raven flew off with the very last pearl. I was sentenced to be led through the market place and whipped with a knout.'

The yega baba was taken to the town gate and shot.

DMITRY
KONSTANTINOVICH
ZELENIN

(1878–1954)

Dmitry Zelenin was born in the Vyatka province, to the west of the Urals. The son of a sacristan, he was educated in a seminary and then at the university of Yuryev (now Tartu) in Estonia. After graduating in 1903, he taught at St Petersburg University and then, in 1916, took up a professorship at Kharkov University. From 1925 until his death, he was a professor at Leningrad University and a research fellow at the Institute of Ethnography of the Academy of Sciences.

Between 1901 and 1916 he published two collections of folktales and five other books in the field of folk literature and ethnography, and he continued to work in the fields of dialectology, social linguistics and ethnography until his last years. It was said, only half-jokingly, that he was as productive as all the other members of the Institute of Ethnography put together. But, like Onchukov, he was able to publish only a small part of what he wrote. His Russian Ethnography *was published in German translation in Leipzig in 1927, but the original manuscript was somehow lost. When this important work was finally published in Russia in 1991, it was in a back-translation from German. Zelenin's* Selected Works *was published in 2004, but his* Ethnographical Dictionary *still remains unpublished.*

A review of Zelenin's Selected Works *includes this haunting account of a talk given by Zelenin at the Soviet Academy of Sciences in 1950, three years before Stalin's death: 'His old shabby suit made him stand out startlingly among the other well-dressed professors. [. . .] On the conference programme the theme of his talk – something to do with primitive rituals – had seemed ordinary enough. But as he began reading his paper about primitive people creeping along on their stomachs and licking the heels of their leaders, it was impossible not to make certain very definite associations. People's faces took on a stony look. There is no knowing whether Zelenin chose this theme entirely consciously or whether in his simplicity of heart he simply failed to realize the glaring parallels.'*[1]

By the Pike's Command

1. There was Omelya Lelekoskoy. All he did was sleep on the stove. And he shat big turds – great piles of them, like sheaves of hay. He had to sleep in the middle of the stove – there was no room anywhere else.

His sisters-in-law told him to go to the Danube to fetch water. 'But how can I? I've got no bast sandals, no foot cloths and no coat. I've got nothing at all – not even an axe.' One sister-in-law began poking his forehead with a stick; another began poking and prodding him on the arse. He found some foot cloths and he found some worn-out sandals. He put on the sandals, he put on a coat, he tied the foot cloths, he put on a cap and he stuck a blunt axe under his belt. He took two pails from on top of the chicken coop. And he took a yoke.

He reached the Danube. He scooped one of his pails through the water, but he didn't scoop up anything at all. He put that pail down and drew his other pail through the water. He caught a pike. 'Ah, my little pike! Now I shall eat you!' 'No, dear Omelyanushko, don't eat me!' 'Why not?' 'Because if you don't, you'll be happy!' 'How come?' 'Because the buckets will go back on top of the hen coop all by themselves!'

The pails made their way back, and Omelya ran along behind them, batting turds along the ground with the yoke. On he ran, laughing away. The pails got back on top of the hen-coop and he got back on top of the stove.

2. The day after this Omelya was sent to the forest to get fire-wood. But he had never done this before; never had he seen how people chop firewood. 'How can I? There's no mare. There's no

collar for the mare, no saddle girth, nothing at all!' 'We've told you already. The mare's in the stables, her collar's hanging on the wheel spoke, under the bridge into the barn. And the sleigh's under the bridge into the barn too. Everything's ready and waiting for you!' He went into the stables – the mare wasn't there, her collar wasn't there, nothing was there. He opened the gates and stood under the bridge. 'By my father's blessing, by my mother's blessing, by the pike's command, let everything be ready – bridle, shaft, saddle girth and all!'

Omelya got up onto the footboard and off he went: 'By my father's blessing, by my mother's blessing, by the pike's command, let the sleigh drive off on its own!' Off he went, singing songs. But it was market day in the village. Everyone wanted to watch him drive by. He crushed whole crowds of people.

He drove into a sweet-scented forest. He found a dry tree that was still standing. It was very broad. He got to work with his axe, but the tree was too strong – he couldn't chop even a splinter from it. 'By my father's blessing, by my mother's blessing, by the pike's command, let the wood chop itself! Let it pack itself onto the sleigh and tie itself tight!'

The pike chopped a load that stood so high you couldn't reach to the top of it. And it was tied so tight you couldn't even slip a finger between the logs.

The pike went on ahead, clearing the fallen branches. And Omelyanushko stood there on the footboard, singing so loud it made the crowns of the trees shake. Crowds of people ran out into the road again and he crushed everyone that was left.

3. The tsar heard news of all this. From the porch of his royal palace he dispatched a whole regiment of soldiers. Up they marched to the porch of Omelyanushko's hut. 'Is Omelyanushko at home?' 'Yes, where would I go? I'm lying at home, lying on the stove.'[1] The soldiers began to rush about. Some fired cannons, others swung hatchets. But what did he care? All he did was play about with his bits of shit. And then: 'By my father's blessing, by my mother's blessing, by the pike's command!' Omelyanushko had only to lift his hand – and he felled the whole regiment.

The tsar sent a second regiment of soldiers. They hurried up to the hut. 'Is Omelyanushko at home?' 'Yes, I'm at home, lying on top of the stove. There's no one can scare me – I don't doff my cap to no-one.' This second regiment didn't even go into the hut. They turned tail.

On the third day the tsar sent two million soldiers. 'Are you coming?' 'Yes, I'm ready now!' By then the soldiers were dismantling the hut, log by log. 'By my father's blessing, by my mother's blessing, by the pike's command, get going, stove, and take me with you!'

The pike knocked down the wall, and the stove set off. It stopped by the tsar's porch. 'Ignorant lout, do you know how many of my soldiers you've killed?' 'But your most royal Highness, what have I done? Whom have I seen? Where have I been?' 'Be off with you, you foulness and filth! Away with you and your stench!' The tsar was already feeling sick.

But Marya Chernyavka was in a room up above. Soldiers had been bringing her food and drink. And then Omelya had come. She had opened the carved windows. Omelya took just one look at her. 'Be bound to me – be my betrothed!' Her heart fell ill. No longer did she eat or drink when the soldiers brought her food.

'She no longer eats or drinks,' the soldiers said to the tsar. 'All she does is weep. Her eyes are all red. She keeps rubbing them with her muslin sleeves.' 'Go and ask her,' said the tsar, 'if he said anything to her.' The soldiers asked her, and she answered, 'He said, "Be bound to me – be my betrothed!" And then my heart fell ill. Since then I haven't eaten or drunk.' The tsar heard this, then said to two of his soldiers, 'Go and find him. Bring him to me. Don't let him go.'

4. 'Well, Omelyanushko, are you ready?' 'Yes!' 'Let's go then!' 'Why?' 'Because Marya Chernyavka is longing for you. She won't eat or drink. Her father has sent for you!' 'By my father's blessing, by my mother's blessing, by the pike's command, go with me, stove! Come on lads, sit here on the stove with me – it'll be warmer for you!' And so some of them just sat there and smoked, while others took care of the fire and threw on more wood.

They drew near the palace gates. The pike took a besom broom and swept away all the turds; now the stove was as clean as a clean floor. They came to the porch. 'Soldiers, bear food and drink to him! But first bear him in on your hands! I'm off to the forge – there I shall forge their wedding bands!'

The tsar went to the forge and forged six large hoops. He stuffed Omelya and Marya Chernyavka into a forty-bucket barrel, bound the barrel with these six hoops and cast the barrel into the Danube River.

5. Who knows how long they floated there? 'What can we do, Omelyanushko? I feel lonely and full of grief. I want to set eyes again on the fair light of the world!' 'Pray to God! Morning is wiser than evening.' 'Maybe we've been brought to land? Maybe we've been brought to yellow sand?' 'No, my silly girl, we're stuck on a sand bank, the barrel will never float free now.' 'I feel lonely and full of grief.' 'Pray to God! Morning is wiser than evening.'

'By my father's blessing, by my mother's blessing, by the pike's command, may this barrel be cast onto dry land, onto yellow sand!' And the pike cast them onto dry land – them and their barrel.

'What can we do, Omelyanushko? I feel lonely and sick and full of grief. I want to set eyes again on the fair light of the world!' Somehow Omelya bored a hole in the bottom of the barrel. Along came a wolf and he began to crap. Omelya caught him by the tail and didn't let go. The wolf took fright and off he ran. He knocked the barrel against a pine tree, against a second pine, against a fifth and a tenth pine. The barrel fell apart. The wolf had set them free.

6. 'Marya Chernyavka!' 'What?' 'You stay here! I'll go and have a look at that mountain. I'll see what it's like there.' 'Will you be long?' Off Omelya went. For a month and a half he tried to climb the mountain. He tried and tried, but he couldn't get up it. 'By my father's blessing, by my mother's blessing, by the pike's command!' The pike pulled him up. He stood on top of the mountain. 'May a city stand here – a city finer than my

father-in-law's! And with heaps of grain that reach to the barn roofs!' He got all this done, then went back for Marya.

They came to the mountain. She climbed up one stone, then up another, and then fell back down again – back to the foot of the mountain. She'd all but torn her dress to shreds. She struggled and struggled, but what could she do? 'By my father's blessing, by my mother's blessing, by the pike's command!' And the pike pulled them both up to the top.

'Omelyanushko!' she said. 'It's a fine city, but we can't live without food!' 'Pray to God. He'll provide food and drink!' They came to the first barn. She crossed herself. 'It's all right,' she said. 'I can see we won't be dying of hunger!' She came to a second barn – and she fell to her knees and prayed. Omelya took her into a third barn. Lord God! In that barn there was still more grain.

There they were. He took her into a hut. 'Light the stove,' he said, 'and cook some breakfast!' She did as he said. All Omelya had to do himself was put the bread in his mouth. 'Well then,' he said. 'You eat and drink. I shall go and call up an army.'

7. Three mornings he called up hosts of soldiers. Soon there was nowhere in the city to billet them all. He called up hosts and hosts. 'Well, Marya Chernyavka, these next three evenings I shall call up provisions!' He sat down, he called up provisions. Lord God! Soon there was nowhere in the city to store them all.

'Now I'll go to the market and buy some fine bulls – after all, I have to feed everyone!' He bought twenty-five of the most expensive bulls. 'Now cook them! I'll go and sort out tables and tablecloths.' The beef was soon cooked, and he himself did everything else. 'Sit down, soldiers! Sit down, my children! Eat and drink! As you served the fair tsar, so you must serve me! Do not betray me!'

He fed them well. 'Now then, off you go! When my father-in-law's soldiers start shooting, keep all their bullets and shells! Keep them there on your knees! Don't shoot! Wait till I give the order – shoot then!' The enemy soldiers fired their guns. They did all their shooting and then they ran out of bullets. They had nothing left. 'Well, my children, now you can pick them off. They'll fall over like sheaves of wheat in the drying barn!' His soldiers got to work. The whole city fired their guns and killed all the father-in-law's soldiers.

'Now you must come and visit! Now you must come and be my guest!' Omelya said to his father-in-law. 'But you must be sure to close your eyes.' The father-in-law closed his eyes. Soon he was sitting there on a bench, eating and drinking. 'I've been here thousands of times, but I've never seen a mountain here before. Where did this mountain come from? Where did this city come from? Where have you come from yourself?' In came Marya Chernyavka. 'It's me, father,' she said. 'And this is Omelyanushko.'

All proper hospitality was shown him. 'Take him away – outside the city! Sit him on the gates, shoot him and scatter his ashes!' And so they did. They took the tsar away, shot him and scattered his ashes.

PART FOUR

NADEZHDA TEFFI

(Nadezhda Aleksandrovna Lokhvitskaya,
1872–1952)

At the beginning of the twentieth century, the magic tale represented what was most glamorous and exotic in Russia's far
distant past. In the 1920s and 1930s, to Nadezhda Teffi and
her fellow Russian émigrés in Paris and elsewhere, the magic
tale represented not so much Russia's historical past as the irre-
trievable world of their own childhood and youth.

Teffi's real surname was Lokhvitskaya. She was born in
St Petersburg into a distinguished family that treasured literature; she and her three sisters all became writers. Her elder
sister was well known as a poet, and each of her younger sisters
published articles in periodicals and had plays performed in
theatres. In 1907, Nadezhda began to write under the name
'Teffi'; this is sometimes thought to come from the English
'Taffy', but she herself, in her story 'Pseudonym', said it derives
from 'Steffi', a familiar form of 'Stepan' – the name of one of
her friends. After the Revolution, Teffi settled in Paris. There
she was an important literary figure; she ran a salon and, for
the rest of her life, contributed weekly columns and stories to
leading émigré periodicals with impressive regularity.

Teffi wrote in a variety of styles and genres: political feuil-
letons published in the Bolshevik newspaper New Life (Novaya
Zhizn') during her brief period of radical fervour after the 1905
Revolution; Symbolist poems that she declaimed or sang in
Petersburg literary salons; popular one-act plays, mainly satir-
ical treatments of topical subjects – one was entitled 'The Woman
Question'; and a novel titled simply Adventure Novel (1930).
Her finest works, however, are her short stories and her Mem-
oirs (1928–9), a witty yet tragic account of her last journey

across Russia, before going by boat from the Crimea to Istanbul in 1919.

Writers of the stature of Bunin, Bulgakov and Zoshchenko admired Teffi; she also always had a wide readership. In pre-Revolutionary Russia, candies and perfumes were named after her; after the Revolution, her stories were published and her plays performed throughout the Russian diaspora. During the first four decades after her death, however, she was almost forgotten. This was probably in part because she was a woman; in part because she was considered 'lightweight' (critics noticed her wit more than her perceptiveness); and in part because both Western and Soviet scholars tended to ignore émigré literature. Since the early 1990s Teffi has been published more and more widely. Nevertheless, her earlier, lighter work is still better known than the more profound stories she wrote in the 1930s.

Throughout her career, Teffi retained an interest in all aspects of the folktale: its language, its rhythmic structure, the power of its images and its moral truthfulness. 'When the Crayfish Whistled' is one of Teffi's best-known early stories; its theme – the danger of our wishes being granted – is a common theme in oral tales. 'A Little Fairy Tale' is a concise primer of Russian folklore, refracted through two distinct prisms: that of Soviet life in the first years after the Revolution and that of émigré life in France. 'Baba Yaga' was first published as a large-format picture book for children. Teffi follows Afanasyev's well-known version; her mastery of folktale diction and rhythm is perfect. 'The Dog' is from The Witch, *the collection Teffi herself considered her best.*

Each of the stories in The Witch *is devoted to a particular character or theme from Russian folklore. 'The Dog' is not a 'magic tale' in the sense that this term is used by folklorists. It is in many respects realistic and it is embedded in a particular historical moment. We have included it because it provides a fine example of a writer drawing on folklore not for ornament but as a source of psychological truth. Just as D. H. Lawrence sometimes draws on the paranormal, so Teffi draws on folklore to convey how, at moments of crisis, we can be overwhelmed by the most primitive aspects of the psyche.*

And the last piece, an article written in 1947 and also titled 'Baba Yaga', exemplifies the extent of Teffi's capacity for thoughtful empathy. In her 1932 version of this story she describes the cat wiping tears from his eyes — perhaps the one detail that clearly distinguishes Teffi's version from that of a folk narrator. In this article, she goes still further, entering into the thoughts and feelings even of the archetypal Russian witch.

When the Crayfish Whistled:
a Christmas Horror

The Christmas tree shone its last; the guests went back to their homes.

Little Petya Jabotykin was diligently pulling the birch-bark tail off his new rocking horse and listening to what his parents said as they took down the beads and stars and put them away until the following year. Their conversation was very interesting.

'Never again,' Papa Jabotykin pronounced solemnly, 'am I having a Christmas tree. It's a waste of money and it affords us no enjoyment.'

'I'd imagined we'd be getting something from your father,' said Maman Jabotykin, seizing her chance.

'A likely story! We'll get something from my father the day crayfish start to whistle.'

'And I thought he'd be giving me a real live pony,' said Petya, looking up at his father.

'A likely story! My father will give you a pony the day crayfish start to whistle.'

Father was sitting with his feet far apart and his head bent down. His moustache was drooping, as if damp, and his sheep-like eyes were fixed gloomily on one spot.

Petya glanced at his father and decided this was a safe moment to talk to him.

'Papa, why crayfish?'

'Hm?'

'When crayfish start to whistle – that's when everything's going to happen?'

'Hm?'

'But when will they start to whistle?'

The father was about to give a frank answer to his son's question when he remembered that a father's duty is always to be strict. He gently cuffed Petya on the back of the head and said, 'Off you go to bed, piglet.'

Petya went to his bedroom, but he did not stop thinking about crayfish. On the contrary, the thought of them was now so firmly lodged in his head that nothing else in the world any longer held any interest for him. The rocking horses did not get their tails pulled out; the clockwork soldier's spring remained unbroken; the clown's squeak-box remained in its correct place, in the pit of his stomach. Petya's room, in short, was the abomination of desolation. Because the young master had no time for such trifles. He was pacing about, wondering what could be done to make crayfish hurry up and start whistling.

He went to the kitchen and asked the advice of Sekletinya the cook. She said, 'They don't whistle because they've got no lips. The day they grow lips, that'll be the day they start whistling.'

Neither she nor anyone else could say any more.

Petya grew; and as he grew, he pondered this more and more deeply. 'There really must be a reason,' he thought, 'why people say that, when crayfish whistle, your wishes will be granted.'

If a crayfish's whistle was merely a symbol of impossibility, then why didn't people say: 'When elephants fly' or 'When cows chirrup'? No! Hidden within this common saying must lie some profound understanding, the wisdom of the people. It was imperative to look into all this more deeply. Crayfish can't whistle because they have neither lips nor lungs. Well and good. But surely it was not impossible for science to bring about changes to the organism of the crayfish? Surely, by means of genetic selection and other influences it was possible for science to compel a crayfish to acquire lungs?

Petya devoted his whole life to this problem. He studied occultism, the better to understand the mystical link between the crayfish's whistle and human happiness. He researched the constitution of the crayfish, its life, habits, origin and potentials.

He married, but not happily. He hated his wife for breathing with lungs, which crayfish do not possess. He divorced his wife – and spent the rest of his life in the service of an idea.

On his deathbed, he said to his son, 'My son! Listen to my testament. Work for the happiness of your neighbour. Study the crayfish's physical constitution, research the crayfish, force the little bastard to change his nature. Occult sciences have revealed to me that a true wish, an ardent and sincere human wish, will be granted every time a crayfish whistles. Unless you're a complete swine, how can you think of anything now except this whistle? Shortsighted little people build hospitals and imagine they're benefiting their neighbours. That kind of work is of course easier than changing the nature of the crayfish. But we – we are Jabotykins! Generation after generation of us will work at this, and we shall achieve our goal!'

When he died, his son took it upon himself to continue his father's work. His grandson did the same, and his great-grandson, finding it difficult to work as a serious scientist in Russia, moved to America. Americans don't like long names and the great-grandson was soon rechristened. Mister Jabotykin became Mister Jeb, and so this splendid family disappeared from view, forgotten by their Russian relatives.

Many, many years went by. Much was new in the world, but the overall extent of human happiness had not changed since the day when Petya Jabotykin, while pulling the birch-bark tail off his horse, had asked, 'Papa, why crayfish?'

Just as before, people wanted more than they could get; just as before, they suffered, consumed by wishes that could never be fulfilled.

But then newspapers started publishing a strange announcement: 'Ladies and gentlemen! Prepare yourselves! The work of many generations is nearing completion! The joint-stock company "Mister Jeb and Co." wishes to announce that on December 25th of this year a crayfish will whistle for the first time and this will result in the most heartfelt wish of every one person in a hundred (1 per cent) being granted. Prepare yourselves!'

At first this announcement attracted little attention. 'Probably it's just some kind of swindle,' people thought. 'These American companies are all the same. They promise miracles – and in the end they all turn out just to be promoting some new kind of shoe polish.'

But the nearer it came to the promised date, the more interest this American venture began to evoke. People were shaking their heads and saying that it was anybody's guess: they'd have to wait and see.

And when the story was taken up by journalists, when newspapers began to print portraits of the great inventor and photographs of every corner of his laboratory, no one any longer felt ashamed to admit that they believed in the coming miracle.

Soon the newspapers were even showing a picture of the crayfish that was promising to whistle. It looked more like a district police officer from the southwest of Russia than like a cold-blooded animal. Goggly eyes, a jaunty moustache and a generally dashing expression. It was wearing a kind of knitted jacket with laces, and either its tail was hidden in something like cotton wool or else it didn't have one at all.

This image enjoyed great popularity. It appeared on postcards in the most fantastic colours – green with light-blue eyes, lilac with gold specks, and so on. The crayfish's portrait could be seen on the label of a new brand of rowanberry vodka. There was a new Russian airship that was the same shape as the crayfish and moved only backwards. And no lady with any self-respect would think of wearing a hat that wasn't adorned with a pair of crayfish claws.

That autumn 'Mister Jeb and Co.' issued their first shares, which shot up in value so fast that even the most stolid of dealers began to speak of them in a respectful whisper.

Time passed; time sped; time flew. At the beginning of October, forty-two different gramophone firms sent representatives to America, to record the sound of the crayfish's whistle and broadcast this sound throughout the world.

Nobody stayed in bed on the morning of 25 December. Many people had been up all night, doing complicated calculations and arguing about how many seconds would have to pass before a whistle in America could affect life on our own meridian. Some said that it would take no longer than it takes to transmit electricity. Others retorted that an astral current was quicker than an electric current, and that since this was clearly a matter of astral currents, rather than any other kind of current, then it followed that . . . and so on . . .

From eight in the morning the streets were swarming with people. Mounted policemen were affably keeping the crowds in order, gently backing into them with the hindquarters of their horses, and the crowds for their part were buzzing with joyful anticipation.

It was announced that, as soon as the first telegram arrived, a cannon would be fired.

People waited excitedly. The young were exultant and ecstatic, laying plans for their radiant future. Sceptics grumbled and said it would be better to go home and have breakfast, since it was quite obvious that nothing whatsoever was going to happen and wasn't it really rather silly to keep on fooling about like this?

At precisely two in the afternoon came the clear, resonant boom of a cannon, answered by thousands of joyful Oohs and Aahs.

But then came something unforeseen and rather strange, an event that no one could recognize – or wanted to recognize – as a link in a chain by which each and every one of them was bound: a certain, tall, stout colonel suddenly began to swell up in a very odd way. As if deliberately, he inflated like an elongated balloon. His coat split, ripping apart along the back seam, and then the colonel, as if glad to have overcome an unpleasant obstacle, burst with a loud pop, spattering in all directions.

The crowd reeled back. People screamed. People took to their heels: what on earth was happening?

A pale little soldier gave a crooked smile, his lips trembling. He scratched behind one ear and gave a helpless shrug: 'All right – get out the handcuffs! It's me what did it! I wished a curse on him, I wished he'd pop it!'

But no one listened to the soldier or laid a finger on him. By then everyone was staring in horror at an attenuated old lady in a fox-fur cloak who had suddenly begun to let out wild howls. Spinning round like a top, she was sinking into the earth right in front of their eyes.

'The bitch – the earth's swallowed her up!' someone mumbled by way of farewell.

The crowd was seized by a mad panic. Not knowing where to turn, everyone began to run. People were knocked to the ground; people trampled on one another. Two women, choking on their own tongues, let out a death rattle, and an old man began to wail over their bodies: 'Chastise me, O Orthodox brothers. My women are dead and I shall be locked up in prison for the rest of my days!'

A nightmarish evening was followed by a ghastly night. Nobody slept. Everyone was remembering their own black wishes and anticipating the fulfilment of the wishes of others.

People were dying like flies. The only person in the entire world to benefit from the crayfish's whistle was a little girl in Northern Guinea; her head cold cleared up thanks to a wish from her aunt, who was fed up with her endless sneezing. Every other good wish (if indeed there were any such wishes) was evidently too feeble and half-hearted to be granted by the crayfish's whistle.

The end was approaching rapidly. Humanity would have perished utterly but for the greed of Mister Jeb and Co. Wanting to ramp the price of their shares still higher, they exhausted the crayfish, forcing the creature, by means of special pills and electrical stimulation, to let out a whistle that was beyond its strength.

The crayfish croaked it.

On its tombstone (the prize-winning work of a famous sculptor) were carved the words: 'Here lies the crayfish that whistled – the property of "Mister Jeb and Co." – a crayfish that satisfied human souls and fulfilled their most ardent wishes. Pray never, never awake again!'

A Little Fairy Tale

Everyone was busy at home and Grisha was allowed to go out for a walk on his own. But only on one condition: that he didn't go too far into the forest. He didn't speak French well and he had been at this French dacha for only three days. How would he be able to ask anyone the way if he got lost? It was best to be careful.

And so, on this condition, he was allowed out.

But Grisha was not a particularly obedient boy, and he always thought he knew better than anyone else what he should and shouldn't do.

And so, when he came to the first trees, he calmly turned off the path and went straight into the densest part of the forest.

The trees grew close together. And between them, twining around the trunks, were thick brambles. There were moments when Grisha found it hard to fight his way through.

He had eaten his fill of blackberries and he had ripped his stockings and torn all his clothes very badly. He was beginning to wonder how to get back to the path when he realized that, to his right, the forest seemed to be thinning out a little. Yes, he could see more light over there. It must be the way back to the path.

He struggled through the undergrowth and came out into the open.

But instead of getting back to the path, he found himself in a small glade.

In the middle of this glade was an old moss-covered tree stump. Beside it flowed a small gurgling brook, half-hidden by forget-me-nots.

Grisha felt tired. He sat down on the grass, leaned back against a little mound and even closed his eyes.

'First I'll have a proper rest,' he said to himself. 'Then I'll find my way back to the path. What's the hurry? When I get back, I'll just get a caning because of my stockings and the state of my clothes and because *why did you have to go into the forest when we told you not to?*'

Grisha closed his eyes.

A cricket in the grass sang, 'Grrrree-eesh! Grrrree-eesh!'

A bee buzzed by. It was as if someone had twanged a string: 'Dzzz-oon.'

From somewhere in the bushes a bird asked, 'Soo-oon? Soo-oon?'

And then, as if imitating its own song, it repeated, 'Oo-oon? Oo-oon?'

And then, articulating the words with absolute clarity, some kind of pipe or flute sang out:

> *Deep, deep in the forest,*
> *Between blue forget-me-nots,*
> *I'll catch you on my hook,*
> *Hook you on my line.*
> *And soon, stranger, soon*
> *You'll be dancing to my pipe,*
> *Dancing to my tune.*

This surprised Grisha, but by then he was feeling too drowsy even to open his eyes.

Then there seemed to be someone laughing. And then a loud click as something landed smack in the middle of Grisha's forehead.

A hazelnut!

A fresh, green hazelnut, still wrapped in its outer leaves.

Grisha looked round – but no one was there.

This was getting stranger and stranger. Where had the hazelnut come from? There was nothing near him except a tree stump, forget-me-nots and dense brambles.

He stretched, then closed his eyes again.

Bang!

Another hazelnut, also smack in the middle of his forehead. This time it really hurt.

Grisha leaped to his feet. He turned round. Looking at him from out of the tree stump were two quick, bright eyes. They were gleaming; it was as if they were laughing. Grisha looked more closely. There, hiding inside the tree stump, was a very small man.

He was a strange little man – entirely naked. He looked sunburnt, brown all over. His legs were shaggy, as if he were wearing thick woollen stockings and had pulled them up above his knees. He had thick lips and two tufts of hair sticking up over his forehead. He was looking straight at Grisha, and it seemed as if he might burst into laughter any moment. He seemed to be shaking all inside him. And it was almost impossible to look at this little man without laughing oneself. Grisha could feel a tickling in his throat, and his legs were starting to twitch.

Not taking his eyes off Grisha, the little man suddenly put a small green pipe to his lips. And the pipe began to sing. It sang the following words:

> The bear, the goat and her kids,
> The vixen and her cubs,
> The wolf and the blind mole –
> Caught now on my hook,
> Hooked now on my line.
> And soon, stranger, soon
> You'll be dancing too,
> Pirouetting to my pipe,
> Dancing to my tune.

Grisha was astonished. 'Are you Russian?' he asked.

The little man laughed.

'*You'll be dancing too!*'

'So you're Russian, are you?'

The little man removed the pipe from his lips.

'I'm not Russian,' he said. 'I'm internashional.'

This annoyed Grisha. 'You're making fun of me. We've been taught every nation in the world – and there isn't any nation called internashional!'

But the little man didn't take offence. He didn't seem in the least bothered by Grisha's reply. He just narrowed his eyes and thought for a moment. 'So you're Russian, are you?' he said. 'Excellent. You can do me a great service, and in return I'll show you the way out of the forest.'

'All right,' said Grisha. 'What you want me to do?'

The little man thought, scratched one of his feet against the other and said, 'A relative of mine's come on a visit. From Russia. She's a refugee. Heaven knows what she's after, I can't make head or tail of anything she says. It's a nightmare. You go and have a word with her! Maybe the two of you will be able to understand each other.'

The little man led Grisha through the forest. Anyone would have thought he was walking about his own apartment. He knew every twist and turn of the way. He knew which bough to slip underneath, which tree stump to walk round, which bush marked a fork to the left or the right.

After maybe a long time – or maybe a short time – the little man led Grisha into a dense hazel thicket. He parted the branches. Grisha saw an ant hill. And sitting on top of this ant hill was an old woman. Her hair was dishevelled and she was dressed in rags. Her fingers ended in claws, like the claws of a crow, and her face was all hidden behind a great mat of hair.

Grisha looked at the woman, and somehow he felt scared.

He did not move. He did not speak.

The old woman shook her hair. All of a sudden, like the wind in a chimney, she boomed out: 'Seems I can smell the smell of a Russian!'

She parted her great mat of hair. Now he could see her big green eyes, her hooked nose and the yellow fang jutting out of her mouth.

Grisha shook from head to toe and howled, 'Baba Yaga!'

He wanted to run away, but terror rooted him to the spot.

But Yaga was smiling, her yellow fang wobbling about.

'Good day,' she said, 'my fine warrior! You're lucky I've lost my appetite or I'd have you for supper. Why are you gawking at me like that? I'm in an extremely difficult position here, and there isn't even anyone I can have a moan to. This here shyster doesn't understand a thing I say.' Yaga pointed one thumb over her shoulder, towards the little man who had brought Grisha there, and spat on the ground. 'And everything I owned has gone to the winds. The government even requisitioned my copper mortar. If it weren't for my broomstick, I'd never have got away at all. I'm just grateful for old Leshy![1] He serves at that Enlightenment Commissariat of theirs and he managed to sort me out a visa.'[2]

Yaga hunched up in despair, resting her cheek on her bone leg.

'Our whole clan's been liquidated. Kaput! Done away with! They've taken Koshchey the Deathless off to London – Europe needed living proof that even under the new regime not everybody kicks the bucket! Tom Thumb, the little slyboots, has wormed his way into counter-espionage. Little Humpbacked Horse got eaten in Moscow by people who were fed up with fasting.[3] And Sleeping Beauty's on the staff of the Council of People's Commissars;[4] she's manning the telephone. As for the bog devils, they've joined a choir, they sing in the new-style churches. Yes, nowadays bride and groom carouse and say their marriage vows beneath a New Year tree. And the bogles sing for them – well, everyone has to make a living somehow. And as for Zmey Gorynych[5] – tough as they come, but not even he could resist temptation. He signed up with the Cheka[6] to supervise the disposal of dead bones. Kikimora's working in the area of State aesthetics.[7] As for the poor werewolf – he's snuffed it. He'd become a quick-change artist – he was turning his coat twenty times a minute – and the public still wasn't satisfied. He said he couldn't keep up – and then he just keeled over.'

Baba Yaga began to cry.

'I'm unhappy; I'm in a bad way. What am I going to do? There isn't even going to be any proper snow here. How am I going to whirl up a whirlwind? How can I sweep over my tracks with a broom? All this is going to be the end of me, it's clear as daylight.'

Baba Yaga was weeping, sobbing and sobbing. Grisha was

still frightened, but he felt sorry for Baba Yaga; he could even feel his nose starting to prickle.

Yaga wiped away her tears with a burdock leaf and said to Grisha, 'You go home, my fine warrior. Go your own way. I haven't even got anything here I could roast you in. There are no proper stoves anywhere. They seem to have installed some kind of central heating in this forest of theirs – damn them!'

Grisha turned round. The strange little man was nodding to him from behind a bush.

'All right? Could you understand what she said?'

'Yes.'

'Hm. I couldn't understand a word myself.'

The little man grabbed Grisha by the hand and whirled him back through the forest. Together they ran and span through the trees – through bushes, over stumps and jagged roots. The little man was singing and laughing:

> *I caught you on my hook,*
> *By a forest brook,*
> *And you were dancing too,*
> *Dancing to my tune.*

He span Grisha round like a top, gave him a shove in the back and was gone. And then, somewhere far away in the forest there was a hoot and the sound of something rolling over.

Grisha looked round. He could see familiar bushes – and, beyond them, the path back to the dachas.

He plodded back.

At home he got it in the neck – for his ripped stockings, for his filthy clothes, and because *why did he have to go into the forest at all*?

And above all – for telling such a pack of lies.

There is, evidently, no justice in the world.

Baba Yaga

(1932 picture book)

Once upon a time there lived a man and his wife. And they had a daughter. She was a good little girl.

Both mother and father loved their little girl. They took good care of her and even spoiled her. The mother would bake pies for her, and the father would stroke her hair and say, 'Grow up healthy and strong, my clever darling. Grow up to be kinder and wiser than anyone in the world!'

And so they lived until the girl's mother died. The father grieved and grieved, but in the end he found himself another wife. Now the little girl had a stepmother.

This wicked stepmother took against the little girl. She nagged at her day after day, and she beat her. After a while she took it into her head to do away with the girl altogether.

When the father had gone away for a while, the stepmother said to the girl, 'Go and call on my sister, your auntie. Ask her for a needle and thread so I can sew you a shirt.'

This auntie, the stepmother's sister, was a baba yaga. She was Baba Yaga, Bone-Leg.

But the little girl was no fool. First of all, she went to speak to her real auntie.

'Good day, auntie!' she said.

'Good day, my darling! What's brought you here?'

'I wanted to tell you that my stepmother's sending me to her sister. I've got to ask for a needle and thread so she can sew me a shirt.'

Her auntie heard what she had to say, then told her what she must do.

'A birch tree will lash you across the face, my darling, but you must tie a little ribbon round it. The gate will creak and squeak. It will hit you and bang you, but you must pour oil on its hinges. Dogs will want to tear you apart, but you must throw them some bread. A tomcat will want to scratch you in the eye, but you must give him some ham. If you do as I say, if you don't muddle or forget anything, you'll come back safe and sound. God go with you!'

The little girl thanked her dear auntie and got ready to leave. She took with her a length of ribbon, a little bowl of oil, a hunk of bread and some ham.

She walked and walked. She walked, walked and walked. She walked all the way to the forest.

By the edge of the forest she saw a little hut with no doors or windows.

The little girl thought for a moment. Then she said, 'Little hut, little hut, turn your face towards me and your back to the forest!'

The little hut turned around.

There was Baba Yaga, Bone Leg. She was sitting and sewing. She looked fierce and angry.

The little girl bowed to Baba Yaga. 'Good day, auntie!' she said.

'Good day, my dear,' grunted Baba Yaga.

'My stepmother's sent me to you. She wants a needle and thread so she can sew me a shirt.'

'All right,' said Baba Yaga. 'But sit down for a while first. You can do a little embroidery for me.'

The little girl sat down at the embroidery frame. Yaga went outside and said to her maid, 'Go and heat up the bathhouse so you can wash my niece for me. Make sure the steam's good and hot, so you can steam every one of her little bones. I'll be frying her tonight for my supper.'

Baba Yaga had a loud voice. It was like the wind when it howls in the chimney. The little girl heard every word. She sat there shaking, more dead than alive. But she said to the maid, in a quiet voice, 'Dear maid! Don't light the wood but pour water over it instead. And when you bring the water for steam, carry it inside in a sieve.'

And then she gave the maid a present: her own little kerchief.

Baba Yaga was waiting. She was growing impatient. She wanted to eat the little girl up.

She went to the window and asked, 'Are you still working, my girl? Are you still sewing?'

'Yes, auntie, I'm still working hard. I'm still sewing.'

'Keep sewing then. And mind you don't tangle the threads.'

Baba Yaga stepped back from the window. The little girl caught sight of the tomcat. He was black and he had yellow eyes. He was walking about the room with his tail straight up in the air, his eyes half-closed, twitching his whiskers and scratching the floorboards with his claws.

The little girl remembered what her auntie had told her. She gave the cat some ham and said, 'Dear puss, sweet puss, tell me what I must do. Teach me what to do to get out of here!'

And the cat replied, in a human voice, 'Here are a comb and a towel for you. Take them and run. Baba Yaga will chase you. And you must put your ear to the ground and listen. When you hear her come close, you must throw down this towel. It will turn into a wide, wide river. But if Baba Yaga's very cunning, if she manages to cross the river, if she starts to catch up with you again, then you must put your ear to the ground a second time. When you hear her come close, you must throw down this comb. It will turn into a deep, dense forest, and she'll never be able to make her way through it.'

As the girl ran out of the hut, some fierce dogs appeared. Barking and snarling, they seemed to appear out of nowhere, out of thin air. They leaped at the girl. They wanted to tear her to pieces.

The girl was terrified, but she remembered what her auntie had told her.

'Good dogs!' she called out. 'Good dogs! Don't bark and don't snarl! Don't scare me or scar me! Let me pass! And here's some bread for you.'

She threw the dogs some bread, and they let her pass.

The girl ran on further. When she reached the outer gate, it creaked and squeaked, then banged shut. It didn't want to let her pass.

The girl remembered what her auntie had told her and poured oil onto the hinges.

'Gate, gate!' she called out. 'Don't creak and don't squeak! Let me pass quietly and don't call your mistress!'

The gate was very happy to feel the oil on its hinges. It opened wide and let the girl pass.

The girl ran on. Suddenly there was a birch tree barring her path. It appeared out of nowhere, out of thin air. It was waving its branches about, trying to lash her across her eyes.

The girl was terrified, but she remembered her auntie's instructions and tied her little ribbon around the trunk of the birch tree.

'Let me pass, silver birch! Let me pass!'

The birch tree let the girl pass.

And all this time the tomcat had been sitting at the embroidery frame. But he hadn't done any sewing. He had just tangled everything up.

Baba Yaga went to the window. 'Are you still working hard, my girl?' she asked. 'Are you still sewing, dear niece?'

'Yes, I'm still working, mean auntie. I'm still sewing, cruel auntie.'

Yaga was surprised by the girl's harsh voice. She rushed into the hut and realized that the girl was not there.

Baba Yaga was furious. She was angry with the cat, and she was angry that she had spent all day sharpening her teeth to no purpose. She started thrashing the cat. She beat him and flogged him and cursed him:

'How dare you, you thieving brute of a cat? How dare you let her go without scratching her eyes out?'

The cat wiped away his tears and said to Yaga in a human voice, 'I've served you for many years, Yaga, and you've never given me even an old bone you've picked clean – but the girl gave me a piece of good ham!'

Baba Yaga rode off. Next it was the turn of the dogs. She beat them and lashed them till their coats were matted like felt:

'You faithless windbags! All bark and no bite! How dare you let the girl out of the hut without tearing her flesh into shreds?'

The dogs took offence. They said, in human voices, 'We've served you for many years, Yaga, and you haven't once thrown us so much as a burnt crust – but the girl gave us good bread!'

Yaga gave up beating the dogs. Now it was the turn of the gate:

'How dare you, you wretched gate? How dare you not creak and squeak and call out to me? How dare you let that girl out? I'll take an axe to you and hack you to pieces! Soon you'll be splinters of firewood!'

In a human voice, the gate replied, 'I've served you for many years, but you haven't once even given me water. But the little girl poured oil onto my hinges!'

Next, Yaga was yelling at the birch tree:

'How dare you, you wretched birch? I'll rip you out of the ground and use all your twigs to make besom brooms! How dare you let the girl pass? How dare you not lash her across the face?'

In a human voice, the birch replied, 'I've served you for many years. You've never once even tied a thread round my trunk, but the little girl gave me a pretty ribbon!'

Yaga stopped shaking the birch tree and turned instead to her maid, 'Lazy, sponging slut! How dare you let the little girl out of the hut? How dare you leave me without any supper?'

She punched the maid with her fists. She gnashed her teeth at her. She kicked her in the back with her bone leg.

And the maid replied, 'I've served you for many years. You've never once given me so much as a torn rag, but the little girl gave me a pretty kerchief!'

Yaga wanted to gnaw her maidservant to death, but she didn't have time. She had to catch up with the little girl.

Yaga crawled down into the storeroom. She got out her copper mortar and rolled it along the ground. She found her pestle and her broom. She got into the mortar – and off she went, crashing and rumbling.

Yaga hurtled on in her mortar, spurring it on with her pestle, sweeping up her tracks with her broom.

The little girl felt the earth start to shake. She put her ear to the ground and listened: Yaga was catching up with her. She was very close indeed.

The little girl remembered what the cat had said and threw down the towel he had given her.

The towel fell on the grass and turned into a broad, broad river. It was so broad that you wouldn't be able to cross it even in three days.

Baba Yaga hurtled up to the edge of the river and stopped. What could she do? How could she cross the water in a copper mortar?

Baba Yaga ground her teeth, banged her pestle and returned home. Then she herded her oxen together, drove them to the river and ordered them to drink up the water.

The oxen drank and drank. They drank and drank until they had drunk the river dry.

Baba Yaga got back into her mortar. She set off again over dry land. The mortar roared and rumbled. She spurred it on with her pestle and swept up her tracks with her broom.

The little girl felt the earth start to shake. She put her ear to the ground and listened: Yaga was catching up with her again. She was very close indeed.

The little girl remembered what the cat had said, took the comb and threw it down on the path behind her.

And straight away a dense, dark forest rose out of the earth. It was so dense and so dark that not even a worm would have been able to worm its way through – let alone a human being.

But Baba Yaga knew nothing of this. She hurtled on in her mortar, spurring it on with her pestle. She was determined to catch up with the girl.

'I didn't get any lunch,' she was thinking, 'but it doesn't matter. There'll be all the more room for my supper.'

Her mortar knocked and banged and rumbled. Pillars of dust twisted into the sky.

Yaga hurtled on towards the forest – but there was no way through. There was no way she could pass through the trees.

Baba Yaga got out of her mortar, ran to the very edge of the forest and began gnawing the trees. She gnawed and gnawed – but after gnawing for a long time she had felled only ten oaks. All she had really done was to make her teeth even sharper.

Yaga made her way back home.

The girl's father was also on his way back to his hut. When he got in, he asked, 'Where's my daughter?'

The stepmother replied, 'She's gone to her auntie's.'

The father didn't believe this.

And then, all of a sudden, there was his daughter. Her face blank from terror, she came running in as fast as her legs would carry her.

'Where have you been, my darling?' he asked her.

'My stepmother sent me to my auntie's to ask for a needle and thread so she could sew me a shirt. But this auntie is a Baba Yaga, Bone Leg, and she wanted to eat me.'

'Dear daughter, how did you manage to get away from her?'

And the girl told her father everything: how her real auntie had given her wise advice, how the tomcat had pitied her and given her a comb and a towel, how the maid had disobeyed Baba Yaga and not heated the bathhouse. She told her father about the gate and about the dogs and about the birch tree.

Her father was very angry when he learned that his wife had wanted to feed his daughter to Baba Yaga. He took a large stick and drove the wicked stepmother out of the hut.

And he and his daughter lived and prospered.

I was there, and I drank mead and beer. It ran down my beard but did not pass my lips.

The Dog

(a story from a stranger)

Do you remember that tragic death? The death of that artful Edvers? The whole thing happened right in front of my eyes. I was even indirectly involved.

His death was extraordinary enough in itself, but the strange tangle of events around it was still more astonishing. At the time I never spoke about these events to anyone. Nobody knew anything except the man who is now my husband. There was no way I could have spoken about them. People would have thought I was mad and I would probably have been suspected of something criminal. I would have been dragged still deeper into that horror – which was almost too much for me as things were. A shock like that is hard to get over.

It's all in the past now. I found some kind of peace long ago. But, you know, the further my past recedes from me, the more distinctly I can make out the clear, direct, utterly improbable line that is the axis of this story. So, if I am to tell this story at all, I have to tell you all of it, the way I see it now.

If you want to, you can easily check that I haven't made any of this up. You already know how Edvers died. Zina Volotova (née Katkova) is alive and well. And if you still don't believe me, my husband can confirm every detail.

In general, I believe that many more miracles take place in the world than we think. You only need to know how to see – how to follow a thread, how to follow the links in a chain of events, not rejecting something merely because it seems improbable, neither jumbling the facts nor forcing your own explanations on them.

Some people like to make every trivial event into a miracle.

Where everything is really quite straightforward and ordinary, they introduce all kinds of personal forebodings and entirely arbitrary interpretations of dreams, made to fit their stories. And then there are other, more sober, people who treat everything beyond their understanding with supreme scepticism, dissecting and analysing away whatever they find inexplicable.

I belong to neither of these groups. I do not intend to explain anything at all. I shall simply tell you everything truthfully, just as it happened, beginning at what I myself see as the story's beginning.

And I myself think the story begins during a distant and wonderful summer, when I was only fifteen.

It's only nowadays that I've become so quiet and melancholic – back then, in my early youth, I was full of beans, a real madcap. Some girls are like that. Daredevils, afraid of nothing. And you can't even say that I was spoiled, because there was no one to spoil me. By then I was already an orphan, and the aunt who was in charge of me, may she rest in peace, was simply a ninny. Spoiling me and disciplining me were equally beyond her. She was a blancmange. I now believe that she simply wasn't in the least interested in me; but then neither did I care in the least about her.

The summer I'm talking about, my auntie and I were staying with the Katkovs, who lived on a neighbouring estate, in the province of Smolensk.

It was a large and very sweet family. My friend Zina Katkova liked me a lot. She simply adored me. In fact the whole family were very fond of me. I was a pretty girl, good-natured and lively – yes, I really was very lively indeed. It seemed I was charged up with enough joy, enough zest for life to last me till the end of my days. As things turned out, however, that proved to be far from the case.

I had a lot of self-confidence then. I felt I was clever and beautiful. I flirted with everyone, even with the old cook. Life was so full it filled me almost to bursting. The Katkovs, as I've said, were a large family and – with all the guests who had come for the summer – there were usually about twenty people around the table.

After supper, we used to walk to a little hill – a beautiful, romantic spot. From it you could see the river and an old abandoned mill. It was a mysterious, shadowy place, especially in the light of the moon, when everything round about was bathed in silver, and only the bushes by the mill and the water under the mill-wheel were black as ink, silent and sinister.

We didn't go to the mill even in daytime – we weren't allowed to, because the wooden dam was very old and, even if you didn't fall right through it, you could easily sprain your ankle. The village children, on the other hand, went there all the time, foraging for raspberries. The canes had become dense bushes, but the raspberries themselves were now very small, like wild ones.

And so we would often sit in the evenings on the little hill, gazing at this old mill and singing all together, 'Sing, swallow, sing!'

It was, of course, only us young who went there. There were about six of us. There was my friend Zina and her two brothers – Kolya, who was the elder by two years, and Volodya, who is now my husband. At the time he was twenty-three years old, already grown-up, a student. And then there was his college friend, Vanya Lebedev – a very interesting young man, intelligent and full of mockery, always able to come up with some witticism. I, of course, thought he was madly in love with me, only trying his best to hide it. Later the poor fellow was killed in the war ... And then there was one more boy – red-haired Tolya, the estate manager's son. He was about sixteen years old and still at school. He was a nice boy, and even quite good looking – tall, strong, but terribly shy. When I remember him now, he always seems to be hiding behind somebody. If you happened to catch his glance, he would smile shyly and quickly disappear again. Now, this red-haired Tolya really was head-over-heels in love with me. About this there could be no doubt at all. He was wildly, hopelessly in love with me, so hopelessly that no one even had the least wish to make fun of him or to try to laugh him out of it. No one teased him at all, though anyone else in his position would have been granted no mercy – especially with people like Vanya around. Vanya even used to make out that Fedotych the old cook was smitten with my charms: 'Really, Lyalya, it's time you satisfied poor Fedotych's passion. Today's fish soup is pure salt.[1] We can't go on like this. You're a vain girl. *You* may enjoy his suffering – but what about *us*? Why should *we* be punished?'

Tolya and I often used to go out for walks together. Sometimes I liked to get up before dawn and go out to fish or pick mushrooms. I did this mainly in order to astonish everyone. People would walk into the dining room in the morning for a cup of tea and say, 'What's this basket doing here? Where have all these mushrooms come from?'

'Lyalya picked them.'

Or some fish would suddenly appear on someone's plate at breakfast.

'Where's this come from? Who brought it?'

'Lyalya went fishing this morning.'

I loved everyone's gasps of astonishment.

So, this redheaded Tolya and I were friends. He never spoke to me of his love, but it was as if there were a secret agreement between us, as if everything was so entirely clear and definite that there was no need to talk about it. Tolya was supposed to be a friend of Kolya Katkov, although I don't really think there was any particular friendship between them. I think Tolya just wanted to be a part of our group; he just wanted the opportunity to stand behind someone and look at me.

And then one evening we all of us, including Tolya, went off to the hill. And Vanya Lebedev suddenly decided that each of us should tell some old tale or legend, whatever they could remember. The scarier, the better – needless to say.

We drew lots to decide who should begin. The lot fell to Tolya.

'He'll just get all embarrassed,' I said to myself, 'and he won't be able to think of any stories at all.'

But, to our general astonishment, Tolya began straight away: 'There's something I've been meaning to tell you all for a long time, but somehow I've never got round to it. A story about the mill. The story's quite true – only it's so strange you'd swear it was just a legend. I heard it from my own father. He used to live six miles away, in Konyukhovka. It was when he was a young man. The mill had been out of use for a long time even then. And then an old German with a huge dog suddenly came along and rented the mill. He was a very strange old man indeed. He never spoke to anyone at all; he was always silent. And the dog was no less strange; it would sit opposite the old man for days on end, never taking his eyes off him. It was only too obvious that the old man was terribly afraid of the dog, but there seemed to be nothing he could do about it. He seemed quite unable to get rid of the dog. And the dog just kept on watching him, following the old man's every movement. Every now and then the dog would suddenly bare its teeth and growl. But the peasants who went there for flour said the dog never attacked any of them. All it ever did was look at the old man. Everyone found this very odd. People even asked the old man why he kept such a devilish creature. But there was no chance of getting any reply out of him. He simply never answered a word . . . And then it happened. All of a sudden this dog leaped on the old man and bit through his throat. Then the peasants saw the dog rushing away, as if someone were chasing it. No one ever saw the dog again. And the mill's been empty ever since.'

We liked Tolya's old legend. Vanya Lebedev, however, said, 'That's splendid, Tolya. Only you missed out a few things. And really it should be more scary. You should have added that the mill has been under a spell ever since. Whoever spends one whole night there will be able, if ever he wishes, to turn himself into a dog.'

'But that's not true,' Tolya replied shyly.

'How do you know? Maybe it *is* true. We simply don't know. I've got a feeling that that's the way it is. It's just that no one's tested this out yet.'

We all laughed. 'But why? What's so special about turning into a dog? If one could turn oneself into a millionaire, that would be different. Or some hero or other, or a famous general – or a great beauty for that matter. But who wants to turn into a dog? Where would that get you?'

No one told any more stories that evening. We talked about this and that, then went our separate ways.

The following morning Tolya and I went into the forest. We picked some berries, but there were too few to take back to the dining room so we decided I might as well eat them myself. We sat down beneath a fir tree, me eating berries and him just looking at me. Somehow this began to seem very funny.

'Tolya,' I said, 'you're staring at me the way that dog of yours looked at the miller.'

'Really I wish I could turn into a dog,' he answered glumly, 'because you're never going to marry me, are you?'

'No, Tolya, you know I'm not.'

'You see, if I remain a man, it'll be impossible for me to be near you all the time. But if I turn into a dog, no one can stop me.'

I had a sudden idea. 'Tolya, darling! You know what? You could go to the mill and spend the night there. Please do! Turn into a dog, so that you can always be near me. You're not going to say you're scared, are you?'

He turned quite white – I was surprised, because all of this was just stuff and nonsense. I was joking. Neither of us, it went without saying, believed in that mysterious dog. But he, for some reason or other, turned pale and replied very gravely, 'Yes, all right, I'll go and spend the night at the mill.'

The day went by in its usual way and, after my morning walk, I didn't see Tolya at all. In fact, I didn't even think of him.

I remember some guests coming round – newlyweds from a neighbouring estate, I think. In short, there were lots of people – lots of noise and laughter. And it was only in the evening, when everyone except family had left and we youngsters had set out for our usual walk, that I began to think about Tolya again. It must have been when I saw the mill – and when someone said, 'Doesn't the mill look dark and spooky this evening?'

'That's because we know the kind of things that go on there,' replied Vanya Lebedev.

Then I started looking for Tolya. Turning round, I saw him sitting a little apart from the rest of us. He was completely silent, as if deep in thought.

Then I remembered what he'd said, and somehow this made me feel anxious. At the same time, I felt annoyed with myself for feeling anxious, and this made me want to make fun of Tolya.

'Listen, ladies and gentlemen!' I called out merrily. 'Tolya's decided to conduct an experiment. Transformation into a dog. He's going to spend the night at the mill.'

No one paid much attention to any of this. They probably thought I was joking. Only Vanya Lebedev answered, saying, 'Yes, why not? Only please, dear Anatoly, be sure to turn into a hunting dog. That really would be a great deal more acceptable than a mere mongrel.'

Tolya didn't say anything in reply. He didn't even move. When we were on our way home, I purposely lagged behind a little and Tolya joined me.

'Well, Lyalechka,' he said. 'I'm going. I'm going to the mill tonight.'

Looking very mysterious, I whispered, 'Go then. You must. But if, after this, you have the nerve *not* to turn into a dog, please never let me set eyes on you again!'

'I promise to turn into a dog,' he said.

'And I,' I said, 'will be waiting for you all night. As soon as you've turned yourself into a dog, run straight back home and scratch on my shutter with your claws. I'll open the window, and then you can jump into the room. Understand?'

'Yes.'

'Off you go then!'

And so I went to bed and began to wait. And just imagine – I couldn't get to sleep. Somehow I was terribly anxious.

There was no moon that night, but the stars were shining. I kept getting up, half-opening the window and looking out. I felt very scared of something. I felt scared even to open the shutters – I just looked out through a chink.

'Tolya's a fool,' I said to myself. 'What's got into him? Sitting on his own all night in a dead mill!'

I fell asleep just before dawn. And then, through my dreams, I hear a scratching sound. Somebody's scratching on the shutter.

I jump out of bed to listen better. Yes, I can hear the sound of claws against the shutter. I'm so scared I can hardly breathe. It's still dark, still night-time.

But I braced myself, ran to the window, flung open the shutters – and what did I see? Daylight! Sunshine! And Tolya's standing there laughing – only he's looking very pale. Overcome with joy, I grab him by the shoulders, then fling my arms round his neck.

'You scoundrel! How dare you not turn into a dog?'

He just kissed my hands, happy that I had embraced him.

'Lyalechka,' he said, 'can't you see? Or maybe you just don't know how to look properly. I *am* a dog, Lyalechka. I am your faithful hound forever. How can you not see it? I shall never leave you. But someone's put an evil spell on you that stops you from understanding.'

I grabbed a comb from the table, kissed it and threw it out the window.

'Fetch!'

He rushed off, found the comb in the grass and brought it to me between his teeth. He was laughing, but there was something in his eyes that almost made me burst into tears.

All this happened as summer was drawing to a close.

Three or four days after that night, my aunt and I went back to our own village. We needed to get ready to return to Petersburg.

Volodya Katkov rather surprised me. He had got hold of a camera from somewhere, and during the days before our departure he kept on and on taking photographs of me.

Tolya kept at a distance. I barely saw him. And he left before me. For Smolensk. He was studying there.

Two years went by.

I only once saw Tolya during that time. He had come to Petersburg for a few days to attend to some practical matter, and he was staying with the Katkovs.

He had changed very little. He still had the same round, childish face, with grey eyes.

'Greetings, my faithful hound! Let me take your paw!'

He didn't know what to say. Terribly embarrassed, he just laughed.

Throughout his visit Zina Katkova kept sending me little notes: 'You really must come round this evening. Your hound keeps howling.' Or: 'Come round as soon as you can. Your hound is wasting away. Cruelty to animals is a sin.'

Everyone kept quietly making fun of him, but he behaved very calmly indeed. He didn't seek me out, and he went on hiding behind other people's backs.

There was just one occasion when Tolya seemed to go a bit wild. Zina was telling me that, since I had such a wonderful voice, I really must go and study at the Conservatoire – and Tolya suddenly came out with, 'Yes, I knew it! The stage! How utterly, utterly wonderful!'

Immediately after this little outburst, needless to say, he seemed terribly embarrassed again.

He was only in Petersburg for a few days. Soon after he had left, I received a huge bouquet of roses from Eilers.[2] We were all racking our brains for a long time, wondering who on earth could have sent it, and it was only the following day, as I was changing the water in the vase, that I noticed a little cornelian dog, tied to the bouquet by a thin gold thread.

I didn't tell anyone the flowers were from Tolya. I somehow started to feel awfully sorry for him. I even started to feel sorry for the dog. It had little shiny eyes, as if it were crying.

And how could someone as poor as Tolya have found the money for such an expensive bouquet? It was probably money his family had given him to go to the theatre with, or to buy things he really needed.

Expensive and splendid as they were, there was something tender and painful about these flowers. It was impossible to reconcile their air of sorrow with the impression created by Tolya's round, childishly naïve face. I even felt glad when the flowers withered and my aunt threw them out. I somehow hadn't dared to throw them out myself. As for the little cornelian dog, I tucked it away in a drawer, to try and forget about it. And I forgot about it.

Then came a very chaotic period in my life. It started with the Conservatoire, which disappointed me deeply. My professor was full of praise for my voice, but he said I needed to work on it. This, however, wasn't my way of doing things at all. I was used to doing nothing very much and receiving ecstatic praise for it. I would squeak out some little song and everyone would say, 'Oh! Ah! Such talent!' As for systematic study, that was something entirely beyond me. It also turned out that the generally held belief in my great talent was somewhat exaggerated. In the Conservatoire I did not stand out in any way from the other girls. Or if I did, it was only because I didn't even once bother to prepare properly for a lesson. This disappointment did, of course, have its effect on me. I became anxious and irritable. I found solace in flirtations, in pointless chatter and in endlessly rushing about. I was in a bad way.

I heard only once from Tolya. He sent me a letter from Moscow, where he had gone to continue his studies.

'Lyalechka,' he wrote, 'remember that you have a dog. If ever you are in need, just summon it.'

He did not include his address, and I did not reply.

The war began.

The boys from my old circle all turned out to be patriots, and they all went off to the Front. I heard that Tolya went too, but somehow I hardly thought about him. Zina joined the Sisters of Mercy, but I was still caught up in my mad whirl.

My studies at the Conservatoire were going from bad to worse. And I'd fallen in with a wild, Bohemian crowd. Aspiring poets, unrecognized artists, long evenings devoted to discussing matters erotic, nights at the 'Stray Dog'.[3]

The 'Stray Dog' was an astonishing institution. It drew in people from worlds that were entirely alien to it. It drew these people in and swallowed them up.

I shall never forget one regular visitor. The daughter of a well-known journalist, she was a married woman and the mother of two children.

Someone once happened to take her to this cellar, and one could say that she simply never left. A beautiful young woman, her huge black eyes wide open as if from horror, she would come every evening and remain until morning, breathing the alcoholic fumes, listening to the young poets howling out verses of which she probably understood not a word. She was always silent; she looked frightened. People said that her husband had left her and taken the children with him.

Once I saw a young man with her. He looked rather sickly. His dress, and his general air, were very sophisticated, 'Wildean'.

Looking cool and indifferent, he was sitting beside her at a table, and he seemed to be either writing or sketching something on a scrap of paper just under her nose. These words or signs evidently agitated her. She kept blushing and looking around: had anyone seen anything? She would grab the pencil from the young man and quickly cross out what he had written. Then she would wait tensely while he lazily scribbled something else. And then she would get agitated again and snatch back the pencil.

Something about this degenerate young man was so horrible, so deeply disturbing that I said to myself, 'Can there, anywhere in the world, be a woman so idiotic as to allow that creature to come anywhere near her? A woman who would trust that man in any way, let alone be attracted to such a repulsive little reptile?'

In less than a fortnight I proved to be just such a woman myself.

I would prefer not to dwell on this disgusting chapter of my life.

Harry Edvers was a 'poet and composer'. He composed little songs, which he half-read, half-sang, always to the same tune.

His real first name and patronymic were Grigory Nikolayevich. I never discovered his surname. I remember I once had a visit from the police (this was later, under the Bolshevik regime) to ask if a certain Grigory Ushkin was hiding in my apartment. But I don't know for sure if it was him they were inquiring about.

This Harry entered my life as simply and straightforwardly as if he were just entering his room in a hotel, opening it with his own key.

Needless to say, it was in the 'Stray Dog' that we first became acquainted.

I was on stage part of that evening, and I sang Kuzmin's little song, 'Child, don't reach out in spring for the rose'.[4] At the time it was still very much in vogue. At the end of the first phrase someone in the audience sang out, 'Rose lives in Odessa.'

It had been someone sitting at the same table as Harry. As I was on my way back to my seat, Harry got to his feet and followed me. 'Please don't take offence,' he said. 'That was Yurochka – he was just playing the fool. But you really shouldn't be singing Kuzmin. You should have been singing my *'Duchesse'*.

And so it began.

Within two weeks I had had my hair cropped and dyed auburn, and I was wearing a black velvet gentleman's suit. A cigarette between my fingers, I was singing the drivel Harry had made up:

> *A pale boy composed of papier-mâché*
> *Was now the favourite of the blue princess.*
> *He had a certain* je-ne-sais-quel *cachet*
> *Betokening voluptuous excess.*

I would raise my eyebrows, shake the ash from my cigarette and go on:

> *The princess had the bluest, sweetest soul,*
> *A dainty, pear-like soul – a true* Duchesse *–*
> *A soul to savour, then to save and seal,*
> *A soul for lovers of* vraie délicatesse.

And so on, and so on.

Harry listened, gave his approval, made corrections.

'You must have a rose in your buttonhole – some quite extraordinary, unnatural rose. A green rose. Huge and hideous.'[5]

Harry had his retinue of followers, an entire court of his own. All of them green, unnatural and hideous. There was a green-faced slip of a girl, a cocaine addict. There was some Yurochka or other, 'whom everybody knew'. There was a consumptive schoolboy and a hunchback who played quite wonderfully on the piano. They all shared strange secrets that bound them together. They were all agitated about something or other, all suffering some kind of torment and, as I now realize, often just making mountains out of molehills.

The schoolboy liked to wrap himself up in a Spanish shawl and wear ladies' shoes with high heels. The green-faced girl used to dress as a military cadet.

It is not worth describing all this in detail. These people really don't matter; they're neither here nor there. I mention them merely to give you some idea of the circles into which I had descended.

At the time I was living in furnished accommodation on Liteiny Prospekt. Harry moved in with me.

He latched on to me in a big way. I still don't know whether he truly fancied me or whether he just thought I was rich. Our relationship was very strange. Green and hideous. I don't propose to tell you about it now.

The strangest thing of all is that when I was with him, I felt repelled by him. I felt a sharp sense of disgust, as if I were kissing a corpse. But I was unable to live without him.

Volodya Katkov came back on leave. He rushed in to my apartment, full of joy and excitement. He exclaimed at my red hair. 'Why on earth? What a one you are! Still, you really are awfully sweet!'

He turned me around, to look at me from all sides. It was clear that he really liked me. 'Lyalechka, I'm only here for a week, and I'm going to spend every day of it with you. I've got a lot to say to you. It can't be put off any longer.'

And then in came Harry. He didn't even knock. And I could see that he took an immediate dislike to Volodya. He must have felt jealous. And so he sprawled out in an armchair and began nonchalantly doing something he had never done before: addressing me with extreme familiarity, not as *vy* but as *ty*.

Volodya must have felt very confused indeed. For a long time he kept silently looking from me to Harry, and then from Harry to me again. Then he stood up decisively, straightened his field jacket and said goodbye.

It greatly upset me to see him leaving like this, but I too had been confused by Harry's rudeness. There was nothing I could think of to say, and I was unable to prevent Volodya from leaving. There had, I felt, been a terrible misunderstanding, but it seemed utterly impossible to do anything to put it right.

Volodya didn't call again. Nor did I expect him to. I felt that he had gone away, that his heart had gone away, forever.

Then came a period of isolation.

In spite of everything he had done to avoid this, Harry was about to be sent to the Front. He went to Moscow to make representations.

I was on my own for more than a month.

It was an anxious time for me, and I had no money. I wrote to my aunt in Smolensk province, but I received no answer.

Eventually, Harry returned. Entirely transformed. Tanned and healthy-looking, wearing a classy sheepskin coat, trimmed with astrakhan, and with a tall Caucasian hat, also astrakhan.

'Have you come from the Front?'

'In a way,' he answered. 'Russia needs not only sacrificial cannon fodder but also brains. I'm supplying the army with motorized vehicles.'

Harry's brain may have been working magnificently, and it may have been needed by Russia, but he was still short of money.

'I need ready cash. Can you really not get hold of any for me? Are you really that lacking in patriotism?'

I told him about my misfortunes and about my aunt. He seemed interested and asked for her address. After hurrying about the city for a few days, he set off again. I had discovered by then that the secret of his new weather-beaten 'soldierly' look was contained in two little pots of pink and ochre powder. To give him his due, this really did make him look very handsome.

By this time the mood of our little world of aesthetes had turned distinctly counter-revolutionary. Before leaving, Harry had composed a new little ditty for me:

> *My heart hangs on a little white ribbon.*
> *White, white, white – remember the colour white!*

I was now wearing a white dress when I performed; we were all pretending to be countesses or marquises. The song was received well. So was I.

Soon after Harry had left, Zina Katkova came back unexpectedly from the Front. She at once began telling me a story I found terribly upsetting.

'Our field hospital,' she said, 'had been set up on the edge of a forest. There was a great deal to do, but we had to leave the next morning. We were being rushed off our feet. At one moment I went out for a smoke – and suddenly there was a young soldier calling my name. Who do you think it was? It was Tolya. Tolya the Dog. "Forgive me, darling," I say, "I'm in a desperate rush." "But I just want to know how things are with Lyalechka," he answers. "She isn't in trouble, is she? For the love of God, tell me everything you know." But just then I heard someone shouting for me. "Wait, Tolya," I say. "The moment I've got this done I'll be straight back." "All right," he says, "I'll wait for you by this tree. We certainly won't be going anywhere before tomorrow." And so I rushed back to my wounded. It was a terrible night. The Germans had got the range of our position, and at dawn we had to pack in a hurry. We didn't lie down for even a minute. I got a bit behind with everything and I had to run to get to our roll call. It was a miserable morning – endless grey drizzle. I'm running along – and suddenly – oh Lord! What do I see? Tolya standing by a tree, all grey and ashen. He had been waiting for me all night long. He looked so pitiful. His eyes were sunken, as if staring out from under the earth. And the man was smiling! Probably he'll be killed soon. Just think – he had been standing there all night long in the rain! Just to hear news of you! And I couldn't even stop for one moment. There was no time for anything. He thrust a slip of paper at me with his address. I shouted over my shoulder, "Don't worry about Lyalya. I think she's getting married soon." And then I worried I'd done the wrong thing. I might have upset him. Who knows?'

This story of Zina's greatly disturbed me. I was in a bad way and I needed the friendship of a good man. And where would

I find a better man than Tolya? I felt moved. I even asked for his address and tucked the slip of paper away.

After that visit I really felt I didn't like Zina any longer. First, she had grown ugly and coarse. Second (and really, no doubt, I should have put this first), she treated me very coldly. More than that, she went out of her way to show her complete lack of interest in me and my whole manner of life. It was the first time, for example, that she had seen me with short red hair, but for some reason she behaved as if this wasn't in the least surprising or interesting. I naturally found this hard to believe. How could she not want to know why I had suddenly cut my hair short? It was obvious that her apparent lack of interest in how I looked was simply a way of expressing contempt for me and my dissipated life – as if, from her exalted heights, she barely even noticed my foolish antics.

She did not even ask whether I was still having singing lessons, or what I was up to in general. To get my own back, I did my best to wound her: 'I just hope the war comes to an end soon. Otherwise you'll lose every last semblance of humanity. You've become a real old harridan.'

I then gave a mannered smile and added, 'I for my part still acknowledge art alone. Your deeds will all pass away, since no one needs them. Art, however, is eternal.'

Zina looked at me with a certain bewilderment and left soon afterwards. No doubt, she wanted nothing more to do with me.

That evening I wept for a long time. I was burying my past. I understood for the first time that all the paths I had taken, all the paths I had followed to reach my present position, had been entirely destroyed – blown up like railway track behind the last train of a retreating army.

'And what about Volodya?' I thought bitterly. 'Is that how a true friend behaves? He didn't ask any questions; he didn't find out anything for sure; he just took one look at Harry, turned round and left. If they all think I've gone mad, that I've lost my way, then why don't they come closer and help instead of just walking away? Why don't they support me and try to make me see reason? How can they be so cool and indifferent? How, at such a black and terrible time, can they abandon someone they were once close to?'

'Very virtuous they all are!' I carried on. 'And they certainly make sure their virtue gets noticed. But is it really so very praiseworthy? How many temptations are there going to be for a woman with a face like Zina's? And Volodya's always been cold and narrow-minded. His petty little soul's as straight and narrow as they come. When did *he* last feel intoxicated by music or poetry? How much more I love my dear Harry, my dear and dissolute Harry, with his tender little song:

> My heart hangs on a little white ribbon.
> White, white, white – remember the colour white!

They would say this is rubbish. *They* would rather have Nekrasov – and his plodding, four-square poems in praise of civic virtue.'

My green and hideous monsters now seemed nearer and dearer to me than ever.

They understood everything. *They* were my family.

But this new family of mine was now disappearing too. The cocaine addict was now fading away in a hospital. Yurochka had been packed off to the Front. The consumptive schoolboy had volunteered for the cavalry, because 'he had fallen in love with a golden horse' and could no longer bear being with people.

'I've ceased to understand people or have any feelings for them,' he kept saying.

From Harry's large retinue there remained only the hunchback.

He used to play 'Waves of the Danube'[6] on a beaten-up piano in a tiny cinema grandiloquently called 'The Giant of Paris' – and he was slowly starving to death.

This was a very difficult time for me. I was kept going only by my anger towards those who had wronged me and by my overwrought and carefully nurtured tenderness towards my one and only Harry.

At last, Harry returned.

He found me in a very anxious state. I greeted him so joyfully that he was positively embarrassed. He hadn't realized I could be like this.

His behaviour was enigmatic. He kept disappearing for days on end. It seemed he really was buying and selling something.

After bustling about for a couple of weeks, he decided that we must move to Moscow: 'Petersburg is a dead city. Moscow's seething with life. There are cafés springing up everywhere. You can sing there. You can read poems. One way or another you can earn a few roubles.'

Moscow also apparently offered more scope for his own new commercial activities.

We packed up and moved.

Life in Moscow really did turn out to be more animated, more exciting and more fun. There were a lot of people I knew from Petersburg. It was a familiar world and I found my place in it easily.

Harry kept on disappearing somewhere or other. He seemed preoccupied and I saw very little of him.

And he forbade me, incidentally, to sing his 'Little White Ribbon'. Forbade me. He didn't *ask* me not to sing it – he *forbade* me. And he seemed very angry: 'How can you not understand that that song has now become superfluous, superficial and utterly inappropriate?'

And he also happened to ask several times whether I knew the address of Volodya Katkov. I put this down to jealousy on his part.

'He's somewhere in the south, isn't he, with the Whites?'

'Of course.'

'And he's not meaning to come here?'

'I don't know.'

'And none of his family are here?'

'No.'

He was strangely inquisitive.

Just what Harry was doing with himself was hard to understand. It seemed he was once again selling or supplying something. The good thing was that every now and then he would bring back some ham, flour or butter. Those were hungry days.

Once, as I was going down Tverskaya Street, I caught sight

of a shabby figure that looked at me intently and then hurried across to the other side of the road. I felt I had seen this person before. I went on looking. It was Kolya Katkov! Volodya's younger brother, the comrade of my dog Tolya. Why hadn't Kolya said anything? He had clearly recognized me. Why had he been in such a hurry to slip away?

I told Harry about this encounter. For some reason my story made him very agitated. 'How can you not understand?' he said. 'He's a White officer. He doesn't want to be noticed.'

'But what's he doing here in Moscow? Why isn't he with the White Army?'

'They must have sent him here on some mission. How stupid of you not to have stopped him!'

'But you just said he doesn't want to be noticed!'

'Makes no difference. You could have asked him back. We could have sheltered him here.'

I was touched by Harry's generosity. 'Harry, wouldn't you have felt scared to be sheltering a White officer?'

He blushed a little. 'Not in the least,' he muttered. 'If you see him again, you really must bring him back with you. Yes, you really must!'

So Harry was capable of heroic deeds! More than that, he was even eager for a chance to prove his heroism!

It was a hot, sultry summer. A peasant woman who traded apples 'from under her coat' suggested I go and live in her dacha just outside Moscow. I moved in with her.

Now and again Harry made an appearance. On one occasion he brought some of his new friends along too.

They were the same young Wildean *poseurs* as before. Green faces; the eyes of cocaine addicts. Harry too had recently taken to snorting a fair amount.

Most of his conversations with these new friends of his were about business.

Soon afterwards someone I knew showed up. He was from Smolensk province, from near our family home, and he brought me a strange little letter from my aunt.

'I've been carrying this letter around for the last two months,' he said. 'I tried to find you in Petersburg, but I'd given up all hope. It seemed I was never going to find you. Then, quite by chance, I met an actress who told me your address.'

'Evidently my letters aren't reaching you,' my aunt wrote. 'But at least the money is in your hands now, and it's a comfort to me to know this. I like your husband very much. He seems very enterprising – a man with a future.'

What all this meant was quite beyond me. What husband? What money? And just what was it my aunt found so comforting?

Harry appeared.

'Harry,' I said, 'I've just received a letter from my aunt. She says she's glad the money is in my hands now.'

I stopped, because I was struck by the look on his face. He was blushing so intensely that it had brought tears to his eyes. Finally I grasped what had happened: Harry had gone to see my aunt and had introduced himself as my husband – and the silly old woman had given him my money!

'How much did she give you?' I asked calmly.

'Around thirty thousand. Nothing much. I didn't want us to squander it all on trifles, and so I put the money into this automobile business.'

'Mister Edvers,' I said, 'in the whole of this story there is only one thing I find truly surprising: the fact that you can still blush.'

He shrugged his shoulders.

'What I find surprising,' he said, 'is that you haven't once wondered what we've been living on all this time and how we found the money to move here from Petersburg.'

'So I've been paying my way, have I? Well, I'm glad to know that.'

He left. A few days later, however, he made another appearance – as if this conversation hadn't happened at all. He even brought his friends again – two of the friends who had come the time before. They had brought with them some vodka and something to eat with it. One of them began making advances to me. They addressed each other – jokingly, I imagine – as 'comrade'. Edvers too was a 'comrade'. They asked me to sing. My admirer – whom I prefer not to mention by name – really appealed to me. There was something weary and depraved about him, something that reminded me of people from our 'hideous-green' Petersburg world. Without giving it any particular thought, I sang our 'Little White Ribbon': '*My heart hangs on a . . .*'

'It's a sweet tune, but the words are idiotic!' said Harry. 'Wherever did you get hold of such antediluvian nonsense?'

And he quickly changed the subject, evidently afraid I would tell everyone he had written the words himself.

Three days later I was supposed to be singing in a café. Our manager got very embarrassed when he saw me and muttered something about it no longer being possible for me to sing that night. I was very surprised, but I didn't insist. I sat down in a corner. Somehow nobody seemed to notice me. The only person who did was Lucy Lyukor. In a poisonous tone of voice, the little poetess said, 'Ah, Lyalya! I hear you haven't been wasting time. They say you've dyed your little white ribbon red!'

Sensing my bewilderment, she explained, 'Only the other day you were singing for a group of Chekists.[7] I don't imagine you treated them to your Little White Ribbon!'

'What Chekists?'

She gave me a sharp look, then named the comrade who had been making advances to me.

I did not reply. I just got up and left.

I was terribly frightened by what had happened. Now Harry really had landed me in the dirt!

The incident with my aunt had not shocked me so very deeply. Nobody in our Bohemian world was particularly scrupulous about money. Though it was unpleasant, of course, that he had kept the whole business a secret from me. This, however, was another matter altogether. How could I stay with him now? He was crazed with cocaine and he was in cahoots with the Cheka. No, I couldn't let comrade Harry call the tune any longer. Had he not been trying to use me to lure White officers into a trap? It was not just out of the goodness of his heart, I now realized, that he had wanted me to invite Kolya Katkov to stay.

I was in despair. Where could I go? There was not a single close friend or relative I could turn to, no one I could count on to show me even just a little everyday kindness. My aunt? But I would have to obtain a travel permit, and besides, I didn't have a kopek to my name.

I went back home.

There was no sign of Harry. It was several days since I'd last seen him.

I did all I could. I went the rounds of different institutions. I wrote petitions and applications. I tried to get myself registered with the newly reconstituted Artists' Union. Then it would be easier for me to get a travel permit.

And then one day I was walking down the street and all of a sudden ... You could have knocked me down with a feather. Kolya. Kolya Katkov. There he was – right in front of my eyes.

'Kolya!' I shouted.

He appeared not to see me and quickly turned down a side-street. After a moment's thought, I followed him. He was waiting for me.

I now realized why I had been slow to recognize him the previous time. He had grown a beard.

'Kolya,' I said. 'What are you doing here? Why are you in Moscow?'

'I'm leaving today,' he replied. 'But you shouldn't have let it be seen that you know me. Isn't that obvious?'

'You're leaving today?' I exclaimed – and felt more despairing than ever. 'Kolya!' I said, 'for the love of God, save me! I'm lost.'

He evidently began to feel pity for me.

'There's nothing I can do now, Lyalechka. I'm a hunted beast. And anyway, I'm leaving today. There really is nothing I can do. I'll ask someone to call round.'

I remembered Harry and the people he now brought to my lair.

'No,' I said, 'you mustn't send anyone round.'

And then I had another thought, a thought that brought warmth to my heart.

'Kolya,' I said, 'is there any chance you'll be seeing Tolya?'

'It's certainly possible,' he answered.

'Tell him, for the love of God, that Lyalya is calling on her dog for help. Remember my words and repeat them exactly.

Promise me. And tell him to leave a note for me in the café on Tverskaya Street.'

'If all goes well,' he said, 'I'll be seeing him in about five days time.'

Kolya was in a great hurry. We parted. I was crying as I walked down the street.

Back home I thought everything over very carefully and decided not to say anything to Harry. Instead I would try and trick him into handing over some of the money – money that did, after all, belong to me!

My efforts to get hold of a permit met with success, and soon nearly everything was ready.

And then the day came . . .

I'm sitting in the dacha on my own, leafing through some papers in my desk, when I begin to feel that someone is looking at me. I turn around – a dog! Large, brownish-red and thin, with matted fur – a German Spitz or Chien-Loup. It's standing in the doorway and looking straight at me. 'What's going on?' I think. 'Where on earth's this dog come from?'

'Kapitolina Fedotovna!' I call out to my landlady. 'There's a dog in here!'

Kapitolina Fedotovna comes in, very surprised. 'But the doors are all shut,' she says. 'How did it get in?'

I wanted to stroke the dog – there was something so very expressive about the way it was looking at me – but it wouldn't allow me to. It wagged its tail and retreated into a corner. And just kept on looking at me.

'Maybe we should give it something to eat,' I say to Kapitolina. In reply, she mutters something about there not being enough food any longer even for human beings, but she brings some bread anyway. She throws a piece to the dog. The dog doesn't touch it.

'Better throw the dog out!' I say. 'It's acting strange. It might be sick.'

Kapitolina flung the door open. The dog went out.

Afterwards we recalled that it never once let us touch it. Nor did it once bark, nor did it ever eat. We saw it – and that was all.

Later that day Harry appeared.

He looked awful – well and truly exhausted. His eyes were bulging and bloodshot, his face taut and sallow.

He walked in, with barely a word to me.

My heart was beating frantically. I had to speak to him – for the last time.

Harry slammed the door. He was terribly edgy. Something had happened to him – or else he had overdone the cocaine.

'Harry,' I said finally. 'We need to talk.'

'Hang on a moment,' he said confusedly. 'What's the date today?'

'The twenty-seventh.'

'The twenty-seventh! The twenty-seventh!' he muttered despairingly.

What was so astonishing about this I really don't know, but his repeated exclamation made the date stick in my mind. And subsequently this turned out to be very important.

'What's that dog doing in here?' he shouted all of a sudden.

I turned round – there in the corner of the room was the dog. Taut, pointing, it was looking at Harry intently, as if it were nothing but eyes – as if its eyes were now its entire being.

'Get that dog out of here!' Harry screamed.

There was something excessive about his fear. He rushed to the door and flung it open. Slowly the dog began to move towards the door, not taking its eyes off Harry. It was slightly baring its teeth, its hackles raised.

Harry slammed the door after it.

'Harry,' I began again. 'I can see you're upset, but I just can't put this off any longer.'

He looked up at me, and then his whole face suddenly twisted in horror. I could see he was now looking not at me but past me. He seemed to be looking at the wall behind me. I turned round: there outside the window, with both paws on the low sill, was the reddish-brown dog. It dropped back down at once, perhaps startled by my movement. But I managed to glimpse its raised hackles, the muzzle it had thrust alertly forward, its bared teeth, the terrible eyes it kept fixed on Harry.

'Go away!' Harry shouted. 'Get rid of it! Drive it away!'

Trembling all over he rushed into the hallway and bolted the door.

'This is terrible, terrible!' he kept repeating.

I sensed that I too was shaking all over, and that my hands had gone cold. And I understood that we were in the middle of something truly awful, that I ought to do something to calm Harry, to calm myself, that I had chosen a very bad moment indeed, but for some reason I was quite unable to stop and I hurriedly, stubbornly, went on:

'I've taken a decision, Harry.'

His hands trembling, he struck a match and lit a cigarette.

'Oh have you?' he said with a nasty smirk. 'How very interesting.'

'I'm leaving. I'm going to my aunt's.'

'Why?'

'It's better not to ask.'

A spasm passed across his face.

'And if I don't let you?'

'What right do you have to stop me?'

I was speaking calmly, but my heart was racing and I could hardly breathe.

'I have no right at all,' he answered, his entire face trembling. 'But I need you here now, and I won't let you go.'

With these words he pulled out the drawer of my desk and immediately saw my new passport and papers.

'Ah! So it's like that, is it?'

He snatched the entire sheaf and began tearing the papers first lengthways and then crossways.

'For your dealings with the Whites I could easily . . .'

But I was no longer listening. I leaped on him like a madwoman. I was shrieking; I was clawing at him. I hit him on his hands and arms. I tried to tear the papers out of his hands.

'Chek-ist! Thief! I'll kill you! I'll kill you!'

He grabbed me by the throat. Really he was not so much strangling me as just shaking me; his bared teeth and staring eyes were wilder and more terrible than anything he actually did. And the loathing and hatred I felt for those wild eyes and that gaping mouth made me begin to lose consciousness.

'Somebody help me!' I gasped.

Then it happened – something truly weird. There was the sound of smashing glass, and something huge, heavy and shaggy jumped into the room and crashed down on Harry from one side, bringing him to the floor.

All I can remember is Harry's legs twitching. They were poking out from under the red, tousled mass that covered his body, which was almost completely still.

By the time I came to, it was all over. Harry's body had been removed; the dog had torn his throat out.

The dog had disappeared without a trace.

Apparently, some boys had seen a huge hound, leaping across fences as it ran past.

All this happened on the twenty-seventh. That is important; much later, when I was a free woman, in Odessa, I found out that Kolya Katkov had passed on to Tolya my appeal for help, and that Tolya had dropped everything and rushed to my rescue. That meant trying to slip through the Bolshevik front line. He was tracked down, caught and shot – all on the twenty-seventh. The twenty-seventh, that very day.

That's the whole story; that's what I wanted to tell you. I've made nothing up; I've added nothing; and there's nothing I can explain – or even want to explain. But when I turn back and consider the past, I can see everything clearly. I can see all the rings of events and the axis or thread upon which a certain force had strung them.

It had strung the rings on the thread and tied up the loose ends.

Baba Yaga

(1947 article)

In the words of the old magic tales: 'Baba Yaga has one bone leg. She rides around in a mortar and pushes herself along with a pestle, and she sweeps up her tracks with a broom.'

And in the words of teachers of literature: 'Baba Yaga is the goddess of whirlwinds and snowstorms.'

In the books we had when we were children, Baba Yaga was depicted as a thin, unkempt old woman, with evil green eyes, with grey tousled hair and a fang sticking out of her mouth. She was gaunt and bony. She was very, very scary – and she ate children.

The word 'goddess' conjured up images of beauty – of Venus or Diana. We'd seen statues of them, images of perfection. We'd heard people say, 'She looks like a goddess.' And then it turned out that our own goddess, our own Russian goddess, is this terrible witch – this hideous, vicious old woman. It seemed ridiculous and absurd.

But if we're going to be honest about it, can any of our ancient gods be called beautiful? Lel', perhaps, the god of spring? But he wasn't very popular and didn't survive in folk memory. Few people have even heard of him.

The figures who have survived are the house spirit, the forest spirit and Baba Yaga. All have turned negative.

The house spirit is a stern little monster. He used to look after hearth and home, but he behaved like some old-style landowner. He brawled. He made a racket. He tormented the horses, got up to all kinds of mischief in the stables, and he pinched the girls till they were black and blue all over. He had a sense of justice, but he was scary, wilful and autocratic: 'Maybe I'll take a liking to you, or maybe I won't. And if I don't, you'll soon wish you were dead.'

As for the forest spirit, you have to be feeling brave even to mention him. He made wild hooting noises, he led people into impassable thickets, he made them lose their way. He did not have a single good deed to his name. He had an evil temper. All he ever wanted was to scare people, to lead them astray, to bring them to a bad end and then plait a tangle of grasses and weeds over the scene of the crime.

Only the spirit of the pools and rivers was in any way beautiful. But if she allowed herself to be seen, it was so that her tender beauty would lure people to their doom. She made people feel pity for her – that was how she touched them so deeply. You would see her sitting there on a branch – a little woman, though she wasn't really a woman at all, since her lower half was the tail of a fish. And so there she would be, sitting just above the water, hiding this tail of hers in the weeds. A little woman, shy, tender and delicate – and always weeping bitterly. Had she merely sat there and beckoned, most people wouldn't have come any closer. But how could they help coming closer when they saw her weeping? They felt pity for her. Her lure was pity. A very dangerous goddess indeed.

But Baba Yaga is the most terrifying of them all, and the most interesting. And the most Russian. Other nations did not have goddesses like Baba Yaga.

Baba Yaga lived on the edge of the forest, in a windowless, doorless hut that stood on chicken's legs. Though, in fact, the hut always did have a door – facing the forest. So the brave young hero, having somehow learned the words of the spell, had only to say, 'Little hut, little hut, turn your face towards me and your back on the forest!' And the hut would turn round.

Baba Yaga lived alone. Alone except for a tomcat. Total solitude was too much even for Yaga. The cat gave off a sense of warmth and cosiness. It purred and it had soft fur. That was why Yaga liked to have a cat around.[1] As for people, she hated them and never sought them out. People came to her of their own accord to discover various wise secrets, and they always managed to cheat her. She knew only too well that every human approach brought with it deception and hurt.

'I can smell the smell of a Russian' meant that she could expect trouble.

Some 'brave young hero' would tell her a pack of lies, make some false promises, discover from her all that he needed to know, cheat her and somehow manage to slip away. She could expect neither gratitude nor honest payment.

And every time she heard the words of the spell, every time the hut turned round on its chicken's legs, Yaga knew there was going to be trouble. And every time, she still stupidly believed in the honesty of the human soul: 'It's just not possible. They can't all be like that.'

One day a poor little orphan girl turns up. Her stepmother has thrown her out; her stepmother has sent her off to a certain death. Baba Yaga knows very well that no human whelp, however little, however poor and pitiful, is without its share of guile. And as well as guile, this little pup of a girl will have brought with her a little comb, a little towel and a piece of fatback. The girl will feed the fatback to the cat – and the cat will betray his owner. That warm, soft, purring puss, that flatterer and caresser – he too will betray her. And the squeaking gates will betray her – the girl has only to smear them with oil. Wherever she looked, Yaga saw treachery and betrayal. It was a sad and tedious business.

There she sat, cross as cross can be, sharpening the fang that stuck out of her mouth.

'I should eat up every one of these boys and girls. But they're cunning, they don't give me a chance. They show up at the door, they pay homage to my great wisdom, they cheat and they lie – and then they take to their heels, every time.'

The treacherous cat and the dishonourable gates release the cunning little runt of a girl. Yaga rushes off in pursuit. The girl throws down her comb – and a dense forest appears. Yaga gnaws her way through the trees. The girl throws down her towel – and a broad, flowing river appears. Yaga begins to drink up the river – but the girl is soon far away, out of reach. And the vile little creature has run off with all Yaga's secrets.

So there she was again – back in her hut with its chicken's legs. Staring into the forest. B-o-r-e-d. Waiting for winter.

Spring always brings with it anxiety. Nature's busy having a good time. People and animals make love. They give birth to cunning little children. All this is bad news. Then comes summer. In the summer heat the forest seethes with life. And the forest does what it has to do; the wind scatters its seeds. The forest feels pleased with itself. Stupid old fool of a forest. It loves life, the immortality of the earth.

Then it's autumn. The first dusting of snow. Yaga cheers up. And then – at last – winter.

The winds begin to blow. The eight grandsons of the God Stribog.[2] Fierce and vicious – creatures after her own heart. Very soon blizzards would be covering up paths; whirlwinds would be whirling their crystal dust, snowstorms singing their songs. At last!

Baba gets into her mortar and pushes off with her pestle. The mortar knocks against hillocks; it bumps, leaps and jumps; it soars up and flies through the whirl of snow. She has strands of ice in her hair; you can see her bony, protruding knee. She is terrible and powerful; she is free as free can be. She flies over the earth like the song of the storm.

Who has ever seen her? As knights dying on a battlefield glimpse the Valkyries, so those who are freezing to death see Yaga through their closed eyes.

Yaga leaps out of her mortar. She sings and dances. She seizes a soft young birch. She twists, twirls, bends and snaps it. There's a loud moan, and powdered snow flies up into the air like silver smoke. Then Baba Yaga throws herself at a scarecrow. He's stuffed with straw and he's been wrapped round some rosebushes for the winter. She throws her arms around him and dances with him. Wild and drunken, she shakes him, then hurls him against the ground.

'Let me go,' begs the scarecrow. 'Don't torture me. I don't want you! I've got a rose for a heart.'

Baba Yaga howls and weeps. On she whirls, crazed and vicious. Roaming the fields and valleys again, looking for someone new to torment.

A traveller! He's just got out of his sleigh, he's looking for the road. Aha! She spins him round, knocks him into a snow-drift, flings snow into his eyes.

Where was he going? To some Masha or other. Some sweet, jolly, warm little Mashenka. What does he want with her now? He's all white now, whiter than white. His eyelashes and eye-brows are white. White, icy curls are poking out from under his cap. Wonderful, free and wonderful is the song of the blizzard. It enchants him. Mashenka? What does she matter to him now? No more than a colourful rag on a fence. Can he even remember her? Eyes of green crystal are looking into his soul. He feels both terrified and full of joy, and his soul sings and laughs. For never, never has it known such ecstasy.

Baba Yaga! Terrible old hag! Accursed man-eater! Oh, how wonderful you are with your song and your crystal eyes! You are a GODDESS. Take me into your death – it is better than life.

The blizzard falls silent. It's warm and dark in the little hut on chicken's legs. The broom stands in the corner, exchanging winks with the pestle. The faithless cat is purring sleepily, stretching his back, pretending . . .

Baba Yaga is lying on the stove. Water drips onto the floor from her icy hair. Her bony leg is sticking out from some rags.

Sad and tedious. Everything is so sad and tedious.

PART FIVE

PAVEL PETROVICH BAZHOV

(1879–1950)

The year 1936 saw the publication not only of Teffi's The Witch *but also (in Yekaterinburg, from 1924 to 1991 known as Sverdlovsk, in the Urals) of the first of Pavel Bazhov's cycle of tales about the Mistress of the Copper Mountain, a beautiful and alluring – yet often surprisingly honourable – figure who is seen as presiding over the region's metal ores and semi-precious stones. Though little known in the English-speaking world, these tales have always been hugely popular in Russia; between 1942 and 2004 at least two new editions were published each year, most of them intended for children.*

Bazhov's work is not easily categorized. 'The Mistress of the Copper Mountain' was originally intended for an anthology of Urals folk literature; it was apparently commissioned from Bazhov as an example of 'workers' folklore'. But publication of the anthology was delayed and the story was first published, in a prestigious Moscow literary journal, as a tale written by Bazhov and only later, when the Urals anthology finally appeared, as a tale recorded by Bazhov. It eventually became clear that these tales are original literary creations, though they do indeed incorporate elements drawn from oral folklore.

In 1937 or 1938 (the dates are unclear), at the height of the Purges, Bazhov only narrowly avoided arrest. He and his wife Valentina then withdrew from the world, staying out of sight in their own home. For several months, perhaps even a year, neither of them appeared on the street; their only link with the outside world was through Valentina's sister. During this period of self-confinement, Bazhov wrote his two greatest tales, 'The Stone Flower' and 'The Mountain Master'. Like the artist Boris

Sveshnikov, who produced his finest drawings while in a labour camp in the mid 1940s, and like Mikhail Bulgakov, who completed his third draft (the last complete draft) of The Master and Margarita in what could be called 'inner exile' in 1937, Bazhov seems to have achieved an extraordinary degree of creative freedom while in the eye of the storm, at the height of the Great Terror.[1]

There are many parallels between Bazhov himself and the tales' young hero, Danilushko. Both disappear, for some time, from the everyday social world – Bazhov into his own house and garden, Danilushko into the realm of the Mistress of the Copper Mountain. Just as Bazhov, during his period of self-confinement, reaches a level of creativity that he was never able to attain before or afterwards, so Danilushko spends time in a magical glade – the heart of the Mistress's realm – that the Mistress does not allow him ever to remember. And like a returning prisoner, Danilushko is ordered not to speak of where he has been. The parallel between Danilushko in his underground realm and a Gulag inmate working in a mine is remarkably close. Nevertheless, this parallel went unnoticed, or at least unremarked upon, and we cannot even be sure that Bazhov was aware of it himself; it seems to have been 'hidden in plain view' – as one can say both in English and in Russian.[2] The Malachite Casket was published as a book in 1939, and a second, expanded edition was awarded the Stalin Prize in 1943.

Bazhov's own life story was as dramatic as any of his tales; after confinement within the magic kingdom of his own home, he awoke to sudden fame. Mark Lipovetsky has suggested that his tales owe much of their popularity to their resonance with the fantasies and terrors of the time.[3] The Soviet Union was, after all, a world where vast numbers of people lived through experiences that the citizens of most countries encounter only in nightmares or fairy tales. There is nothing unusual – from a historical point of view – about mass murder, but only in Stalin's Russia were hundreds of thousands of people snatched up without warning, swept away to a distant realm of snow and ice and then returned to their homes after the passing of ten, twenty, even thirty years. Early Soviet propaganda claimed that, thanks to the Party, fairy tales had become reality; there may be more truth in this than is immediately apparent. If folk-tales have remained important in Russian culture, this may not be only because Russia remained a predominantly peasant country for so long. It may also be because the dramatic extremes of folktale, more than most supposedly realist literature, encapsulated people's real, lived experience.

As for the Mistress of the Copper Mountain herself, similar though she may be to the seductive mermaids or rusalki of Russian folklore (see Appendix, pp. 424–5), she is still more similar to a poet's Muse. Born in 1879, Bazhov was a young man during the heyday of Symbolism – the period commonly known as the Silver Age of Russian Literature. His tales are a late bloom from this period; like many of Teffi's stories, they draw much of their power from the tension between Symbolist aspiration and the reality of the era.

Bazhov's tales speak for themselves. His own life story, however, deserves to be told in more detail. Anna Gunin, the translator of the four tales included in this collection, has provided the following account.

Pavel Bazhov was born in 1879 into a line of Urals ironworkers. His father and grandfather were serfs, spending their working lives in the region's iron factories. Encouraged by a teacher at a local elementary school, the young Bazhov began memorizing entire volumes of Pushkin. A friend of the family, Nikolay Smorodintsev, persuaded Bazhov's parents to continue their son's education. A gymnasium school would have been beyond their means, but with Smorodintsev's help, Bazhov gained a place at the Yekaterinburg pre-seminary school, normally reserved for the sons of clergy. At fourteen, Bazhov enrolled at the Perm seminary, which he attended for six years. The seminary housed a clandestine library, with books on populist and Marxist politics, economics and science, and for three years Bazhov was in charge of this. At the seminary Bazhov learned Greek, Latin and Old Church Slavonic; he was introduced to poets and thinkers of antiquity, and he expanded his knowledge of Russian literature, discovering the short stories of Chekhov, in particular, who became his favourite author. He excelled in his studies, graduating third in his year, and he yearned to go to university. The seminary, however, would not support further secular study, and Bazhov decided to work as a teacher.

In 1905 Bazhov was arrested for subversive political activities and spent two weeks in prison. He later described himself as having been an 'anarcho-populist' revolutionary. Two years later he began teaching in a girls' school, and here, among his pupils, he met his future wife, Valentina. They married in 1911. Over a fifteen-year period, Bazhov spent his summers hiking and cycling through the Urals, an area that had long enjoyed a relatively independent existence and still had its own distinct culture. There he gathered folklore and observed the lives of local people, studying the various metal and stone workers at their trade and learning from them the details of their crafts.

Bazhov's literary activity began with the 1917 October Revolution, when he started editing army and civilian newspapers and writing sketches and short stories. Later, he wrote, 'It is likely that I would not have written any literary works if the Revolution had not taken place.' During the Civil War, Bazhov headed army political units, helped to set up partisan units in Siberia and Altai and oversaw initiatives to eradicate illiteracy. For seven years from 1923 he worked for The Peasants' Gazette (Krestyanskaya gazeta), travelling to villages and factories to gather material for reports on the lives of the workers.

Initially Bazhov had been linked to the Socialist Revolutionary Party, or SRs, but in 1918 he joined the Communist Party. During the Civil War he was taken prisoner by the Whites and escaped. In the 1930s, when former SRs were being persecuted, he wrote to the Party administration denying formal membership of the Socialist Revolutionaries. Nevertheless, he was twice expelled from the Communist Party, in 1933 and in 1937. Bazhov had worked as a censor, and both expulsions resulted from denunciations by an author whom he had censored. On the second occasion, a book he had edited was described as 'counter-revolutionary' and 'Trotskyist'; it was based on a collection of the memories of various revolutionaries, some of *whom had been declared 'enemies of the people' just as the book came off the press. The book was removed from circulation and Bazhov was fired from his job as editor of a publishing house. A year later, when the men responsible for his expulsion had themselves been declared 'enemies of the people', his case was reopened and his Party membership restored, although the book remained banned. After this, Bazhov stopped writing non-fiction.*

At the height of the Purges, Bazhov received a summons to the NKVD.[4] *He packed a small suitcase and arrived at the appointed time, but after waiting for several hours in the corridor he realized that, in the general confusion, they had forgotten about him. Bazhov quietly slipped home and spent a year in hiding, afraid to go out into the streets. With no income of his own, his family was supported by his sister-in-law's modest teacher's salary. Bazhov dug in the vegetable patch by day, composing stories, and he devoted his nights to writing them out. Thus emerged the stories that made up the first edition of* The Malachite Casket.

On his sixtieth birthday, in 1939, the first copy of The Malachite Casket *came off the press. And in 1943 Bazhov was awarded the Stalin Prize, in response to which he told a friend: 'Hailed today, jailed tomorrow.'*

The Mistress of the Copper Mountain

One day, two men from our town went to look at their grass. Their meadows, however, were a fair distance away. Somewhere beyond Severushka.

It was a holiday, and the heat was sweltering. Both men worked in the mountain, that is to say at Gumeshki. They mined malachite ore, and also lapis lazuli. And when they struck nuggets and nodules of copper and the like, then that too.

One was a young lad, not yet married, and there was a hint of green in his eyes already. The other was a little older. He was completely burnt out from work. His eyes were all green, and there was a dusting of green over his cheeks. And he was forever coughing.

It was good to be in the forest. The birds were singing gaily, there was a haze rising from the earth and the air was gently scented. The lads felt warm and drowsy. They reached the Krasnogorsk mine. In those days they mined iron ore there. Well, our lads lay down on the grass under a mountain ash and went straight to sleep. But the young lad suddenly awoke – as if someone had jabbed him in the side. He looked: in front of him, sitting on a heap of ore near a large stone, was a woman. She had her back to the lad, but he could see from her plait that she was a maiden. The plait was blue-black and, rather than hanging loose as our lasses' plaits do, it seemed stuck to her back. It was tied with ribbons that shimmered now red, now green. Light shone through them and they were tinkling very softly like copper leaf. The lad marvelled at the plait, and carried on looking at her. The girl had a pleasing figure and was not too tall, and she was such a bundle of energy that she could not keep still for a moment. She would lean forward as though searching for something underfoot, then spring back again; she would bend to one side, then the other. She would jump to her feet and wave her arms about, then lean forward again. In a word, the girl was quicksilver. He could hear her babbling something, but in what language and to whom he couldn't make out. Only she said everything with a laugh. She seemed full of mirth.

The lad had been about to say something to her, when all of a sudden it hit him:

'Oh my, it must be the Mistress herself! Just look at her clothes. How could I not have noticed? It was her plait had me spellbound.'

Her clothes were indeed of a kind you could never find in all the world. Her dress was of silken malachite. There really is such a thing. Stone, but like silk to the eye. And it even feels like silk.

'What terrible luck!' thought the lad. 'How can I get away before she notices me?' You see, he'd heard about this Mistress – this malachite girl – from the old men. They'd said that she loves to play tricks on people.

He had barely thought this when she turned around. She looked cheerfully at the lad, grinned and said teasingly, 'Stepan Petrovich, what are you doing staring at a maiden's beauty for free? People pay money for looking, you know. Come closer. Let's have a little chat.'

The lad was terrified, of course, but he didn't show it. He steeled himself. She might be a mysterious power, but all the same she was a girl. Well, and he was a lad – and that meant he was ashamed to appear scared in front of her.

'I don't have time for chatting,' he said. 'We've overslept as it is, and we're on our way to check the grass.'

She laughed, then said, 'That's enough of your play-acting. Come here, I have a proposition for you.'

Well, the lad saw there was no way out. He began to walk towards her, and she gestured with her hand, as if to tell him to walk round the other side of the ore heap. He walked round and there he saw vast numbers of lizards. And they were all

different. Some were green, some were sky-blue merging into
indigo, and there were others that looked like clay or sand
speckled with gold. Some glistened like glass or mica; others
were like faded grass, but they too were adorned with patterns.

The girl laughed.

'Don't tread on them,' she said, 'Stepan Petrovich, my soldier. See how big and heavy you are, compared to my little
ones.' And she clapped her hands together, and the lizards scattered, freeing a path.

The lad walked closer, then stopped. Then she clapped her
hands once more and said, laughing away, 'Now there's nowhere
for you to step. If you flatten one of my servants, you'll find
yourself in trouble.'

He looked down – now he couldn't see the ground at all.
The lizards had all flocked to one spot, and the ground had
become like a patterned floor. Stepan looked: Good grief – so it
was copper ore! Every kind, and all burnished. There was mica,
and blende, and all sorts of glittering stones, with some that
looked like malachite.

'Well, have you recognized me yet, Stepanushka?' the malachite girl asked, and she let out a peal of laughter.

Then, after a pause, she said, 'Don't be frightened. I won't
do anything bad to you.'

This riled the lad. The girl was mocking him. He grew
mighty angry, and he even shouted, 'I work in the mountain –
who do you think *I'm* going to be afraid of?'

'Good,' answered the malachite girl. 'That's just what I need,
a man who's not afraid of anyone. As you go down into the
mountain tomorrow, you'll see your factory steward. Now
here's what you must say to him – and mind you don't forget
the words: "The Mistress of the Copper Mountain has ordered
you, you rank old goat, to clear out of the Krasnogorsk mine.
If you go on breaking up this iron cap of hers, she will drive all
the copper in Gumeshki so deep that you won't be able to reach
it at all."'

She narrowed her eyes and went on, 'Have you understood,
Stepanushka? You say you work in the mountain, that you're
not afraid of anyone? Then do as I bid and say those words to

the steward. And now be on your way – and mind you don't say anything to the man you came with. He's burnt out from work, no need to get him mixed up in this. I've already told the lapis lazuli to help him a little.'

Again she clapped her hands, and the lizards all scattered. Then she leapt to her feet, gripped a stone with both hands, hopped up onto it and, just like a lizard, scurried across it. Her hands and feet were now green paws, a lizard's tail was poking out, there was a black stripe going halfway up her spine, while her head was still human. She ran to the summit, turned back and said, 'Don't forget what I told you, Stepanushka: "She orders you, you rank old goat, to clear out of Krasnogorsk." Do what I ask, Stepanushka, and I'll marry you!'

This made the lad furious. He spat on the ground.

'Ugh, what an abomination! Marry a lizard!'

Seeing this, she burst into laughter.

'All right,' she shouted, 'we can talk about it later. Maybe you'll change your mind!'

And she vanished behind the hill, with just a flash of her green tail.

The lad was left all alone. Down at the mine everything was quiet. The only sound was his companion snoring gently behind the heap of ore. He went and woke him. They made their way to the meadows and inspected the grass, then towards evening they turned back for home. Stepan, though, could think about only one thing: what was he to do? To speak like that to the steward would be a grave matter indeed, and, as it happened, the steward really was rank – they said there was something rotting in his insides. The thought of not saying anything was no less frightening. She was, after all, the Mistress. She could change any ore you like into mere blende. How would he ever get his work done then? And worse still, he was ashamed of looking a vain braggart in front of the girl.

He thought and thought, then plucked up his courage: 'Come what may, I'll do as she bids.'

The next morning, as the men were gathering at the hoist, the factory steward approached. Everyone took off their caps, of course. Then they fell silent, but Stepan walked up to him

and said, 'Yesterday I saw the Mistress of the Copper Mountain, and she bade me say this to you. She orders you, you rank
old goat, to clear out of Krasnogorsk. If you ruin this iron cap
of hers, then she'll drive all the copper in Gumeshki so deep
that nobody will be able to reach it.'

The steward's moustache began to quiver.

'What's this? Are you drunk, or have you gone plain crazy?
What mistress? And who do you think you're speaking to? I'll
have you left in the mountain to rot!'

'Your will is your will,' said Stepan, 'but that is what she
bade me say.'

'Flog him,' yelled the steward, 'then take him into the mountain and chain him up at the workface! So he doesn't peg out,
feed him some dog oats, and show him no mercy if he doesn't
meet his task. And if he puts a foot wrong, whip him without
pity!'

Well, of course, they flogged the lad and took him into the
mountain. The mining overseer, who was also an absolute
scoundrel, took him to the very worst stope of all. It was wet
there, and there was no decent ore – the place should have been
abandoned long ago. They shackled Stepan to the workface,
using a long chain so as not to stop him from working. Well,
this was in the days of serfdom, you know. There were all manner of abuses against folks. And the overseer said, 'You can cool
off here a bit. Your quota will be such-and-such an amount of
pure malachite' – and he named some unimaginable quantity.

There was nothing for it. As soon as the overseer left, Stepan
began swinging his pick, he was a spirited lad, after all. He
looked about – and things suddenly didn't seem so bad. The
malachite was just falling off the rock; it was as though someone was tossing it down to him. And the rock face was now
quite dry; the water had all disappeared.

'Now this is good,' he thought. 'Seems the Mistress hasn't
forgotten about me.'

Barely had he thought this when something flashed. He
looked up – and there was the Mistress, right in front of him.

'Well done, Stepan Petrovich!' she said. 'You have shown
yourself to be honourable. You weren't afraid of the rank old

goat. You spoke out, good and proper. Now come and look at my dowry. I don't go back on my word either.'

And she knitted her brows a little as though something were troubling her. She clapped her hands, and the lizards came running. They released Stepan from his chain, and the Mistress instructed them: 'Now, I want double the quota. And make it the very finest malachite, silken grade.' Then she said to Stepan, 'Well, my betrothed, let's go and look at my dowry.'

So off they went. She walked on ahead, and Stepan followed. Wherever she went, the way ahead opened to her. There was one large room after another, and in each one the walls were different. One was entirely green, the next was yellow with gold flecks. In another the walls were covered with copper flowers. Other rooms were deep blue from lapis lazuli. In short, words cannot describe how beautifully the chambers were decorated. And the dress the Mistress wore kept changing. One moment it glinted like glass, the next it suddenly paled, then it began to sparkle with diamond dust, or turn from red to copper, then shimmer silken green again. They walked on and on. Then she stopped.

'From here on,' she said, 'there is mile upon mile of speckled yellow and grey stone. Not worth seeing. And here we are right below Krasnogorsk itself. It's my most treasured place after Gumeshki.'

Stepan saw a vast room, with a bed, tables, little stools – all made from copper nuggets. The walls were of malachite and diamond, and the ceiling was dark crimson tinged with black, with copper flowers on it.

'Let's sit here and talk,' she said. They sat down on the stools, and the malachite girl said: 'Have you seen my dowry?'

'I have,' said Stepan.

'So, what do you think *now* about marrying me?'

Well, Stepan didn't know what to reply. He had a betrothed. A good lass, an orphan. Needless to say, though, she was nowhere near as beautiful as the malachite girl! She was just a simple ordinary person. Stepan hemmed and hawed, then said: 'You've a dowry fit for a tsar, but I'm just a simple worker.'

'My dear friend,' she said, 'please don't beat about the bush.

Tell me straight, will you take me in marriage or not?' And this time she knitted her brows a little more.

'Well,' Stepan answered bluntly, 'I cannot, because I'm promised to another.'

He said this and thought, Now she'll really flare up. But she seemed quite delighted.

'Well done,' she said, 'Stepanushka, I praised you for your speech to the steward, but for this you get double the praise. You didn't covet my riches, you didn't give your Nastasya away in exchange for a girl of stone.' The lad's betrothed was, indeed, called Nastasya. 'Here's a present for your betrothed,' she went on – and she gave him a large malachite casket. Inside it was every sort of feminine finery. Rings, earrings, bracelets and the like, items that not even the wealthiest of brides would have possessed.

'But how can I climb up out of here carrying this great chest?' the lad asked.

'Don't you fret about that. It will all be taken care of. I'll rescue you from the steward, and you and your young wife will need for nothing, but listen now – you must heed what I say: do not, ever again, remember me. This is the third test I'm setting you. And now you must have something to eat.'

She clapped her hands again, and the lizards came running – they set the table full of dishes. She fed him with good cabbage soup, fish pie, mutton, buckwheat and the like, everything that graces the Russian table. Then she said, 'Well, farewell, Stepan Petrovich. Be sure not to remember me.' And she was in tears. She put out her hand, and the tears drip-dripped, and on her palm they hardened into grains. There was a good handful of them. 'Here – may these bring you profit. People pay huge sums for these stones. You will be rich.' And she gave them to him.

The stones were cold, but her hand was hot, just like a living hand, and it was trembling a little. Stepan took the stones, bowed low and asked, 'Where am I to go?' He too was cheerless. She pointed the way with one finger and a tunnel opened before him. Inside the tunnel it was as light as day. Stepan walked through the tunnel, and once again he saw all manner of earthly treasures. He emerged right at the stope. He stepped out, the tunnel closed up, and everything was as it had been before. A lizard ran up and fitted the chain to his foot, and the casket with the gifts suddenly became small; Stepan hid it in his bosom. Soon the overseer appeared. He had come to have a laugh, but he saw Stepan with a huge heap of malachite, far more than his quota – and all of it the very finest grade. 'What's all this?' he thought. 'Where's it all come from?' He clambered into the stope where Stepan had been working, inspected it all and said: 'In a stope like this, anybody could hew all the malachite he liked.' He led Stepan to another stope, and he put his nephew where Stepan had been.

Stepan went back to work again the next day. Once again, the malachite was tumbling down, and he also began coming across nodules and nuggets of copper, while the other lad – the nephew – well what do you know, he didn't find anything at all, it was all just dead rock and blende. At this point the overseer realized what was up. He ran to the steward and said, 'No doubt about it. Stepan has sold his soul to an evil spirit.'

The steward replied, 'Who he sells his soul to is his affair, but we need to make our profit. Promise him that we'll grant him his freedom if he finds a two-ton malachite boulder.'

The steward told them to unchain Stepan. And he ordered them to stop all work at Krasnogorsk.

'Who knows?' he said. 'Perhaps the fool was talking sense. In any case, the iron ore we're striking now is all mixed up with copper – it mucks up the pig iron.'

The overseer explained to Stepan what was required of him, and the lad answered, 'Who would say no to freedom? I'll do my best, but whether I find it – that depends on what my luck will bring me.'

Soon Stepan did indeed find them the boulder they wanted. It was hauled up to the surface. They congratulated themselves for being so clever, but they did not give Stepan his freedom. They wrote about the boulder to the squire, and he arrived from that San Petersburgh itself. After hearing the whole story, he called Stepan over.

'Tell you what,' he said, 'I give you my word as a nobleman

to set you free if you can find me a malachite mass that can . . . well, be hewn into pillars no less than thirty feet high.'

Stepan answered, 'I've already been duped once. Now I've learnt my lesson. First write me a manumission paper, then I'll do my best and we'll see what happens.'

The squire, of course, started shouting and stamping his feet, but Stepan would not budge: 'Oh I nearly forgot – write my betrothed a paper too. Else what kind of a muddle would that be – me free, but my wife still in bondage.'

The squire saw that the lad was not going to yield. He wrote him a certificate.

'Here,' he said. 'But be sure to do your very best!'

Stepan just said the same as before: 'Now that depends on what my luck will bring me.'

Stepan found the malachite, of course. No wonder, seeing as he knew all the insides of the mountain like the back of his hand and the Mistress herself was helping him. They hewed this malachite into tall pillars, hauled the pillars up to the surface, and the squire sent them to the top church in San Petersburgh itself.[1] And the first boulder which Stepan found sits in our city to this day, so they say. They preserve it as a marvel.

Stepan was now a free man, but the riches in Gumeshki quite disappeared. They struck plenty of lapis lazuli, and even more blende. But nobody found so much as a trace of nuggets or nodules of copper, the malachite came to an end and water began to take over the mine. Well, from that time onwards Gumeshki fell into decline, and then it was entirely flooded. They said it was the Mistress, furious about the pillars, that they'd been put in a church. She didn't like that at all.

Stepan did not have a happy life either. He married, started a family and built a house, all good and proper. He might have lived there in comfort and been happy, but he became downhearted and his health started failing. He was pining away by the minute.

The ailing man took it into his head to get a fowling piece and take up hunting. It was always the Krasnogorsk mine he went to, and he always came home empty-handed. One autumn day he left and didn't return. His family waited and waited for him . . . Where had he vanished to? They got together a search party, of course. And there at the mine they found him, lying dead near a tall stone, with a sort of smile on his face, and his little rifle close by on the ground, still loaded. The people who first found him described how, not far away from him, they'd seen a huge green lizard the likes of which just aren't found in our parts. It was sitting as if keeping watch over the dead man; it had raised its head and tears were dripping down. As the people ran closer, it leapt up onto a stone, then disappeared. And when they got the dead man home and started to wash him, they saw one hand was closed into a fist, and inside the fist they could just make out some little green grains. A whole handful of them. There happened to be someone knowledgeable there. He peered at these grains from an angle and said, 'But it's copper emerald! That's a rare stone, and precious. What a fortune you've been left, Nastasya. Only where did he get such stones from?'

Nastasya, his wife, said that the dead man had never mentioned any such stones. He had given her a casket when they were still engaged. A large casket made of malachite. There had been plenty of fine things in it, but no stones like that. No, she had never seen any like that.

They tried to release those stones from Stepan's dead hand, but the stones crumbled to dust. No one had any idea where Stepan had got them from. Later they did some digging at Krasnogorsk. Well, there was nothing but ore, just plain brown ore, with a coppery shine. Only later did someone realize that Stepan's stones had been the tears of the Mistress of the Copper Mountain. He had not sold them to anybody; he had kept them and hidden them from his family; he had had them with him when he met his death. Well, what do you make of that?

So that is what she's like, the Mistress of the Copper Mountain!

A bad man who meets her will have nothing but woe, and there will be little joy for a good man.

The Stone Flower

Mramorskoye was not the only place renowned for its stoneworkers. They say that our towns too had their share of craftsmen. The only difference being that our men worked mostly with malachite, as it was plentiful enough, and scarce a higher grade to be found. Now, out of this malachite they produced some beautiful pieces. Such rare trinkets that you'd be struck with wonder: how ever did they manage that?

There was at that time a master craftsman called Prokopich. The best in the trade; no one could surpass him. But he was getting on in years.

And so the squire went and ordered his steward to send some young lads to train with this Prokopich: 'Let him hand them down his art, to the finest detail.'

Only Prokopich – perhaps loath to share his skills, perhaps for some other reason – taught poorly indeed. He was nothing but roughness and wallops. He would plaster a lad's head with bumps, he'd fair rip off his ears, and then he'd say to the steward, 'This one's no good . . . His eye is poor, he has a clumsy hand. He's not got it in him.'

The steward evidently had orders to keep Prokopich happy.

'If he's no good, then he's no good . . . We'll give you another.'
And he'd send him a new boy.

The kids got to hear about Prokopich's teaching methods. Early in the morning they'd start wailing away, desperate to avoid being sent to him. Nor did the fathers and mothers much like handing over their beloved children to such vain torment, and they began to cover for them as best they could. And besides, this malachite craft was an unhealthy business. The malachite was sheer poison. It was no surprise that people tried to shield their kids.

The steward, nevertheless, minded the squire's instructions and kept on sending apprentices to Prokopich. And Prokopich would torture the lads in his usual way, then send them back to the steward: 'This one's no good . . .'

The steward started to get mad at him: 'How much longer is this going to go on? This one's no good, that one's no good, when will you find one who *is* any good? Take the lad on!'

Prokopich stuck to his guns: 'What's it to me? Were I to teach the kid for ten years, nothing would come of it.'

'Look, which lad do you want?'

'I wouldn't complain if you sent me none at all, I wouldn't miss them.'

And so Prokopich and the steward got through one kid after another, all with the same result: their heads were covered in bumps, and all they thought about was escape. Some even spoiled their work on purpose so that Prokopich would send them away.

And then it was the turn of Danilko the Scrawny. An outright orphan was this little lad. Twelve years old he would have been, perhaps more. He stood tall and thin as can be; it was a wonder he kept body and soul together. Well, he had a pleasant face. His hair was lovely and curly, his eyes sparkled blue. First they had taken him in as a servant in the squire's house, for fetching the tobacco box or a handkerchief, running errands and the like. Only the little orphan had no talent for such work. Other kids would do everything at the double. At the snap of a finger they would stand to attention and ask: 'What is your bidding?' But this Danilko was always hiding away in a corner; standing stock still, he'd be staring wide-eyed at some picture or ornament. They'd shout for him, but he wouldn't move an inch. To start with, of course, they used to give him a beating, but then they gave up on him: 'What a holy fool! A real slowpoke! You'll never make a decent servant out of *that* lad.'

They didn't bother sending him to the factory or to the mines in the mountain: he was frail and skinny, he wouldn't have lasted a week. The steward put him to work as a herdboy, but

Danilko wasn't cut out for that. The lad tried mighty hard, but he always made a mess of things. He seemed to be constantly thinking about something or other. He'd fix his gaze on a blade of grass – and the cows would all wander off! The old herdsman he'd been put with was a gentle soul. He pitied the orphan, yet at times even *he* scolded him: 'Whatever will come of you, Danilko? You will ruin yourself, and you'll bring my old back under the whip too. Now, where's the good in that? Tell me what it is you're brooding over, at least.'

'I don't really know myself, Grandad . . . Nothing special . . . I got a bit lost in looking. There was a wee insect crawling across a leaf. It was bluish-grey, and peeping out from under its wings was a bit of yellow. The leaf was a nice broad one . . . Its edges were jagged, like curved little frills. The outside was darker, but in the middle it was green as can be, as if freshly painted . . . And this wee bug was crawling along.'

'Sometimes I wonder if you're a fool, Danilko. Is it your business to examine insects? If it crawls, let it crawl – your job is to watch the cows. Look, now, get this folly out of your head, else I'll have to tell the steward!'

There was just one thing that came naturally to Danilushko. He had learnt to play the cow horn – a thousand times better than the old man! Sounded just like proper music. In the evenings, as they herded the cows, the girls and women would beg, 'Play us a tune, Danilushko.'

And he would start playing away. His tunes were unfamiliar. Almost like the rustling of the trees, or the babbling of the river, or all manner of birds calling to one another – in any case, they sounded good. On account of these songs the women began to be mighty well-inclined to Danilushko. One would darn his kaftan, another would cut him some canvas for foot cloths, or sew him a new shirt. As for feeding him, this went without saying – each would give him as much as they could of whatever was sweetest and tastiest. The old herdsman also took a liking to Danilushko's tunes. Only this is where things began to go a little wrong. Danilushko would start playing and he'd forget everything – it was as if the cows weren't there at all. And this playing brought him misfortune.

Danilushko must have been engrossed in his playing, and the old man must have nodded off. A number of the cows strayed from the herd. When Danilushko and the old man began to round up the herd, they realized that some cows were missing. They dashed off in search, but it was no use. The cows had been grazing near Yelnichnaya ... The most wolf-ridden and desolate backwoods around ... They only found one of the missing cows. They drove the herd home and explained what had happened. Everyone set out from the town on foot and on horseback to search, but they could not find a single cow.

Well, everyone knows what punishment you could expect in those days. Whatever the misdeed, you bared your back. To make matters worse, one of the cows belonged to the steward himself. There would be no clemency. First the old man got a flogging, then came Danilushko's turn, but the lad was mere skin and bone. The squire's flogger even let slip, 'Just look at him, one flick of the whip and he'll flake out – if he doesn't give up the ghost altogether.'

Nevertheless, he struck him without pity, and Danilushko kept silent. The flogger struck him a second time, and a third time – the boy stayed silent. At this point the flogger flew into a rage and began thrashing him with all his might, shouting, 'I'll make you scream all right! I'll make you yelp!'

Danilushko was trembling all over, tears were running down his cheeks, but he stayed silent. He bit his lip and steeled himself. And so he fainted, and he hadn't let out so much as a whisper. The steward, who was there, of course, was astonished: 'What a stoical lad we have here! Now I know what to do with him, if he comes through alive.'

Danilushko convalesced in bed. Granny Vikhorikha set him on the path to recovery. Vikhorikha took the place of a doctor in our towns, and she was renowned far and wide. She knew the power in herbs: which were for toothache, which for strains, which for aches ... She gathered the herbs herself, at the time when each was at its most potent. From these herbs and roots she would prepare tinctures, boil up tisanes and add them to ointments.

Danilushko lived well at Granny Vikhorikha's. The old woman

was gentle with him, and she liked to talk, and the entire hut was filled with herbs and roots and all kinds of flowers that had been hung up to dry. Danilushko was curious about these herbs: What was this one called? Where did it grow? What kind of flower did it have? The old woman would tell him all about it.

One time Danilushko asked, 'Granny, do you know all the flowers in these parts?'

'I wouldn't like to boast,' she replied, 'but I think I know all the revealed ones.'

'What?' asked Danilushko. 'Are there ones that aren't revealed?'

'Aye, there are,' she replied. 'Have you heard of the fern flower, said to appear on Ivan Kupala Day?[1] That flower is magic; it will find you buried treasure. But it's harmful to man. And then there's the touch-me-not's flower that's like a running flame. Catch it and any lock will open for you. It's a thieves' flower. And then there's the stone flower that's said to grow in the malachite mountain. It's at full strength on the Day of the Snake.[2] Unlucky is he who sets eyes on the stone flower.'

'Why is he unlucky, Granny?'

'That I do not know, son. It's what I was told.'

Danilushko might have stayed longer at Vikhorikha's, but the steward's informants saw that the lad was beginning to walk a little and they went straight to the steward. The steward summoned Danilushko and said to him, 'Now you'll go to Prokopich to be trained in the malachite craft. It's just the work for you.'

Well, what could he do? Danilushko went along, even though he was still swaying in the wind.

Prokopich took one look at him and said, 'This really is going too far. Even strong, hearty lads find my training too much for them. How am I ever going to be able to take this one to task? He's barely breathing.'

Prokopich went to see the steward: 'What do I want with a frail lad like this? If I give him one blow too many, he'll kick the bucket – then I'll really have to answer for it!'

But it was no use. The steward wouldn't listen: 'Your job is to teach, not to argue! He's a sturdy little lad. Never mind that he looks scrawny.'

'Well, it's up to you,' said Prokopich, 'if that's what you've decided. I'll teach him, if I won't have to answer for it.'

'There's no one to answer to,' said the steward. 'He's all alone, this little lad, you can do as you please with him.'

Prokopich went home and found Danilushko standing by the workbench, inspecting a small slab of malachite. There was a notch on it, indicating where the edge was to be chiselled. Now Danilushko was staring at this spot and shaking his head. Prokopich wondered what this new lad was looking at so intently. He asked sternly, in his usual manner, 'What do you think you're doing? Who asked you to touch that piece? What is it you're staring at?'

Danilushko answered, 'To my eye, Grandad, the edge oughtn't to be chiselled from this side. See, there's a pattern here, it'll get cut off.'

Prokopich, of course, began shouting at him: 'What's this? Who do you think you are? A master craftsman? Never made a thing in your life, and here you are, offering your opinion already! What do *you* think you know about all this?'

'All I know is that this piece has been ruined,' Danilushko replied.

'And you're saying it'll be me who's ruined it, eh? You, a mere kid, telling me, one of the finest masters! I'll show you damage, all right . . . Yes, you're in for it now!'

He shouted a lot and kicked up a din, but he didn't lay a finger on Danilushko. You see, Prokopich himself had been thinking a lot about this slab, trying to decide from which edge to start chiselling. Danilushko's words had hit the mark. After a while Prokopich stopped his shouting and began to speak a little more gently: 'Well, then, would the new master care to show us how he would do it himself?'

Danilushko began demonstrating and explaining: 'Here's the pattern you could have. Or even better, you could cut the slab a bit narrower, chisel the edge off your new margin, and just leave a little twist along the top.'

Prokopich raised his voice again: 'Well, I never! You sure

have amassed a lot of knowledge! Mind you don't fritter it all away!' But to himself he was thinking: 'The lad speaks truth. Something could likely be made of him. Only how am I going to teach him? Just one knock will send him to the grave.'

After thinking a little, he asked, 'Whose boy are you, then, my clever one?'

Danilushko told his story: 'Well, I'm an orphan. I don't remember my mother, and as for my father I don't know anything about him. I don't even know his name, so people just call me Danilko the Scrawny.' He went on to say he had worked as a servant and why he'd been booted out, how later in the summer he had herded the cows and why it was he'd been flogged.

Prokopich felt sorry for him: 'You've not had a sweet life, I see, lad, and now you've ended up with me. Our trade's a harsh one.'

Then, as if something had made him angry, he started to grumble: 'Now, that's enough! See how talkative you are! Any fool can work his tongue – it's what he does with his hands that counts. We've talked the entire evening away! And you're meant to be my student! Wait till tomorrow – then I'll see what you're fit for. Sit down to supper – after that it'll be time for bed.'

Prokopich lived alone. His wife had died long ago. Old Mitrofanovna who lived nearby used to come round and help out. In the mornings she boiled and baked, and tidied the hut, while in the evenings Prokopich looked after things himself.

After they had eaten, Prokopich said, 'You can sleep here on this bench.'

Danilushko took his shoes off, put his knapsack under his head and covered himself with his kaftan. He curled up a little against the autumn cold, then quickly fell asleep. Prokopich also lay down, but he was unable to sleep: he couldn't get the conversation about the malachite pattern out of his head. He tossed and turned. He got up, lit a candle, went over to the workbench – and began to measure the malachite slab this way and that. He covered up one edge, then the other. He increased the margin, then reduced it. He held it this way, turned it the other way, but no matter what he did, it was clear that the lad had understood the pattern better.

'Well Danilko the Scrawny, who'd have thought it!' Prokopich marvelled. 'Barely arrived, and he's already teaching an old master. What an eye he has! What an eye!'

He went quietly to the storeroom and brought out a pillow and a large sheepskin coat. He slipped the pillow under Danilushko's head and covered him with the sheepskin coat.

'Sleep well, my sharp-eyed one!'

Danilko did not wake; he just turned over onto his other side. Now that he was warming up, he stretched out under the sheepskin coat and started to whistle lightly through his nose. Prokopich had no children of his own, and this Danilushko had already touched his heart. The master stood and marvelled at him, while Danilushko went on whistling, still peacefully asleep. Prokopich kept wondering what he should do: how could he get this gaunt, sickly little fellow back on his feet?

'How can he study our craft with health like that? The dust is sheer poison, he'll just wither away. First he needs a good rest and to get his health back – then I'll start teaching him. It looks like he's got real talent.'

The next day he said to Danilushko, 'At first you'll just be helping out around the house. That's my routine with someone new. Understand? To start with, you can go and fetch some guelder berries. They'll be all coated in hoarfrost – just right for pies. Only don't wander off too far. However much you collect, that will be fine. Take some bread with you – the forest will give you an appetite – oh, and you must drop in on Mitrofanovna. I told her to bake you a couple of eggs and give you a container of milk. Understand?'

The next day he said, 'Go and catch me a nice loud goldfinch and a lively little linnet. You must bring them back by this evening. Understand?'

When Danilushko had caught them and brought them back, Prokopich said: 'They'll do all right, but you can find better. Go and catch some more.'

And so it went on. Every day Prokopich would set Danilushko work to do, but really it was all just fun and games. When the snow fell and a neighbour was going out to fetch firewood, Prokopich sent Danilushko to lend him a hand. Well, what help could Danilushko be? On the way into the forest he sat in the front of the sledge and held the reins, and on the way back he followed the cart on foot. He would go for a walk, then have a good supper and sleep like a log. Prokopich gave him a fur coat, a warm cap and mittens, and he ordered some new felt boots for him. Prokopich, you see, lived quite comfortably. He was a serf, but he paid a quit-rent and he earned a little. He grew mighty fond of Danilushko. To tell it straight, he treated him like a son. Well, and there was nothing he begrudged him, and he was determined not to let him start working before he was ready.

Living in this style, Danilushko soon started to recover his strength, and he too grew fond of Prokopich. Well, of course he did! He was grateful to Prokopich for his concern, and it was his first taste of a life like this. The winter passed. Danilushko lived free as a bird. One moment he would wander down to the pond, the next he'd be in the forest. Only Danilushko was also taking in the craft. He would come home and they'd start talking straight away. He would tell Prokopich about one thing and another, and then he'd ask, 'What's this for?' or, 'How did you do that?' Prokopich would first explain and then demonstrate. And Danilushko would take it all in. Sometimes he'd have a go himself. 'Here, let me try . . .' Prokopich would watch. Where necessary, he'd correct him and show him how to do it better.

One day, however, the steward saw Danilushko down at the pond. He went and asked his informants, 'Whose lad is he? The number of times I've seen him down by the pond! Playing about with a fishing rod on workdays – and he's hardly a kid any more . . . Someone's hiding him from work.'

The informants asked around, then spoke to the steward. The steward didn't believe them. 'Go and fetch the lad,' he said. 'I need to look into this myself.'

They went and fetched Danilushko.

'Whose boy are you?' asked the steward.

Danilushko replied, 'I'm apprenticed to a master in the malachite craft.'

The steward grabbed him by the ear. 'Is this how you study, you scoundrel!' And he led him by the ear to Prokopich.

Prokopich saw things were amiss, and he did his best to cover for Danilushko: 'It's I who sent him out to catch some perch. I had a terrible craving for fresh perch. Because of my ill health it's the only thing I can eat. So I ordered the boy to catch some for me.'

The steward did not believe him. And he could see that Danilushko was a new man now: he'd got his strength back, and he had proper boots on his feet and he was wearing a good shirt and trousers. So he decided to test Danilushko: 'Right, then, show me what the master has taught you.'

Danilushko slipped on his apron, went to the workbench and began explaining and demonstrating. Whatever the steward's question, he was ready with an answer. He described how to rough out the stone, how to saw it, how to cut the chamfer, when and with what to glue it together, how to burnish it, how to mount the stone on copper or wood. In a word, he explained everything.

The steward tested and tested him, then said to Prokopich, 'Looks like this one's turned out all right!'

'I'm not complaining,' answered Prokopich.

'That's just it, you're not complaining – you're spoiling the lad! He was sent to you to learn your craft, but all he does is sit by the pond with a fishing rod! You be careful! I'll give you fresh perch to remember for the rest of your life – and there won't be anything for the lad to smile about either!'

After making these threats he left, leaving Prokopich still marvelling: 'When did you learn all that, Danilushko? I didn't think I'd taught you anything yet.'

'Oh but you did! You explained and demonstrated,' said Danilushko, 'and I remembered it all.'

Tears rolled down Prokopich's cheeks – his heart was truly touched.

'My son,' he said, 'dear Danilushko ... Whatever else I know, I will share it with you ... I won't keep anything from you ...'

Nevertheless, that was the end of Danilushko's life of freedom. The very next day the steward sent for him and began giving him tasks for his training. At first, of course, it was simple things: women's brooches, jewellery boxes. Then it was lathe work: candlesticks and all sorts of finery. And then it was carving. Little leaves and petals, patterns and flowers. The malachite craft is painstaking work. A piece may seem trifling – yet the number of hours the craftsman has slaved over it! And so Danilushko grew into manhood.

And when from a single piece of stone he fashioned a bracelet in the form of a snake, the steward acknowledged him as a fully-fledged master. He wrote to the squire: 'We now have a new master in the malachite craft: Danilko the Scrawny. He works well, only he's very young so he's a bit slow. Do you wish to leave him at his training or release him on a quit-rent basis, like Prokopich?'

Danilushko was not really working slowly at all, but with astonishing deftness and speed. Prokopich had shown his usual cunning. When the steward set Danilushko a task to be completed, say, in five days, Prokopich had been going along and saying, 'He can't manage that. It will take him a fortnight. The lad's still studying, after all. If he does it in a rush, he'll just end up wasting good stone.'

Well, the steward would argue a while, but he'd end up allowing him a few more days. And so Danilushko was able to take it easy. He even, without the steward getting to hear about it, learned some reading and writing. It was just the bare minimum, of course, but he knew his letters. Here, too, Prokopich was helping him. But when, on top of all this, Prokopich tried to do the tasks the steward had set Danilushko, the boy did not allow it:

'What are you doing, Uncle? You can't take my place at the workbench! Look, your beard's turned green from malachite dust, your health's not what it used to be, but you can't say this work's doing *me* any harm!'

By then Danilushko had indeed grown strong and sturdy. People still called him Danilushko the Scrawny, but only out of habit. How he had changed! Tall and ruddy, curly-headed and merry. In a word, enough to make the girls swoon. Prokopich began talking about brides, but Danilushko would just shake his head: 'What's the hurry? First let me become a true master, then we can think about brides.'

In reply to the steward's report, the squire wrote:

'Let that Danilko who is apprenticed to Prokopich make a footed chalice for my house. Then I shall decide whether to release him on a quit-rent basis or let him continue with his training. Only be sure that Prokopich does not give him a hand. If you fail to do this, there will be a penalty to pay.'

When the steward received this letter, he called for Danilushko and said, 'You're going to be working here, with me. You'll be given a workbench and all the stone you need.'

When Prokopich heard about this, he was upset. What could all this mean, he wondered. What was going on? He went to the steward, but the steward wouldn't even listen to him . . . He just shouted, 'It's none of your business!'

So Danilushko went to work at the steward's. Before he left, Prokopich warned him: 'Take your time, Danilushko! Don't show them all you can do!'

At first Danilushko was on his guard. He was spending most of the time measuring things up and looking them over, but he soon grew tired of working so slowly. Whether or not he was working, he still had to put in his time at the steward's; he still had to be there from morning till night. Well, out of boredom Danilushko went and started working flat out. In no time at all he'd completed the chalice. Acting as if everything was normal, the steward said, 'Make another one just the same!'

Danilushko made a second one, then a third. Only when he'd finished the third one did the steward say, 'I won't let you get away with it this time! I've caught you and Prokopich at your game. After I wrote to him, the squire gave you a deadline for one chalice, but you've turned out three. Now I know what you're capable of. You won't be able to trick me any more – I'll teach that old dog to pander to you! I'll make an example of him!'

So he wrote to the squire about what had happened and sent him the three chalices. Only the squire – perhaps because he happened to be in a good mood, perhaps because he was annoyed with the steward for some other reason – did the very opposite of what the steward was expecting.

He set Danilushko a piffling quit-rent and he allowed the lad to remain with Prokopich – if the two men were working together, perhaps they would be able to come up with something new. Along with the letter he sent a drawing. It showed a chalice with all sorts of fiddly bits. Along the rim was a carved border, around the middle was a lattice ribbon of stone and on the foot were some little leaves. In a word, it was a real concoction. And on the drawing the squire had written: 'Even if it takes you five years, I want it done exactly as shown.'

So the steward had to take back his words. He told Danilushko what the squire had written, handed him the drawing and sent him back to Prokopich.

Danilushko and Prokopich brightened up again, and they began working with renewed enthusiasm. Danilushko soon set to work on this new chalice. It had any number of intricacies. The least slip and the piece would be ruined; you'd have to start all over. Still, Danilushko had sharp eyes, his hand was sure and he had strength enough – the work was going well. Only one thing riled him: while there was no end of challenges, the chalice had absolutely no beauty at all. He spoke to Prokopich, but Prokopich merely seemed puzzled: 'What's it to you? If that's what they've drawn, then it must be what they want. Goodness knows how many pieces I've turned and carved, but where they end up, I've no idea.'

Danilushko tried talking to the steward, but that got him nowhere. The steward merely stamped his feet and waved his hands about. 'Are you crazy? That drawing cost a mint. It was likely done by the best artist in the entire capital. Who do you think you are to question it?'

Then he must have remembered what the squire had said – that between them, the two men might be able to come up with something new. He went on, 'I'll tell you what . . . Make this chalice from the squire's drawing, and if you want to think up another of your own design, that's up to you. I won't stop you. There's no shortage of stone. Whatever you need I'll provide.'

At this point Danilushko sank into thought. It's been said many times that any fool can knock another man's work, but to create something of your own means many a night of tossing and turning. Danilushko continued to work on the squire's chalice, but his mind was elsewhere. He was thinking away, wondering what flower and leaf would best suit the malachite stone. He became pensive and gloomy. Prokopich noticed, and asked, 'Are you all right, Danilushko? Take it easy with this chalice. What's the hurry? You should go out and enjoy yourself sometimes – it's not right to do nothing but sit there, day in, day out!'

'You're right,' said Danilushko. 'I ought at least to go down to the forest. Perhaps I'll spot what I'm after.'

From then on he began going to the forest almost every day. It was the time for haymaking and picking berries. The wild grasses and herbs were in flower. Danilushko would stop in a hayfield or a forest glade and stand there staring at something. Then he would wander the hayfields again, examining the grass as though searching for something. There were a lot of people about making hay or gathering herbs and berries. They would ask Danilushko, 'Lost something?' He would smile joylessly and say, 'No, I haven't lost anything, there's just something I can't find.'

'There's something not right with the lad,' these folks began saying.

He'd go back home, make straight for the bench and sit there till morning. As soon as the sun came up, he'd be off to the forest and hayfields again. He began bringing home all sorts of little leaves and flowers, more and more of them from poisonous plants that the cattle avoided: white hellebore and hemlock, moonflower and marsh tea, and various kinds of sedge. His face became drawn, his eyes began to look troubled, his hands lost their boldness. Prokopich well and truly started to worry. Danilushko said to him, 'The chalice gives me no peace. My only wish is to bring out the full power of the stone.'

Prokopich tried to talk some sense into him:

'Why does it bother you so much? You're well fed, what else do you need? Let the squires amuse themselves however they like. What matters for us is to be left in peace. If they think up some design, then we'll do as they ask, but why go out of your way for them? You're just giving yourself an extra burden, that's all.'

But Danilushko would not budge.

'It's not that I'm trying to please the squire,' he said. 'I just can't get this chalice out of my head. I see what fine stone we have, and what do we do with it? We turn it and carve it and burnish it, but all in vain. But I've a yearning now to make something that will allow me to see the full power of the stone and reveal it to others.'

After a while Danilushko went and sat down to work on the chalice from the squire's drawing. Now and again he laughed: 'A stone ribbon with little holes, a carved rim . . .'

All of a sudden he abandoned this chalice and began work on something else. And he just went on standing there at the bench, not taking a moment's rest. He said to Prokopich, 'I shall make the chalice in the shape of the moonflower.'

Prokopich tried to talk him out of it. At first Danilushko did not want to listen. Three or four days later, however, after making a slip, he said, 'All right then. First I'll finish the squire's chalice, then I'll start on my own. Only you mustn't try to stop me . . . I really can't get it out of my head.'

'All right,' said Prokopich. 'I won't bother you.' To himself, however, he was thinking: 'The lad's calming down, soon he'll forget about this chalice of his. He needs a wife, that's what. Once he's got a family to provide for, that'll clear his head of all this nonsense.'

Danilushko started on the chalice. It was a lot of work; it was going to take him more than a year. He worked hard at it, and he didn't bring up the moonflower even once. Prokopich began to talk about marriage: 'What about Katya Letemina, how about her for a bride? She's a good girl . . . There's not a word can be said against her.'

Prokopich was being artful. He had long since noticed that Danilushko had his eye on this girl. And she for her part was certainly not turning away from him. That's why Prokopich, as if just in passing, had mentioned her. But Danilushko stood firm: 'Wait! First let me get this chalice out of the way. I'm fed up with it. Any moment now I might make a slip with the hammer and crack it, and all you can do is harp on about marriage! Katya and I have agreed everything already. She's going to wait for me.'

Well, Danilushko finished the chalice from the squire's drawing. Of course, they didn't tell the steward, and they decided to have a little party at home. Katya, his betrothed, came with her parents; the other guests were mostly malachite masters. Katya marvelled at the chalice: 'How ever did you manage to carve out that pattern without breaking the stone anywhere? It's so smooth and perfectly turned!'

The master craftsmen also gave their approval: 'It's exactly the same as the drawing. There's really nothing one can fault. You've done a perfect job – and you've done it so fast. If you go on working like this, we'll have a hard time keeping up with you.'

Danilushko listened to all this. Then he said, 'That's just it – there's nothing to fault. It's smooth and even, the pattern's come out perfectly, it's been carved just like the drawing, but where's the beauty in it? Look at a flower – even the plainest flower brings delight to your heart. Well, who could this chalice bring delight to? What's it for? Anyone who looks at it will marvel, just like Katya did, at the master's eye and hand, at the patience he must have had not to chip the stone anywhere—'

'And where he has slipped up,' the masters laughed, 'he'll have glued it together and covered it with polish, and no one will ever know the difference.'

'Exactly . . . But where, I ask, is the beauty of the stone? There was a vein here, and I have to drill holes in it and cut flowers into it. Why? What are they doing here? The stone's been ruined. And what a stone it was! The finest stone! The very finest!'

He was getting worked up. He had clearly had a bit to drink.

The craftsmen gave Danilushko the same advice that Prokopich had repeated time and time again: 'Stone's stone, and there's nothing more to it. Our job is simply to turn it and carve it.'

Only there was an old man there. Long ago he had taught

Prokopich and the other masters. They all called him Grandad. He was very old and frail indeed, but he understood what was being said, and he advised Danilushko: 'My dear son, you stay away from that path! Don't even think of it! Else you'll end up as one of the Mistress's mountain masters . . .'

'What masters are they, Grandad?'

'Ah . . . the masters who live inside the mountain, nobody sees them . . . Whatever the Mistress desires, they will create it. Once I chanced to see their work. Now that was true craftsmanship! Bears no resemblance to what we do here.'

Everybody became curious. They asked what it was he had seen.

'It was a snake,' he said. 'A snake bracelet.'

'Well? What was it like?'

'Nothing like our own work, I tell you. Any master would know at a glance that it was from somewhere else. Our snakes, no matter how perfect they are, they're stone – but this one seemed alive. The black pattern on its back, its little eyes . . . It looked as if it might bite you at any moment. Well, to them that's just child's play! They've seen the stone flower, they understand true beauty.'

The moment the old man mentioned the stone flower, Danilushko immediately began questioning him. The old man answered candidly enough, 'I don't know, dear son. I've heard that such a flower exists. Our craftsmen must never set eyes on it. Whoever so much as glimpses it, the whole world will go dark for him.'

Danilushko replied, 'I'd like to see it.'

At this, Katya became agitated: 'What are you saying, Danilushko! Surely you're not weary of this world already, are you?' She started crying. Prokopich and the other craftsmen were not slow to grasp why. They began to poke fun at the old master: 'Grandad, you're going soft in the head. You and your fairy tales! Why lead the lad astray?'

At this the old man lost his temper. Banging his fist on the table, he said,

'There *is* such a flower! What the lad says is true: we don't understand the stone. Well, that flower shows us true beauty.'

The masters laughed: 'You've had one too many, Grandad!'
But he kept on: 'The stone flower exists!'

The guests left, but Danilushko was unable to forget this conversation. He began going back to the forest, wandering about near his moonflower, and he was no longer saying anything about a wedding. Prokopich began to press him: 'Why bring shame upon the girl? How many years are you going to keep her waiting? Soon people will start laughing at her. It's not as though there's any shortage of gossips round here!'

Danilushko returned to his old refrain: 'Wait a bit longer! I just need to decide what I want and then find the right stone.'

And he began going to the copper mine at Gumeshki. Sometimes he'd go right down into the mine and explore the workface; sometimes he would stay at the surface and sort through the stones he found there. Once, as he was turning over a stone and examining it, he said aloud, 'No, not this one . . .'

No sooner had he spoken than a voice said, 'You need to look somewhere else . . . at Snake Hill.'

Danilushko looked round – no one was there. Who could it be? Someone playing a joke . . . Only there didn't seem to be anywhere they could be hiding. He looked around again and set off back home. Once again someone called out, 'Did you hear, Master Danilko? Snake Hill, I tell you.'

Danilushko looked around. He could just about make out a woman, but she was no more than a bluish haze. And then there was nothing.

'What's this?' he thought. 'It couldn't be her, could it? Perhaps I really should go to Snake Hill?'

Danilushko knew Snake Hill well. It was near by, not far from Gumeshki. Now the hill is no more, it was all levelled long ago, but in earlier times they used to take stone from the top of it.

Well, the next day Danilushko went to Snake Hill. The hill was small but steep. From one side it looked like it had been sheared off. The rock face couldn't have been better: the strata were all beautifully clear.

Danilushko went up closer and found a large malachite rock. It had been torn out of the hill. It was a huge stone, too heavy for him to lift, and it seemed to have been worked into the shape of a little bush. Danilushko began to examine his find. It was exactly what he needed: the colour was deeper at the bottom, the veins were all just where he wanted them. Well, it was perfect . . . Danilushko was overjoyed, he ran for a horse, brought the stone home and said to Prokopich, 'Just look at this stone! It could have been made for me. Now I'll get the work done in no time. Then we can have the wedding. Katya must be well and truly fed up with waiting for me. Well it's not been easy for me, either. It's only this job that's been stopping me. Now I can finish it off!'

So Danilushko set to work on the stone. He worked around the clock. Prokopich said nothing: perhaps the lad would calm down when he had realized his dream. The work was going quickly. Danilushko had finished the bottom of the stone. It was the spitting image of a moonflower bush. The broad leaves, the jagged edges, the veins – everything was perfect. Even Prokopich said the bush seemed alive – so alive you wanted to reach out and touch it.

But as Danilushko began work on the very top part, he got stuck. He had turned the stem: the leaves lying close against the sides were so slender it was a miracle they held fast! The cup was just like the cup of a real moonflower, but something was wrong . . . It had gone dead; it had lost its beauty. Now Danilushko was unable to sleep at all. He would sit at the chalice, trying to decide how to put it right, what to do to make it better. Prokopich and the other masters couldn't believe it – what more could the lad want? He had made a chalice the likes of which no one had ever seen, yet he was unhappy. The lad's wits were wandering, he needed treatment. Katya heard what people were saying and she took to weeping. This made Danilushko begin to see reason.

'All right,' he said, 'I'll stop. It's clear I can't reach any higher, I'm never going to capture the power of the stone.' And now it was he who was impatient to get married. But what was there to be impatient about when the bride had got everything ready long ago? They chose the day and Danilushko became more cheerful. He told the steward about the chalice. The steward rushed round to look at it: yes, it was quite something! The steward wanted to send the chalice to the squire straight away, but Danilushko said, 'Wait a little, it still needs a few finishing touches.'

It was autumn. The wedding was to be held around the time of the Day of the Snake. Someone happened to mention that all the snakes would soon be gathering in one spot. This made an impression on Danilushko. He remembered all the talk about the malachite flower. It was as if something were pulling him: 'Perhaps I should go one last time to Snake Hill? Maybe there's still a chance I could learn something there?' And he remembered the stone: 'It's as if someone had put it there specially for me! And that voice telling me to go to Snake Hill!'

And so Danilushko went. The ground had already begun to frost over, and there was a dusting of snow. Danilushko went up to the steep slope where he had found the stone. He looked around. Right at the spot where the stone had been there was now a big hollow, as if someone had been quarrying. Without stopping to think about who this could have been, Danilushko stepped down into the hollow. 'I'll sit down and have a rest from the wind,' he thought. 'It's warmer down here.' Beside one of the walls of the hollow he saw a grey rock shaped like a chair. Danilushko sat on it, and fell deep into thought. He was looking down at the ground; he just couldn't stop thinking about that stone flower. 'If only I could have just one glimpse of it!'

All of a sudden it felt warm, as if summer had returned. Danilushko looked up: sitting opposite him, by the far wall, was the Mistress of the Copper Mountain. Danilushko knew her at once by her beauty and her malachite dress. Only he thought, 'Maybe I'm just dreaming this. Maybe there isn't really anyone at all.' He went on silently sitting there, looking right at the spot where the Mistress was sitting, acting as if he saw nothing. She, too, was silent, as if lost in thought. Then she asked, 'So, Master Danilko, did your moonflower chalice not work out?'

'No,' he answered. 'It didn't.'

'Don't be downhearted! Try again! You shall have stone according to your wish.'

'No,' he answered, 'I can't go on. I'm worn out, and it's all gone wrong. Show me the stone flower.'

'That's easily done,' she said, 'only you'll end up regretting it.'

'Are you saying you won't let me leave the mountain?'

'What do you mean, not let you leave! The way is open, it's just that people always return to me.'

'Show me the flower, I beg you!'

Once again she tried to dissuade him: 'Why not try once more to do it on your own!' She talked about Prokopich: 'He took pity on you, now it's your turn to pity him.' She talked about his betrothed: 'The lass adores you, but you always have your eyes elsewhere.'

'I know,' Danilushko shouted, 'but without the flower, life is nothing to me. Show it to me!'

'In that case,' she said, 'let us go to my garden, Master Danilko.'

She stood up. At that moment there was a rustling noise like a landslide. Danilushko saw that the walls of the hollow had disappeared. Towering above him were tall trees, only they weren't like ordinary trees – these trees were made of stone. Some were marble, some were of serpentine. Yes, every kind of stone. And they were alive, with branches and little leaves. They were swaying in the wind; there was a sound as if someone was tossing handfuls of shingle about. The grass below was also of stone. Azure, red, many-coloured . . . Though there was no sun to be seen, everything was lit up like just before sunset. Little golden snakes were fluttering and dancing between the trees. They radiated light.

And so the Mistress led Danilushko to a large clearing. Here the earth was like ordinary clay; on it, though, were bushes as black as velvet. And adorning these bushes were large green bell-shaped malachite flowers, and in each bell was a little antimony star. Above these flowers glimmered fiery bees, and the little stars were quietly chiming; it was as if they were singing.

'Well, master craftsman Danilko, have you had your look?' asked the Mistress.

'How would I ever find the stone to make anything like this?' replied Danilushko.

'Had you thought up this flower yourself, I'd have given you the stone, but now I can't.'

With that, she gave a wave of her hand.

Once again there was a rustling noise – and once again Danilushko was sitting on the chair-shaped stone in the hollow. The wind was whistling. Well, as we know, it was autumn.

Danilushko went back home. That very evening his betrothed was holding a party. At first Danilushko sang and danced and seemed full of cheer, but then it was as if a cloud came over him. Katya took fright: 'What's happened? You look like you're at a funeral!'

He said, 'My head's hurting. All I can see is black and green and red. I can't see light anywhere.'

The party came to an end. As was the custom, the bride and her girlfriends began to walk the groom back to his home. It was no distance at all, just one or two houses away. Katya said, 'Let's go the long way round, girls. We'll walk to the end of the street, then come back down Yelanskaya Street.'

To herself she was thinking: 'Perhaps he just needs some air, maybe he'll perk up again once he's outside.'

Her girlfriends were happy enough to go along with this. 'Yes,' they called out. 'Of course, we must walk him home properly. He lives awfully close – we haven't yet had time to sing him a proper parting song.'

It was a quiet night, and snow was falling – just right for a walk. And so on they went. The bride and groom walked ahead, while the bride's girlfriends and the young men who had been at the party fell a little behind. The girls started up their parting song. It was long and plaintive, like a funeral lament. This was the last thing Katya wanted. Her Danilushko had been gloomy enough anyway: why did they have to go and sing him a funeral song?

She tried to distract Danilushko. He talked a little, but then he turned sad and silent again. In the meantime Katya's girlfriends had come to the end of their parting song and moved on to more cheerful ones. The girls were lively and full of laughter, but Danilushko seemed more dejected than ever. No matter how she tried, there was nothing Katya could do to cheer him up. And so they came to his home. The friends of the bride and groom began to go their separate ways, while Danilushko silently, without observing the rituals, walked the bride back to her door and then went back home again.

Prokopich had long since gone to bed. Danilushko quietly lit a lamp, dragged his chalices into the middle of the hut and stood there looking at them. Just then Prokopich was seized by a coughing fit. He was choking and gasping. You see, he was old and he had become quite ill. This coughing cut through Danilushko's heart like a knife. Memories of the whole of his life with Prokopich flashed through his mind. He felt terribly sorry for the old man. As for Prokopich, when he had finished coughing, he asked, 'What are you doing with the chalices?'

'Oh, I'm just wondering if it's time to hand them over.'

'You should have done that long ago,' said Prokopich. 'They're simply taking up space here. And there's certainly nothing you can do to improve them.'

Well, they talked a little longer, then Prokopich fell back to sleep. And Danilushko lay down too, only he couldn't get to sleep at all. He tossed and turned, got up again, lit a lamp, had another look at the chalices and walked over to Prokopich. For a while he just stood there, looking down at the old man and sighing . . .

Then he took a hammer and smashed it down onto the moonflower. The chalice shattered with a crunch. As for the other chalice, the one made from the squire's drawing, he didn't even touch it. He merely spat into the centre of it and ran out of the hut. And from that moment Danilushko was nowhere to be found.

Some said that he had gone crazy and disappeared into the forest; some said that the Mistress had taken him as one of her mountain masters.

But really it was all very different. And that is another story.

The Mountain Master

Katya, Danilko's betrothed, remained unmarried. It was two or three years since Danilko had gone missing, and she had passed the usual age for marrying. In our parts, among the factory folk, a girl over twenty was considered past her prime. Young lads would seldom marry such girls – more often the girls would end up marrying widowers. This Katya, though, was a comely girl, and the young men were still asking for her hand. But her reply was always the same: 'I'm promised to Danilko.'

They tried to talk her round: 'Well, it can't be helped! You were promised to him but you never married. No use thinking about all that now. The man died long ago.'

Katya would not budge: 'I'm promised to Danilko. And maybe he will come back after all.'

'He is not among the living,' they would repeat. 'That's for sure.'

But she held fast: 'No one has seen him dead. To me he's as alive as ever.'

They decided the lass was not quite right in the head, and they left her alone. Others even started to mock her; they began calling her the corpse's bride. The name stuck. From then on, it was as if she had no other name but Katya Corpse-Bride.

Then there was an outbreak of some kind of disease, and Katya's elderly parents both died. She had a large family: three brothers, all of them with wives, and a number of married sisters. They fell out over who should live in their father's house. Seeing they had reached a deadlock, Katya said, 'I'll go and live in Danilushko's hut. Prokopich is quite elderly now. At least I'll be able to look after him.'

Her brothers and sisters tried, of course, to dissuade her:

'It's not proper, sister. Prokopich may be elderly, but think what people might say.'

'Why should I care?' she replied. 'It won't be me spreading gossip. And anyway, Prokopich is hardly a stranger to me. He's a foster father to my Danilko. I shall call him Papa.'

And so she left. It has to be said that her relatives did not try all that hard to stop her: with one less person, after all, things would be quieter. Prokopich, for his part, was pleased.

'Thank you, Katya, for not forgetting me,' he said.

And so they began to live together. Prokopich would sit at the bench, and Katya would run about doing the chores – working in the vegetable plot, boiling and baking, and the like. Keeping house for two is, of course, not so very difficult ... Katya was a sprightly girl; she'd get through the work in no time. When she'd finished, she would sit down to her own handiwork: sewing, knitting, making things to keep for a rainy day. Everything went smoothly to begin with, although Prokopich was getting weaker and weaker. He would spend a day at the workbench, then two in bed. Long years of work had worn him out. Katya began wondering how they would manage.

'This sewing and knitting won't earn us a livelihood, but it's the only craft I know.'

So she said to Prokopich, 'Papa! Teach me to make something simple.'

This made Prokopich laugh: 'Whatever next! Working with malachite is no job for a girl. Never heard of such a thing in all my life.'

Well, all the same, she began to watch Prokopich at his craft. Wherever she could, she helped him out. She would saw the stone; she would do some polishing. And Prokopich began to show her a few other things. Not real craftsmanship. Simple things like how to turn a plaque, make handles for knives and forks and other items people needed. Mere trifles, of course, but enough to make a difference if times grew hard.

Prokopich died not long after. Then Katya's brothers and sisters began to press her more than ever: 'There's nothing for it. Now you really do have to get married. How will you be able to live on your own?'

Katya cut them short: 'That's my worry, not yours. I don't need your suitors. Danilushko will come back. He'll master his craft in the mountain and come back.'

Her brothers and sisters gesticulated excitedly: 'Are you in your right mind, Katya? To talk like that is sinful! The man died long ago, but you're still waiting for him! Watch out, or you'll start seeing things.'

'I'm not afraid of that,' she replied.

'But what are you going to live on?'

'You don't need to worry about that either,' she answered. 'I shall manage on my own.'

The brothers and sisters took this to mean that Prokopich had left her some money. They started up again: 'You're a fool! If there's money around, you're going to need a man in the house even more. Somebody – God forbid – might try to steal the money. They'll wring your neck like a chicken. And you've barely even lived . . .'

'I shall live,' she answered, 'as long as I am fated to.'

The brothers and sisters went on for some time with their hullabaloo. Some of them were shouting, some trying to talk her round, some crying, but Katya stood firm: 'I'll get by on my own. No need for any of your suitors. I already have a betrothed.'

Her family, of course, were incensed: 'If you need help, don't come running to us!'

'Thank you,' she replied, 'my dear brothers, my sweet sisters! I won't forget. And don't you forget either. If you happen to pass this way, then you must walk straight past my door!'

She was laughing at them. The brothers and sisters left in a fury, slamming the door behind them.

Katya was left all on her own. At first, of course, she cried, but then she said, 'No! I won't give in!'

She dried her eyes and set about the housework, scrubbing and scouring till everything was clean. When she had finished, she went to the workbench. Here, too, she began arranging everything to suit her; she put the tools she most needed close by, and put the rest to one side. Once everything was in order, she wanted to get down to work: 'I can at least have a go at making a wall-plaque.'

She went to get a stone, but there were none that seemed right. There were the remnants of Danilushko's moonflower chalice, but Katya wanted to keep them; she had tied them up in a special bundle. And, of course, there was all the stone that Prokopich had left. But the pieces he had been working on during his last months had been large ones. Those stones were all too big. He'd already used up the offcuts and leftovers for smaller items. 'Seems I'll have to go down to the mine,' Katya said to herself. 'Maybe I'll find what I need there.'

She had heard Danilko and Prokopich talk of getting their stone from Snake Hill. So that's where she went.

Around Gumeshki, as always, there were lots of people: some sorting through the ore, some carting it away. They stared at Katya, wondering what she was doing with her basket. Katya didn't like being gawped at. Instead of looking for stone there, she walked round to the far side of the hill where there was still forest. Katya made her way through the forest until she reached Snake Hill itself, and there she sat down. She felt grief-stricken; memories of Danilushko were coming back. She sat on the stone, and her tears began to flow. There was no one else nearby, she was surrounded by trees, and she wept without restraint, her tears dripping down onto the earth. She cried for some time, and then she saw: right by her feet there was now a large piece of malachite. But it was lodged in the earth. How could she get it out without a pickaxe or a crowbar? She tried to shift it a little. It seemed not to be too firmly embedded. So she started scraping the earth away with a little stick. She scraped away all she could and then began trying to shake it free. Suddenly it yielded, and there was a sound from underneath, like a branch snapping. The stone was a small slab, three fingers thick, the breadth of a palm, and no more than two spans long. Katya gazed at it in wonder: 'It's exactly what I was thinking of. I'll be able to get a good number of plaques from it when I saw it up. And there'll hardly be any waste.'

She brought the stone home and got straight down to work. Sawing takes time, and there was the housework to attend to as well. She'd look up from her work and realize the whole day had gone by; there was no time to mope about. But the moment she sat down at the bench, she would always remember Danilushko: 'If only he could see that there's a new worker now! Sitting where he and Prokopich used to sit!'

Of course, a few louts made their appearance. It was bound to happen ... On the eve of some holiday Katya was sitting working late into the night when three lads climbed over the fence. They wanted to give her a fright, or maybe worse – who knows? Anyway, they were all drunk. Katya was sawing away and she didn't hear them come into the entrance room. She heard nothing until they started trying to break into the main room: 'Open up, Corpse-Bride! You have guests from among the living!'

At first Katya simply said: 'Go away, boys!'

Well, that didn't have much effect. They carried on bashing away at the door – it seemed as if it might give way any moment. At this point Katya undid the latch, flung open the door and shouted, 'Well, come on in. Who wants his forehead smashed first?'

The lads gawped – she was holding an axe.

'Don't fool around with *that*!' they said.

'Who's fooling around?' she answered. 'Cross the doorstep and you get your head smashed in.'

They may have been drunk, but the lads could see that she wasn't joking. She was a fully-grown woman, with broad shoulders, a determined look in her eyes, and she clearly knew what to do with an axe. They did not dare enter. They hollered a bit and then left. They even went about telling people what had happened. Soon people started teasing them – three of them and they'd run away from a girl! This, of course, was not to their liking, so they spun a yarn about how Katya had not been alone. No, standing behind her had been a corpse: 'It was so terrifying that you couldn't help but run for your life!'

There's no knowing how many people believed the lads, but from then on the rumours began to spread: 'There's an evil spirit in that house. It's not for nothing she chooses to live all alone.'

Katya heard all this, but it didn't bother her. 'So much the better,' she thought. 'Let them spin their yarns! If they start to feel a bit frightened, maybe it'll stop them from coming a second time.'

The neighbours were also astonished to see Katya at the workbench. 'Trying her hand at a man's craft!' they scoffed. 'Whatever will come of it?'

This stung Katya more. She herself began to wonder whether or not she could cope with all the work on her own. Well, nevertheless she got a grip on herself: 'It's just wares for the market! Is that so demanding? Just needs to be smooth ... I can do that, can't I?'

Katya finished sawing up the stone. The pattern fitted remarkably; it seemed almost to be telling her where to make the crosswise cuts. Katya marvelled at how cleverly everything was turning out. She divided the stone along the markings, then started turning. The work wasn't especially tricky, but it wasn't beginner's work either. At first she found it a struggle, but then she got the hang of it. The plaques came out superb, and with no waste at all. The only stone she lost was the dust from the turning.

Katya finished the plaques. She marvelled once again at what a fine stone she had found, and then began thinking about where to sell her wares. Prokopich had sometimes taken trifles like this to town and delivered them all to one shop. Katya had often heard about this shop. So she decided to travel to town. 'I'll go and ask,' she said to herself. 'Maybe they'll take my work regularly.'

She locked up the hut and set out on foot. No one in Polevskoy even noticed that she had left. Arriving in town, Katya asked where the shop was and went straight there. She looked around: the place was crammed with stone objects of every kind, and there was an entire glass case full of malachite plaques. The shop was crowded with people. Some were buying, others were bringing their wares. The shopkeeper seemed stiff and haughty.

At first Katya felt too frightened to approach him, but then she plucked up her courage and asked, 'Do you need any malachite plaques?'

The shopkeeper pointed to the glass case: 'Malachite plaques! Can't you see how many I've got?'

The other craftsmen delivering their work joined in: 'Any number of folk have started making plaques recently. The stone just gets wasted. What they don't realize is that to make a plaque you need a good pattern.'

One of the craftsmen was from Polevskoy. He said in a quiet voice to the shopkeeper: 'She's a bit nutty, this girl. Her neighbours have seen her working at the lathe. Seems she's managed to knock something out . . .'

So the shopkeeper said: 'Right then, show me what you've brought.'

Katya handed him a plaque. The shopkeeper looked at it, then stared straight at Katya and said, 'Who did you steal it from?'

Katya, needless to say, felt insulted. In a very different tone, she said, 'What right do you have to speak like that to someone you don't even know? Look – if you're not blind! Who could I possibly have stolen this number of plaques from, all with the same pattern? Answer me that!' And she emptied all her wares onto the counter.

The shopkeeper and craftsmen looked at the plaques: they did indeed all share the same pattern. And the pattern was exquisite. In the centre there was a tree; there was a little bird perched on one of the branches, and another little bird below, all crystal clear and cleanly finished. The customers heard them all talking and drew closer to have a look, but the shopkeeper quickly covered up all the plaques and said, 'You can't see anything when they're all in a jumble. Wait a moment and I'll put them on display. Then you'll be able to choose what you want.' And to Katya he said, 'Go through that door. I'll pay you straight away.'

Katya went through, and the shopkeeper followed. He locked the door and said, 'What are you asking for them?'

Katya had heard Prokopich mention how much he used to

get. So she named the same price. The shopkeeper just laughed: 'You must be kidding! I only ever paid that much to a craftsman from Polevskoy, Prokopich, and his adopted son Danilko. Well, and they were true masters!'

'That's how I know the price,' she replied. 'I'm from the same family.'

'Oh, I see!' the shopkeeper said in surprise. 'So this is Danilko's work, is it?'

'No,' she replied, 'it's my own work.'

'But he left you the stone?'

'I found it myself.'

The shopkeeper clearly did not believe her, but he didn't try to beat down the price. He paid up, fair and square, and he even said, 'If you make any more like these, be sure to bring them to me. I'll take them straight away and I'll always give you a good price.'

Katya went out of the shop overjoyed, thinking she'd been given a fortune. The shopkeeper put the plaques on display. The customers came crowding round: 'How much are they?'

The shopkeeper, of course, had known what he was doing. Naming a price ten times higher than he'd paid Katya, he announced, 'Never been a pattern like it. It is the work of Danilko the master from Polevskoy. There's no one can match him.'

Katya got back home. 'Well, who'd have thought it?' she kept marvelling. 'My plaques turned out the best of the lot! It was a fine piece of stone I found. What a stroke of luck!' Then it dawned on her: 'Could it have been Danilushko sending me a message?'

And she got herself ready and left for Snake Hill.

But the malachite master who had tried to embarrass Katya in front of the town trader had also got back from the town. He envied Katya the rare pattern she had found. 'I ought to find out where she gets her stone from. Maybe Prokopich or Danilko told her about some new site!'

He saw Katya hurrying off somewhere, and he followed her. He watched her skirt around Gumeshki and make her way somewhere behind Snake Hill. The craftsman continued to follow her, thinking, 'On that side it's all forest. I'll be able to creep right up to this new pit of hers.'

They entered the forest. Katya was only a short way ahead and she had relaxed her guard; she wasn't listening out or looking around her. The craftsman was delighted: without the least effort he was about to discover a new source of stone. And then all of a sudden there was a noise nearby – the craftsman even took fright. He stood stock still: what had it been? While he was trying to work this out, Katya disappeared. The craftsman ran every which way through the forest, until he finally emerged at Seversky Pond, well over a mile from Gumeshki.

Katya had no idea that anyone had been spying on her. She climbed the hill and reached the spot where she had found the first stone. The hollow seemed a little bigger now, and at its edge there was a stone just like the first one. Katya shook it about, and it came loose. Once again, there was a noise like a branch snapping. Katya picked up the stone and then she began sobbing and wailing, much as women weep and wail over the dead. 'O my true love, my heart's desire . . .' she called out through her tears. 'Who did you leave me for?'

After she had finished lamenting, her pain seemed to ease a little, and she stood in thought, looking in the direction of the mine. She seemed to be in some kind of a clearing. All around her the forest was dense and tall, but over towards the mine the trees were thinner. The sun must have been about to set. On the floor of the clearing darkness was creeping in from the forest, but over towards the mine there was still sunlight. The place was ablaze, and the stones were all shining.

Katya was intrigued. She wanted to get closer. She took a step, and something crunched underfoot. She drew her foot away, looked down – and saw that there was no ground beneath her feet. She was standing on some kind of tall tree, on its very crown. All around her were the tops of other trees. Down below, in the gaps between the trees, she could see plants and flowers, and they were nothing like the kind we have in our parts.

Anyone else in Katya's shoes would have taken fright. They would have started screaming and shrieking, but Katya had only one thought: 'It's happened! The mountain's opened up! Oh, if only I could see Danilushko!'

No sooner had she thought this than, down below her, through the gaps in the trees, she saw someone who looked like Danilushko, and he was stretching his arms up towards her and he seemed to be wanting to say something. Everything went dark and Katya leaped towards him – from the top of the tree!

She fell to the ground just where she had been standing. On coming to, she said to herself, 'So I really have started seeing things. I'd better go back home straight away.'

She knew she should go, but she just sat there, hoping the mountain might open again, hoping to catch another glimpse of Danilushko. There she sat until it was quite dark. Only then did she set off back home, thinking, 'Well, it's really happened! I've seen Danilushko!'

The craftsman who'd been spying on Katya had already got back. He checked Katya's hut – and found it locked. So he hid by the side of the path, hoping to see what she'd bring back with her. As Katya approached, he stepped out and barred her way. 'Where have you been?' he asked.

'To Snake Hill,' she replied.

'At night? Why?'

'To see Danilko.'

The craftsman shied away in fear. The following day the entire town was talking and whispering about her: 'Corpse-Bride really has gone crazy now. She goes to Snake Hill in the middle of the night to wait for a dead man. In the state she's in she could end up setting fire to the town.'

Once again her brothers and sisters hurried round and began nagging at Katya and trying to talk sense into her. Only she wouldn't listen to them. She just showed them the money and said, 'Where do you think I found this? They turn down work from good craftsmen, but look what they paid me for my very first piece of work! How do you explain that then?'

The brothers had heard about her good fortune. One of them said, 'You had a stroke of luck. I don't see what's so very strange about that.'

'Luck like that doesn't happen,' she replied. 'It was Danilko himself who planted the stone and drew the pattern on it.' The brothers laughed, and the sisters once again flapped their hands about excitedly: 'Now she's well and truly lost her wits! We'd better tell the steward. Maybe she really will go and set fire to the town!'

Of course, they didn't tell the steward at all. They'd have felt ashamed to betray their own sister. But as they left Katya's house, they agreed to keep an eye on her. They decided that one of them would have to follow her wherever she went.

Katya saw her relatives out, locked the door and began sawing the new stone. As she worked, she told herself, 'If this stone turns out as good as the last one, then I'll know it wasn't a dream, and that I really did see Danilushko.'

She worked as fast as she could. She couldn't wait to see how the pattern would turn out. It was the dead of night, but she remained at the workbench. One of her sisters woke up, saw a light in the hut, ran to the window, peeked through a chink in the shutter and said in amazement, 'She doesn't even sleep! What a curse the girl is!'

Katya finished sawing the first slab: there was a pattern! And it was even better than on the first stone. A bird was flying down from a tree, its wings spread, while another bird was flying from below to meet it. The pattern was repeated five times. And there were clear marks showing her where to make the crosswise cuts. Katya didn't pause to think. She just leaped to her feet and dashed off. Her sister followed, knocking at her brothers' doors as she ran by, urging them to hurry. The brothers came running; other people joined them. By then it was already growing light. They saw Katya running past Gumeshki. Everyone rushed after her. It was clear she didn't know she was being followed. She ran past the mine, and then slowed her pace a little as she skirted Snake Hill. The crowd held back a little, waiting to see what she would do next.

Katya walked up the hill, just as she had done before. She looked up: all around her now she could see a wondrous forest. She touched a tree. It was cold and smooth like polished stone. The grass underfoot was also of stone, and it was still dark everywhere. 'I must have found my way into the mountain,' Katya said to herself.

By then everyone else had become thoroughly terrified: 'Where's she vanished to? A moment ago she was right here, and now she's gone!'

They all started rushing about. Some went up the hill, some walked around it. Everyone was calling out, 'Can you see her anywhere? Can you see her?'

Katya, meanwhile, was walking through the stone forest, wondering how she could find Danilko. She walked and walked, and then she called out, 'Danilko, answer me!'

Something stirred in the forest. The boughs seemed to be rapping out: 'Not here! Not here! He's not here!' Only Katya didn't give up. 'Danilko, answer me!' she called again.

The forest answered once again: 'Not here! Not here! He's not here!'

Katya called out a third time: 'Danilko, answer me!'

And then there she was – standing in front of Katya – the Mistress of the Mountain herself! 'What are you doing in my forest?' she asked. 'What do you want? Are you looking for a good stone? Take any stone you like – and then leave!'

'I don't want any of your dead stone!' replied Katya. 'Give me my living Danilushko. Where are you hiding him? What right do you have to lure away a man who's already betrothed?'

She was a brave lass. She went straight for the jugular – and with the Mistress right there in front of her! The Mistress, however, was unruffled. 'Is there anything else you want to say?' she asked.

'Yes – give me back my Danilko! I know you've got him here . . .'

The Mistress broke into laughter and said, 'You foolish girl, don't you know who you're speaking to?'

'Of course I do,' she shouted, 'I'm not blind. But I'm not afraid of you, you home-wrecker! Not in the least! No matter how clever you've made things down here, all the same Danilko yearns for me. I know it – I've seen him. Understand?'

The Mistress replied, 'Let's hear what Danilko himself has to say.'

Until then the forest had been in darkness, but now it seemed to come alive. It became light. The grass underfoot was ablaze with coloured lights, and each tree was more beautiful than the next. Through the gaps between the trees Katya could see a clearing, and in it were stone flowers, and above them, like sparks of fire, were golden bees. It was all so beautiful that you could gaze for a hundred years and still not gaze your fill. And there in the forest was Danilko. He was running straight towards her. Katya leaped towards him:

'Danilushko!'

'Wait,' said the Mistress. And then she asked: 'Well, master Danilko, the choice is yours. If you go with her, you will forget all that is mine; if you stay here you must forget about her and everyone else too. Which is it to be?'

'I cannot forget about other people,' he answered, 'and not a minute goes by without me thinking of Katya.'

The Mistress smiled brightly and said, 'You've won, Katerina! Take your master craftsman. And for being so brave and steadfast, I shall give you a gift. Let all that is mine remain in Danilko's memory. Everything except this – which he must completely forget!' And the clearing with its miraculous flowers suddenly faded away – like a light that has been extinguished. The Mistress pointed them in the right direction and added, 'Danilko, don't tell anyone about the mountain. Say that you went to study with a distant master. And you, Katerina, don't think for one moment that I lured your betrothed away. He came of his own accord, in search of what he has now forgotten.'

At this Katya bowed and said, 'Forgive me my rough words!'

'That's all right,' she answered. 'How can they hurt a woman who is made of stone! I'm telling you for your own sake, so that the two of you may live without discord.'

Katya and Danilko set off through the forest. It grew darker and darker, and the ground underfoot became more and more pitted and rugged. They looked around and saw they were at the Gumeshki mine. It was still early, and there was no one about. They quietly made their way home. All the people who had gone after Katya were still wandering about the forest, calling out, 'Can you see her anywhere? Can you see her?'

They searched and searched but could see no sign of her. Then they went back home – and saw Danilko there in the hut, sitting beside the window.

They took fright, of course. They crossed themselves and recited all kinds of chants and spells. Then they saw that Danilko was filling his pipe. This calmed them down: the dead, after all, do not smoke pipes.

One by one they began walking closer. They saw that Katya was there in the hut too. She was busy at the stove, and she seemed in high spirits. They hadn't seen her like that in a long time. This emboldened them, and they entered the hut and began asking, 'Where have you been all this time, Danilko?'

'I was in Kolyvan,' he replied. 'I'd heard about a master stoneworker there, they say he's the finest there is. Well, I fancied studying a little with him. Old Papa, may he rest in peace, tried to talk me out of it. But I went off without his permission, I told no one except Katya.'

'But why did you smash the chalice?' they asked.

Danilko's eyes misted over a little. After a while he said, 'Oh, I don't know . . . I came back from the party . . . Perhaps I'd had too much to drink . . . The chalice hadn't turned out like I wanted it, so I went and smashed it. It's the kind of thing that happens to every craftsman at one time or another. Nothing odd about it.'

Then the brothers and sisters started questioning Katya: why hadn't she told them about Kolyvan? But there was no getting anything out of Katya. She just said, 'Well, that's a bit rich. Didn't I keep telling you that Danilko was still alive? And what did you do? You all tried to thrust suitors at me and lead me astray! Come and sit at the table. I've just baked some eggs.'

And that brought an end to the matter. Everyone sat there for a while, chatting about this and that. Then they went off to their homes. In the evening Danilko went to the steward to announce his return. The steward kicked up a bit of a fuss, of course. But they sorted things out in the end.

Danilko and Katya began living together in a hut of their

own. People say that they lived happily and in harmony. Everyone in the trade called Danilko the 'Mountain Master'. There was no one who could hold a candle to him. And so he and Katya prospered. Only from time to time, Danilko would sink deep into thought. Katya, of course, understood what he was thinking about, but she said nothing.

Golden Hair

It happened in the days of old. Back then there wasn't a Russian to be seen in these parts. And the Bashkirs lived a good way away, too. They needed open country for their cattle, you see; they needed broad glades and open steppe. They could find all that over by the river Nyazya, and along the Uraim basin, but what good was this part of the world to them? To this day the trees grow tall and thick, but at that time the forest was so dense that you couldn't even walk through it, let alone ride. The only people who ever entered the forest were the hunters.

They say there was a hunter among the Bashkirs who went by the name of Aylyp. There was no man stronger or more daring. He could kill a bear with a single arrow or grab an elk by the antlers and throw it over his shoulder – and that would be the end of the creature. As for wolves and the like, it was the same story. Once Aylyp had set eyes on a beast, it never got away.

One time Aylyp was riding through open country when he spotted a fox. For a hunter like him, a fox was a paltry catch. All the same, he said to himself, 'I'll have some fun, I'll strike her down with my whip.' Aylyp kicked the horse into a gallop, but he couldn't catch up with the fox. He got ready to draw his bow, but the fox had vanished. Well, what of it? If she had escaped, then good luck to her! Barely had he thought this when there was the fox again, standing behind a tree stump. She even yapped a little, as if to say: 'Can't catch me!'

Aylyp got ready to loose an arrow – again the fox had gone. He lowered his bow – and there was the fox again, yapping: 'Can't catch me!'

This roused Aylyp's spirit: 'We'll see about that, ginger!'

The broad glades ended; from here on, it was dense forest. But this did not stop Aylyp. He dismounted and chased after the fox on foot – but still he had no luck. He knew the fox was somewhere near, but still he couldn't shoot her. Nor was he about to give up. A fine hunter like he was – and unable to kill a fox! In the end Aylyp found himself in a part of the forest he didn't know at all. And the fox had vanished. Aylyp searched and searched, but there was no sign of her.

'Might as well see where I am,' he said to himself.

He found a tall larch and climbed to its very top. He looked around: not far away was a little river gushing down the side of a mountain. The river was babbling merrily away to the stones and in one place it was shining so brightly that it hurt his eyes. 'Whatever can that be?' he wondered. And then he saw: behind a bush, sitting on a white stone, was a maiden of the most unimaginable beauty. She had tossed her plait over her shoulder and the end of the plait was floating in the current. She had golden hair and her plait was ten fathoms long. The river was almost ablaze from this plait; it was more than his eyes could bear.

Aylyp stared in wonder at the maiden, and she looked up and said, 'Hello, Aylyp. I've been hearing about you for a long time from my nanny the fox. So, it seems that you're the biggest and the handsomest, the strongest and the luckiest of all. Will you take me for your wife?'

'What is your bride price?' he asked.[1]

'How could anyone pay for me,' she answered, 'when my papa owns all the gold in the world? Anyway, he won't give me away willingly. You'll have to kidnap me, if you are bold and smart enough.'

Aylyp was overjoyed. He climbed down from the larch, ran to where the girl was sitting, and said, 'If this is your desire, then I'm more than willing. I'll carry you off in my arms, I won't let anyone snatch you away.'

Just then the fox gave a yap. She was right there by the stone. She struck her snout against the ground, turned into a wizened little old woman, stood up and said, 'Oh, Aylyp, Aylyp, you speak idle words! You boast of your great strength and luck, but you couldn't hit me with one of your arrows!'

'You speak the truth,' he answered. 'But it's the first time I've slipped up like that.'

'Indeed. But the task ahead is going to be a good deal harder. This maiden is the daughter of Poloz the Snake. Her name is Golden Hair. Her hair is of pure gold – it chains her to the spot. She sits here washing her plait in the river, but its weight never lessens. Here, try lifting her plait – you'll see if you're strong enough to carry her away.'

Aylyp – who was indeed a man apart – hauled her plait out of the water and began winding it around his own body. He wound it round several times, then said to the maiden, 'Now, my bride, my dear Golden Hair, we are closely bound by your plait. No one can separate us!'

With these words, he lifted the maiden up in his arms and was on his way. The little old woman chased after him and pressed a pair of scissors into his hands: 'Do at least take these with you, O Nimble-Wits.'

'What do I want scissors for? I've got a knife, haven't I?' And Aylyp would have refused the scissors. But his bride, Golden Hair, said, 'Take them, they'll come in useful. *You* may not need them, but *I* will.'

So Aylyp set off through the forest. From the top of the larch, he had worked out roughly which way to go. At first he walked at a good pace, but after a while he began to find it hard going, for all his matchless strength. His bride saw that he was growing tired, and she said, 'I'll walk, and you can carry my plait. That will be easier. We must get further away, or else Papa will notice I'm gone and quick as a flash he'll pull me in.'

'What do you mean – pull you in?' asked Aylyp.

'He has the power to pull down into the earth any gold he desires. If he wants to take my hair, no one can stand in his way,' she replied.

'That remains to be seen!' said Aylyp. Golden Hair just smiled wryly.

And talking away in this manner, they walked on and on. Golden Hair kept repeating, 'We must get further away. Perhaps we can get beyond the reach of Papa's power.'

They walked and walked until they were ready to drop.

'Let's rest a little,' said Aylyp. But the moment they sat on the grass, the earth began to pull them in. Golden Hair managed to grab the scissors and cut through the hair that Aylyp had wound around him. That is what saved him. Her hair disappeared into the ground, while he remained up above. He had been pulled into the ground, but only a little way. As for his bride, she had vanished. Vanished as though she had never been. Aylyp pulled himself up out of the hollow, and thought, 'What in the world is this? My bride has been snatched from my arms and I don't even know by whom. Shame on me! No, I can't let this happen! I'll find her even if it costs me my life.'

And he began to dig where Golden Hair had been sitting. He dug for a day, and he dug for a second day, but to little avail. Aylyp had strength aplenty, but his only tools were a knife and a cap. It was hard to get much done with those!

'I'd better mark the spot and go back home for a spade.'

No sooner had he thought this than there was the fox – the fox who had lured him into the forest. She struck her snout against the ground, turned into a wizened old woman, stood up and said, 'Hey, Nimble-Wits! Decided to mine for gold or something?'

'No,' he answered. 'I'm looking for my bride.'

'Your bride,' she said, 'has been sitting for a long time in the same place as before, weeping away and washing her plait in the river. Her plait has grown. Now it's twenty fathoms long. Not even you have the strength to lift it now.'

'What should I do, Auntie?' asked Aylyp.

'That's better,' she said. 'First ask, then act. Now here's what you must do. You must go back home and live as you did before. When three years are up, if you have not forgotten your beloved Golden Hair, I'll be back for you. But if you go in search of her on your own, you'll never see her again.'

Aylyp wasn't a man who was used to waiting – he was used to getting what he wanted then and there – but this time it seemed there was nothing for it. Down at heart, he set off back home.

Oh, how those three years dragged! One spring came after another, and Aylyp took no joy in them – he just wanted them to be over. People began to wonder what was the matter; they could see that their Aylyp was no longer his usual self. His kinsfolk began asking him straight out, 'Are you ill?'

In response, Aylyp would grab five strapping men with one hand, lift them up into the air, spin them around and say, 'Ask me again and I'll hurl you the far side of that hill!'

Not once did he stop thinking about Golden Hair. She was always there in his mind. How he yearned to catch even a distant glimpse of her, but then he would remember the old woman's instructions and he dared not disobey.

But one day during the third year a girl caught Aylyp's eye. She was a young little thing, black-haired, cheerful as a blue tit. She too would gladly have done nothing but hop about and waggle her tail. This lass barged in on Aylyp's thoughts. 'Everyone else my age has wives and families by now,' he began telling himself. 'But what about me? I found a bride and let her slip through my fingers. It's a good thing no one knows about it: I'd be a laughing stock! Perhaps I should marry this black-haired lass? I can't be sure of getting that other one, while with this one I need only to pay the bride money and she's mine. Her father and mother will be more than happy, and by the look of it, she won't be shedding tears either.'

He would muse like this for some time. Then he'd remember his Golden Hair, but in a different way. It was no longer so much a matter of feeling sorry for her, more a matter of feeling galled that she'd been snatched from his arms. No, that was more than he could bear!

As soon as the third year was up, Aylyp caught sight of the fox. This time, instead of readying an arrow, he followed the fox, taking care to leave signs behind him: notches in trees, marks chiselled on stones, and the like. They came to the same little river. There he saw Golden Hair. Her plait was now twice as long. Aylyp walked up and bowed: 'Hello, my bride, my sweet Golden Hair!'

'Hello Aylyp!' she answered. 'Don't be upset that my plait has grown longer. It's much lighter now. You were clearly thinking about me very hard. Every day I could feel it becoming lighter and lighter. It was only towards the end that something seemed to go wrong. Could it be that you started forgetting? Or was there someone else who got in the way?'

And she smiled wryly as though she already knew. At first Aylyp felt ashamed. Then he made up his mind and told her everything: how his eye had been caught by the black-haired girl, how he had thought about marrying her.

Golden Hair replied, 'It is good that you've been honest with me. I believe you. We'd better leave straight away. Perhaps this time we really will manage to get beyond the reach of my father's power.'

Aylyp hauled the plait out of the river, wound it around himself and took the scissors from the nanny fox. They set off through the forest. Following the signs Aylyp had left, they made swift progress. They walked on and on until evening. When it was quite dark, Aylyp said, 'Let's climb up a tree. Maybe your father's power won't be able to reach us there.'

'You may be right,' replied Golden Hair. But how could the two of them climb the tree when they were bound together as if by a cord? 'We must cut off my plait,' said Golden Hair. 'There's no point in dragging all this weight about. It'll be plenty long enough if we leave it down to my heels.'

Aylyp was loath to. 'No,' he said. 'Better to leave it. Your hair's so fine and soft. It's lovely to stroke.'

So Aylyp unwound the plait from around his body. Golden Hair was the first to go up the tree. But she was a woman and she wasn't used to climbing trees . . . Aylyp helped her as best he could, and in the end she managed to get up into the lower branches. Aylyp quickly went up after her and hauled the whole of her plait off the ground. They climbed a little higher to where the branches were densest and settled down for the night.

'We'll stay here till dawn,' said Aylyp, and he tied his bride's plait to the branches so that she wouldn't fall to the ground if she dozed off.

'That's a good tight knot!' he said. 'Now get some sleep, and I'll keep watch. I'll wake you at dawn.'

Golden Hair, sure enough, soon fell asleep, and Aylyp began to drift off too. Then he felt so very, very sleepy that he was unable to shake it off. He rubbed his eyes, shook his head, twisted and turned, but there was nothing he could do about it. And so he nodded off. An eagle owl started flying about the tree they were in, hooting uneasily, 'Wuwhoo! Wuwhoo!' as if telling him to be on guard. But Aylyp slept on, oblivious to the world, snoring gently and dreaming that he was riding towards his tent and that his wife Golden Hair was coming out of the tent to welcome him. She was the fairest and loveliest of all – and her plait was like a golden snake, rippling as if it were alive.

At the stroke of midnight, with a sudden crackle, the branches they were lying on caught fire. Aylyp was scorched and flung to the ground. All he saw was an enormous ring of fire shining out of the earth and his bride turning into a cloud of tiny golden sparks. The sparks flew towards the ring and then were extinguished. Aylyp rushed over – but there was nothing there. And everywhere was pitch dark. He fumbled about on the ground . . . There was grass, small stones, forest debris. Then he felt the end of the plait. It was two fathoms long, perhaps more. Aylyp cheered up a little: 'She's left me a keepsake. It's a sign from her. So it seems her father's power over the plait *can* be broken.'

No sooner had he thought this than there was the fox, yapping at his feet. She struck her snout against the ground, turned into a wizened old woman, stood up and said, 'Hey, Nimble-Wits! What do you want most, the plait or the bride?'

'I want my bride with the golden plait that's twenty fathoms long,' he replied.

'Too late,' she said. 'It's thirty fathoms now.'

'Never mind about that,' said Aylyp. 'All I want is to get her back.'

'Well, why didn't you say so? Here are my last words of advice. Go home and wait three years. I won't come for you any more, you can find the way by yourself. See that you come exactly on time, not a moment early or late. And go and bow down to Grandfather Eagle Owl. Perhaps he'll sharpen your wits for you.'

With these words she vanished. When it became light, Aylyp set off back home, thinking to himself: 'Which eagle owl did she mean? There are any number of them in the forest! Which one is it I should bow to?'

He thought and thought, then he remembered: while they were in the tree, an eagle owl had been flying about very close to them and calling, 'Wuwhoo! Wuwhoo!' as if telling him to be on guard.

'She must have meant that one,' Aylyp decided, and he turned and went back to the tree. He sat there till evening, then called out, 'Grandfather Eagle Owl! Sharpen my wits! Show me the way.'

He called and he called, but nobody answered. But by then Aylyp had learned patience. He waited a second day, then called out again. And again there was no answer. Aylyp waited a third day. In the evening he called out, 'Grandfather Eagle Owl!'

And at that very moment he heard a voice from up in the tree: 'Wuwhoo! Here I am. Who's looking for me?'

Aylyp told him about what had happened and asked for his help. Eagle Owl replied, 'Wuwhoo! It will be hard, my son!'

'That doesn't matter to me,' Aylyp answered. 'I'll give it all the strength and patience I have, if only I can win back my bride.'

'Wuwhoo! I'll show you the way. Listen carefully!'

And Eagle Owl gave him instructions, step by step: 'In these parts, Poloz the Snake possesses great power. Here he is master of all the gold: he can take it away from anyone at whim. And any place which bears gold, Poloz can encircle with his ring. You can ride for three whole days, but you still won't be able to escape. There is only one place in our parts where Poloz's power has no effect. If you know how, you can flee from Poloz with your gold. But the price is high, and there's no road back.'

Aylyp began to beg him: 'Be kind. Please show me this place.'

'I cannot show you,' he answered, 'because you and I have different sight: my eyes see nothing by day, whereas yours will not see where I fly by night.'

'What can I do then?' asked Aylyp.

Grandfather Eagle Owl said, 'I'll tell you a clear sign to look out for. Make your way to the lakes. In the middle of one lake you'll see a rock that juts up like a hill. On one side there are pine trees growing, but the other three sides are entirely bare, like walls. This is the place. Whosoever reaches this rock carrying gold will find a passage leading down below the lake. And there they will be beyond Poloz's reach.'

Aylyp turned this all over in his mind – and suddenly he realized: it was Lake Itkul. He was overjoyed, and he called out, 'I know that place!'

The eagle owl said, 'Well, be on your way, and take care not to slip up.'

'Don't worry – I'll be careful.'

The eagle owl added in parting, 'Wuwhoo! Remember, once you have escaped from Poloz, there is no road back.'

Aylyp thanked Grandfather Eagle Owl and made his way home. He soon found the lake with the stone in the middle. Then he thought: 'We'll never run all that way in a day. I'll have to make a trail we can ride down.'

So Aylyp set to work clearing a trail. It is no easy task to cut your way through dense wood singlehanded, and over sixty miles of it! There were moments when he could barely keep going. Then he'd take out the plait end – at least he still had that – he'd gaze at it admiringly and stroke it, and his strength would return and he'd get back to work. The three years went by in a flash, and he only just managed to get everything ready in time.

The appointed hour came and Aylyp set out for his bride. He hauled her plait out of the river, wound it around his body – and away they ran. They reached the trail Aylyp had made, where he had left six horses ready and waiting. Aylyp mounted one horse, placed his bride on another and took the reins of the other four. They rode off at a swift gallop. Whenever their horses tired, they mounted another pair and galloped on. Ahead of them ran the fox. She sped on and on, skimming the ground, spurring the horses on, as if to say, 'Can't catch up with me!' By evening they had reached the lake. Aylyp climbed straight into a canoe and ferried his bride and the fox to the rock in the lake. As they reached the shore, a passage opened in the rock; and just as they went down into the passage, the sun sank below the horizon.

And what happened next was truly extraordinary!

No sooner had the sun set than Poloz the Snake encircled the entire lake with a triple band of fiery rings. Golden sparks skittered across the water in all directions, yet Poloz was unable to drag his daughter back up to the surface. And the eagle owl was doing what he could to make things harder for him. He perched on the rock in the lake and began hooting over and over: 'Wuwhoo! Wuwhoo! Wuwhoo!'

He would hoot like this three times, and the fiery rings would dim a little and seem to cool. And when the rings flared up again and golden sparks began skittering across the water, the eagle owl would start up his cry again.

Night after night Poloz went on trying, but to no avail. His power had no effect.

Ever since then, gold has washed up on the shore of the lake. Even in places where there are no traces of old rivers, people find gold. It only comes in little flakes and threads, never in nuggets – let alone in nuggets of any size. So how did the gold get there? Well, they say that Poloz pulled it from his daughter's plait. And there is certainly a great amount of this gold. Later, within my memory – oh, the number of quarrels over these shores that broke out between the Bashkirs and the Russians from the Kasli foundry!

And so Aylyp and his wife remained under the lake. There they had meadows, herds of horses and flocks of sheep. In other words, a life of freedom.

They say that every so often Golden Hair comes out onto the rock. People have seen her. It seems she appears at daybreak and sits there with her plait coiled around the rock like a golden snake. They say it's a wondrous sight!

Not that I've ever seen it myself. Not even once. I wouldn't want to lie to you.

PART SIX

FOLKTALE COLLECTIONS FROM THE SOVIET PERIOD

During the ten years immediately after the Revolution, different approaches to the study of folklore were allowed to exist side by side. Members of the 'historical school' analysed the heroic songs known as byliny primarily as reflections of historical reality. Members of the 'Finnish school' tried to reconstruct the history of individual tales by considering both historical and geographical factors and comparing all available versions in different languages; it was a member of this school, N. P. Andreyev, who first translated Antti Aarne's index of tale-types into Russian. Still more important than the historical or Finnish schools were the Formalists, who, as their name implies, were concerned primarily with matters of form. Vladimir Propp's Morphology of the Folktale is the one work of Soviet folktale scholarship to have been widely translated and have been incorporated into international literary discourse.

From the mid 1930s, however, official Soviet attitudes towards folklore grew ominously contradictory. On the one hand, in his keynote speech at the first Congress of Soviet Writers in 1934, no less a figure than Maksim Gorky stressed both the artistic value and the 'life optimism' of folk art and literature. This led to massive official support for the collection of folklore. In the words of Felix J. Oinas, 'the executive committee of the Moscow Oblast organized wide collecting of folklore in all of its area in 1934–35. Local centers of folklore were founded in numerous districts [. . .] The local intelligentsia, university students, and students of trade schools were mobilized for active collecting. The influential party papers, such as Pravda and others, published both appeals for collecting and samples of collected materials.'¹ On the other hand, a great deal of folk literature was, in reality, unacceptable to the Soviet authorities. Some was obscene, some religious, and some simply frivolous. Just as, during the nineteenth century, Afanasyev was held responsible for the anti-clerical humour that imbues many of his tales, so Soviet folklorists ran into difficulties because of the genuinely spiritual attitudes underlying much of the art and literature they collected.²

We have already seen that both Onchukov and Zelenin were able to publish only a little of what they collected after the 1917 Revolution. It is clear that some of the later, probably no less gifted, collectors did not even dare to note down ideologically suspect material. Nevertheless, if only because of Russia's size and backwardness, peasant culture survived tenaciously. Great resources were allocated to the collection of folklore, and many folklorists were extremely dedicated. In spite of everything, they collected many interesting tales.

ERNA VASILYEVNA
POMERANTSEVA

(1899–1980)

*During a career that lasted more than five decades, Pomerant-
seva published over 300 books and articles. She taught in
various higher education institutes in Moscow and continued
to lead folklore-collecting expeditions until her final years.*

The Cat with the Golden Tail

Well then, once upon a time there lived an old man and an old woman, and they had three daughters. And there, in that forest beyond the mountain, lived a bear, and the bear had a cat with a golden tail. And one day the bear said, 'O cat with a golden tail, find me a bride!'

So the cat with the golden tail set off to search for a bride. He began walking about the garden outside these people's hut, wandering about among their cabbages. One of the girls caught sight of him through the window. 'Papa!' she shouted. 'There's a cat with a golden tail! He's running about the kitchen garden!'

'Run and catch him! Run and catch him!'

The girl rushed off after him. The cat ran down between two rows of vegetables; the girl ran after him. The cat ran along a path; the girl ran along the path, too. The cat jumped over a ditch; the girl jumped over the ditch after him. The cat ran into a hut; the girl ran into the hut after him.

The bear was lying on a bed. 'What a fine wife you've brought me!' he said. 'Now we can live well! You, my dear mistress, can give me food and water, and I'll bring you firewood. And here are some keys for you. You may go into *this* barn, and you may go into *this* barn, too – but don't go into *that* barn or I'll kill you.'

So the girl went into the first barn and into the second barn. The first barn was full of grain, and the second was full of meat, fatback and honey. She really wanted to go into the third barn, just for a look. She went in and found three big barrels. She opened the first barrel and dipped a finger inside to see what was there. She looked at her finger and saw it had turned to gold. The vat was full of gold – golden water. The girl felt frightened. She tied a piece of rag round her finger and sat down to do some sewing. Then Misha the bear came home. He saw her bandaged finger and asked, 'Why, mistress, have you bandaged your finger?'

'I cut it. I was slicing noodles and I cut my finger.'

'Let me have a look at it!'

'Ow, it hurts! It hurts!'

'Let me have a look at it!'

He pulled off the bandage and saw her gold finger. 'So you went into the third barn, did you?' He cut her up straight away, then threw her into the third barn, just behind the vat.

Now the bear was on his own again. 'O cat with a golden tail, find me a bride! O cat with a golden tail, find me a bride!'

'Stop killing the brides. I won't look for you unless you stop.'

'O cat with a golden tail, find me a bride!'

'Oh, all right then.'

So the cat began walking about the old man's vegetable garden, wandering about among the cabbages. One of the girls caught sight of him through the window. 'Papa! Mama!' she shouted. 'It's the cat with the golden tail!'

'Run and catch him! Run and catch him!'

The girl rushed off after the cat. The cat ran down between two rows of vegetables; the girl ran after him. The cat ran along a path; the girl ran along the path, too. The cat jumped over a ditch; the girl jumped over the ditch after him. The cat ran into a hut; the girl ran into the hut after him.

The bear was lying on a bed. 'What a fine wife you've brought me!' he said. 'Now we can live well! You, my dear mistress, can give me food and water, and I'll bring you firewood. And here are some keys for you. You may go into *this* barn, and you may go into *this* barn too – but don't go into *that* barn or I'll kill you.'

So the girl went into the first barn and into the second barn. The first barn was full of grain, and the second was full of meat, fatback and honey. She really wanted to go into the third barn, just for a look. She went in and found three big barrels. She opened the first barrel and dipped a finger inside to see

what was there. She looked at her finger and saw it had turned
to gold. The vat was full of gold – golden water. The girl felt
frightened. She tied a piece of rag round her finger and sat
down to do some sewing. Then Misha the bear came home. He
saw her bandaged finger and asked, 'Why, mistress, have you
bandaged your finger?'

'I cut it. I was slicing noodles and I cut my finger.'

'Let me have a look at it!'

'Ow, it hurts! It hurts!'

'Let me have a look at it!'

He pulled off the bandage and saw her gold finger. 'So you
went into the third barn, did you?' He cut her up straight away,
then threw her into the third barn, just behind the vat.

Now the bear was a widower again. He felt lonely. 'O cat
with a golden tail, find me a wife! O cat with a golden tail, find
me a bride!'

'No, I'm not going. Why do you keep killing them?'

'I won't do it any more. I'll even love them and cherish
them.'

The cat went off to the old man's garden and began wandering about among the carrots. The third daughter saw him and
shouted out, 'Papa! Mama! It's the cat with the golden tail!'

'Run and catch him! Run and catch him!'

The girl rushed off after the cat. The cat ran down between
two rows of vegetables; the girl ran after him. The cat ran along
a path; the girl ran along the path, too. The cat ran down a furrow; the girl ran down the furrow, too. The cat jumped over a
ditch; the girl jumped over the ditch after him. The cat ran into
a hut; the girl ran into the hut after him.

The bear was lying on a bed. 'What a fine wife you've brought
me!' he said. 'Now we can live well! You, my dear mistress, can
keep the stove going and cook for me, and I'll bring you firewood. And here are some keys for you. You may go into *this*
barn, and you may go into *this* barn too – but don't go into *that*
barn or I'll kill you.' And the bear went off to collect firewood.

The girl went into the first barn and into the second barn.
The first barn was full of grain, and the second was full of
meat, fatback and honey. After that, she wanted very much to

go into the third barn, to see what was there. She turned the key in the lock and saw the vats. She dipped a stick into one vat and it turned to gold in her hand. She dipped a stick into the second vat and saw that it had turned to silver. She dipped a stick into the third vat and it began to move. Then she looked behind the vat. 'Oh,' she thought, 'there are my sisters. They've been killed.' She dipped the stick into the fourth vat and it stopped moving – the water in this vat was the water of death. And so the girl went to one of her sisters, put her head back on her neck and sprinkled her with the water of death. Her sister's head grew back on, but she was still dead. Then she sprinkled her with the water of life – and her sister came to life again.

'One way or another, I'm going to rescue you. I'll bake some pancakes and put you in the basket with them. I'll get the bear to take the basket to our home and put it down in the garden. I'll tell him our Mama's died and that the pancakes are for the wake.'

The bear got back home and found his wife baking pancakes. 'Oh, what a splendid mistress I have now! What have you been doing with yourself?'

'Oh, this and that. You can see: I've been everywhere and I've found everything I need.'

'You didn't go into the third barn, did you?'

'No, I don't know what you've got there.'

'Give me something to eat.'

'First take this basket of pancakes. Our mother's died and we must remember her. Take this basket and throw it down in the garden.'

'All right.'

The girl put her sister into the basket and covered her up with pancakes and little pies. 'So, off you go. The basket's full. But it's a gift for the wake – mind don't you go eating any of it yourself. I'm climbing up onto the roof to keep an eye on you better!'

The bear slung the basket onto his back, but it was heavy and he felt tired. 'A little pastry would be tasty,' he said aloud, meaning to sit down for a while on a tree stump. 'Perhaps I'll try one little pie!'[1]

But the sister inside the basket said, 'Get up, get up, you lazy bear! Don't you dare touch the food you bear!'

'Sharp eyes, sharp eyes, I'll leave the pies,' said the bear. He had gone a long way and he was surprised that his wife could still see him.

In the end the bear got to the edge of the garden and threw down the basket of pies beside one of the outbuildings. The dogs leaped out at the bear. The bear ran into the forest, and the girl jumped out of the basket and ran back into her home.

The bear got back home. There was his wife – still hard at work. 'My Papa's died,' she said. 'Now we have to remember him, too.'

'All right. Just say when you're ready – and I'll take the basket.'

The girl baked some more pancakes. 'All right, Mikhail Mikhailovich. Here's the basket. But don't you dare touch the food you bear, don't you dare try a single pie. I'm climbing up onto the roof – to keep an eye on you better!'

The bear slung the basket onto his back, but it was heavy and he felt tired. 'A little pastry would be tasty,' he said, meaning to sit down on a tree stump. 'Perhaps I'll try one little pie!'

But the sister inside the basket said, 'Get up, get up, you lazy bear! Don't you dare touch the food you bear!'

'Sharp eyes, sharp eyes, I'll leave the pies,' said the bear. The bear had gone a long way and he was surprised that his wife could still see him.

In the end the bear got to the edge of the garden and threw down the basket beside one of the outbuildings. Bits of pancake and pie flew in every direction. The girl leaped out of the basket and the dogs leaped out at the bear.

On the third day the girl said to the bear, 'Now my brother's died. We have to remember him.'

'All right. Bake the pancakes and pies and I'll take the basket.'

Now in their yard they had a learned cock. The girl said to this cock, 'Once I'm in the basket you must cover me up with the pancakes and pies. And in return I'll give you some grain.' First, though, she took a pestle, dressed it in her own clothes and put it on top of the roof. Then she got into the basket and the cock covered her up with a layer of pancakes and pies. (And she'd taken some of the gold.)

The bear took the basket and set off. He walked a long way and he began to feel tired. 'A little pastry would be tasty,' he said. 'Let me just try one little pie!'

But the girl said, 'Lazy bear, lazy bear! Don't you dare touch the food you bear.'

'Sharp eyes, sharp eyes!' said the bear. 'I'll leave the pies.'

In the end the bear got to the edge of the garden and threw down the basket beside one of the outbuildings. The dogs leaped out after him. He ran all the way to his hut. And there, up on the roof, was his wife! 'What are you doing, up there so high? I haven't touched a single pie!' She went on standing there; she didn't say a word. 'Get down off the roof, I'm telling you. Get down or I'll beat you!' Still not a word. The bear got very angry. He took a big pole and poked it at her. The pestle began to roll – bump, bump, bump – down off the roof. The bear tried to stop it. He tried to stand his wife up again. 'Careful, my dear! You'll be smashed to pieces!' But the mortar fell down from the roof, too – and went smack into the bear's snout. That was the end of the bear, and it's the end of this story, too.

IRINA VALERYANOVNA
KARNAUKHOVA

(1901–59)

Karnaukhova was born in Kiev; her father was a railwayman, her mother had worked as a journalist. In Petrograd after the Revolution, Karnaukhova worked briefly as a literary translator. In 1921 she moved to Moscow, where she studied in the Institute of the Word, a school for writers set up under the auspices of the Commissariat of Enlightenment. Among the teachers at this institute were Olga Ozarovskaya and the twin brothers Yury and Boris Sokolov, who had published an important collection of folktales and songs in 1915. In the summer of 1923, Karnaukhova was one of the many guests of the legendarily hospitable poet Maksimilian Voloshin, at his home in the village of Koktebel in the Crimea; there Karnaukhova often narrated folktales. Between 1926 and 1932 she took part in several major expeditions to the north of European Russia; the tales she collected were published in 1934 with an introduction by Yury Sokolov. This collection stands out both for the interest of the tales themselves and for the vividness with which Karnaukhova describes her informants.

During the second half of her life, Karnaukhova worked as a children's writer. Some of her work was original, while some drew on themes from folklore.

Mishka the Bear and Myshka the Mouse

Once there was a man who had married for a second time. He had a daughter, and his wife had a daughter, too. The wife took against her husband's daughter. She nagged and nagged; she was pestering the life out of her. And she gave her husband a hard time, too.

'Take that girl away into the forest,' she said. 'Let there be neither sight nor sound of her in this hut.'

The woman packed a basket for her stepdaughter. It was full of all kinds of horrible things – dirt and sand instead of food and drink. And then the old man had to take his daughter to a hut in the forest. He took her there in a sleigh and left her there on her own. The girl opened the basket and felt surprised by her stepmother's kindness. There in the basket were all kinds of good things: butter and buckwheat and cheesecakes. (The dirt and sand had been turned into good food.) The girl lit the stove and began to make herself some buckwheat porridge. Then a little mouse popped out of a hole and said, 'Give me a little porridge, girl!'

The girl gave the little mouse some porridge. The mouse ate, wiped her face with her tail and said, 'Thank you, my beauty. And now I shall do you a good turn. Soon a bear will come to this hut and play blindman's bluff with you. Don't be afraid, but just hide under the floor. I'll pretend to be you.'

The girl agreed. Evening drew in. The bear came in and said, 'Greetings, my beauty! Let's play blindman's bluff!'

The girl blindfolded the bear and hid beneath the floor. And the little mouse began scampering about, knocking against the floorboards. The bear chased after her. He didn't give up easily.

'You're very smart,' he said in the end. 'You're too quick for me. I've had enough.'

The girl came up from under the floor and removed the bear's blindfold. The bear gave her a whole basket of silver. And off he went – back into the forest. In the morning Masha made some more porridge, ate some herself and gave some to the little mouse. The mouse said, 'This time the bear will go under the floor. You must sit on top of the stove. I'll do the same as I did yesterday.'

In the evening the bear came in.

'Greetings, my beauty! Let's play blindman's bluff! If I catch you, I'll eat you. If I don't catch you, I'll give you some gold.'

The girl blindfolded the bear and then sat on top of the stove. And the little mouse began scampering about, knocking against the floor. The bear crept under the floor. He didn't give up easily.

'You're very cunning,' he said in the end. 'I've had enough, my beauty. You've worn me out.'

The girl removed the bear's blindfold. The bear piled up a great heap of gold for her in one corner of the hut.

In the morning Masha made some more porridge, ate some herself and gave some to the little mouse. The mouse said, 'Today the bear will climb up onto the stove. I'll pin you up on the wall. And then I'll pretend to be you.'

In the evening the bear came in.

'Greetings, my clever one! Let's play blindman's bluff! If I catch you, I'll eat you. If I don't catch you, I'll reward you well.'

The girl blindfolded the bear. The little mouse pinned her up on the wall and began to play. The little mouse climbed up onto the bench – and the bear climbed up onto the bench, too. The little mouse hid in a corner – and the bear was right there on her heels. Then the bear climbed up onto the stove to rest.

'You're very cunning,' he said. 'I've had enough, my beauty. This time you really have worn me out.'

The girl removed the bear's blindfold. The bear gave her some perfect pearls.

*

Meanwhile the stepmother was telling her old man what to do:

'Go on then. Go into the forest and bring back your daughter's braids!'

The old man drove off into the forest. He found his daughter alive – and the hut full of all kinds of good things! He packed them all onto the sleigh.

The stepmother was baking pancakes for the girl's wake. She could hear the knocking and rattling of the old man's sleigh. And then the dog started barking:

'Woof, woof, woof! The old man's daughter's all clothed in gold! The woman's daughter's dressed all in dirt!'

And there was the old man's daughter with all her silver and gold and her perfect pearls. The stepmother was furious.

'Take my own daughter to that hut!' she yelled.

She packed her daughter a basket full of cheesecakes and butter. The old man took her to the hut and left her there on her own. The girl opened her basket. There was nothing in it but dirt and sand. The girl started trying to make porridge. After a while she had a little taste. Out jumped the little mouse.

'Give me some porridge, girl!'

The girl slapped the little mouse on the forehead. The little mouse ran back to her hole. Along came the bear.

'Greetings, girl! Let's play blindman's bluff! If I catch you, I'll eat you. If I don't catch you, I'll reward you well.'

The girl blindfolded the bear – and off she ran. She ran into a corner – and the bear ran into the corner too. She jumped onto the bench – and the bear jumped onto the bench too. After a while the bear caught her, skinned her, hung her skin up on a rail and ate up everything else. He even gnawed at her bones.

The old man came to fetch the girl – and all he could do was put her bones in a sack.

The girl's mother was baking pastries stuffed with fish. She was preparing a festive meal, but then the dog started barking:

'Woof, woof, woof! The old man's daughter's all clothed in gold! The woman's daughter's dressed all in dirt!'

The woman rushed outside. She saw the bones and howled. And that's the end of the story.

Jack Frost

Once upon a time there was a widower who had taken a second wife. He had a daughter of his own, and his wife had a daughter, too. Well, everyone knows what it's like to live with a stepmother. Do too much – you get beaten. Do too little – you get beaten. Do things just right – and you still get beaten. Well, the unkind woman said to her husband, 'Take that daughter of yours away into the forest. Yes – into the forest and into the frost.'

The man wasn't very happy about this, but what could he do? He took his daughter off into the forest. He took her into the forest, left her beneath a bush and went back home. Somewhere up above her the girl could hear Jack Frost. He was creaking and cracking among the twigs and branches. The girl said to him, 'Please, Jack Frost! Don't creak and don't crack so, Jack Frost! I've no belt on my waist, no shoes on my feet and no shirt on my back, O Jack Frost.'

Jack Frost began to feel sorry for her. He turned milder. Once again the girl said, 'Please, Jack Frost! Don't creak and don't crack so, Jack Frost! I've no belt on my waist, no shoes on my feet and no shirt on my back, O Jack Frost.'

Jack Frost turned milder still. The girl repeated, 'Please, Jack Frost! Don't creak and don't crack so, Jack Frost! I've no belt on my waist, no shoes on my feet and no shirt on my back, O Jack Frost.'

At that, Jack Frost turned as mild as mild can be. He even threw the girl a chest full of fine, warm clothes: a shirt, a marten-fur coat, a silk shawl. She put on all he had given her, then sat there in the warm.

In the morning the woman said to her husband, 'Well, now you must go and bring back your daughter's bones.'

The man went off into the forest and found his daughter alive. She was sitting on the ground, surrounded by chests and trunks. He brought her back home, along with everything she'd been given. The stepmother was furious. 'My own daughter must go and get a rich dowry, too!' she yelled. And she told her husband to take her daughter into the forest.

The man left the girl beneath the same bush in the forest. Along came Jack Frost. The girl said, 'Stop that racket, Jack Frost! I've no belt on my waist, no shoes on my feet and no shirt on my back, Jack Frost.' (In fact her mother had given her some warm felt boots and wrapped her up tight in a fur coat and a shawl.) This angered Jack Frost. He began to creak and crack and snap more fiercely than ever. The girl said, 'Stop that, Jack Frost! Stop that racket, Jack Frost! I've no belt on my waist, no shoes on my feet and no shirt on my back, Jack Frost.'

Jack Frost grew still more angry. He turned as fierce as fierce can be. And the girl froze to death.

In the morning the woman said to her husband, 'Well, now you must go and fetch my daughter, along with all her chests and trunks full of fine clothes.'

The man set off. He found the dead girl. She couldn't speak, but her bones were still cracking and snapping.

Snake-Man

Twelve young girls went to bathe in the lake. Eleven laid their smocks together; the twelfth flung her smock to one side. Then they all bathed. Eleven came out, put their smocks on and left. The twelfth found a huge snake on her smock.

The girl felt scared. The snake said, 'I won't leave your smock till you promise to marry me.'

What could the girl do? She promised to marry him.

That evening the girl and her mother closed all the doors and windows and put out the fire. They sat and waited, wondering what would happen. The snake came. It slithered round all the doors and windows, hiss-hiss hissing, hissing like the rain. They sat there trembling: were there any chinks or holes anywhere?

On the second evening the girl and her mother closed all the doors and windows and put out the fire. They sat and waited, wondering what would happen. The snake came. It slithered round all the doors and windows, hiss-hiss hissing, hissing like the rain. They sat there trembling: were there any chinks or holes anywhere?

And it was the same on the third evening – the girl and her mother closed all the doors and windows and put out the fire. They sat and waited, wondering what would happen. The snake came. It slithered round all the doors and windows, hiss-hiss hissing, hissing like the rain. They sat there trembling: were there any chinks or holes anywhere?

But the girl felt so scared that she said, 'Let me go, Mama. It's better I marry him.'

And so she married him. But really her husband was a man – a man under a spell. In the daytime he was a water snake. In the evening she would call him, 'As a snake, leave the lake! Be a man, on dry land!'[1]

He would appear as a snake, then turn into a young man.

It was not long before they had two children. One more – and the snake would have remained a man for good. But the mother pitied her daughter for being married to a snake. She asked, 'How do you call him up?'

'As a snake, leave the lake!' said the daughter. But she didn't say the next words – they were secret.

The mother took a sharp scythe, went to the bank and called out, 'As a snake, leave the lake!'

Out of the lake came the snake. And the mother went and chopped his head off. The daughter came running – but it was too late. She called her children and sent them away as white swans. And she herself turned into a grey cuckoo forever.

The Herder of Hares

There was once a herder. He wandered about all the time singing songs. And in the same place there was a landlord. He knew
sorcerer's spells. Something about the herder enraged him.
Why was the herder always singing? What made him so happy?

The landlord went and said to the herder, 'Come and herd
for me, herder!'

'All right.'

'You must take good care of my livestock. If you succeed, I
agree to pay you a hundred roubles. But if you fail, then I cut
three strips from your back.'

'That's all right by me,' said the herder.

The landlord then gave him a hundred hares. 'Take them out
into the forest to feed – but I want them all back home by this
evening. Lose a single hare and I cut a strip from your back –
and you can go to the devil's mother without a coin in your
purse.'

'Very well,' said the herder. 'But don't be too hasty, your
Excellency. Don't be too quick with your curses.'

And so he drove the hares into the forest. Off they all ran,
every which way. All you could see was their tails. But the
herder just lay down and slept. You could hear the son of a
bitch whistling through his nose and snoring.

Evening set in. The herder awoke, sat up, took out his pipe
and began to sing:

> *Hares, hares, hares,*
> *Eating without a care –*
> *Here, here, here!*

The hares all came running out of the forest. The herder gathered them all together and drove them back home. The landlord turned black with fury: 'How have you done that, you wretch? Well then, go and sleep now – and tomorrow I'll give you a real task.'

In the morning he gave the herder two hundred hares: 'If you bring them all back, good luck to you! But lose a single hare and I cut a strip from your back – and off you go without any pay.'

The herder drove the hares into the forest. But the landlord had a word with his wife. 'This herder,' he said, 'is going to bring us to rack and ruin. He brings back every last hare. And he never stops singing. Go and buy one of the hares from him.'

His wife washed and put on her very best dress. And off she rode into the forest. She rode up to the herder but found him asleep. He was whistling through his nose.

'Greetings, young man,' she said, 'but what are you doing here?'

'I'm herding my little hares, my beauty!'

'Oh, can't you sell me just one of your little hares? City dwellers love what comes from the wild.'

'My hares, young lady, are forbidden hares. They're not for sale.'

'What then do you bid me do?'

'You must agree, my beauty, to sleep with me.'

The woman was young, the herder was handsome, and her husband was very severe. And he had ordered her to pay whatever price the herder asked. She agreed. And so they took joy in each other. And the herder said, 'You're a sweet lady. Here's a little hare for you, in return for our pleasure.' And he gave her a little hare. She felt very glad and tucked the hare away in her bosom. And he lay down and went back to sleep – the sweet young lady had tired him.

Evening set in. The herder awoke, sat up, took out his pipe and began to sing:

> Hares, hares, hares,
> Eating without a care –
> Here, here, here!

The hares all came running out of the forest. The one he had given the young lady came, too. The herder set off back home. The landlord was waiting in the gateway. He counted the hares: every last hare was present. What could he do?

In the morning he gave the herder three hundred hares. But as soon as the herder had left, he had a word with his young daughter. 'Go to him in the forest, Masha. Do whatever it takes to get one of the hares from him!'

His young daughter dressed herself up and set off. She walked and walked until she came to the forest. There was the herder, whistling through his nose.

'What are you doing here, young man?' she asked.

'I'm herding hares, young lady.'

'Won't you show me just one of your hares?'

'Why not? Money's a key to every door.'

'How much do you need?'

'Only my hares are not money hares. They're forbidden hares.'

'What do you bid me do?'

'To see one of my hares, you must lift your dress to your knee.' She lifted her dress. He let out a whistle and a hare ran up.

'Oh what a darling little hare! Mayn't I hold it in my hands?'

'To hold it between your hands, you must lift your dress to your belly button.'

She felt ashamed. But what could she do? She was afraid of her father. She lifted her dress to her belly button. Then she said, 'But mayn't I hold it close?'

'To hold it close, you must lift your dress to your breasts.'

She was ashamed, but what could she do? She lifted her dress up to her breasts. There between her breasts was a birthmark. He saw her birthmark. But he didn't force himself on her. No, he just let her go very politely.

Evening set in. The herder awoke, sat up, took out his pipe and began to sing:

> *Hares, hares, hares,*
> *Eating without a care –*
> *Here, here, here!*

The hares all came running out of the forest. And the hare the daughter was holding came, too. The herder drove all the hares back home. The landlord was waiting in the gateway. He counted the hares: every last hare was present. He felt angrier than ever.

In the morning he gave the herder five hundred hares. 'Bring them all back – and we'll settle up. Lose even one – and it's a strip from your back.'

As soon as the herder had left, the landlord changed his clothes, put on a wig, took a skinny old mare and set off for the forest. He found the herder asleep. He woke him.

'What are you doing here?'

'Herding hares.'

'Will you sell me a hare?'

'How much will you give me?'

'A hundred roubles.'

'No.'

'A thousand roubles.'

'No.'

'What do you want for it then?'

'Just kiss your mare under her tail.'

What could the landlord do? He didn't want to pay this herder his wages. And so he lifted the mare's tail and kissed her on the arse. His face got all smeared with horseshit. But the herder gave him his hare, and so off he went, feeling very pleased with himself. But the herder just played on his pipe and the hares all came running. He drove them back home and found the landlord white with fury.

'The day before yesterday,' said the landlord, 'you were one hare short.'

'What day was that? The day your wife and I—'

'Alright, alright . . . but yesterday—'

'The day your daughter lifted—'

'Alright, alright . . . but today—'

'The day you—'

'All right, you son of a bitch. Let me give you your wages.'

And so the herder outwitted the landlord. And he went on singing. Yes, he felt merrier than ever.[1]

A Cock and Bull Story

There once lived three brothers. They went into the forest to fell trees. They chopped and chopped, and it grew late. They wanted to kindle a fire, but they had no light. And so they climbed up a fir tree, and one of them caught sight of a light.

The eldest brother said, 'All right, I'll go and ask for a light.'

So off he went. He came to a blazing fire. The forest spirit was lying beside it. And there were some foxes and pine martens and a big heap of logs.

'Give me a light,' he said.

'Tell me a cock and bull story,' said the forest spirit, 'and I'll give you a flame. But if you can't speak true baloney, then I'll tear a strip from your back.'

'Once my dad had a worker who loaded forty cartloads of hay.'

'Fool! I've loaded forty-one cartloads myself.'

He cut a strip from the brother's back and sent him back where he'd come from.

Then the second brother went to ask for a light. He walked and he walked and he came to the bonfire.

'Give me a light,' he said.

'Tell me a cock and bull story,' said the forest spirit, 'and I'll give you a flame. But if you can't speak true baloney, then I'll tear a strip off your back.'

'My dad had a worker once, and he chopped a hundred cartloads of logs.'

'Fool! I've chopped a hundred and one cartloads myself.'

He cut a strip from the brother's back and sent him back where he'd come from.

Then it was the turn of the youngest brother. So off he went. He came to a blazing fire. There was the forest spirit – the *leshy* – lying beside it. And there were some foxes and pine martens and a big heap of logs.

'Greetings, fellow! Give me a light!'

'If you tell me a cock and bull story,' he said, 'I'll give you a flame. But if you can't speak true baloney, then I'll tear a strip off your back.'

'I'll tell you your story,' said the youngest brother. 'Only don't interrupt me. If you interrupt once, then the foxes and martens are mine.'[1]

'Very well.'

'And so we were all living together – thrice-nine brothers by the name of Ivan, a sister with no name at all, and our mother Malanya. A father was born to us – the size of a mouse, with a nose like a house.[2] And so off we went to christen our father. I mounted our mare, took her tail between my teeth – and off I rode. (*The forest spirit remains silent. He doesn't interrupt.*) We came to a river. My mare almost flew – and tore her belly in two. Her front legs were on the far shore, and her rear legs where they had been before. I cut off a twig, cleaned it and sewed up my mare's belly. And on I rode. Someone told me that, over the seas, flies and mosquitoes were dear and calves were cheap. So I caught twenty hundredweight of flies and mosquitoes. Then I swapped the flies for calves and the mosquitoes for bulls. I set off back home with them all. I drove them as far as the sea, but there wasn't a boat to be seen – neither sail nor steam. I took one bull by the tail, whirled it, whirled it and hurled it across the waters. And I did the same with the others. I hung on tight to the last calf and ended up on this shore too. I looked at my old mare and saw the twig had grown into a fir tree. It had grown and grown and grown right up into the sky. And so into the sky I climbed. There I saw that the saints were all barefoot. They were lying about on the grass, eating their own tears and afraid to walk. Well, I took pity on them. I began killing my bulls, making shoes from their hides and lugging them high into the skies. I shoed the last saint – and began to feel faint. I wanted to get back down again, so I made a rope out of rain. (*As for the forest spirit, he doesn't say a word. He doesn't interrupt.*) I was slipping down, but then a storm got up. It shook the rope and it broke my bones. I swung, swung, swung – and fell into a bog. I fell so deep that all you could see of me was my hair. A wolf took to walking over my head. Then it was weaving its nest there. Well, I began waving my hands. I waved and waved and I waved them free. I grabbed the wolf by the tail, and he pulled me out. (*The forest spirit doesn't dare say a word.*) I ripped open the wolf's tail – and there I found chests and caskets and all kinds of papers. And one of these papers says that the *leshy* here in this very forest owes my father one thousand roubles.'

'That's a lie! That's a lie!' said the forest spirit. (He couldn't bear it.) 'That's a lie.'

The youngest brother collected the foxes and martens, took a light and made off.

A Marvellous Wonder

Once there lived a rich merchant. He was about to travel abroad, to trade there. And he asked his young wife, 'What shall I bring back for you as a present?'

'I've got all I need already. But if you want to amuse me, then bring me a marvellous wonder.'

'All right,' he said.

And off he went. Now this wife of his had a friend, a young steward who was her lover. They had been waiting for the merchant to leave, so they could love each other. She had asked for a marvellous wonder so that her husband would have to search for a long time and not come back home. As soon as he left, they began eating and drinking and enjoying themselves in every way. They knew no shame, yes, they forgot it completely.

The merchant made a great deal of money. He went to look for a present for his young wife. He looked and looked, but there was nothing she did not have already. Nowhere could he find a marvellous wonder.

Sad as sad can be, he was walking down a street. Towards him came an old man.

'Why so sad, merchant?'

'Because my wife asked me to bring her a marvellous wonder – but where can I find one?'

'That's no sorrow. I can sort one out for you straight away.' The old man led him into his hut.

'See who's walking round the yard?' he said.

'There's a goose walking round the yard,' said the merchant.

'Hey, goose!' said the old man. 'Come in out of the yard.'

In out of the yard came the goose.

'Hey, goose!' said the old man. 'Get into the pan.'

The goose got into the pan.

The old man lit the stove and put the pan into the oven.

'Hey, goose!' said the old man. 'Roast yourself nicely for me.'

The goose roasted itself till it was crisp and brown.

'Well then, young man, sit down and have supper with me. Only don't throw the bones under the table. Pile them up into a single pile.'

The merchant sucked the bones clean and put them one by one on the table. When they'd finished, the old man said, 'Up you get, goose!'

The goose stood up, whole and hale.

'Hey, goose, out you go into the yard!'

Out into the yard went the goose.

'This is truly a marvellous wonder,' said the merchant. 'How much do you want for it, old man?'

'Nothing at all. Just take it home and say to your wife, "I've brought you a marvellous wonder, a wonderful goose. The name of the goose is 'A lesson for a young wife'".'

Off went the merchant. He got back home and said to his wife, 'I've brought you a marvellous wonder.'

'What kind of a wonder?'

'A wonderful goose. Its name is "A lesson for a young wife".'

Along came the goose.

'Hey, goose!' said the old man. 'Get into the pan.'

The goose got into the pan.

'Hey, goose!' said the old man. 'Roast yourself in the stove.'

The goose roasted itself. They took it out of the stove and ate it.

'Up you get, goose!'

The goose stood up.

'Hey, goose, out you go into the yard!'

Out into the yard went the goose.

Then the merchant went off to his store. Along came the wife's lover. They loved each other. They enjoyed themselves. Then the lover said, 'I'd like something to eat.'

'Now I'm going to give you a marvellous wonder – a meal you will marvel at.'

The wife called out through the window, 'Hey, goose, come in out of the yard!'

In came the goose.

'Hey, goose, get into the pan!'

But the goose didn't want to get into the pan. The wife thought her friend would laugh at her. She got cross and hit the goose with the pan. And then she and the pan were stuck fast, stuck fast to the goose.

'Hey, friend!' she called out. 'Unstick me!'

Her friend tried to pull her away, but he couldn't. He was stuck fast, stuck fast to the wife.

'Goose!' she called out. 'Dear lesson for a young wife, release us! Let us go free now.'

But the goose went out into the yard, and they went out after it. They were running along behind it, calling out, 'A lesson for a young wife! A lesson for a young wife!'

Just then the merchant came along and saw his wife and the young steward stuck fast together.

'Hm!' he said. 'Who'd have thought it? A lesson for a young wife!'

He pulled them apart and gave them a good thrashing. He gave them such a thrashing that they quite forgot about having any more fun together.

So there you are – a lesson for a young wife!

FYODOR VIKTOROVICH TUMILEVICH

(1910–79)

Fyodor Tumilevich lived most of his life in Rostov, on the mouth of the Don. A teacher of folklore in the university and the teacher-training institute, he published several volumes of the folktales and folksongs of the Don Cossacks.

The Snake and the Fisherman

There were once two fishermen who were neighbours. They caught fish and sold them, but then there were no more fish and they still had to find a way to live. Their wives kept saying, 'Go on, go and hire yourselves out as labourers!'

In the end they listened to their wives and went off to look for work. They walked for a day, and for a second day, and for a third day. They were tired of walking, but there was no work anywhere. They looked and looked, but no work could they find. They came to one small village, spent the night there and went on their way. On they went through the steppe. It was a hot day and they felt thirsty. They saw a stream, went up to it, drank their fill and went on further. It was not long after noon; the sun was high in the sky.

They felt tired and hungry.

'I'm tired. I can't go on any further,' said one of them. 'Let's have a rest.'

'No, you rest if you like – but I'll go on to the next village and ask for some bread.'

So one fisherman went on into the village, while the other stayed where he was. He saw a stone and sat down on it. But lying underneath this stone was a snake. The fisherman was squashing this snake. He heard a voice from underneath the stone, 'Set me free, fisherman!'

The man felt sorry for the snake. He got to his feet and lifted up the stone. The snake slid out and wrapped itself round his neck. It was about to bite him, but he asked, 'What are you doing, snake? People repay good with good, but you want to repay good with evil. Don't bite me.'

The snake slid back down onto the ground and said, 'Let's go on our way, man. If we meet anyone, we'll ask what they do: how do *they* repay good?'

The man agreed, and they set off together. After a while, they met a bull coming towards them. The fisherman said to the bull, 'Tell us. How do people repay good?'

The bull replied, 'People repay good with evil. I plough my master's land for him, I sow it and I fetch water for him. But when the time comes, my master will slaughter me, cook my meat, take off my hide, spread it out on the ground and walk on me.'

'Well, fisherman,' said the snake. 'You must let me bite you.'

'No, snake, let's go on further.'

They went on. After a while, they met a horse. The fisherman said to the horse, 'Tell us, horse. How do people repay good? The snake and I have been arguing. I say that good is repaid with good, but the snake says it is repaid with evil.'

The horse listened, then replied, 'I've served my master for twenty years. I'm old now. He doesn't feed me any longer, and he threatens to slaughter me and skin me. You're wrong – people repay good with evil.'

'Well, fisherman,' said the snake. 'Did you hear what the horse says? I must bite you now.'

'No, snake, let's ask a third time.'

After a while, they saw a donkey coming towards them. They said to the donkey, 'Tell us, donkey. How do people repay good?'

The donkey replied, 'With evil.'

After that, the fisherman said to the snake, 'Now you can bite me.'

But the snake said, 'No, fisherman, I shall believe you. I shall repay your good with good.'

The snake led the man back to the stone, slid underneath it, gave the man a little gold and said, 'Come to me whenever you need money.'

The fisherman took the gold and left. He gave up working. Instead, he lived off this gold. When he had spent all the gold, he went back to the snake and the snake gave him some more.

He spent all that too, then went back to the snake once again. The snake gave him more gold. The fisherman went off, thinking, 'Why does the snake give me so very little?'

He spent all this gold too. Off he went to the snake again, thinking, 'Why does the snake give me so very little? I'll kill it. Then I can take all the gold, and I'll start to live well.'

So the fisherman thought. But the snake could hear the fisherman's thoughts. The fisherman went up to the snake, and the snake bit him. And the fisherman died.

A. V. BARDIN

(1888–1962)

Bardin lectured at the Orenburg (between 1938 and 1957 the city was called Chkalov) Pedagogical Institute. He was both a collector of the region's folklore and an active participant in the creation of what is sometimes called 'Soviet fakelore'. His Folklore of the Chkalov Province *was published in 1940; his* Soviet Folklore of the Chkalov Province *in 1947. Even by the standards of his time, Bardin appears to have been shockingly blatant in his readiness to create 'fakelore'; in 1947, as the Stalin cult was at its apogee, he was criticized for requiring all his students to compose (!) 'folklore' about Soviet achievements.[1] The following brief tale is, no doubt, entirely genuine – there are many folktales in a similar vein – but it is obvious enough that the hostile treatment of the rich peasant would have made this a particularly safe tale to publish in Soviet times.*

The Everlasting Piece

A man was returning home after his twenty-five years as a soldier. He walked all through the day. Night fell. He climbed up onto a tall oak, and after a while, he saw an old man down below. The old man's hair was as white as the moon and he had a long white beard. The old man went right up to the oak tree and sounded a horn. Out of nowhere appeared twelve wolves. The old man took a loaf of bread from his bag, divided it into thirteen pieces and gave one piece to each wolf. Then he gave the remaining piece to the soldier. The soldier took the piece of bread and greedily began eating it. But, no matter how much he ate, the piece did not get any smaller. At dawn the old man sounded his horn again and the wolves ran off in different directions. The soldier climbed down from the oak and went on his way. In time he came to a village. He asked a rich peasant to let him stay the night in his hut. The soldier went into the hut and sat down at the table. He had walked a long way and he was hungry. He took out the piece of bread and began to eat. The rich peasant saw that the piece of bread was not getting any smaller. 'Sell me that piece of bread, soldier!' he said.

'No,' said the soldier, 'it's an everlasting piece. With it, I'll be all right. I need never go hungry again.'

The peasant began to question the soldier: how had he acquired this piece of bread that would last forever? The soldier told him. And when morning came, the soldier went on his way.

In the evening the rich peasant went into the forest, climbed up into the oak and waited for the old man. He did not have to wait long. The old man went right up to the oak tree and sounded his horn. Twelve wolves came running up to him. The old man took a loaf of bread from his bag, divided it into eleven parts and gave them to the wolves. One wolf was left without any bread. The old man pointed up at the peasant. The wolf leaped up into the oak and tore the rich peasant to pieces.

DMITRY MIKHAILOVICH BALASHOV

(1927–2000)

Balashov's father was an actor and his mother an artist. As well as publishing collections of folk ballads, songs and stories, Balashov wrote historical novels. From 1972 he lived in a village on the shore of Lake Onega, and from 1983 in Novgorod. In 2000, while in his home in a village in the Novgorod region, he was murdered; it is not known why.

How a Man Pinched a Girl's Breast

Once there were two neighbours. One was rich and the other was poor. The poor neighbour had a son, but the rich neighbour had a daughter. One evening the daughter went off to a party, but before the party she and the poor neighbour's son had been in the bathhouse and he had pinched her. Yes – his father had been bringing back the hay, he had been mowing the hay – and the poor neighbour's son had gone and pinched her on the breast. And she had said to him, 'Come round, friend, in the evening!'

'The rich girl is calling me,' he said to himself. 'I'll go as quick as I can.'

He ate and drank and put on his best clothes. Along he went – but everyone there was already on horseback. Out from the bathhouse she came and struck him with a whip. 'Once a young lad,' she said, 'but now a fine stallion!'

She mounted him – and off she rode. Forty of them came together in the steppe – forty such maidens on forty such stallions. And they galloped and galloped. Which of them could strike their stallion the most? Which of them could make their stallion run wildest?

Towards morning they all went back to their homes. But first they all gathered at the same bathhouse. The girls struck their whips and said, 'Once a fine stallion, but now a young lad!'

Now young lads once again, back home they all went, swaying as they walked. They had galloped all through the night – those girls had worn them out. 'Come round, friend, in the evening!' called out the rich neighbour's daughter.

'No,' he thought. 'I've had enough.'

Back home he went. His father began to scold him: 'What have you been doing? Out revelling all night! It's already time we were off to the forest – and you're only just back from your revels!'

But the stepmother took the lad's side. 'You were young once,' she said to her husband. 'You used to go out all night too!'

The father went off to the forest, but the young lad stayed at home. And the stepmother began asking questions: 'Where were you? What have you been up to?'

'Well, yesterday we were bringing in the hay, and the neighbour's daughter was there, and she said to me, "Come round, friend, in the evening!" So I go to the bathhouse, but she strikes me with a whip and says, "Once a young lad, but now a fine stallion!" And she mounted me and was off. And there were forty of them out in the steppe, and they rode us all night, and towards morning they all went back to the same bathhouse as before and they struck us with their whips and said, "Once a fine stallion, but now a young lad!" And off we all went, swaying as we walked.'

'Did she tell you to come again?' asked the stepmother.

'Yes, she did. She called out, "Come round, friend, in the evening!" – but I'm not going.'

'No,' said the stepmother. 'You must go. I'll tell you what to do.'

Evening set in. The father came back from the forest. The young lad got ready. The stepmother gave him six bricks and a rooster, put an awl in his right hand and gave him three iron skillets to put on his head.

'Now,' she said, 'you must go before anyone's there, before they come to the party. Sit on the floor, make these bricks into a wall and put the skillets on top of your head like a roof. Tuck the rooster against your left side and hold the awl in your right hand. When they fly in and insult you, when they rush into the bathhouse, you must poke the rooster. The rooster will crow and they'll all rush out of the bathhouse again. And when the girl is left behind on her own, you must seize her by her braid. You must catch her and not let go. There in your hands she'll turn herself into one creature after another. She'll turn into a mouse, then a rat, but you mustn't let go. Just keep hold of her braid. Then she'll turn into a spindle. You must snap the spindle, pick it up again and say, "One end be a beautiful maiden, the other end be a heap of gold!" Then strike her with the whip and say, "Once a fair maiden, now a young filly!" '

He collected all this stuff and went off to the bathhouse. He put the bricks all round him, he put the skillets on top of his head, he took hold of the rooster and the awl – and there he sat. And then there they all were! They opened the door and flew in as ravens.

'But now he's waiting in a city of stone,' they said. 'He's sitting under a roof of iron.'

And they began pecking at this roof of his. But he prodded the rooster with his awl, and the rooster crowed. They all rushed out of the bathhouse. The girl was left behind on her own. He seized her by her braid. There in his hands she began turning herself into one creature after another. She was a mouse, then a rat, and who knows what else. But he didn't let go. Then she turned into a spindle. He took the spindle, snapped it in half and said, 'One end be a fair maiden, the other end be a heap of gold!'

And she turned into a fair maiden. And he led her out of the bathhouse, struck her with a whip, mounted her and rode off. He rode into open steppe. He rode and rode. He beat her and whipped her. He galloped and galloped for all he was worth. He made her fair sweat, he did, but he never went anywhere near those other forty. And in the meantime those forty were arguing. Was he riding on her? Or was she riding him? There was no way they could tell.

'Beyond thrice-nine seas, beyond thrice-nine lands, in the thrice-ninth tsardom, in the thrice-ninth country, lives a lad who has never been baptised and who has never prayed. Let him tell us!'

They found a little lame girl, and she ran off and dragged this lad along, but he wouldn't say anything. (This lad, you see, was a friend of the poor man's son.) They dragged the lad back where he'd come from. Then they said, 'Beyond thrice-nine seas, beyond thrice-nine lands, in the thrice-ninth tsardom, in the thrice-ninth country, lives a lass who has never been baptised and who has never prayed. Let her tell us!'

And once again the little lame girl ran off and she dragged this girl along to them. And then they learned that it was *he* who had been riding on *her*. Well, they all rode about for a while and then they rode home. All of them went home, but he was the last of all. He struck his filly with a whip and said, 'Once a young filly, now a fair maiden!'

And then she said, 'Come and ask for my hand and I'll be your wife. You have made me human again.' (There had been an unclean spirit in her, you see.)

By the time he got back home, it was already light. The father had gone off into the forest. The stepmother asked, 'Well, who was the rider and who was ridden? Did you ride on her, or did she ride you?'

'I rode on her. The girls wanted to know. They tried all they could to find out and they brought along a lad from beyond thrice-nine seas, from beyond thrice-nine lands, but he didn't say. Then they brought a lass from beyond thrice-nine seas, from beyond thrice-nine lands, a lass who had never been baptised and who had never prayed. It was this lass who told them – yes, that's how they found out. And then we all rode back home, and I was the last of all. And then she said, "Send your mother to ask for my hand and I'll marry you. You've made me human."'

The stepmother gave him something to eat and drink, then put him to bed.

Back came the father. He began scolding his son.

The stepmother took the lad's side. 'You were young once,' she said to her husband. 'You used to go revelling too!'

They sat down to eat and drink. The stepmother said, 'It's time your son married. Else he'll be going out revelling night after night.'

'All right then. What's stopping him?'

'Well, shall I ask for the hand of our neighbour's daughter?'

'A likely story!' laughed the father. 'As if our rich neighbour's going to give his daughter to our poor son!'

'I'll go round and ask,' said the stepmother.

The father told her not to go. 'We're poor and needy,' he kept saying, 'but our neighbours are rich.' But the stepmother slipped round all the same. And so she talked about this, and she talked about that, and then she asked if her stepson could marry their daughter.

'Do you think we've raised our daughter just for your son?' laughed the father.

But then the daughter opened the door. 'Papenka,' she said, 'let me marry him. He's my groom. He's made me human.'

After that, the father didn't say another word. There was a merry feast and a wedding.

PART SEVEN

PART SEVEN

ANDREY PLATONOVICH PLATONOV

(1899–1951)

Andrey Platonov, the greatest Russian prose-writer of the last century, is still best known for the extraordinary novels and stories he wrote in the late 1920s and early 1930s. His later work, more optimistic in tone and apparently simpler, has often been wrongly seen as representing a compromise with the demands of the Soviet authorities. In reality, it is no less profound than his earlier work and it deals with the same themes – perhaps still more subtly. Platonov is as remarkable for his persistence as for his boldness. The entire body of his work can be seen as a single book – and The Magic Ring, *his small collection of versions of Russian magic tales, can be seen as the final chapter of this book.*

The son of a railway worker who also gilded the cupolas of local churches, Andrey Platonov was born at the turn of a century – on 1 September 1899 – and between town and country, on the edge of the central Russian city of Voronezh. This seems fitting; in his mature work Platonov seems to delight in eliding every conceivable boundary – between animal and human, between the animate and the inanimate, between souls and machines, between life and death. He was almost certainly an atheist, yet his work is full of religious symbolism and imbued with deep religious feeling. He was a passionate supporter of the 1917 Revolution and remained sympathetic to the dream that gave birth to it, yet few people have written more searingly of its catastrophic consequences.

Platonov's relationship with the official Soviet literary world was no less complex. Some of his works were published and immediately subjected to fierce criticism; others were accepted for publication yet published only thirty or forty years after his death. Platonov was never himself arrested but, in 1938, his fifteen-year-old son, Platon, was sent to the Gulag – probably in order to put pressure on Platonov himself; Platon was released in late 1940, only to die three years later of the tuberculosis he had caught in the camps. During the Second World War Platonov worked as a correspondent for Red Star *(the newspaper of the Red Army) and published several volumes of stories, but in 1946 he was again subjected to vicious criticism. After this, he could no longer publish work of his own. He did, however – perhaps largely through the support of the influential Mikhail Sholokhov[1] – manage to publish his versions of traditional folktales: a collection titled* Bashkir Folktales *in November 1947, and* The Magic Ring *in October 1950. The first of these seven retellings of Russian skazki, 'Finist the Bright Falcon', was also published separately, in three different editions, in 1947 and 1948.*

Platonov had evidently been giving serious thought to the folktale for at least ten years before this; between 1938 and 1940 he had reviewed several different anthologies. He formulates his thoughts most clearly, however, in a review (published in October 1947) of Aleksey Tolstoy's versions of Russian folktales – a review that Platonov must have written around the same time as he was working on his own versions. Platonov begins by criticizing most previous collections – even Afanasyev's. Though he refers to it as one of the best works of Russian folklore, he expresses regret that Afanasyev, for all his love of folktales, was not himself an artist: 'If we remember such an ideal "reworker" of folk themes as Pushkin, and the quality of the skazki *he created, then everyone will understand our view that only an artist – and only a great artist at that – is up to the task of "composing" or "reworking" a* skazka.' *Platonov then affirms that the aim of such great artists as Pushkin and Lev Tolstoy – and Aleksey Tolstoy in his own time – has always been 'the restoration, the recreation – from all the variants the people has created on a particular theme – of the very best root variant of a particular tale'. Platonov continues, 'But these writers do still more – they enrich and inform a popular* folktale with the power of their own creativity and endow it with the definitive, ideal combination of meaning and form that will allow this tale to continue to exist for a long time or forever.' Platonov concludes, 'But a first small volume of folktales is only a beginning; it is essential to publish the entire corpus of Russian folktales. This body of work, in addition to its artistic and ethical value, must also serve as a material repository for the treasure of the Russian language, our people's most precious possession.'

Platonov justifiably saw himself as a successor, in this respect, to Pushkin and Lev Tolstoy.[2] His own skazki are witty and vigorous, and he has a remarkable ability to penetrate deep into the structure of a particular word, image or motif and bring out its deeper meaning. At the same time, Platonov is entirely himself in these skazki and one could even say that in them he has returned to his origins. Much of his work contains elements of folktale, and the surrealism of some of his earlier stories and novels is closer to that of folktale than to that of the self-conscious and intellectual French literary movement. And the themes of his skazki are the themes of his work as a whole; 'No-Arms' seems especially important for being the only work in which two of his deepest and most constant themes – orphanhood and the loss of limbs – are resolved optimistically.

In June 1940, in the journal Children's Literature, Platonov published an enthusiastic review of the first edition of Pavel Bazhov's The Malachite Casket. He wrote of one tale that it is 'presented in the true, living language that gives a sense of the time and place of the action, of the individuality of the teller and of the philosophy of the people who created this tale. For each image, concept or action there is a uniquely exact and unrepeatable verbal form. The word serves as an organic part of a given action and belongs to it and to it alone. Any slightest discrepancy between word and fact has the effect of distorting the fact itself; everything then vanishes – both truth and art. The Malachite Casket contains very few such infringements of the organic structure of speech – so few that they are not worth mentioning.'[3]

The particular quality of Platonov's own skazki becomes

*most apparent if we compare them with the many folklore-
inspired works of art and music from the first two decades of
the twentieth century – and above all with the works associated
with Diaghilev and the Ballets Russes. The mood of Stravinsky's ballets is one of violence and erotic excitement. The
dominant colour in the sets and costumes designed by Roerich,
Goncharova and Stravinsky's other collaborators is a brilliant
red. The image that epitomizes this period – an image painted
by Leon Bakst, Natalya Goncharova, Kuzma Petrov-Vodkin,
Valentin Serov and Viktor Vasnetsov among others – is that of
the firebird.*[4] *The mood of Platonov's* skazki *is very different.
The virtues he celebrates are patience, endurance, kindness and
forgiveness. He turns to Russian folklore as a source not of
pagan vitality but of what can best be called Christian values.
And his counterpart to the Firebird is Finist the Bright Falcon.
The Firebird leaves behind her a tail feather that shines as
bright 'as a thousand candles'; it is no wonder that the bedaz-
zled Tsar sends his sons out to capture her. Finist, by contrast,
leaves behind him the plainest, greyest and most ordinary of
feathers; only Maryushka, his 'destined one', has the perspicu-
ity to grasp what this feather, with its promise of love and
perhaps even of rebirth, is truly worth. The name Finist is
derived from Phoenix, the bird that is reborn out of its own
ashes; Finist and the Firebird appear to be male and female
aspects of one and the same bird. Where Stravinsky, Diaghilev,
Goncharova and others saw an image of alluring glamour, Platonov saw a symbol of quiet hope, of the possibility of new life
springing even from grey ash. Afanasyev's version, incidentally,
makes no mention of the colour of Finist's feather; in choosing
to describe it as grey, Platonov appears – as so often in* The
Magic Ring *– not to be adding something of his own to the oral
versions but to be revealing their inner logic.*

*Platonov's language is idiosyncratic yet also strangely imper-
sonal; I have heard it described as 'the language that might be
spoken by the roots of trees'. Tragic though it is that Platonov
was unable to publish original works during his last five years,
there is something fitting about his having ended his career as a
semi-anonymous reteller of folktales. During the decades after*

his death his skazki *were often included, without acknowledgement, in anthologies of literature for Soviet schoolchildren; Platonov's name may, for a decade after his death, have been almost forgotten, but even then millions of children were reading his work. This would perhaps not have surprised Platonov; like the soldier-storyteller in 'Wool over the Eyes', he knew that 'a story's stronger than a Tsar'.*

Platonov's courage and endurance were remarkable. These skazki *were written after he had been diagnosed with the tuberculosis he had caught from his son and from which he himself would die in January 1951. It is unlikely that he intended it as such, but the following paragraph about a plane tree, written in 1934, now seems to be a description of Platonov himself: 'Zarrin-Tadzh sat on one of the plane tree's roots (...) and noticed that stones were growing high on the trunk. During its spring floods, the river must have flung mountain stones at the very heart of the plane, but the tree had consumed these vast stones into its body, encircled them with patient bark, made them something it could live with, endured them into its own self, and gone on growing further, meekly lifting up as it grew taller what should have destroyed it.'*

Finist the Bright Falcon

Once there was a peasant who lived in a village with his wife and three daughters. The daughters grew bigger and he and his wife grew older – until the day came when it was the wife's turn to die. The man was left to bring up his daughters alone. All three were beautiful, and each as beautiful as the others, but they were different in nature.

The old man was well off and he cherished his daughters. He wanted to find some lonely old widow or other to look after the household, but Maryushka, the youngest daughter, said, 'Father, there's no need to find an old widow. I can look after the home on my own.'

Maryushka was diligent and hard-working. The two elder daughters, for their part, said nothing.

And so Maryushka took the place of her mother. She knew how to do everything, and she did everything well. And if there was any task she couldn't do, she was quick to get used to it – and in no time at all she would be doing this task well too. Her father watched; he was glad that his daughter was so clever, obedient and hard working. She was beautiful, too – and her kindness made her yet more beautiful. Her sisters were also beautiful, but they never thought they were beautiful enough, and they were always trying to add to their beauty with pink powders and white powders and all kinds of new outfits. Often they spent a whole day trying to make themselves prettier – but, come evening, they still looked the same as they had in the morning. They'd realize they'd wasted a whole day and got through whole pots of powders without becoming any the prettier and they would get crosser and crosser. As for Maryushka, she would be tired out – but then she knew that she'd fed the livestock and cleaned and tidied the hut, that she'd cooked the supper and kneaded the dough for tomorrow's bread and that her father would be pleased with her. She would look at her sisters with kind eyes and not say a word. This made her sisters crosser still. They thought that Maryushka had not looked like this in the morning, that she had grown prettier during the day – only they couldn't understand how.

One day the father had to go to market. He said to his daughters, 'Well, children, what shall I buy you? What can I get to make you happy?'

The eldest daughter said, 'Buy me a shawl, Father, one with big flowers embroidered on it in gold.'

'You can buy me a shawl, too, Father,' said the middle daughter, 'one with big flowers embroidered on it in gold and with red in between the flowers. And buy me some tall boots as well, with soft calves and with dainty high heels that tap on the ground.'

This upset the eldest daughter. Her heart was greedy. She said to her father, 'And buy the same for me, Father. Yes, buy me some tall boots with soft calves and dainty high heels that tap on the ground. And buy me a ring too – buy me a ring with a precious stone to put on my finger. After all, I'm your only eldest daughter.'

The father promised to buy everything that his two elder daughters required. Then he said to his youngest daughter, 'Maryushka, why aren't you saying anything?'

'I don't need anything, Father. I never leave the house. I don't need any fine clothes.'

'Maryushka, don't say such things! How can I leave you out? I can't not get you a fairing.'

'I don't need a fairing,' said the youngest daughter. 'But, dear Father, buy me a feather of Finist the Bright Falcon, if it's not expensive.'

The father rode off to market. He bought all the presents his elder daughters required, but nowhere could he find a feather of Finist the Bright Falcon.

'No,' the merchants all said, 'nothing of the kind exists. There's no demand.'

The father did not want to upset his clever, hard-working youngest daughter, but what could he do? Back home he went – without having bought a feather of Finist the Bright Falcon.

But Maryushka was not upset at all.

'Never mind, Father,' she said. 'You'll be going to market again – one day you'll find yourself buying me my feather!'

Time passed – and the father needed to go to market again. He asked his daughters what presents they wanted; he was a kind and good father.

The eldest daughter said, 'Last time, Father, you brought me some little boots. Now you must get the blacksmiths to heel them with little horse-shoes.'

The middle daughter heard her sister and said, 'And do the same for me, Father. Else the heels just tap on the ground. I want them to ring. And so I don't lose the little nails from the horse-shoes, buy me a little silver hammer so I can hammer them in.'

'And what shall I buy you, Maryushka?'

'Have a look round, Father. See if you can find a feather of Finist the Bright Falcon.'

The old man rode off to the market. He soon finished his business and bought his two elder daughters their presents. Then he looked for Maryushka's feather. He looked and looked. He looked till nightfall, but the feather was nowhere to be found. No one was selling it.

Again he came back with no present for his youngest daughter. He felt sorry for Maryushka, but she just smiled at her father. She was happy simply to be seeing her dear father again.

Once again the time came for the father to go to the market.

'Well, dear daughters, what gifts would you like me to buy you?'

The eldest daughter thought and thought, but she couldn't think what she wanted. 'Father!' she said. 'Buy me something!'

The middle daughter said, 'Buy me something too, Father, and then buy me something else on top of that something.'

'What about you, Maryushka?'

'Just buy me a feather of Finist the Bright Falcon, Father.'

The old man rode off to the market. He finished his business and bought his two elder daughters their presents. But he didn't buy anything for his youngest daughter. Nowhere in the market was there any such feather.

On his way home the father saw someone walking along the road. It was an old old man, even older than he was – an ancient old man.

'Greetings, Grandad!'

'Greetings, my friend! Why are you looking so sad?'

'How can I not look sad? My daughter keeps asking me to buy her a feather of Finist the Bright Falcon. I've searched and searched, but it's nowhere to be found. And it's for my youngest daughter, the one I cherish most of all.'

The old old man thought for a while – and then said, 'Well, so be it!'

He untied his knapsack and took out from it a little box.

'Keep the box somewhere safe,' he said. 'Inside it is a feather from Finist the Bright Falcon. Now then, don't forget my words: I have a son, and I cherish him as you cherish your daughter. It's time he got married, but he doesn't want to marry and I can't force him. And he keeps saying, "If anyone asks for this little feather, give it to them. She who asks for this feather will be my bride."'

The old old man came to the end of his words – and suddenly he wasn't there any more. He had vanished. Had he ever really been there at all?

Maryushka's father was left with the feather. It was a grey and ordinary little feather, but nowhere had he been able to buy it. The father remembered what the old old man had said and thought, 'Well, it seems this will be my Maryushka's fate: to marry an unknown stranger – a man she's never known and never seen.'

The father returned home. He gave the elder daughters their presents, and he gave his youngest daughter the little box with the little grey feather.

The elder daughters put on their fine dresses and began to make fun of their sister. 'Stick that sparrow's feather into your hair,' they said, 'and you'll find you look fairer than fair!'

Maryushka did not say a word, but when everyone had lain down to sleep, she took the plain, grey feather of Finist the

Bright Falcon, placed it on the table in front of her and sat
down to wonder at it. Then she picked the little feather up in
her hands, held it for a while to her breast, stroked it and inadvertently dropped it onto the floor.

Straight away someone knocked at the window. The window opened, and in flew Finist the Bright Falcon. He flew down
to touch the floor – and turned into a handsome young man.
Maryushka closed the window, and she and her young man
began talking their talk. When it was nearly morning, she
opened the window. The young man bowed down to touch the
floor – and turned into a bright falcon. The falcon left one little
plain grey feather as a keepsake and flew off into the blue sky.

Three nights Maryushka welcomed the falcon. All day he
flew about the sky, over fields and forests, over mountains and
oceans; towards evening he flew to his Maryushka and turned
into a handsome young man.

The fourth night the elder sisters heard Maryushka's quiet
voice. They also heard the voice of a strange young man. In the
morning they asked, 'Well, sister, who is it you talk to at nights?'

'I say a few words to myself,' Maryushka answered. 'I have
no friends and I work all day. There's no time to talk. In the
evenings I talk to myself a little.'

The elder sisters listened to their younger sister and did not
believe her. They said to their father, 'Father, our Marya's got
herself a young man. They see each other at night and talk to
each other. We've heard them.'

'You shouldn't be listening,' said the father. 'Why shouldn't
our Maryushka have a young man? There's nothing wrong in
that. She's a pretty girl, and she's of the right age. Very soon it
will be your turn too.'

'But it's my turn now. I'm older than Marya and I should be
marrying first. Marya hasn't waited her turn – she shouldn't
have found her betrothed before me.'

'True enough,' agreed the father. 'But fate's fate – what does
fate know about turns? One girl stays an old maid to the end of
her days, while another is courted by everyone.'

So the father spoke, but as he spoke he was thinking, 'Could it be that the words of the old old man who gave me the feather are coming true now? Maybe they are, and maybe it's no bad thing – I just pray fate has sent her a good man!'

But the two elder daughters had wishes of their own. Towards evening they took some knives from the kitchen, pulled off the handles and went into Maryushka's room. Then they stuck these knives, together with some sharp needles and bits of old glass, around the frame of the window. Maryushka was out in the shed just then, looking after the cow, and she didn't see any of this.

And then, when it was dark, Finist the Bright Falcon flew down to Maryushka's window. He flew to the window – and struck against the sharp knives and needles and slivers of glass. He struggled and struggled and tore open all his chest. But Maryushka was worn out from her day's work and she'd dozed off while she was waiting for Finist the Bright Falcon. She didn't hear him beating his wings in the window.

Then Finist said in a loud voice, 'Goodbye, my fair maiden! If you need me, you will find me, even though I am far away! But on your way to me you will wear out three pairs of iron shoes, you will wear down three iron staffs against the wayside grass and you will gnaw your way through three stone loaves.'[1]

Maryushka heard Finist's words through her sleep, but she was unable to awake or get to her feet. Only the following morning did she awake, and then her heart filled with grief. She looked at the window – and there was Finist's blood, drying in the sun. Then she began to weep. She opened the window and buried her face in the spot where she could see the blood of Finist-Falcon. Her tears washed away the falcon's blood, and she herself – as if she had washed in the blood of her betrothed – grew still more beautiful.

Maryushka went to her father and said, 'Don't be angry with me, Father – but give me leave to set out on a distant path. If I stay alive, we'll see each other again. But if I die, then that's how it was fated.'

The father didn't want to give his dearest, youngest daughter leave to set off who knows where. But how could he keep her

at home against her will? He knew that a girl's loving heart is
more powerful than the will of a mother or father. He bid his
beloved daughter farewell.

The blacksmith forged Maryushka three pairs of iron shoes
and three iron staffs. She took three stone loaves. Then she
bowed to her father and her sisters, paid a last visit to her
mother's grave and set off in search of Finist the Bright Falcon.

Maryushka walked and walked. She followed her long path
for more than a day, more than two days, more than three
days. She walked for a long time. She walked through open
steppe and dark forests. She crossed high mountains. Birds
sang songs to her in the fields; the dark forests treated her
kindly; from high up in the mountains she wondered at the
whole world. She walked so far that she wore out one pair of
iron shoes and one of her iron staffs. She had gnawed her way
through a whole stone loaf, but there was still no end to her
path. Nowhere was there any sign of Finist the Bright Falcon.

Maryushka let out a sigh, sat down on the ground and was
just putting on her second pair of iron shoes when she saw a
little hut in the forest. Night had already fallen.

Maryushka said to herself, 'I'll go into that little hut and ask
if they have seen my Finist the Bright Falcon.'

Maryushka knocked at the hut. In it lived an old woman.
Whether she was kind or wicked Maryushka did not know.
The old woman opened the door. Before her stood a beautiful
young maiden.

'Grandmother, let me stay the night with you!'

'Come in, my little dove, and be my guest! Are you going far?'

'Far or near, Grandmother, I don't know. I'm looking for
Finist the Bright Falcon. You haven't heard anything of him,
have you, Grandmother?'

'What do you mean? I'm old, I've been in the world a long
time, I've heard of everyone. You've got a long way to go, my
dear.'

In the morning the old woman woke Maryushka and said to
her, 'You must go on your way now, my dear. You must go and
speak to my middle sister. She's older than me and she knows
more. Maybe she can set you on a good path and tell you where

your Finist now lives. But so you don't forget me, take this silver distaff and golden spindle. They will spin you a gold thread out of plain flax. Take care of my gift as long as it's dear to you. But if you no longer need it, give it away.'

Maryushka took the gift, wondered at it and said to her host, 'Thank you, Grandmother. Now tell me which way I should go!'

'I'm going to give you a little ball of yarn that rolls all by itself. Whichever way the ball rolls, that's where you should go. And when you need a rest, just sit down on the grass. The ball will stop and wait till you're ready.'

Maryushka bowed to the old woman and set off after the ball. She walked on and on – she lost count of how many days she had walked. She did not spare herself – even though the forests she walked through were dark and terrible, even though the fields were full of thistles instead of wheat, even though the mountains were gaunt and rocky and no birds sang in the sky above her. Maryushka walked ever further – and ever faster. Before she knew it, she had to change her shoes again. She had worn out a second pair of iron shoes; she had ground away a second iron staff; she had gnawed her way through a second stone loaf.

Maryushka sat down to change her shoes. She looked round. Night was setting in. Not far away was a black forest, and on the edge of the forest was a little hut. In the window a light was being lit.

Her little ball rolled up to this hut. Maryushka followed it and knocked on the window. 'Good people!' she called out. 'Let me come in!'

An old woman came out onto the porch. She was older than the woman who had taken Maryushka in before.

'Where are you going, fair maiden? Who in the world are you searching for?'

'I'm searching for Finist the Bright Falcon, Grandmother. I stayed the night with an old woman in a forest. She had heard of Finist but never seen him. She told me that maybe her sister would know more.'

The old woman invited Maryushka into her hut. In the

morning she woke her guest and said, 'You'll have to go a long way if you're going to look for Finist. I've often heard about Finist, but never have I set eyes on him. You must go now to our eldest sister – she's sure to be able to help you. And so you don't forget me, take this as a gift. It'll be a keepsake in joy, and a help in need.'

And the old woman gave her guest a silver saucer and a golden egg.

Maryushka asked the old woman's forgiveness, bowed to her and set off after the little ball.

Maryushka walked on. The earth she was walking over was no longer the earth she knew.

No longer was there any open steppe around her – only forest. And the further the ball rolled, the taller the trees grew. It turned dark. She could no longer see the sun and the sky.

But Maryushka went on through the darkness. She walked and walked – until she had worn out her last pair of iron shoes, until she had ground down her last iron staff, until she had eaten the last crumb of her last stone loaf.

She looked around her: what was she to do? She saw her little ball. It was lying beneath the window of a little hut in the forest.

Maryushka knocked at this window. 'Kind people,' she called out, 'shelter me from the dark night!'

Out onto the porch came an ancient old crone – the very eldest sister of all the old women.

'Come inside, my little dove!' she said. 'What a long, long way you've come! No one lives beyond me in the world – I'm as far as you can go. Tomorrow you'll have to head in a different direction. But who are your people and where are you going?'

'I'm not from these parts, Grandmother,' replied Maryushka. 'I'm searching for Finist the Bright Falcon.'

The eldest of the old women looked at Maryushka and said, 'So you're looking for Finist the Falcon, are you? I know him, yes, I know him all right. I've been living a long time, so long I've got to know everyone. I remember everyone.'

The old woman put Maryushka to bed. In the morning she woke her up and said, 'It's a long time since I've done anyone any good. I live alone in the forest. I remember everyone, but no one remembers me. I shall do you a good turn – I can tell you where your Finist the Bright Falcon lives. But even if you find him, it will be hard for you. Finist-Falcon's married now. He lives with his wife. It will be hard for you. But still, you have a good heart – and a good heart always brings with it good sense. And good sense makes light work of even the very hardest of tasks.'

'Thank you, Grandmother,' said Maryushka. And she bowed low, right down to the ground.

'You can thank me afterwards. Now here's a little present for you. Take this golden needle and embroidery frame: hold the frame – and the needle will sew of itself. Well, be off with you now. You'll see what to do next as you go along.'

The little ball didn't roll any further. The eldest old woman came out onto the porch and showed Maryushka which way to go.

Maryushka set off as she was, with no shoes on her feet. 'How am I to keep going?' she wondered. 'The earth here is hard and strange underfoot. I must learn to get used to it.'

She walked a short way. She came to a clearing. In it stood a splendid house. It had a tower, and the porch and the window frames were finely carved. A rich, important-looking woman was sitting by one of the windows. She was looking at Maryushka: what was this young girl doing here?

Maryushka remembered: she had nothing to put on her feet and she had gnawed her way through her last stone loaf.

'Greetings, mistress!' she said. 'Do you need any work done – in return for bread and shoes and clothing?'

'I do,' replied the important-looking woman. 'But do you know how to take care of the stove and fetch water and cook dinner?'

'I lived with a father and no mother. I can do everything.'

'And can you spin and sew and embroider?'

Maryushka remembered the presents the three old grandmothers had given her.

'Yes,' she said.

'Go along to the kitchen then,' said the mistress of the house.

And so Maryushka began to work as a servant, a stranger in a rich household. Her hands were honest and diligent – there was no task they couldn't perform.

The mistress of the house could hardly believe her luck. She had never had a maid who was so hard-working, so kind and so quick-witted. She ate plain bread, and she washed it down with kvass. She never even asked for tea. The mistress began to boast to her daughter:

'Look what a good maid I've found. She's clever and willing and she's got such a sweet face.'

The mistress's daughter looked at Maryushka.

'Bah!' she said. 'Maybe she does have a sweet face, but I'm more beautiful than her and my skin's whiter.'

That evening, when she'd finished her household tasks, Maryushka sat down to do some spinning. She sat down on the bench, got out the silver distaff and golden spindle and began to spin. She span – and the thread she span from the flax tow was not an ordinary thread, but a golden thread. She span – and as she span, she looked into the silver distaff and there in the distaff she could see Finist the Bright Falcon. There he was – alive and looking at her. Maryushka looked at him and began to speak to him:

'Finist, Finist my Bright Falcon, why have you left me alone? Why have you left me to weep bitter tears for you? It was my sisters who separated us, my sisters who shed your blood.'

Just then the mistress's daughter came into the servants' hut. She stood at a distance, watching and listening.

'Who are you weeping for?' she asked. 'And what is that trinket you're playing with?'

Maryushka replied, 'I'm weeping for Finist the Bright Falcon. And I'm spinning a thread. I shall embroider a towel for Finist, so he can wash his bright face in the morning.'

'Oh!' said the mistress's daughter. 'Why don't you sell me your trinket? Finist is my husband. I shall spin a thread for him myself.'

Maryushka looked at the mistress's daughter. She stopped her golden spindle and said, 'I don't have any trinkets. What I have here in my hand is my work. And the silver distaff and the golden spindle are not for sale. A kind old grandmother gave them to me as a gift.'

This upset the mistress's daughter. She didn't want to let a golden spindle slip through her fingers.

'If they aren't for sale,' she said, 'then let's do a swap. Give them to me as a gift – and I'll give you a gift too.'

'All right!' said Maryushka. 'Allow me to take one quick look, just out of the corner of my eye, at Finist the Bright Falcon.'

The mistress's daughter thought for a moment, then agreed to this.

'All right then. Give me your trinket.'

She took the silver distaff and the golden spindle. 'Why shouldn't the girl look at Finist for a few minutes?' she said to herself. 'He won't come to any harm – I'll give him a sleeping potion. And with this spindle my mother and I will soon be swimming in gold!'

Around nightfall Finist the Bright Falcon returned from the heavens. He turned into a handsome young man and sat down, together with his wife and his mother-in-law, to a family dinner.

The young mistress ordered someone to fetch Maryushka: she could wait on them at table. Like that, she could have a look at Finist, in keeping with their agreement. Maryushka appeared. She waited on the family all through the meal, served all their dishes and did not once take her eyes off Finist. But Finist did not respond; it was as if he were not there. He did not recognize Maryushka. She was worn out from the long path, and longing had changed her face.

The family finished their meal. Finist got to his feet and went to his chamber to lie down for the night.

Maryushka said to the young mistress, 'There are a lot of flies about tonight. I'll go into Finist's chamber to keep them off him. Otherwise he won't be able to sleep.'

'Let her!' said the old mistress.

Once again, the young mistress thought for a moment.

'All right,' she said, 'but first let me go in myself.'

And she followed her husband into his chamber and added some sleeping drops to his glass of water. 'Maybe,' she was thinking, 'this maid has another trinket she'll be willing to swap.'

'Go along now,' she said to Maryushka. 'Go and keep the flies off my husband.'

Maryushka went into Finist's chamber and quite forgot about the flies. There was her beloved friend. He was fast asleep – and she could not wake him from his sleep. She looked and looked at him – but, no matter how long she looked, she still hadn't looked her fill. She bent down over him. She was breathing the same air as him. She whispered, 'Wake up, my Finist. Wake up, my Bright Falcon. Here I am – I've come to you. I've worn out three pairs of iron shoes, I've worn away three iron staffs and I've gnawed my way through three stone loaves!'

But Finist remained fast asleep. He did not open his eyes or say a word in answer.

Then the young mistress, Finist's wife, came in.

'Well,' she asked. 'Have you been keeping the flies off him?'

'Yes, they've all flown out of the window.'

'Well then, it's time you went back to the servants' hut for the night.'

The following evening, after she had done all her housework, Maryushka took out her silver dish and her golden egg. She rolled the golden egg around – and a new golden egg rolled off the dish. She rolled the egg around a second time – and another golden egg rolled off the dish.

The young mistress saw all this.

'Oh!' she said. 'You've got another trinket, have you? Sell it to me. Or you can swap it for anything you like.'

'I can't sell you the silver dish and the golden egg,' said Maryushka. 'A kind old grandmother gave them to me as a gift. Now let me give them to you in turn. Here you are!'

The young mistress took the silver saucer and the golden egg. She was delighted.

'Maryushka,' she said, 'maybe there's something you'd like for yourself. You can ask for whatever you want.'

'There's very little I want. Just let me keep the flies off Finist again tonight, after you've put him to bed.'

'All right,' replied the young mistress. She was thinking, 'My husband won't come to any harm from being looked at by a strange girl. Anyway, I'll give him a sleeping potion and he won't even open his eyes. And who knows? Maybe this servant girl has brought some other little trinket with her!'

Around nightfall Finist the Bright Falcon came back again from the heavens. He turned into a handsome young man and sat down to dine with his family. The young mistress called Maryushka in to wait on them. Maryushka laid the table, served all the dishes – and didn't once take her eyes off Finist. But Finist looked without seeing. His heart did not know her.

Once again the young mistress gave her husband a sleeping potion and put him to bed. Once again she sent Maryushka the maid to him, to keep off the flies.

Maryushka went in to Finist's room. She began calling him and weeping over him. She thought he'd wake up any moment, take one look at her and know her for his Maryushka. She called and called. She wiped the tears from her own face so that they would not fall on Finist's white face and wet it. But Finist went on sleeping. He did not wake up and open his eyes to her.

On the third evening, when she was done with her household tasks, Maryushka sat down on the bench in the servants' hut and took out her golden needle and embroidery frame. She held the frame in her hands, and the needle sewed of itself.

As Maryushka sat and worked, she kept saying, 'Show yourself, show yourself, my beautiful pattern. Embroider yourself for Finist the Bright Falcon. Fill him with wonder.'

The young mistress was waiting not far away. She went into the servants' hut and saw Maryushka with her golden embroidery frame and her golden needle that sewed by itself. Her heart went wild with envy and greed, and she said, 'Oh Maryushka, oh my darling Maryushka, give me this trinket of yours or take anything you like in exchange for it! I've got a golden spindle, I can spin thread and I can weave cloth, but I've got nothing to embroider it with. If you don't want to swap it, then sell it to me! I'll pay any price you ask!'

'No,' said Maryushka, 'that's impossible. I can't sell you my golden needle and my golden embroidery frame, and I can't swap them for anything either. The very kindest and oldest of the old grandmothers gave them to me as a gift. I can only give them to you.'

The young mistress took the golden needle and the golden embroidery frame, but she had nothing to give Maryushka in return. She said, 'You can go along, if you like, and keep the flies off my husband. You used to ask to do that.'

'All right,' said Maryushka with a sigh. 'I'll go.'

After supper the young mistress decided not to give Finist a sleeping potion, but then she changed her mind and put one in his drink after all. 'Why let him look at the girl?' she thought. 'He'll be safer asleep.'

Maryushka went in to where Finist was sleeping. Now her heart could no longer bear it. She dropped down to the floor, her head against his white breast, and lamented:

'Wake up, wake up, my Finist, my Bright Falcon. I've walked across the whole earth to find you. Three iron staffs have worn themselves down beside me, the hard ground has ground them to nothing. My feet have worn out three pairs of iron shoes and I have gnawed my way through three stone loaves. Awake, my Finist, wake up, my Falcon! Take pity on me!'

But Finist was asleep. He sensed nothing. He did not hear Maryushka's voice.

Maryushka wept over him for a long time. She tried and tried to wake him up, but she could do nothing – his wife's sleeping potion was too strong. But then one of Maryushka's hot tears fell on Finist's chest, and a second fell on his face. The first tear burnt his heart; the second tear opened his eyes. He awoke at once.

'What is it?' he said. 'What is it that's burnt me?'

'Finist, my Bright Falcon!' answered Maryushka. 'Awake to me – I'm here now! I've searched and searched for you. I've worn iron shoes and iron staffs to nothing. Iron couldn't last out the journey. Only I could. And now I've been calling you for three nights, and all you've done is sleep. You haven't awoken. You haven't answered my voice.'

At last Finist the Bright Falcon knew his Maryushka, his fair maiden. At first he was so overjoyed that joy made him unable to speak. He just clasped Maryushka to his white breast and kissed her.

When he came to, when he took in that his Maryushka was with him again, he said, 'Be my grey dove, my faithful love!'

There and then he turned into a falcon, and Maryushka into a dove.

They flew away into the heavens and flew side by side all through the night, until dawn.

While they were flying, Maryushka said, 'Falcon, falcon, where are you flying to? Your wife will miss you!'

Finist the Falcon heard what she said and answered, 'It's to you I'm flying, my fair maiden. And as for a wife who sells her husband for a spindle, a saucer and a needle – she doesn't need a husband and she won't miss him.'

'What made you marry a wife like that?' asked Maryushka. 'Was it against your will?'

'No, but it was against my fate, and without my love.'[2]

And they flew on further, side by side.

At dawn they dropped down to earth. Maryushka looked around – there was her father's house, just as it had always been. She wanted to see her father, and there and then she turned into a fair maiden. And Finist the Bright Falcon struck against the damp earth and became a little feather.

Maryushka took the feather, hid it in her bosom and went to her father.

'Greetings, daughter! My youngest, my beloved! I thought you were gone from the world. Thank you for coming home, for not forgetting your father. But where have you been all this time? Why didn't you hurry back sooner?'

'Forgive me, Father. I did only what I had need to do.'

'Well, needs must. I'm glad the need has passed.'

That day was a holiday. A big fair had opened in town. Her father was about to set out on his way there. And her two sisters were going with him to buy themselves presents.

Her father asked his little Maryushka to come too.

'I'm worn out from the road, Father,' she replied. 'Anyway, I've nothing to wear. Everyone at the fair will be dressed in fine clothes.'

'Maryushka, I'll buy some fine clothes for you,' said her father. 'At the fair there'll be plenty to choose from.'

'We can lend you some of our own,' said the elder sisters. 'We've got more than we need.'

'Oh thank you, sisters!' Maryushka replied. 'But your clothes won't suit me – your bones aren't my bones. Anyway, I'd rather stay here at home.'

'All right, do as you please,' said her father. 'But what shall I bring you back from the fair? Tell me. Don't treat your father unkindly.'

'Dear Father, there isn't anything I want. I've got everything already. It's not for nothing I wandered so far and wore myself out on the road.'

The father rode off to the fair with his two elder daughters. Straight away Maryushka took out her little feather. It struck against the floor and turned into a handsome young man – Finist, only he was now more handsome than ever. Maryushka gazed at him in wonder but was so happy she couldn't think what to say.

'Don't look so full of wonder, Maryushka. It's your love that's made me like this.'

'I may be wondering at you,' said Maryushka, 'but really you remain always the same to me. I love you however you seem.'

'Where's your dear father?'

'He's gone to the fair. So have my elder sisters.'

'Why haven't you gone with them, my Maryushka?'

'I've got Finist, my Bright Falcon. What do I need from the fair?'

'I don't need anything either,' said Finist. 'Your love has made me rich.'

Finist turned around and whistled out of the window. At once there appeared fine clothes and adornments, and a golden carriage. They dressed, sat down in the carriage, and the horses were off like lightning.

They reached the fair just as it opened. There were mountains of all kinds of costly goods and foods, and the buyers were still on their way.

Finist bought everything there was in the fair, all the foods and all the goods. He ordered everything to be taken by cart to the village where Maryushka's father lived. The only thing he did not buy was the cartwheel grease. He left that on the stalls.

He wanted all the peasants who came to the fair to be guests at his wedding and to get to it as quickly as possible. For that, they'd need to grease the wheels of their carts.

Finist and Maryushka set off back home. They went fast. The horses could hardly breathe for the wind.

Halfway back Maryushka saw her father and her elder sisters. They were still on their way to the fair. Maryushka told them to turn round and go home, to her wedding with Finist the Bright Falcon.

In three days everyone who lived within fifty miles had arrived. Finist and Maryushka were married. It was a splendid wedding.

Our grandfathers and grandmothers all went to this wedding. They feasted a long time and drank toasts to the bride and groom. They would have stayed till winter, but the time came to bring in the harvest. The wheat was already starting to shed its grain. And so the wedding ended and the guests all left.

The wedding came to an end. In time even the wedding feast was forgotten, but Maryushka's true and loving heart is remembered forever throughout all Russia.

Ivan the Giftless and Yelena the Wise

In a certain village there once lived a peasant woman, a widow. She lived long, bringing up her son Ivan.

And then the time came – Ivan had become a man. His mother was glad he was fully grown now, but she did wish he hadn't grown up so very hapless. No matter how he tried, her son could do nothing right. All he did went askew; nothing went true.

He would go out to plough. His mother would say to him, 'Plough a bit deeper this time, son. The soil on top's been worn out.' Ivan ploughed as deep as he could, cutting right down into the clay and turning it up on top. Then he sowed the grain – and nothing came of it, the seeds were all wasted.

It was the same with everything else. Ivan always did his best, but he had little wit and nothing that could be called luck. But his mother was already old and she no longer had the strength to work. How were they to live? And they were very poor; they owned nothing at all.

One day they ate their last crust of bread. The mother thought and thought: how was her hapless son going to live? She had to get someone to marry him. A wise wife can turn even the daftest, most luckless of husbands into a deft worker who can earn his keep. But then who would want to marry her son? Not even a widow, let alone a fair maiden, would want her hapless son for a husband.

While his mother grieved, Ivan just sat on the earth wall outside, without a care in the world.

Suddenly he looked up and saw a little old man, a frail old man covered in moss. Earth had eaten into his face; it had been driven there by the wind.

'Give us a bite to eat, my son,' said the little old man. 'I've grown thin from the road and I've eaten the last crumb in my pouch.'

'Grandad, we haven't a morsel left in the hut,' said Ivan. 'We didn't know you were coming or I'd have saved our last crust for you. I wouldn't have eaten it yesterday. But come along in. At least I can give you a good scrub and wash your shirt for you.'

Ivan heated up the bathhouse, scraped all the dirt off the old man, beat him with a besom so he'd work up a good sweat, washed his shirt and trousers and laid out a bed for him in their hut.

The old man slept well. When he woke in the morning, he said, 'I'll remember your kindness, the good turn you've done me. If ever you're in trouble, just go into the forest. When you come to where the path forks, you'll see a grey stone. Give the stone a push with your shoulder and call out, "Grandad!" I'll come straight away.'

With that the old man went off. As for Ivan and his mother, life got still worse for them. They had eaten every last crumb, every last scrap from their larder.

'You just wait here for me, Mother,' said Ivan. 'I won't be gone long. Maybe I'll be able to bring you some bread.'

'A likely story!' answered his mother. 'Where's a man with your luck going to get bread? Get something to eat for yourself if you can, but don't worry about me. I'll be dying hungry – no doubt about it. Now if only you could find yourself a good wife. Marry a wife with a head on her shoulders – you see – and you need never go hungry again!'

Ivan sighed and went off into the forest. He came to where the path forked and pushed the stone with his shoulder. The stone yielded a little – and there before Ivan appeared the old man.

'What do you want?' said the old man. 'Or have you just come to visit?'

The old man took Ivan into the forest. After a while they came to some fine huts. The old man went straight inside one of them, taking Ivan with him; evidently he was the master there.[1]

The old man called his cook and the boy who worked with her in the kitchen and said they'd like to start with some roast sheep. He served his guest himself. Ivan ate all he was given and asked for more: 'Tell them to roast another sheep and to bring me a loaf of bread.'

The old man told the kitchen boy to roast another sheep and to bring in a loaf of wheaten bread. 'There you are,' he said. 'Take all your heart asks for. Or maybe you've had enough already?'

'Thank you very much,' said Ivan. 'Yes, I've had all I want for myself. But ask your servant to take the sheep and the bread to my mother. She's living all hungry, with no food at all.'

The old man told his kitchen boy to take a whole sheep and two loaves of white bread to Ivan's mother. Then he asked, 'How come you and your mother are living all hungry? You're a man now. Before you know it, you'll find yourself married. How are you going to keep your family?'

'I don't know, Grandad. Anyway, I have no sweetheart.'

'That's a great pity,' said Ivan's host. 'But I can give you my daughter in marriage. She's a clever girl – she's blessed with enough wit for you both.'

The old man called his daughter. In came a beautiful maiden. No one had ever seen such beauty or known it was to be found in the world. The moment Ivan saw her, his heart missed a beat.

The old father looked sternly at his daughter and said, 'Here is your husband, and you are his wife.'

The beautiful daughter merely lowered her eyes and said, 'As you wish, Father.'

And so they got married and began living together. They lived well and there was nothing they lacked. Ivan's wife looked after the hut. As for the old master, he was seldom at home. Most of the time he was wandering the world, searching amid the people for wisdom. Whenever he found some wisdom, he came back home and noted it down in his book.

One time the old man came back with a little round mirror. It was a magic mirror that he'd brought from far away, from a craftsman-magician in the Cold Mountains. The old man brought it back and stored it away.

Ivan's mother was living well now, with plenty to eat, but she went on living in her own hut in the village. Her son wanted her to come and live with him and his wife, but she refused. She didn't like the idea of sharing the home of her daughter-in-law.

'I'm frightened, my son,' she said. 'Your dear Yelenushka's a great beauty. She's rich and from a fine family. What have you done to deserve her? My fate and your father's fate was to be poor, and as for you – you were born with no fate at all.'

And so Ivan's mother went on living in her own little old hut. And Ivan thought about what she'd said. It was true. It seemed he had all he needed. His wife was always sweet to him and she never said a cross word. But it was as if, deep inside him, Ivan always felt cold. The life he was living with his young wife was only half a life; it wasn't the life it should have been.

One day the old man went up to Ivan and said, 'I'm going on a long journey, further than I've ever gone before. I won't be back for a long time. Now I want you to look after this key for me. I used to take it with me, but I'm going such a long way now that I'm afraid of losing it. Take good care of it – and don't open the barn door with it. And if you do go into the barn, don't take your wife inside with you. And if you do end up taking your wife inside, don't give her the brightly coloured dress. I'll give it to her myself – it's for her I'm keeping it – but not till the time's right. Well, take care. Watch you don't forget my words – or you'll lose your life in death!'

With that the old man left.

After some time had passed, Ivan found himself thinking, 'No, it won't do any harm if I just go inside the barn for a look. I won't take my wife with me.'

Ivan went to the barn that had always been kept locked. He opened the door. Inside he saw heaps of gold ingots and stones that flamed like fire. He saw precious goods he didn't even know the names for. And in one corner of the barn was a little storeroom or secret place; there was a door leading into it.

Ivan opened the door. He didn't really mean to, but, before he had even stepped inside, he found himself calling out, 'Yelenushka! Quick! Come here, my darling!'

Inside the storeroom hung a dress embroidered with brilliant stones. It glowed like a clear sky and light flowed over it like a living wind. The mere sight of the dress filled Ivan with joy. It was just right for his wife. It would suit her in every way.

Ivan remembered that the old man had told him not to give this dress to his wife – but all he was going to do now was just show it to her: how could any harm come to the dress just from that? And Ivan loved his wife; her smile was his happiness.

Along came Yelena. She flung up her hands in amazement.

'Oh, my goodness!' she exclaimed. 'What a fine dress!'

And then, before Ivan knew where he was, she was saying to him, 'Help me into the dress. Make sure it hangs straight.'

Ivan forbade her to put the dress on at all. She began to weep.

'So that's how much you love me!' she said. 'Too good a dress for your wife, is it? You might at least let me slip my arms through the sleeves to see how it feels. Maybe it won't be right for me after all.'

Ivan gave his leave.

'All right,' he said. 'See how it feels.'

His wife put her arms through the sleeves. Then she was asking again:

'I can't see a thing. Let me just slip my head through the collar.'

Ivan gave his leave. She put her head through the collar – and quickly pulled the dress down. It wrapped all around her. In one of the pockets she could feel a little mirror. She took it out and looked at herself.

'My, what a beauty!' she said. 'But why's she living with a hapless husband? I wish I were a bird. Then I'd fly far, far away.'

She gave a high-pitched cry, flung up her arms and was gone. She had turned into a dove and was flying where she wished to fly – far, far away into the deep blue sky. The dress she'd put on must have been a magic dress.

Ivan felt very sad. But what was the good of feeling sad? He had no time to waste. He put some bread in his knapsack and set off to search for his wife.

'Wicked creature!' he said. 'Disobeying her father and leaving like that without leave! I'll find her, I'll teach her what's what.'

After saying this, Ivan remembered he had been born hapless, and he began to cry.

He walked along roads, along tracks, along paths. He felt sad and he missed his wife. All of a sudden he saw a pike lying by the edge of a stream. It was dying; it couldn't get back into the water.

'Well,' he said to himself. 'Things may not be looking good for me, but they're still worse for that pike.'

He picked the pike up and released it into the water. It dived deep down, shot up again, stuck its head out of the water and said, 'I won't forget your kindness, the good turn you've done me. If you're in trouble, just say, "Pike, pike, remember Ivan!"'

Ivan ate a piece of bread and went on further. He walked and walked. It was close to nightfall.

Then Ivan saw a sparrow. A kite had caught it and was holding it in its talons. The kite was about to devour it.

'I may be in a bad way myself,' thought Ivan, 'but that sparrow's about to die.'

Ivan scared the kite away. The kite released the sparrow from its talons.

The sparrow perched on a branch and said to Ivan, 'If ever you're in need, just call out, "Sparrow, sparrow, return my good turn!"'

Ivan spent the night under the tree. Come morning, though, he went on his way further. Already he had walked far from his own home; already he had grown tired – and he had become so thin in body that he had to hold his clothes in place with one hand. But there remained a long way for Ivan to go – and he walked on for a whole year and then half a year. He had crossed all of the earth and come to the sea. There was nowhere further for him to go.

He asked someone who lived there, 'Whose land is this? Who are the tsar and tsaritsa here?'

The man replied, 'Our tsaritsa here is Yelena the Wise. She knows everything – she has a book where everything is written down – and she has a special mirror where she can see everything in the world. She can probably even see you right now.'

And he was right. Yelena had already seen Ivan in her little mirror. Her maidservant Darya had wiped the dust off the mirror with a towel and then looked into the mirror herself. First Darya had thought how beautiful she was, and then she had glimpsed a foreign peasant.

'Look!' she said to Yelena the Wise. 'There's a foreign stranger just appeared. He must have come a long way. He's all thin and worn out and his bast sandals are torn to ribbons.'

Yelena the Wise looked in the little mirror.

'A foreign stranger!' she said. 'That's no foreign stranger – it's my own husband who's just appeared.'

Ivan walked towards the palace. The courtyard was surrounded by a wooden fence. On top of each stake was a dead human head. Only one stake was empty, with nothing on it.

Ivan asked about all this: what did it all mean? The man who lived there replied, 'Those are the suitors of our tsaritsa. You haven't seen our tsaritsa. Her beauty is more than words can tell and in wit she's a magician. Suitors keep coming to ask for her hand. They're bold, noble men, but she refuses them all. No suitor will suit her unless he has the wit to outwit her. Whoever fails she executes by death. Now there's only one stake left. That'll be for the next would-be husband.'

'She's my wife,' said Ivan. 'I've come here to be her husband.'

'Then it'll be your head on that stake,' said the man, and went off towards his hut.

Ivan went into the palace. Yelena the Wise was sitting in her royal chamber and she was wearing the dress her father had brought back and hidden in the barn, the one she had clothed herself in without leave.

'What's brought *you* along?' asked Yelena the Wise. 'Why have *you* appeared all of a sudden?'

'I wanted to have a look at you,' said Ivan. 'I've been missing you.'

'Others have been missing me too,' said Yelena the Wise, and pointed to the fence outside, where the dead heads were.

'Aren't you my wife any longer then?' asked Ivan.

'I used to be your wife,' said the tsaritsa, 'but I'm no longer the woman I was then. What do I want with a hapless peasant? If you want me to be your wife, then you must win me again.

And if you fail, it's off with your head! Look – there's still one empty stake left outside.'

'The empty stake doesn't need me,' said Ivan. 'But you watch out – or you'll find yourself needing me more than you ever dreamed. Tell me: what wish do you want fulfilled?'

'You are to fulfil my command – to hide where I can't find you, or so that I can't recognize you if I do. You may go where you please, even to the edge of the world. Outwit me – and I'll become your wife. But if you fail to remain secret, if I divine where you're hidden, it's off with your head.'

'Let me eat your bread and sleep on your straw,' said Ivan. 'And in the morning I'll fulfil your wish.'

That evening Darya the maidservant laid out some straw for Ivan in the entrance room and brought him a thick slice of bread and a jug of kvass. Then Ivan lay down and began to wonder: what would the morning bring?

After a while he saw Darya again. She came in, sat down near the door so that she was looking outside, spread out the tsaritsa's bright dress and began darning a hole in it. She sewed and sewed; she darned and darned. Then she began to cry.

'Why are you crying, Darya?' asked Ivan.

'How can I not cry,' she answered, 'if tomorrow will bring my death? The tsaritsa told me to darn a hole in her dress, but the needle doesn't sew. It only tears the dress even more. The cloth's so tender it just gapes apart. And if I fail to mend the dress, the tsaritsa will have me executed in the morning.'

'Let me have a go,' said Ivan. 'Maybe I can mend it myself. Then you won't need to die.'

'I shouldn't even let you touch this dress,' said Darya. 'The tsaritsa says you're a hapless halfwit. Still, you may as well try. I'll watch.'

Ivan took the dress, sat down again and began to sew. What Darya had said was true: the needle only tore the dress even more. The dress was light as air and there was nowhere for the needle to take hold. Ivan threw down the needle and began to work with his hands, taking each thread in turn and tying it to the end of another thread.

Darya saw what Ivan was doing and got very angry. 'You

fool,' she said, 'what do you think you're doing? There are thousands and thousands of threads there in that hole. How can you tie them all with your fingers?'

'Where there's patience and will, there's always a way,' said Ivan. 'You go and lie down now. Don't worry – I'll be finished by morning.'

Ivan worked on all through the night. From up in the sky the moon was shining down at him, and anyway the dress shone of itself, as if it were alive. He could see every last thread.

Ivan finished a little before dawn. He looked at the work he had done. The hole had gone and the dress was all of a piece.

He picked the dress up. It seemed to have become heavy. He examined the dress. In one pocket he found a book – the book where the old man who was Yelena's father had noted down all of his wisdom. In the other pocket he found the little round mirror the old man had brought back from the craftsman-magician in the Cold Mountains. Ivan looked in the mirror – he could see something there, but it was all very cloudy. Then he looked at the book, but he couldn't understand a word. 'What people say must be true,' Ivan said to himself, 'I'm a hapless halfwit.'

Soon afterwards Darya the maidservant came in. She took the finished dress, looked it over and said to Ivan, 'Thank you. You've saved me from death and I shall remember your kindness, the good turn you've done me.'

Up over the earth rose the sun. It was time for Ivan to go away to a secret place where Tsaritsa Yelena would be unable to find him. He went out into the yard, saw a haystack there and climbed into it. He thought he was completely hidden, but the dogs in the yard all started barking at him and Darya shouted, 'Goodness me – now you really are being a fool! You can't even hide from me, let alone from the tsaritsa. Get out from there – and don't dirty the hay with mud from your sandals!'

Ivan climbed out of the haystack and wondered where to go next. Not far away he could see the sea. He walked to the shore and remembered the pike.

'Pike! Pike!' he said. 'Remember Ivan!'

The pike poked its head out of the water. 'Quick!' it said. 'I'll hide you deep down on the sea bed.'

Ivan threw himself into the sea. The pike pulled him down to the sea bed, buried him deep in the sand and stirred up the water with its tail.

Yelena the Wise took her round mirror and held it to the earth: Ivan wasn't there. She held it to the sky: Ivan wasn't there. She held it to the sea: there too she could see no sign of Ivan – only cloudy water. 'I may be cunning and wise,' the tsaritsa said to herself, 'but it seems this hapless Ivan's not such a simpleton either.'

She opened her father's book of wisdom and read, 'Cunning of mind is powerful, but kindness is more powerful still. Even a beast remembers kindness.' So said the written words, but then the tsaritsa read what was not written. This time the book said, 'Ivan lies buried in the sand on the sea bed. Call the pike and order him to fetch Ivan. Say that if he doesn't, you'll have him cooked for your dinner.'

Yelena sent her maidservant Darya to call the pike and tell him to bring Ivan up from the bottom of the sea.

Ivan appeared before Yelena the Wise.

'Execute me,' he said, 'I'm not worthy of you.'

But Yelena the Wise thought better of it: there was always time enough to have a man executed and, in any case, it wasn't as if she and Ivan were strangers. They had been family; they had shared one home.

'Go and hide again,' she said to Ivan. 'If you outwit me, I'll pardon you. But if not, I'll execute you.'

Ivan went off to look for a secret place where the tsaritsa would be unable to find him. But where could he go? Tsaritsa Yelena had a magic mirror where she could see everything in the world. And if there was anything she couldn't see in this mirror, her wise book would tell her about it.

Ivan called out, 'Hey, sparrow! Do you remember my kindness?'

The sparrow was already there.

'Fall to the ground,' it said. 'Become a grain of wheat!'

Ivan fell to the ground and became a grain of wheat. The sparrow devoured it.

Yelena the Wise turned her mirror to the earth, to the sky, to the water – there was no sign of Ivan. Everything was there in the mirror – except what she needed. The Wise Yelena lost her temper and threw her mirror against the floor, and it smashed into pieces. Then Darya the maidservant came in. She gathered up all the slivers from the mirror and carried them away in the hem of her skirt to the servants' corner of the courtyard.

Yelena the Wise opened her father's book. In it she read, 'Ivan is in the grain; the grain is in the sparrow; and the sparrow is on the fence.'

Yelena sent Darya to call the sparrow down from the fence: the sparrow must give her the grain of wheat or else he'd be fed to the kite.

Darya went to speak to the sparrow. The sparrow heard Darya's words, took fright and threw out the little grain from its beak. The grain fell onto the ground and turned into Ivan. He stood there just as before.

And so Ivan appeared once more before Yelena the Wise.

'Execute me now,' he said. 'It's true: I'm hapless, and you're very wise.'

'Tomorrow,' said the tsaritsa. 'Tomorrow I'll have your head stuck up on the last stake.'

That evening Ivan lay in the entrance room. In the morning he was going to die and he didn't know what to do. Then he remembered his mother. So much did he love her that he felt at peace again straight away.

Then Darya came in with a bowl of porridge.

Ivan ate the porridge. Then Darya said, 'Don't you be afraid of our tsaritsa, Ivan. She's not truly wicked.'

'A husband doesn't fear his own wife,' said Ivan. 'I just wish I had time to teach her what's what.'

'Don't be in a rush to get yourself executed tomorrow,' said Darya. 'Say you've got things to do, that it's impossible for you to die straight away. Say you're expecting your mother to visit.'

And so, when morning came, Ivan said to Yelena the Wise, 'Allow me to live a little longer. I want to speak to my dear mother – she may be coming to see me.'

The tsaritsa gave him a quick look. 'I can't grant you life just like that,' she said. 'You must hide from me a third time. If I can't find you, then you can live. So be it.'

Ivan went out to look for a secret place. He saw Darya the maid coming towards him.

'Wait a moment,' she ordered. 'I'll hide you away. I haven't forgotten your kindness.'

She breathed into Ivan's face and Ivan disappeared. He turned into the warm breath of a woman. Darya breathed in and drew him into her breast. Then she went into the tsaritsa's chamber and took the father's wise book from the table. She wiped the dust off it, opened it and breathed into it. Her breath immediately turned into a new first letter in the book's title. Ivan had become a letter. Darya closed the book and went out.

Soon afterwards Yelena the Wise came in. She opened the book and looked inside: where was Ivan? But the book had nothing to say. Or if it did have something to say, the tsaritsa couldn't understand it; there was no longer any sense in the book. What the tsaritsa didn't know was that every word in the book had changed because of the new letter now in the title.

Yelena the Wise slammed the book shut and struck it against the ground. All the letters scattered out of the book. And when the first letter in the title struck the ground, it turned into Ivan.

Ivan looked at Yelena the Wise. He looked and looked at his wife and couldn't take his eyes off her. The tsaritsa for her part was gazing at Ivan; and, as she gazed at him, she began to smile. And this made her still more beautiful than she had been before.

'And there was I,' she said, 'thinking I had a hapless peasant for a husband – but he hid from the magic mirror and outwitted the book of wisdom!'

And from then on they lived in peace and harmony. One day, though, the tsaritsa said to Ivan, 'What about your dear mother? Why hasn't she come to see you yet?'

'Yes, you're right to ask! And we haven't seen your dear father for a long time either. Tomorrow morning I'll go and fetch them both.'

But by daybreak Ivan's dear mother and Yelena's dear father

were already there; they had come of their own accord to be with their children. Yelena's father knew a close way to their tsardom. They had walked only a short distance and were not in the least tired.

Ivan bowed to his mother; then he turned to the old man and fell down at his feet.

'It's bad, Father. I did what you forbade. Forgive your hapless son.'

The old man embraced and forgave him.

'Thank you, son,' he said. 'There was charm in the forbidden dress and wisdom in the book. The mirror showed all things visible – all that seems in the world. I thought I'd collected a good dowry for my daughter, only I didn't want to give it to her too soon. I thought I'd brought her gifts of every kind, but I'd left out the one kind that matters, the kindness that was there inside you. I went far away in search of this gift, but it was close at hand all the time. It's never a given, nor can anyone give it – it seems we must each seek it out for ourselves.'

Yelena the Wise began to cry. She kissed her husband and begged his forgiveness.

And from then on Yelena and her father and Ivan and his mother all lived together. They lived a splendid life and they're still living it to this day.

The Magic Ring

A peasant woman lived in a village. Together with her lived her son Semyon; he had not yet married. They were very poor. They slept on straw, their clothes were old and patched, and they had nothing to put in their mouths. This was a long time ago, when the peasants had little land and what land they did have was barren. What the peasants managed to sow would be killed by frosts. If it was not killed by frosts, it would be destroyed by drought. If it was not destroyed by drought, it would be drowned by rain. If it was not drowned by rain, it would be gobbled up by locusts.

Once a month Semyon used to go into town on behalf of his mother – to collect her widow's pension of one kopek.

Once he was on his way back home with the money, with the one kopek, when he saw someone strangling a dog with a piece of rope. It was very small, a little white dog, a mere puppy.

'Why are you tormenting the puppy?' Semyon asked.

'That's none of your business. If I want to kill it, I'll kill it.'

'Why not sell him to me for a kopek?'

'All right. Take him!'

Semyon gave the man his last kopek, took the puppy in his arms and set off back home. 'I have no cow and no horse,' he said to himself, 'but I do have a puppy.'

He brought the puppy back home, but his mother just scolded him: 'You fool,' she shouted. 'We've got nothing to eat ourselves – and you have to go off and buy dogs!'

'Don't worry, Mama. Dogs are livestock too. They may not moo, but they know how to bark.'

A month later Semyon went to town again for the pension. It had gone up. This time he was given two kopeks.

On his way back he met the same man. This time he was tormenting a cat.

Semyon ran up to him. 'It's a living being,' he said. 'Why are you torturing it?'

'That's none of your business. It's my cat and I'll do what I like with it.'

'Sell her to me.'

'All right – but a cat's dearer than a dog.'

They settled on two kopeks.

Semyon took the cat and set off back home. His mother scolded her son more than ever. She scolded him right into the evening and began scolding him again early the next morning.

Another month passed by. Semyon went to town again for the pension. It had gone up by another kopek. This time he was given three kopeks.

Semyon made his way out of the town. There on the road stood the same man. Now he was strangling a snake.

Semyon said straight away, 'Don't kill her. She's no common snake – I've never seen a snake like her before. I'm sure she's not poisonous. Why not sell her to me?'

He bought the snake for three kopeks, which was all the money he had in the world. Then he tucked the snake under his shirt and set off back home.

Once the snake had warmed up in Semyon's bosom, she said to him, 'You won't be sorry you spent all your money on me. I'm no ordinary snake – I'm Snake Skarapeya.[1] If it weren't for you I'd have met my death. But I'm alive now and my father will show you his thanks.'

Semyon got back home and let the snake out from under his shirt. The moment his mother caught sight of the snake, she climbed straight up onto the stove. She wasn't even able to scold her son – she was tongue-tied with fright. As for Skarapeya, she slid underneath the stove, curled up there and fell fast asleep.

And so now there were five of them, all living together – a white dog, a grey cat, Semyon and his mother and then Snake Skarapeya.

Semyon's mother didn't like Skarapeya. She was always forgetting her food or not putting out her water. Sometimes she
stepped on her tail.

One day Skarapeya said to Semyon, 'Your mother's not very
kind to me. Take me back to my father.'

The snake slid off along the path. Semyon followed. He followed the snake for a long time – all day and all night, all night
and all day. Now they were deep in the forest. Semyon began
to wonder where he was going and how he would ever find his
way back.

'Don't be afraid,' the snake consoled him. 'There's not much
further to glide. Look – we've already come to the border of the
snake tsardom! And I'm the daughter of the snake tsar – soon
we'll meet my father. But listen now. When I tell my father how
you saved me, he'll thank you and offer you a great deal of
gold. You must refuse the gold. Instead you must ask just for
one thing – the gold ring my father wears on his finger. It's a
magic ring. My father's been keeping it for me, but I want to
give it to you.'

Semyon and the snake tsarevna arrived at the snake tsar's.
The snake tsar was very glad to see his daughter again.

'Thank you for saving my beloved daughter,' he said to
Semyon. 'I'd give her to you in marriage, I'd be only too glad,
but she's already betrothed. Please take as much of my gold as
you wish!'

Semyon refused the gold. Instead, he said to the snake tsar,
'Give me the ring you're wearing – it will be a keepsake for me
to remember your daughter by. Yes, I can see an embossed
snake's head on it, and two green stones that burn like eyes.'

The snake tsar thought deeply, then took the ring from his
finger and gave it to Semyon. As he did this, he whispered in
Semyon's ear, telling him what to do with the ring, how he
should act in order to summon its magic power.

Semyon bid farewell to the snake tsar and his daughter
Skarapeya. Standing nearby was the adopted son of the snake
tsar; his name was Aspid.[2] Semyon said goodbye to him, too.

Semyon went back home, to his mother. The first night, as
soon as his mother had lain down to sleep, Semyon slipped the

snake's ring from one finger to another. Twelve strong men at once appeared before him.

'Greetings, new master!' they said. 'What do you want done?'

'Fill the whole barn with flour, brothers. And make sure there's some sugar too, and some butter.'

'Certainly!' said the young men.

And they vanished.

When he awoke in the morning, Semyon saw his mother dipping dry crusts in water and chewing away at them with her few wobbly teeth.

'What are you doing, mother? Why haven't you mixed some dough and set it to rise? You could be baking some pies for us!'

'Have you lost your senses, my son? It's over a year now since we've had so much as a handful of flour.'

'Just have a look in the barn, mother. Maybe you'll find some flour there after all.'

'What's the good of looking in an empty place? Even the mice out there have all starved to death. I'd do better to block up the barn door for good.'

Off went the mother to the barn. She pushed the barn door. It swung wide open and she fell straight into a mountain of flour.

After that they began to live well. Semyon sold half the flour and, with the money he got for it, bought lots of beef. Even the cat and the dog were now eating rissoles every day. They grew sleek and glossy.

And then one night Semyon saw a vision. The moment he fell asleep he saw a beautiful maiden. It was as if she were there in the room. But when he awoke, she had gone. Semyon began to long for her, but he did not even know where she lived.

He moved the snake's ring from one finger to another.

'What are your orders, master?' asked the twelve young men.

Semyon told them about his vision: he had seen a beautiful maiden. He didn't know where she lived but, wherever it was, that was where he must go.

In the twinkling of an eye Semyon was in another tsardom. He was in the tsardom where the beautiful maiden lived.

He went up to someone who lived there and asked about the beautiful maiden.

'Now which one might that be?' the man asked in reply.

Semyon told him about the maiden.

'That sounds like the tsar's daughter!' the man said.

Semyon transferred his ring from one finger to another and ordered the young men to take him into the palace, to the tsarevna. Straight away he was inside the palace – and there he saw the tsarevna. She was even more beautiful than she had appeared in his dream.

Semyon gave a deep sigh – what else was there for him to do? – and summoned the young men again. He ordered them to take him back home.

Back in his own home he felt sad and lonely. He was longing for the tsarevna. Without her he could hardly eat his bread or drink his beer.

His mother began to worry: 'What's the matter with you, son? Are you ill or are you pining for someone?'

'I'm pining for someone, Mama,' said Semyon. And he told her all that had happened.

His mother was terrified. 'Whatever next!' she said. 'How can a peasant's son even think of loving a tsarevna? Tsars are sly and deceitful people. They'll mock you and abuse you. And a tsar will have you executed sooner than he'll give you the hand of his daughter. Marry a poor peasant's daughter if you want to be happy!'

Semyon just carried on repeating the same thing: 'Go on, Mama, go and ask for the tsarevna's hand.' But his mother kept refusing to go.

Semyon thought for a long time. He thought and thought till he thought something up.

He used his snake ring to summon the twelve young men. The twelve young men appeared just like that.

'What are our orders, master?'

'I want a splendid mansion, and I want it ready by morning. There must be a fine chamber for my mother. And make sure you lay a mattress of down on her bed.'

'All right, master, we'll build you your mansion and we'll fill your mother's mattress with the finest of down.'

Semyon's mother awoke in the morning and could hardly get out of bed – so deep had she sunk into her mattress of down. She looked around her chamber and rubbed her eyes. Was she still dreaming – or was this for real?

Then Semyon came in and wished her good morning. Everything, she realized, was for real. 'What's happened, son?' she asked. 'Where have all these goods come from?'

'From one good,' he replied, 'comes another good. Now you'll be able to live in comfort and I'll be able to marry whomever I like. No one can look down on us now.'

'Well,' thought his mother, 'what a bold, quick-witted son I've got!'

The son then returned to his same request: 'Go on, mother, now you must go to the tsar and tsaritsa. You must ask on my behalf for the hand of their daughter.'

The mother looked all around her. She walked about the mansion. She thought how rich and splendid everything looked.

'All right,' she decided. 'I'll go to the tsar and tsaritsa and ask for the hand of their daughter. We may not be their equals, but we're not far beneath them.'

Off she went.

She walked straight into the imperial hut, into the tsar's front room. The tsar and tsaritsa were drinking tea. They'd poured a little into their saucers and were blowing on it to cool it down. The tsarevna was in her maiden's room, sorting through the chests that contained her dowry.

The tsar and tsaritsa went on blowing into their saucers. They didn't even notice Semyon's mother. Some of the tea splashed onto the tablecloth. And it wasn't just tea – it was tea with sugar! A tsar – and he didn't even know how to drink tea!

'That's tea, you know, not water,' said Semyon's mother. 'Why splash it about?'

The tsar looked at her. 'And what's brought you here?' he asked.

Semyon's mother stepped forward into the centre of the room.

As a matchmaker should, she stood beneath the roof beam –
beneath the mother beam of the hut.

'Good day, Sir Sovereign Tsar,' she said. 'You've got stock
for sale and we've got a buyer. Allow my son to marry your
daughter.'

'Who is this son of yours? Where are his estates and what is
his lineage?'

'He's from peasant stock and he's from a village some way
away. His name is Semyon Yegorovich. Have you not heard of
him?'

The tsaritsa gaped in astonishment. 'What's got into you,
woman? We're knee-deep in suitors – we can pick and choose.
What do we want with the son of a peasant?'

Semyon's mother took offence at this. 'My son's no ordinary
peasant, thank you. He's worth more than ten tsareviches. And
as for a mere tsarevna, a mere girl-daughter . . .'

The tsar thought up a cunning ruse. 'All right,' he said, 'tell
your son to construct a crystal bridge from our palace hut to
his front door. In the morning we'll ride over and take a look at
his rooms. Yes indeed!'

Semyon's mother went back home. As she went in, she nearly
tripped up over the cat and dog. They had grown very sleek.

She shooed them angrily out of the way. 'Eating and sleeping
all day,' she said to herself. 'A fat lot of use those two are!'

Then she spoke to her son: 'It's no good, my son. They didn't
agree.'

'What do you mean? How could they not agree?'

'What did you expect, son? Did you think they were going
to jump for joy? The tsar just made fun of us. He said, "Let him
construct a crystal bridge from our palace to his front door.
Then we can ride over to you across crystal."'

'That's all right, mother. That's child's play.'

That night Semyon cast his ring from one hand to the other
hand. He summoned his young men and ordered them to construct a crystal bridge by the following morning. The bridge
was to go from his own porch to the imperial palace hut, it was
to cross over all the rivers and gullies, and there was to be a

carriage that would travel the length of the bridge under its own power.

Everywhere round about, from midnight until dawn, could be heard the ring of hammers and the rasping of saws. In the morning Semyon went out onto the porch to have a look. The bridge was ready; it was made of crystal and a self-powered carriage was travelling along it.

'Go on, mother,' he said. 'Go and speak to the tsar now. Tell him and the tsaritsa to get ready to come and visit. Say I'll be rolling up any moment to collect them in the self-powered carriage.'

His mother set off.

Crystal is slippery and it was a windy day. The moment she stepped onto the bridge, there was a gust of wind from behind her. She fell down in fright, then slid all the way to the tsar's porch on her backside.

'I called by yesterday,' she said to the tsar, 'and you ordered my son to construct a bridge. Have a look through the window – your bridge is now ready.'

The tsar looked out through the window.

'Well,' he said. 'A real bridge – who'd have thought it? Your son certainly knows a thing or two!'

The tsar put on his crown and his gold brocade trousers. He called the tsaritsa and went out onto the porch. He tested the railings: were they firm? He ran the palm of his hand over the crystal bricks: were they the real thing? 'Well, well, well,' he said to himself. 'Goodness knows how, but the bridge has certainly been built good and proper.'

Just then Semyon rolled up in a wonderful, self-powered carriage. He opened one of the doors and said, 'Greetings to you, Sovereign Tsar, and to your Sovereign Tsaritsa-Wife! Please be seated. Come and be our guests!'

'I'll be only too glad,' said the tsar, 'but my wife may be a little timid.'

Semyon looked at the tsaritsa. She threw up her hands in horror.

'I'm not going. It's awful. It'll drop us down into the river.'

Then the tsar's courtiers and magnates appeared. The eldest

pronounced, 'You must set an example, your Highness. You
have to go. The people mustn't think you're afraid.'

The tsar and the tsaritsa climbed into the carriage – what
else could they do? The courtiers all crowded onto the foot-
boards or hung from the door handles.

The bell rang. The carriage whistled, hummed and roared and
began to shake. In a cloud of smoke and steam it jerked forward –
and then off it went. It rocked and rolled all the way. The tsar
and tsaritsa were glad there was only one bridge to cross.

They reached Semyon's palace. Semyon got out to open the
tsar's door, but the courtiers were there first. They were dragging the tsar and tsaritsa out of the carriage, fanning them and
trying to bring them back to their senses.

The tsaritsa was shouting and screaming. The tsar was quite
silent, but you could see he felt the same as his wife.

'My!' said the tsaritsa. 'I've never been so jolted and shaken
in all my life. Where's that suitor gone – the devil take him! Yes,
young man, you can have the girl – do what you like with her!
And we'll be going back home on foot.'

Everything went as Semyon wished. The tsarevna was given
to him in marriage and they began to live together as man and
wife. Their life began well, there was no gainsaying it.

But then one day something happened. Semyon and his wife
went for a walk in the forest. They walked a long way. They
felt tired, lay down under a tree and dozed off.

Just then Aspid, the adopted son of the snake tsar, happened
to pass by. He saw the ring on Semyon's finger and turned into
a viper from envy. He had hankered after that ring for many
years; he knew its magic power and had kept asking the snake
tsar to give it to him. But the snake tsar had always refused,
and he had never told him the secret of the magic ring's action.

Aspid turned himself into a beautiful maiden. He was even
more beautiful than Semyon's young wife. He woke Semyon
and beckoned to him. 'In a moment,' Aspid was saying to himself, 'that ring will be mine.'

Semyon looked at the unknown beauty who was making
signs to him. 'Be off with you,' he said. 'Wherever you're going,
get going there! You may be comely, you may even be comelier

than my wife, but my wife's dearer to me. No, you won't catch *me* going anywhere with you!'

And Semyon went back to sleep.

Then Aspid turned himself into a handsome young man, a prince of princes. He woke up the tsarevna, Semyon's wife, and began strutting about in front of her.

'What a man!' thought the tsarevna. 'Far more handsome than my husband! A pity he wasn't around earlier – I could have done with a suitor like him!'

Aspid went right up to Semyon's wife and held out his hand to her. The tsarevna got to her feet and glanced down at Semyon. There was dirt on his face and he was blowing it about as he breathed.

'Who are you?' the tsarevna asked Aspid.

'I'm the son of the tsar. They call me the Prince of Princes.'

'And I'm a tsar's daughter!'

'Come along with me then. I'll look after you well.'

'Let's go, my prince!' said Semyon's wife, and gave him her hand.

Aspid whispered something in the tsarevna's ear – and she nodded in agreement. Then he went off alone. What he had instructed her to do was to find out from Semyon the secret of the magic ring's action. Then she was to bring him the ring.

. She and Semyon went back home. She took Semyon by the hand and asked if it was true that he had a magic ring on his finger. If he really loved her, he should tell her about this magic ring: how did the ring act?

Semyon was kind and good. He told his wife everything. 'My wife loves me,' he thought, 'so why shouldn't she know about the ring? She's not going to do me any harm.'

And Semyon put his magic ring on his wife's finger: after all, he could always take it back again when he needed it.

During the night the tsarevna transferred the ring from one finger to another.

The twelve young men appeared straight away. 'Here we are,' they said. 'What can we do for you, new mistress?'

'Here's what you can do for me. Take this mansion and the

crystal bridge and move them to where the Prince of Princes lives.'

And that was that; no longer did Semyon Yegorovich have a wife.

He and his mother awoke in the morning to find everything gone. All they had was a poor hut and an empty barn; everything was as it had been before. There were just the four of them, Semyon and his mother, and the cat and the dog – and there was nothing at all for any of them to eat.

Semyon did not let out a word of complaint, not even a sigh. He recalled what his mother had said: 'Don't marry a tsarevna – it won't bring you happiness.' Why hadn't he listened to his mother?

In his sorrow Semyon looked out of the window. A carriage was approaching; inside it he could see the tsar. Just opposite Semyon's window the carriage stopped and the tsar got out. He looked around: where had everything gone? There was no mansion and no crystal bridge. Nowhere was there anything that gleamed or glittered – only a poor old hut and Semyon watching the tsar through the window.

'What's all this?' shouted the tsar. 'Where's my daughter the tsarevna? What have you done with her, you cheat and deceiver?'

Semyon went out to the tsar and told him the truth: that the tsarevna had taken his magic ring and deceived him.

The tsar did not believe the truth. He got into a rage and ordered Semyon to be thrown into prison until he confessed what he'd done with the tsarevna.

Semyon's mother was left without her son and breadwinner – and very soon she was left with nothing to eat. She called to the cat and the dog and set off begging. She would beg for a crust of bread beneath one window and eat it beneath the next. But it was turning cold and dark. Summer had grown old, too. Winter was drawing near.

The cat said to the dog, 'We won't last much longer like this. We must find the tsarevna and get the magic ring back. Our master saved us from death. Now it's our turn to save him.'

The dog agreed. He sniffed at the ground and ran off. The cat followed.

They had to run a long, long way. And what's quick to say can take many a day.

They ran and ran until they saw the crystal bridge and the mansion that had once been a home to them and Semyon.

The dog waited outside while the cat went in. She stole into the bedchamber of the tsarevna who had deceived Semyon. The tsarevna was asleep. The cat saw the ring glittering between the tsarevna's teeth. Yes, she was keeping it in her mouth; she must have been afraid the ring would be stolen.

The cat caught a mouse, gave him a bite on the ear and told him what he must do to stay alive. The mouse climbed up onto the bed, crept silently over the tsarevna and tickled her in the nostril with his tail. The tsarevna sneezed and her mouth opened. Out fell the ring – and off it rolled across the floor.

The cat seized the ring and leaped through the window. The tsarevna awoke. But by the time she had begun searching her room, the ring was already far away and the mouse that had tickled the tsarevna's nose was quietly gnawing a crust of bread in the kitchen: what would a little mouse know about what had just happened?

The cat and the dog made for home. They ran and ran. They didn't eat or sleep – there was no time. They ran over mountains and they ran through deep forests. They swam across rivers and they crossed open steppe. All the way the cat kept the magic ring under her tongue. She never once opened her mouth.

There before them lay the very last river. Beyond it they could see their own village. They could see Semyon's hut.

The dog said to the cat, 'Sit on my back and I'll swim. And be sure to keep your teeth tight together. Don't drop the ring.'

They began to swim the river. They were half way across. The dog said, 'Careful, puss. Don't speak or you'll drown the ring.'

The cat didn't say a word. They swam a little further. Then the dog said:

'Don't say a word, puss!'

The cat hadn't said anything at all. And then the dog spoke again:

'Don't drop the ring, puss! Keep your mouth shut!'

'But my mouth is shut!' said the cat – and dropped the ring into the river.

As soon as they'd reached the bank, they started cursing and fighting.

'It's all your fault, you stupid chatterbox of a cat!' whined the dog.

'No, it's all *your* fault, you barking blabbermouth,' replied the cat. 'Why did you keep talking when I wasn't saying a word?'

Just then some fishermen dragged in their net and began gutting their catch. They saw the cat and the dog quarrelling and thought they must be quarrelling because they were hungry. They threw them some fish guts.

The cat and the dog caught the fish guts and started to eat. They had only eaten a little when there was a crunch. Something hard. Yes – there was the ring!

They left their food and ran into the village. They ran up to their own hut: was their master there? No, there was no sign of Semyon – and it seemed his mother was still wandering about begging. The cat and the dog ran on into the city, to Semyon's prison.

The cat climbed up and began walking along the top of the outer wall. She was looking for Semyon, but she had no idea where he was. She wanted to purr or mew to him, but the ring was under her tongue and she was afraid of dropping it.

Towards evening Semyon looked out through his prison window. He wanted a glimpse of the wide world – of the bright world outside his prison. The cat saw Semyon. She climbed down a gutter, then made her way along a wall and into his cell.

Semyon took the cat in his arms. 'Well,' he thought, 'she may only be a cat, but she has a loyal, faithful heart. She hasn't forgotten me.'

The cat mewed and dropped the magic ring onto the floor in front of him.

Semyon picked it up and summoned the twelve young men.

They appeared straight away. 'Greetings, dear old master!' they said. 'Tell us what you want done. We won't waste time about it.'

'Take my mansion from wherever it is now,' said Semyon, 'and bring it here. And if there's anyone living in my mansion, bring him or her along too. I'd like to have a look at them. And you can move the crystal bridge here as well, but turn it so that the other end is in the next village instead of by the imperial hut.'

Semyon's orders were carried out to the letter. His mansion was back in place straight away. Inside Semyon found the young tsarevna, together with her Aspid. They left quickly and went to live with the tsarevna's father. Where else could they go?

When Aspid understood just what had happened, when he realized that the tsarevna had lost the ring, his rage transformed him into a viper.

And this time he was unable to turn himself back into a young man, because this rage didn't pass. He couldn't get over his fury with the tsarevna. And so Aspid remained a viper. All he could do was curse and hiss at the tsarevna. This made her old father remember Semyon.

'Yes,' he thought, 'Semyon may only have been a peasant but he was a good fellow. And Aspid may be a tsarevich, but he's a viper.'

And Semyon and his mother, and their cat and dog, were soon all living together again in their mansion.

Semyon now goes every day to the next village. He rides there in his self-powered carriage. With the crystal bridge it's no distance at all.

They say Semyon's going to take a wife from that village – that he's asked for the hand of a young orphan girl who's even more beautiful than the tsarevna.

Soon there'll be a wedding. Semyon and the orphan girl will marry and have children. And that will be the beginning of a new tale.

Ivan the Wonder

All this was a long time ago; there were people living then, too. Among them were a peasant and his wife. Their life was a good life. The wife knew no harm from her husband and they had enough to eat – though not more than enough; the earth did not bear wheat and rye easily. Their land was a distant land, a forest land where people lived humbly.

For nearly five years the husband and wife lived in harmony in every way, but they had no children and one can't live without children; a life without children is no life at all.

The husband began to get angry with his wife, and his wife would keep crying. She would go off to the barn, where no one could see her, and weep alone. She would weep and not tell anyone and not say a word to her husband. And what could she have said to her husband? Nothing: a childless wife is as orphaned as a motherless child.

During the sixth year of their marriage the wife fell pregnant and conceived a child. Now the husband was still more furious. 'This child is no child of mine,' he said. 'It's from someone else. Be off with you. Never let me set eyes on you again!'

Where was the woman to go? Not to her mother and father. In the old days a mother and father would never have allowed a married daughter back into the home. They would have ordered her to return to her husband and do as he said.

The wife resolved, 'I'll go where my eyes look. I'll go into the dark forest. There I'll meet a fierce beast, and the beast will eat me.' And so off into the dark forest she went. She was hungry and her hair was hanging loose, and she was thinking, 'I've lived only a very little of life – but I'm still young, and in my womb I am bearing my first child to his death.'

On she walked into the dark and boundless forest. Here and there she ate a little – a few berries, some roots and herbs that she found in the glades.

The last of her time was coming; soon she would have to give birth. She collected some brushwood and small branches and built herself a little shack. And there she gave birth.

She gave birth to a son, and she gave him the same name as her father: Ivan. She wrapped him in her skirt, warmed him and lifted him to her breast. Ivan drank his mother's milk, slept a little, then stretched out to her breast again. The mother gave him her breast straight away. Ivan emptied it and stretched out to the other breast.

A day passed, and then another day. The mother could see that her son Ivan was growing like leavened dough. By the third day Ivan was already talking to his mother. On the fourth day it was the mother's turn to talk; she told her son everything about how people live in the world and how she herself had lived. The mother felt sad and lonely in the forest – but she could see that her son, though he had lived little, had been born with a quick understanding. And so they went on living in the forest, conversing like equals. Before his mother knew it, she and Ivan were equals no more; he had outgrown her. But very little time had passed; it was only a week or two since Ivan had first come into the world.

Ivan got up off the ground, had a stretch, looked into the forest and saw a grey wolf running along. Ivan walked straight towards the wolf, seized him by the scruff of his neck, held him to the ground and pressed down on him – and that was the end of the wolf.

The mother saw what Ivan had done.

'My son is quick to understand,' she thought. 'And he's strong too! But whether he's kind and good it's still too soon to tell.'

The mother flayed the wolf, then laid out the skin on the floor of their shack. Ivan took the flesh of the wolf outside and threw it down on the ground, not far away.

Two bears came up and tried to snatch the meat, each want-ing it for itself, and they began to fight.

The mother saw the bears and felt frightened.

'The bears will eat us, my son.'

'They won't touch us. I'll share out the meat for them, and they'll quieten down.'

Ivan went out, tore the meat in half and threw it to the bears, giving each an equal portion. Then he went back to his mother. But the bears had seen Ivan tearing the wolf's flesh and the bones flying every which way, and they felt wary: what if Ivan began tearing them in half too? And so the bears went off into the forest, without eating any of the wolf meat at all.

Ivan began wandering about further. To feed his own mother, he needed to gather berries and dig up sweet roots. And besides, he wished to have a look at the earth. He had been born on earth to see light, but all he had seen so far was the mother who had given birth to him and dark forest. His mother, though, had told him that not everywhere was forest, that there was also open steppe.

Ivan went off to look for open steppe. He saw a path. 'I'll walk somewhere trodden,' he thought. 'I've never done that before.' He went a little way. Then he heard a knock and a clatter. The leaves on the trees began to tremble. Ivan stopped; he didn't know what to think.

Wild horses were running past him on their way to a drink-ing place. But Ivan had never set eyes on horses before and he had no idea who these horses were. He seized one horse by the mane, so that it would stop and he could have a good look at it. The horse tried to keep going; it would have torn any other man's arm from his shoulder – but Ivan had been born mighty strong . . . He gave a sharp tug to the horse's mane that made the horse kneel on the ground before him. It looked at Ivan out of the corner of one eye and then got back onto its feet, dumb-struck.

Soon after this Ivan walked up to his mother. He was walk-ing on foot, holding the horse by its mane.

When his mother saw this, she said, 'Why are you leading the horse when you could be riding on it?'

The mother told her son how he should ride on a horse. Ivan leaped onto the horse and shouted into its ear. Frightened by his voice, the horse galloped off. Trees trembled at the mere sight of the horse; bushes flew out from under its hooves.

Ivan came out into open steppe. Here it was bright, and the sky above him was full of space, not like in the forest. The sight of all this filled Ivan with joy. The horse beneath him galloped on ever further. Now Ivan could see strangers walking about, and some kind of huts standing on the ground. They were covered with yellow grass. Ivan had never seen other people before, only himself and his mother. Nor had he ever seen villages, and huts covered with straw.

Right into his horse's ear Ivan shouted, 'Stop!'

The horse was so frightened it stopped then and there.

Ivan told the horse to wait for him while he walked through the village. He felt like having a look at the wide world, at people, at things he had never seen before.

Ivan saw little children walking along the village street. He himself, of course, was a little child, even though he was big and strong.

He went into the street and stood in the middle of the little children. He wanted to play. He lifted up one child and turned the child's head towards him. He wanted to stroke the child or say something childish to it, but then he saw that the child's head had fallen onto the ground. 'What's the matter?' Ivan wondered. 'Why's it flown off like that? Hasn't it grown on properly yet?'

He went up to a little boy the same age as himself and took him by the hand. The boy's whole arm fell off. Ivan began to feel pity for these little children. He picked the head up from the ground, stuck it on the headless child's neck and pressed down on it; it grew back, just as it had been before. Then he put the arm back in place, and it took root too.

Ivan mounted his horse and galloped off. On runs his steed – the earth trembles indeed. If a stove is unsound, it falls to the ground. If a hut has weak walls, to the ground this hut falls.

No good, Ivan realized, came from a gallop like this. He shouted into his horse's ear, 'You there! Wolf meal, grass gobbler! Stop pounding the ground – fly along it instead!'

The horse flew on still faster, no longer even troubling the grass beneath it.

Ivan rode a long way. He looked around him. There was nothing but open steppe, and the sky was touching the edge of the earth. And there on the edge of the earth he could see a little hut. Ivan rode up to the little hut. He tethered his horse and went inside. The table had been laid; on it was both food and wine. Ivan tried the food. He liked it; there were both salty dishes and sweet dishes – everything he could have wanted. Then he tried the wine – and didn't like it at all. It made his mouth feel all bitter. Ivan saw a stick that had been cut and trimmed; it was standing in the corner. He took it in his hand: was it strong? Might it come in useful? He knocked it against a floorboard. From under the floor jumped Yashka-Red-Shirt.

'What are your orders?'

'Well,' Ivan answered, 'what can you do? Show me everything in the world.'

Yashka-Red-Shirt opened a view for Ivan: now Ivan could see everything in the world. As for Yashka himself – he just went back where he'd come from.

Ivan knocked on the floor a second time. Straight away Yashka-Red-Shirt was there in front of him.

'What are your orders?'

'I've looked long enough. Close the view. Let something be left for my mother to look at.'

Now there was nothing. 'I'll go and fetch my mother,' thought Ivan. 'It's lighter living in open steppe.'

But just as Ivan was crossing the threshold, he saw a giant warrior coming towards him. This hut was the warrior's home.

'Who are you and where are you from?' asked the warrior. 'Who asked *you* to come and make yourself at home here, you know-nothing lout?'

'I'm not a know-nothing,' said Ivan. 'I'm my mother's son.'

This angered the warrior. He hit Ivan with his fist.

'Huh!' said Ivan. 'You didn't bring me into this bright world, and you're not going to force me out of this bright world!'

Ivan seized hold of the warrior, lifted him off the ground, swung him horizontally through the air and hurled him somewhere far off. The warrior struck the ground and that was the end of him.

Ivan went over to his horse. He looked up – and saw another giant warrior coming towards him. He was the brother of the one before, but he was still stronger and fiercer.

'Who asked *you* here, you unwashed, know-nothing lout?'

The warrior was about to attack Ivan, but Ivan seized him and threw him against the ground. And that was the end of the warrior – he had breathed his last breath. All Ivan could see was a little steam rising off him. Ivan tried to grab hold of the steam, but he was left empty-handed. It was a shame that nothing remains of a man. What was Ivan to do now? He'd rather the warrior could go on being a warrior. After all, there was nothing that could frighten Ivan. 'But what can I do,' thought Ivan, 'so as not to damage a man to death? It would be better to teach him a lesson first. Then he can be alive and know.'

Up rode another warrior, the brother of the two who were no more.

'What kind of a know-nothing are you?'

'I'm no know-nothing. I'm my mother's son.'

The warrior seized hold of Ivan, meaning to kill him, but Ivan just took him in his arms and began wondering what to do with him. There on the wall he could see a large bag. Ivan stuffed the warrior into the bag, crumpling him so that he would fit in better, and hung the bag back on the wall, on an oak peg. Let the warrior hang there, bent more than double.

Ivan closed the bag with an iron lock and threw the key out of the window.

Ivan went outside into the world. This time there was no one else. He mounted his horse and set off back home.

His mother saw Ivan coming. At first she didn't recognize him, although little time had passed since he had left. It was indeed difficult to recognize Ivan. From fighting against the giant warriors he had matured in strength, and thoughtfulness had come onto his face.

Ivan said to his mother, 'Come with me, mother. I've found you a good life.'

They rode to the hut where the warriors had been living.

Ivan sat on the horse, and he held his mother in his arms so that she would not be exhausted by the journey. When they arrived, Ivan's mother saw at once that it was a good strong hut: yes, brigands always have good huts.

Ivan left his horse outside and led his mother into the hut. They went into the best room. Ivan knocked on the floor with the stick, the same as before. Yashka-Red-Shirt appeared at once: what were their orders?

Ivan said to him, 'Show everything, just as you showed me before.'

Yashka showed them everything in the world – everything that could be seen and that could not be seen. The mother gazed, wondered and was filled with joy. And when she had gazed her fill, Ivan ordered Yashka:

'Lay a meal for us on the table.'

Yashka brought many good things. He put bread and salt, foodstuffs and wine on the table, and then disappeared until they should call him again. It was evident that he was humble, that the warriors had taught him obedience.

Ivan's mother tasted the different foods and washed them down with wine. She felt merry and began to dance. Ivan looked at his mother and felt glad that he had a young mother and that she had a happy heart.

'Life here will be merrier for you,' he said.

'Who knows, my son? It still remains to be seen where life is better.[1] I'm afraid there may be brigands here.'

'You're right,' said Ivan. 'I'll go out on my horse and have a look.'

The mother was left on her own. She walked about the hut and looked everything over like a true housewife, seeing what was stored where and how many goods had been laid in. The hut was spacious. There were two front rooms, a kitchen and storerooms. The mother could see a large bag hanging on the wall: did it perhaps contain something good? She felt the bag. It was kept shut by an iron padlock and the key wasn't there. She remembered about Yashka-Red-Shirt, took hold of the stick and knocked on the floor.

Yashka appeared.

'What are your orders?'

'Find me the key.'

'Straight away.'

Yashka found the key and disappeared again. Ivan's mother opened the iron lock, then watched as a man rose up out of the bag. He had a stretch and pulled back his shoulders; he was strong, handsome and clean-faced. Never had Ivan's mother seen such a man. The men in her village had all been thin and weak. The earth had consumed them with work, and life had eaten them away with its cares. 'So this is what a true warrior looks like!' thought Ivan's mother. 'Probably he has a wife of his own, but I can be a guest to him!'

No sooner had the warrior climbed out of the bag than he sat down and ate what was left on the table; he had become very hungry in the empty bag. The warrior ate; his cheeks grew pinker and drops of sweat began to fall from his forehead.

'Have you had all you want, or do you want more?' asked Ivan's mother.

'I want more,' said the warrior. 'Call Yashka!'

The mother knocked with the stick. Yashka appeared. He brought food, drink and various delicacies. And after that, he came twice more, bringing more food.

'Had enough now?' asked the mother.

She was looking at the warrior and admiring him. Her heart moved towards him; she had begun to love him.

'Well,' said the warrior. 'I have goods of all kinds and a large hut, but the hut has no mistress.'

'You've got Yashka,' said the mother. 'He cooks for you and does everything that needs to be done in the home.'

'Yashka's a servant,' said the warrior. 'Yashka serves me, but he has no soul. He makes himself useful to anyone. But you – I promise you – can be the mistress here in my home.'

'I'd gladly be your mistress,' the mother answered the warrior. 'But I have a son and I have to talk to him and see what he thinks. If he doesn't want you as a stepfather, then you'll never get the better of him. He'll prove stronger than you.'

'We'll do away with your son,' said the warrior. 'We'll rid ourselves of him.'

The mother felt frightened. She began to listen: what would her heart say? And what would her conscience say? Her conscience was saying nothing at all, but her heart was speaking – and her heart loved the warrior. The mother asked, 'And how are you going to do away with Ivan?'

'Let me teach you,' said the warrior.

And he taught her what she must say to her son. Then he climbed back into the bag and hid away.

Ivan came back and found his mother lying ill in bed.

'Are you ailing, mother?'

'Yes, my dear son, I'm ailing. But listen to me – I want to tell you something I heard about long ago. Far away from here – you have to go on foot, you can't get there on horseback – lies a dark forest. And in this forest, together with her cubs, lives a warrior she-wolf. If only you could bring me milk from the breast of that she-wolf! Then I'd drink it and be strong again!'

Ivan listened to his mother and replied, 'I'll bring you whatever you need, dearest mother, even if I have to go to the other world.'

Ivan released his horse – out into the open steppe. 'Let it live free and eat all it wants,' he thought. 'Why should it always have to gallop beneath me?' And he went on foot into the dark forest.

Meanwhile, the warrior, still in his bag, was thinking, 'Soon the wolf will be tearing Ivan to pieces. She can toss a man half a mile just like that. Soon there'll be no one stronger than me in the whole wide world!'

The warrior climbed out of the bag.

'Call Yashka,' he said to his new mistress, Ivan's mother. 'And give me something to eat!'

Ivan, for his part, was making his way through the dark forest. Then he caught sight of the warrior she-wolf. She was dozing beneath a tree, suckling her four cubs.

The she-wolf opened her eyes and looked at Ivan.

Ivan walked up close, sat down beside her and said, 'Give me some of your milk. If you don't, I'll milk you myself. My mother's ailing. She says she needs your milk to get better.'

The she-wolf thought for a moment: other than mosquitoes

and forest birds, no one in the forest ever came near her – but now a man had appeared right by her side. She would have liked to get up and tear this man to pieces, but it would have been a pity to disturb her children: let them go on feeding.

'Where will you put the milk?' asked the she-wolf.

Ivan thought for a moment: he had brought nothing with him.

'Let one of your cubs fill his mouth with milk,' he said. 'Then he can come with me – he can run behind me.'

The she-wolf raised her head off the ground.

'A little child of my own flesh!' she said. 'You cherish your mother, but I cherish my sons. I'm not letting you take one of my sons away.'

Ivan got to his feet, tore up an old oak along with its roots and threw it far into the distance.

'I'll bring your child back,' he said. 'I won't harm him in any way.'

The wolf realized she was no match for Ivan in strength.

'All right,' she replied, 'he can go with you.' Then she licked one of her little cubs and said, 'Serve the man, as you have served me. Fill your mouth with milk, but don't swallow it. Go where you must go, and come back to me soon.'

The little wolf cub sucked till his mouth was full, then got up from the ground. Ivan looked at the cub; he was almost as big as a horse.

He and the cub set off at a walk. Then they began to run, to get everything done sooner.

Towards evening Ivan's mother finished tidying the hut and looked out of the window. There was her son, riding on the back of a wolf: the wolf must have been frightened – he was going at a run.

'See!' she said to her warrior. 'You thought the she-wolf would tear Ivan to pieces, but here he is – riding home on the back of a wolf! Get back into the bag.'

After saying this, she lay down on the bed and began to groan, as if she were ill.

In came Ivan. He took a wooden bowl and told the young wolf-child to pour the milk out from his mouth and into the bowl.

Ivan gave the milk to his mother and said, 'Drink, dear mother. Then your illness will pass.'

His mother replied, 'Wait a little, my son. I've grown weak. I can't swallow anything at all now.'

'As you like, dear mother,' said Ivan. 'But I made the wolf cub gallop through the forest, so you'd have help as soon as possible.'

Ivan went back outside to the wolf cub. His mother took the bowl with the she-wolf's milk and was about to pour it away under the floor. But the warrior peeped out from the bag and said, 'Give it to me to drink. Maybe it will make me stronger.'

And he drank the milk of a wild beast.

The mother lay down again, as if she were ill. Then the warrior said to her, 'You must say to your son Ivan that the she-wolf's milk didn't help you. Let him go tomorrow to fetch milk from a lioness. He won't be able to get the better of the lioness. She'll tear him to pieces and gnaw his bones clean.'

In the morning the mother told her son to go to the lioness. 'Then maybe I'll get to my feet again and go on living.'

Ivan called the wolf cub and went into the forest with him. They walked a short way, they walked a long way – but Ivan did not know where the lioness lived. He asked the wolf cub, but the wolf cub did not know either.

'But my mother's sure to know,' said the wolf cub.

They went to ask the mother she-wolf. She was overjoyed that Ivan had brought back her son, her own little cub. And Ivan asked if she knew where the lioness lived.

'Yes,' answered the she-wolf. 'My son can show you the way.'

The mother she-wolf instructed her cub where they should go in order to find the lioness.

This time the wolf cub as big as a horse ran on ahead, while Ivan followed.

They ran for days and nights, through morning and evening twilights, through noons and midnights. There was no longer anything at all. Ivan could see neither forest, nor grassy steppe; all he could see was bare rock. And there, lying beneath a very large rock, was a lioness. She was giving her dugs to her lion-cub children.

The wolf cub felt wary. He stopped. But Ivan went up close to the lioness, seized her by the jaw and was about to tear her in half, to rip her lion's head from her body. Ivan saw the eyes of the lioness fill with tears. He took his hands away.

'Don't kill me, Ivan-Wonder,' said the lioness. 'Don't make my children into orphans. Tell me what you need.'

'Give me some of your milk. And let one of your children carry it behind me in his mouth.'

'I don't cherish my milk,' said the lioness, 'but I cherish a son of mine a great deal.'

'I'll bring him back to you again,' Ivan promised her. 'And I'll put him back beneath your dug, just as he was.'

This gladdened the lioness, and she let her lion-cub child go with his mouth full of milk.

Ivan set off back home. Now he was one of three.

His mother looked out of the window and saw Ivan coming back home alive, with two wild beasts running behind him. She told the warrior to hide in the bag on the wall and she herself lay down again and began groaning, as if she were ill.

'What are we going to do now?' she asked her warrior of a husband.

The warrior crept back into the bag and answered her from inside it, 'Let Ivan fetch from the eagle an egg that she has not yet sat on. The eagle lives on a cliff. The cliff is on a mountain, and the mountain stands on a hill. Beneath the hill lies an abyss. Ivan will fall from the cliff into the abyss and be dashed to pieces.'

That night the mother gave her warrior husband the milk of the lioness, and in the morning she told Ivan to go and fetch from the eagle an egg that she had not yet sat on. Whoever ate such an egg, she said, was sure to become strong. The milk of the lioness hadn't, after all, made her any better.

Ivan set off to find the eagle. The two beasts went with him. Ivan came to where the lioness lived and said to her, 'I've brought you your son. Tell me now, for you've wandered a long way over the earth: where does the eagle live in her nest?'

The mother lioness instructed her little lion-cub son where to go in the mountains. Then she sent him off with Ivan.

Ivan came to the hill. The hill was steep, but Ivan was agile and patient. He climbed to the top of the hill, and the wolf cub and the lion cub scrambled up after him. But on top of the hill stood a stone mountain, tall and smooth as a wall, and on top of the mountain stood a sheer cliff – and it was there on that cliff that the eagle had her nest. Ivan looked at the mountain of rock and saw that agility was not enough; no degree of agility would help him climb to the top if there were no handholds or footholds. The only way to the top was by flying – but Ivan had no wings. Ivan stood and thought for a while, but he did not grow sad. Instead, he smiled. He had grown quickly in strength, but his good sense and goodness of heart had grown still more quickly. Through work, he understood, the impossible can be made possible.

Then Ivan told the wolf cub and the lion cub that they should each gnaw off one sharp stone. The beasts began gnawing away at the mountain, but they couldn't gnaw their way through the stone; they were still children and their teeth had not grown properly. They ran back down, found some stones in a stream, took them in their jaws and brought them to Ivan.

Ivan began hitting the mountain with these stones and breaking it up. At first only little crumbs broke away, but then bigger pieces came off and soon Ivan had destroyed a whole slab. And with that slab he began knocking big cliffs out of the mountain – and the mountain began to subside until, in the end, Ivan had taken the whole of it apart. When the peak of the mountain was level with Ivan's shoulders, he caught sight of the eagle in a cleft up in the very highest cliff of all. She was sitting there in her nest.

'What is it you want, Ivan the Warrior?' asked the eagle.

'Give me an egg that you haven't sat on,' said Ivan.

'I don't have any,' said the eagle, 'but my sister does. Wait here. I'll fly to my sister on the other mountain and borrow an egg for you. Otherwise you'll be knocking down all our mountains.'

'Yes,' said Ivan, 'I will.'

The eagle flew to her sister on the other mountain and brought Ivan an egg that hadn't been sat on. But her eagle sister hadn't given her one of her own eggs – she had given her the egg of a poisonous snake. She was miserly and she wanted eaglet children to be born from every one of her eggs.

Ivan took the egg from the eagle and set off back towards his mother. And the two beasts, the wolf cub and the lion cub, ran along behind him.

'Go back now to your parents,' said Ivan.

But the two wild beasts replied, 'No, we're not going to. You're kind and good, and we've grown used to you.'

Ivan brought his mother the eagle's egg.

His mother took the egg and said, 'I got better, my son. But now I've gone and caught a chill from the wind and I've fallen ill once more.'

And then, following her husband's instructions, she told Ivan to go to a certain distant tsardom: 'I've heard that everybody there has died. Maybe the tsardom can be yours now.'

Ivan was surprised that his mother should say this: what did he want with someone else's tsardom? But he was afraid of disobeying his mother. He called the wolf cub and the lion cub and set off to this strange tsardom. No sooner had he left his own home than the cowardly warrior got out of his bag and ate the egg of the poisonous snake. He thought that it was the egg of an eagle.

The cowardly warrior had instructed Ivan's mother to send him to this strange, unpeopled tsardom in order that he should die there. Where everyone had already died, he said, there Ivan would be sure to die too.

Ivan walked for a long time, not knowing how to find this strange tsardom. But on the way, his beasts grew up, and their teeth and claws became strong as they walked to this unknown place.

Ivan came to the strange tsardom. In those days, this tsardom lay by the shore of a great sea. Ivan saw sky and sea. He saw rivers, forests and ploughed fields. Everything he saw was good, only there were no people anywhere.

Ivan sat on the shore and wondered what he should do. But there was a deed to be done there and then.

Walking along the shore was a beautiful maiden in a gold

brocade dress. She was walking along the shore and weeping. Never in his life had Ivan seen such a maiden, nor had he ever been in a place where such beauty was to be seen. He had loved only his mother and looked only at her.

'Why are you weeping?' Ivan asked the beautiful maiden.

'I'm afraid of dying,' answered the maiden. 'Get away from here quickly or you'll die too!'

Ivan looked troubled and said, 'No, what you say is not true. I shan't die and I shan't give *you* up to death. But who are you? And who are your parents?'

The maiden wiped away her tears and replied, 'I'm the tsar's daughter. Once we had a tsardom, and once there were people, but a sea monster has eaten all the people. No one is left – only my mother, my father and me. Now the monster's going to eat me, and before the day's over my mother and father will have died of grief, and then there won't be anyone left at all.'

And the beautiful maiden began weeping again.

Just then a terrible sea monster came out of the water. It had three heads and three jaws, and a thousand teeth in each jaw. It had a belly like a hog's and a tail like a snake's.

The monster saw Ivan standing by the young tsarevna. It saw the lion cub and the wolf cub, and it said, 'I was only counting on a little snack, but it seems I can have a full meal.'

The monster rushed at the tsarevna. It wanted to seize her in one of its jaws, but Ivan stood in front of the tsarevna. He put his arms right around the stout monster and began to squeeze. The monster began to wheeze. Straight away it opened two other jaws full of teeth, in order to bite Ivan's head off. The wolf cub leaped on one of the monster's heads, and the lion cub on the other. They began gnawing at the monster. The damp, stout monster was still wheezing, but it was now trying to seize Ivan's head in its third jaw. But at that moment an eagle swooped down from the sky. She perched on the monster's third head and began pecking its eyes until the eyes had quite flowed away. Meanwhile Ivan went on squeezing the monster. Black blood began to stream from it; it grew weak and fell down dead.

The eagle settled on Ivan's shoulder and said, 'Forgive me,

Ivan the Good! My sister deceived me. She didn't give me an eagle's egg – she gave me the egg of a poisonous snake. I've been searching for you all over the earth, so I could warn you. Don't break open that egg! If you break it open, you will turn from kind to cruel, from brave to cowardly, from generous to greedy.'

Then the beautiful tsarevna embraced Ivan and began to weep clear, happy tears, for Ivan had saved her from a terrible death in the jaw of the beast.

Ivan felt sad now that he had fulfilled his work. He was longing to see his mother and he began to make ready to go home. But the beautiful tsarevna asked Ivan to remain forever in their tsardom. She was afraid some other insatiable monster might rise up out of the deep sea.

Ivan looked at the tsarevna and saw that she had become dear to him now. He could have looked at her forever, never taking his eyes off her.

Then he said to her, 'I'll go and see how things are with my mother and then I'll come back to you. But the wolf and the lion and the eagle can stay with you. No one can harm you while they're here.'

And Ivan set off back home.

He caught sight of the hut where his mother lived, and his heart jumped for joy. His mother, however, was sitting at table, opposite her warrior husband who had been in the bag on the wall. They were eating various delicacies and drinking sweet wine; Yashka-Red-Shirt was serving them.

The warrior looked out of the window and saw Ivan. This time the beaten warrior did not hide away in the bag on the wall. The wolf's milk had made him more vicious, the lion's milk had given him strength, and the egg of the poisonous snake had engendered in him an evil fury.

The warrior went out to greet Ivan. He went up close to Ivan and took a swing with one arm, meaning to smash Ivan's head off his shoulders and send it far into the distance – but he himself fell dead. Ivan had got in first: while the warrior was raising his arm, Ivan had knocked his heart out of him.

The mother saw from the hut what had become of her

warrior. She came down from the porch, fell onto the chest of her fallen husband and wept for him. She did not greet her son or look at him.

Ivan walked away from his mother and sank into sad thought. He had recognized the warrior he had defeated and stuffed into the bag, and he now understood that his mother loved this warrior with all her soul.

Ivan felt pity for his mother.

He picked up the warrior's heart from the ground and inserted it into his chest. The warrior breathed a long breath.

Then the mother fell at her son's feet. She began to beg his forgiveness, and she told him all that had happened. Ivan turned away from his mother and walked off where his eyes looked. But his eyes could not see anything then; they were full of tears.

Ivan came back to himself only after he had walked a long, long way. Then he looked around him, saw the great sea in the distance and made his way to the unpeopled tsardom where the beautiful tsarevna lived.

Very soon, as was right and just, Ivan married this tsarevna. Her name was Lukerya. Their wedding was merry, but there were few people: there were no revellers, no one to celebrate the day other than the beautiful Lukerya's mother and father, the bride and bridegroom themselves, and the eagle, the wolf and the lion.

And, in due course, plenty of children were born to Ivan and Lukerya – and from the children came grandchildren, and so the nation got going again.

And then Ivan grew old. He remembered about his mother: was she still alive? Did she have bread?

Ivan left his home and his family. He said goodbye to Lukerya and set off on a long journey, to the hut where his mother lived.

But there was nothing there. There was only open steppe, and there was no sign on the earth of where the hut had stood.

'What about Yashka-Red-Shirt?' Ivan wondered. 'Where's he gone?' And he shouted out to him, 'Answer my call, Yashka! As you used to do!'

And there was Yashka, walking along towards him, the same

as ever, neither young nor old, neither living nor dead – yet obedient as always. And he was leading by the hand a frail old woman, so bent that her face was almost touching the ground.

Ivan saw that this was his mother.

'Greetings, dearest mother!' he said.

His mother stretched out her hands to him – but to the wrong side, not towards where he was standing.

Then Yashka-Red-Shirt said, 'She went blind. She cried her eyes out over you. She can't see anything at all.'

Ivan went down on his knees before his mother, embraced her and kissed her blind eyes.

'Forgive me, mother,' he said. 'Forgive me for getting cross and upset then and putting you out of my mind.'

Ivan lifted his old mother up in his strong arms and carried her back to his own home. There his beautiful wife Lukerya was waiting for him. There his children and grandchildren were all living, and there happiness had been prepared for his poor mother.

Yashka followed Ivan there and asked him, 'And what about me? What are your orders?'

'You can entertain the children!' Ivan said to Yashka.

No-Arms

There was once an old peasant who lived in a village with his wife and their two children. He came to the end of his life and he died. Then it was his old woman's turn to get ready to die – her time had come, too. She called the children to her, her son and her daughter. The daughter was the elder, the son the younger.

She said to her son, 'Obey your sister in everything, as you have obeyed me. Now she will be a mother to you.'

The mother gave a last sigh – she was sorry to be parting from her children forever – and then died.

After the death of their parents, the children lived as their mother had told them to live. The brother obeyed his sister, and the sister took care of her brother and loved him.

And so they lived on without their parents, perhaps many years, perhaps few. One day the sister said to her brother, 'It's hard for me to keep house on my own, and it's time you were married. Marry – then there'll be a mistress to look after the home.'

But the brother did not want to marry. 'The home has a mistress already,' he said. 'Why do we need a second mistress?'

'I'll help her,' said his sister. 'With two of us the work will be easier.'

The brother didn't want to marry, but he didn't dare disobey his elder sister. He respected her as if she were his mother.

The brother married and began to live happily with his wife. As for his sister, he loved and respected her just as before, obeying her in everything.

At first his wife seemed not to mind her sister-in-law. And the sister-in-law, for her part, did all she could to be obliging.

Only soon the wife began to feel upset. She wanted to be first in the home; she wanted her word to count for more than her sister-in-law's. The young master would go off to plough, or to market, or maybe into the forest. And when he came back, he would find trouble. His wife would start complaining to him about his sister: she didn't know how to do anything properly, she had a wicked temper, she'd broken the new pot . . .

The husband said nothing. 'I go out,' he thought, 'and trouble comes in. That's not good at all.'

But a man can't stay at home all the time.

Once more the brother left home; once more he found trouble when he came back.

'It's none of my business – but that sister of yours will make beggars of us all. Just look in the barn! Our cow Zhdanka died yesterday. Your hateful sister fed her something and the cow's fallen down dead.'

His wife didn't say that she'd fed the cow poisonous herbs herself, just to be rid of her husband's sister.

The brother spoke to his sister. 'So you've poisoned the cow, sister. We'll have to earn a lot of money to buy another.'

The sister was innocent, but she took the blame on herself. She didn't want her brother to think ill of his wife.

'I've slipped up, brother,' she said. 'It won't happen again.'

'Well then,' said her brother, 'give me your blessing. I must go and work in the forest and earn a few kopeks. Look after everything at home, sister, make sure nothing goes wrong. When my wife gives birth, help the child into the world.'

Off he rode to the forest – and it was a long time before he returned. While he was away, his wife gave birth to a little son, and his sister helped the boy into the world and took him into her heart. But the boy was not to live long in the world: one night his mother lay on him inadvertently in her sleep, and he died.

Just then the brother came back from the forest. At home he found sorrow. His wife was weeping and howling: 'It's that sister of yours, the snake in the grass. She's smothered our little son, next she'll be the death of me too.'

The brother heard his wife's words and was filled with fury.

He called his sister: 'I thought you were to be a mother to me. I've grudged you nothing, neither bread nor clothes, and I've always obeyed you. And now you've taken away my only son. If he'd lived, he'd have been a comfort to me, a hope to me when I'm old. He'd have fed you, too, when you can no longer work. And you've killed him.'

And he added, 'Never again will you see the light of the world.'

The sister tried to say something in answer, but in his grief and fury the brother didn't listen, and he looked at his sister as if he were a stranger, as if he didn't know her.

Early next morning the brother woke his sister.

'Get ready,' he said. 'We're leaving.'

'But it's early, brother,' said the sister. 'The sky's still dark.'

The brother wasn't listening. 'Get ready,' he repeated, 'and put on your best dress.'

'But, brother, dear brother, today's not even a holiday,' the sister said in answer.

But the brother didn't hear her at all; he was already harnessing the horses.

He took her into the forest and then he stopped the horses. It was still early, barely light.

In the forest stood a tree-stump. The brother told his sister to kneel down and lay her head on it.

The sister laid her arms on the tree-stump, and her head on her arms.

'Forgive me, brother,' she managed to say, and she wanted to add that she was not to blame for anything; maybe he would hear her now.

But the brother had already raised his axe high in the air. He had no time to listen to his sister.

Just then a little bird called out from a branch, and its voice was merry and ringing. The sister wanted to listen to the bird, and she lifted her head, leaving her arms on the tree-stump.[1]

The brother brought his axe down and chopped off both her arms at the elbow. He could have forgiven no one the death of his son, not even his own mother.

'Quick!' he said. 'Be off with you. Go where your eyes look. I'd wanted to cut off your head, but it seems your fate is to live.'

The brother looked at his sister and wept. 'Why is it,' he thought, 'that happiness is just happiness, while one sorrow always becomes two? Now I have no son, and no sister.'

The brother started the horses and rode away; his sister remained alone in the forest. She got up from the ground and set off, with no arms, where her eyes looked. The paths were all long overgrown and she had no idea where they led. Soon there were no longer any paths at all. She was lost, weak from not eating, her dress torn to rags.

Days passed; nights passed. The sister walked on, following where her eyes looked. It was strange not to have any arms, and she missed her brother. She walked on, crying:

> *Winds, winds, unruly winds,*
> *Take my tears to my mother,*
> *Take them to my father.*
> *But I have no mother, I have no father.*
> *Sun, sun, high in the sky,*
> *Give warmth to me, unhappy me.*

The light of the wide world before her was all darkened by tears, and she couldn't wipe them away. She walked on, not seeing how the wind combed her hair and the sun brightened her cheeks, making her pretty and fair of face. It must be true what they say – that good people are made beautiful even by grief, while the evil are disfigured even by beauty.

When her tears dried, there was an orchard in front of her; the forest had gone. And there were apples ripening on the trees – big, juicy ones. Some of them were ripening quite low: yes, she could reach them with her mouth. The sister ate one apple and had a bite of a second, but she didn't touch a third apple, she held herself back: she was eating what belonged to a stranger for the first time, compelled by mortal hunger.

Just then the watchman came up to her and shouted: 'You witch! What's brought you here, snatching other people's apples with your mouth? Thirty years I've been guarding this orchard and not one apple's ever been stolen. And now you come along and start munching. You'll catch it, thief with no arms!'

The watchman cursed her roundly and took the armless woman to the master of the orchard.

Just then the master's young son was sitting in the hut and looking out of the window. He saw a young maiden. She was thin and wretched, quite plain at first glance, but her eyes were lit by such a good and kind soul that this made her more beautiful than any charm could, and there was no woman in the world more beautiful. He marvelled at this strange girl, his heart beating with joy.

'Let her go!' he called out to the watchman.

He went up to the girl and saw she had no arms. And he loved her still more: yes, not even mutilation can disfigure someone you love.

But then the young man felt sad: what would his father say?

He went up to his father, bowed and said, 'Father, I have news for you: news of joy, not of sorrow. Our watchman's caught a girl in the orchard, and now there's no one dearer to me in the world. Don't break my heart, father. Allow me to marry her.'

His father went outside, looked at the girl with no arms, and said: 'What's the matter with you, my son? There are plenty of girls who are prettier than she is – and it certainly won't be hard to find one who's richer. Look at her – an armless cripple! You'll end up walking behind her with a beggar's pouch.'

'There may be prettier girls in the world,' said the son, 'but there are none who are dearer to me. And as for the beggar's pouch, well, father, if that's to be our fate, then so be it.'

The father thought deeply.

'Make up your own mind, son. I have power in my home and power in my garden, but I have no power in your heart. Your heart's not an apple.'

There was an honourable wedding, and the young people began to live together, like all young people. They lived peacefully, they lived happily, but it was not their lot to live together for long: soon they had to part.

War had broken out against the enemy, and the husband of the girl with no arms was taken to serve in the army. As he left, he spoke to his father: 'Take care of my wife, father. Soon she'll be giving birth. Write me a letter then – so I can rejoice in a son or a daughter.'

'Don't grieve, my son,' said the father. 'And don't lay down your life for nothing. You're going to miss your wife, but don't grieve about her – she'll be like a daughter to me.'

And the young man set off to the war. Soon her time came, and his wife without arms bore him a son. She looked at the child. The grandfather looked at the child. The little boy's hands were golden, the moon shone bright on his forehead, and where his heart was, there glowed the sun. Yes, for a mother or a grandfather there is no other kind of child.

The grandfather set off to the city, to sell apples in the market. The mother with no arms called the old watchman and told him to write a letter to her husband. In his time the old man had served in the army too, and he had learned to read and write there. First she told him to write greetings – from herself and from her father-in-law – and then to say that she'd given birth to a fine son, and to say everything about him, why it was that everyone who looked at him felt glad.

The old man folded the letter, tucked it inside his shirt and set off.

He walked through forests; he walked through open steppe. Before he knew it, it was night. Not far away stood a hut. He asked to stay the night there.

The owners invited him in and gave him supper. The husband lay down and fell asleep, but the wife began to question the old man: who were his people? Where had he come from and where was he going? And how had he lived to be old – through good times or bad times, in plenty or in hunger?

The old man told her how he had lived in the past and what he was doing now. 'Now,' he said, 'I'm taking good news to the young master. His wife has borne him a son. And his wife has no arms, but she has a sweet face, and there can't be anyone in the world more gentle-hearted.'

The mistress of the hut looked surprised. 'She hasn't got any arms at all?'

'No,' said the old man. 'They say her own brother chopped them off. I suppose he must have been in a frenzy of rage.'

The woman looked surprised again. 'Goodness me! What villains there are in the world! But what have you done with your news? Take care you don't lose it!'

'Here it is,' said the old man. 'It's in a paper, tucked safe inside my shirt.'

'Why not go and have a good steam?' said the woman. 'You must be worn out by now and you'll have sweated on the road. I'll get the bathhouse stove going right away.'

The old man was glad. 'What can be better than an hour in the bathhouse?' he thought to himself.

The woman heated up the stove. The old man took off his clothes and went to steam his old bones. But it wasn't from respect or kindness of heart that the woman had prepared the bathhouse for the traveller: no, her husband was No-Arms's brother, it was from this very hut that he had taken her to the forest, meaning to put her to death. She found the letter in the old man's undershirt. She read it, threw it into the stove, wrote out another letter and put this new letter where the old one had been. This new letter said that the wife had borne her husband not a son, but something like a piglet in front, like a dog from behind, and with a back like a hedgehog, and as to what should be done with it, let her husband decide.

Morning came, and the old man went on further.

Time passed – and there was the same old man, coming back along the same road. The woman saw him and invited him into her hut.

The old man went inside, to stay the night in a familiar hut. The woman asked him what message he was taking home: what had the young master said to him?

'I didn't see the young master. He was fighting. After the battle was over, they gave me a letter from him. His wishes are there in the letter.'

'What are his wishes?' asked the woman.

'How would I know?' said the old man. 'It isn't for me to read his letter.'

The old man prepared to lie down for the night. Outside it was already dark.

'Let me darn your shirt, grandad,' said the woman. 'Look at what you've done to it on the road!'

But the old man was already asleep. The woman took his shirt and looked inside. There, sewed into the lining, she found the letter. She unstitched it and began to read. The letter was from the husband to his wife with no arms. In it he told her to take care of their child and cherish it, and as for the child being born misshapen, it would be none the less precious and dear to him. The husband of the wife with no arms also asked his own father to look after the child and care for it.

'No,' whispered the woman. 'Your father will not take care of the child.'

And she wrote another letter, as if from the husband of No-Arms. The letter was addressed to his father, with not a word for his wife. In it the husband asked his father to throw his wife out of the house, together with her son. He wanted nothing more to do with her: why should he live with a wife with no arms? She was no wife for a warrior; if he returned whole from the war, he would start a new family.

The woman darned the old man's shirt and sewed her own letter into the lining, keeping the true letter herself.

And the old man went on his way.

He went back to his master, the father-in-law of No-Arms, and gave him the letter.

The old master read the letter and called No-Arms.

'Good day, mistress,' he said.

'Good day, father,' she replied. 'But what kind of mistress am I? I'm the youngest in the home.'

'And I,' the old father-in-law said sadly, 'am no master. When the watchman brought you in, I wanted to send you away, but you stayed. And now I want you to live all your life here in my home, but you are going to leave forever.'

And he told her what his son had written. 'He's told me I must send you away. His heart must have changed towards you.'

In the morning No-Arms tucked her baby son in the folds of her skirt, gripped the hem between her teeth, and left. She went where everyone goes when they have nowhere to go to – where her eyes looked.

And the old father-in-law was left on his own. He began to miss his grandson; he began to miss his daughter-in-law with no arms. He called the old watchman and told him to search for No-Arms and her son and bring them back home. The watchman set off through the woods and fields and wandered about for a long time, calling to No-Arms. But the world is wide – how could he hope to find them? The watchman returned with nothing.

The old orchard keeper began to grieve and pine. One day he lay down to sleep and didn't wake up. His own sorrow was the death of him.[2]

As for No-Arms, she had gone on her way through the wide world, following where her eyes looked. She walked through open steppe; she began to feel thirsty. Then she entered a forest. In the forest was an old grandfather oak tree, and not far from that oak – a well. No-Arms bent down over the well, but the water was too far away, she couldn't drink. No-Arms bent down lower: maybe she could reach it after all. There it was, water. 'At least I can wet my lips,' No-Arms said to herself. Her lips touched the water, she unclenched her teeth, and down fell the child, out of her skirt and into the well. The mother stretched after him, remembered that she was a cripple and began to weep. 'Alas,' thought No-Arms, 'why was I ever born? I can endure both grief and injury, and I've given birth to a child – but now I'm unable to save him!'

And through the water she sees her son, lying at the bottom of the well. And she also sees that her arms have grown; she stretches them out to her son and grabs hold of him. But after she's lifted him out of the water, after she's saved him – once again she has no arms.

And No-Arms walked on further with her son – her son who had been saved. As it got dark, she came to a village and asked to stay the night there. In the morning No-Arms was about to set off again, but the people in that village were kind people;

they took in and welcomed the mother with no arms, so she could live there and bring up her child among them.

No-Arms's son grew up among good people, but the war where his father was fighting had still not finished. In those days wars lasted for many years.

The time came – and No-Arms's son was taken to fight too. His mother fitted him out with everything he might need; the whole village helped her to equip the young warrior. They bought him clothes and victuals. They bought him a horse – let him ride to the war. The mother bid farewell to her only son.

'Go now,' she said, 'and come back alive. Your father's fighting there too. Now it's your turn, my son. If the enemy invades, it will be the end of us; but if you drive them out, we shall never be parted again.'

Off rode her son to the war. His mother was now all alone, and she began to yearn for him. She thought of her son all day and dreamed of him at night. Sometimes he had killed all the enemy and was on his way back to her; sometimes he was lying dead in a field, crows pecking his eyes out.

Her heart couldn't bear it. No-Arms dressed herself as a soldier and set off to the war. When she got there, the soldiers thought she was a man and just said, 'You should be at home, my friend, sitting on the stove. What can a cripple do in a war? You're a brave fellow, but this is no place for you.'

But No-Arms knew what she should do. She began to care for the sick and the dying. Sometimes a man would be about to die – and her good and kind words would keep him alive. Or a soldier would lose heart, she'd walk in front of him towards the enemy, and the despondent warrior would raise his sword again. Yes, that's how it was.

And then one day No-Arms caught sight of her son. He was in the middle of the battlefield, and the enemy were falling dead around him. He was hard pressed. All his comrades, everyone who had fought beside him, had now fallen, and her son stood alone. But in place of the enemies he killed came more enemies, and there was no end to them.

His mother watched: would her son hold out or not? His power was great, but all power can be overpowered. And then a whole dark host fell on him, and she could no longer see if he was alive or dead.

From a distance the commander himself was watching the battle. He said to his aide, 'Find out the name of that warrior of ours over there. Find out whose son he is, and send him help straight away.'

But when would this help come? In time, or too late? Suddenly No-Arms saw her son rise up from the ground. All around him were fallen enemies. And at that moment a black host bore down on him. Her time – the mother understood – had come. She shouted out, 'Stand firm, my son! Stand firm, my only begotten son!' – and rushed to his side.

She didn't stop to think that she had no arms – all she knew was her heart beating away in fury against the enemy and with love for her son – and then she felt her arms again, and the strength in them, as though her brother had never chopped them off. She snatched up the sharp sword of a fallen warrior and started to cut down the enemies crowding around her son. She fought for a long time, defending her son; she was beginning to tire and, as for her son, he was soaked in blood and barely able to stand. Then came the help sent by the commander. Fresh soldiers cut down the remnant of the enemy; those who had fallen at the hands of No-Arms and her son already lay dead. No-Arms's son had fought by his mother's side, but he hadn't recognized her: he had had no time to look at her, and even if he had, he wouldn't have known her – his mother had no arms, while the arms of this warrior were mighty.

Soon after the enemy had been defeated, the war came to an end. The commander at once summoned all his bravest warriors, asking each to say who were his people and who was his father, and giving each a reward. He called No-Arms's son and asked: 'Who are your people, young man? Who are your father and mother? They too must be rewarded, for having raised such a son.'

No-Arms's son hung his head. 'I have no father,' he said, 'and I can't remember him. I grew up alone with my mother. The earth was our bed, and the sky our covering. Good people took the place of my father.'

'The people are a father to all fathers,' said the commander. 'I am less than they and cannot reward them. But your mother must be rewarded for having raised a brave son. Let her appear before me and take her reward in her hands.'[3]

'But she hasn't got any hands, she hasn't got any arms at all,' said No-Arms's son.

The commander looked sadly and penetratingly at the young warrior.

'Go and fetch your mother,' he said. 'Bring her to me.'

No-Arms's son went back to the village to look for his mother. There he learned that his mother had gone to the war, too. She had gone to care for those who had been cut to pieces and mutilated.

He went back and spoke to the commander. His mother had left the village, he told the commander; she was here with the army.

The commander asked everyone who had helped heal the wounded and dying to be brought to him, and he began to reward them for the good work they had done. And when a woman with no arms came up to him, wearing the clothes of a soldier, he looked her in the face and knew her as his wife, and No-Arms recognized him as her husband. No-Arms wanted to embrace her husband – she had been separated from him for a whole age – but she remembered she had no arms. They had withered away again immediately after she had stood by her son in the battle. But No-Arms couldn't bear it, and she reached out towards her husband. She had always loved him; she had never forgotten him. And then, as if from her heart, her arms grew, as strong as they had ever been, and with them she embraced her husband. And from that moment her arms stayed with her forever.[4]

Then the father called for his son and said to him: 'Welcome, my son! I am your father, and you didn't know me, nor I you. Evil people parted us, but there is a power more powerful than evil.'

The son looked at his father and rejoiced. Then he looked at his mother and saw that his mother now had hands and arms. And he remembered that last battle and the warrior who had defended him with his sword. The son fell on his knees before his mother and kissed her hands that had saved him.

Soon afterwards, when peacetime set in, the commander set off to the house where he had once lived with his father, where he had first seen No-Arms and begun to love her. He took with him his wife and his son and rode off to live in peace. After going some distance, they stopped at the hut of No-Arms's brother, because it was on their way.

As soon as the brother's wife saw them, as soon as she saw who had come – No-Arms herself and all her family, all whole and hale, and people of standing – she collapsed at their feet in terror and at once, without being asked, told all she had done to doom No-Arms and her little child.

'Maybe they'll pardon me,' she thought. 'It was a long time ago.'

No-Arms listened to her, and, in answer, told of her own fate, of all she had suffered.

No-Arms's brother bowed to his sister, and said: 'Thank you, sister, for your story – but evil must not be left to bear seed. Forgive me, dearest sister.'

And that night, without his guests knowing, he led from the stables a young mare who wasn't yet broken in. He twisted the reins, and with them he tied his wife to the mare's tail and himself to his wife. He called out – and the horse was off, dragging husband and wife through open steppe, beating them to death against the ground.[5]

In the morning, No-Arms and her husband and son waited for their hosts, but only a mare ran up, alone, without any people, out of the open steppe.

The guests waited and waited – and then rode off, back to their home and to long and happy lives. Unhappiness may indeed live in the world, yet only by chance; happiness must live constantly.

Wool over the Eyes

Once there was a soldier who had served his twenty-five years of service. He was a loyal and honourable soldier, but he liked to play tricks on his comrades. He could say anything in the world and make it seem like the truth; until they came to their senses, his comrades would all believe him.

Now a soldier may have to serve many years, but he has time off, and he, too, wants to have fun. He doesn't have a family, he doesn't have to think about board and lodging, so what does he do after sentry duty? What do you think? He tells stories! And what does he care where his stories take him?

Soldier Ivan had received his discharge. It was time for him to go back home, but his home was somewhere far, far away, and he was long unaccustomed to his kinfolk.

'Well,' he sighed. 'I've served all my life as a soldier. I've served for twenty-five years, but I haven't once seen the tsar! When I get back to my village, my kin are going to ask what the tsar's like. What will I tell them?'

Off Ivan went to see the tsar.

Now the tsar of that land was Tsar Agey – and Tsar Agey loved being told stories. Until he'd listened to a few, he never felt merry. Tsar Agey also liked to tell stories and ask riddles himself. He liked it when people listened to him, and he liked it still more when people believed his stories and couldn't un-riddle his riddles.

Along came Ivan, into the presence of Tsar Agey.

'What do you want, fellow countryman?' asked Agey.

'I want to look at your royal face! Twenty-five years I've served as your soldier, not once have I seen your face.'

Tsar Agey told the soldier to sit down opposite him on a carved wooden chair: 'Sit and look, soldier! Sit on this chair, sit till the devil drags you away by the hair!' And the tsar laughed.

Ivan sat on the carved chair. He felt a little scared in the tsar's royal presence, and he wasn't quite sure if the tsar was in his right mind. 'Why does Tsar Agey sound so delighted about this devil of his?' he kept wondering.

'Well, soldier, I'll ask you a riddle!' said Tsar Agey. 'How great is the world – what do you reckon?'

Ivan looked serious. 'Not so very great, your Majesty! The sun goes all the way round it in under twenty-five hours.'

'True enough,' said the tsar. 'And how much height stands between the earth and the sky? A great height or a little height?'

'The same thing, your Highness – only a very little height. If there's a knock up there, you hear it down here.'

Tsar Agey could see the soldier was speaking truth and this upset him. The soldier was smart. He might even be smarter than the tsar himself.

'Soldier, tell me one more thing. How deep are the depths of the sea?'

'How deep are the depths of the sea? No one knows that. My grandad served at sea, and he went and drowned deep into the water. It's forty years since he drowned – and he's still not found his way back.'

Tsar Agey realized he was never going to outriddle the old soldier. He ordered the soldier to be given some money, so he could set up a home for himself. Then he sat him down at the table to drink some tea.

'Present me a story, soldier. Then I'll let you go home.'

Now a soldier never has any money at all, and he's always glad to be given some. And Ivan had sat long enough in the tsar's royal presence, and anyway it wasn't really tea that he wanted.

'Let me go out for some fun, your Highness. Twenty-five years I've served in your service. Now let me go and live as I please. I'll present you the story later.'

Ivan left the tsar's and went to a tavern. For a day and a night the soldier had fun. He drank away all the money the tsar had given him. He had nothing left but an old half kopek. He drank that away too, but he still hadn't drunk all he wanted. He wanted more.

'More vodka, landlord, and a bite to eat!'

The landlord was afraid of being cheated. 'Are you paying in gold or in silver?' he asked.

'Gold. Silver's too heavy for a soldier to carry about with him.'

The landlord brought the soldier some food and some vodka, then sat down opposite him.

'Where are you going now, soldier?' he asked. 'And what about your kin – are they still living or have they all passed away?'

'I've come from the tsar's royal presence,' said Ivan. 'Where else would a soldier be coming from? And a soldier doesn't need kinfolk. The whole world is his kin. Drink up, landlord – it's on me!'

The landlord drank with the retired soldier.

'I'll charge you a bit less,' said the landlord. 'Yes, I'll give you a discount.'

'Drink up, landlord! And a soldier doesn't need discounts – I'll settle in full! And have a bite to eat!'

The landlord lived well. He was accustomed to good food and good drink – but what he loved more than anything was good talk.

'Tell me a true story, soldier,' he said, 'a story about something that really happened to you.'

'Which story shall I tell you, landlord?'

'Any story you like. What lands you've wandered. What places you've made your home.'

'Well then, let me tell you. Before I served my service I was a bear, and I lived in the forest. And I'm a bear now, too, and I'm on my way back to the forest.'

At first the landlord felt frightened. It was his own tavern, and it was full of goods and wares. He might incur a loss from the bear – how would a bear be able to pay for what he had eaten and drunk?

'My!' said the landlord. 'Is that the truth?'

'It certainly is!' said the retired soldier. 'Can't you see? I'm a bear, and yes, you're a bear too!'

This well and truly shocked the landlord: who would he be able to trade with now that he was a bear?

The landlord looked at the former soldier and pinched himself. Yes, the soldier was a bear – and now he himself was a bear too.

'What are we going to do, soldier? We don't have to run away into the forest, do we?'

'Not now. We might be killed by hunters. There'll be time enough to escape to the forest.'

'But what are we to do now?' said the landlord. 'Oh, how unhappy we are! We're bears!'

The former soldier stayed calm. 'What are we to do now?' he said. 'Let's drink and feast! Be a true host – bid the world be your guest! Bears can't be landlords – and we can't let your goods go to waste!'

The former Ivan was speaking the truth – there was no doubt about it. The landlord gave orders for people to be called from every village and every town, from every hut for miles around.

The guests arrived – people they had called, and far-flung strangers who had heard the call from others. They ate till not a scrap or a crumb remained; they drank till every barrel was drained. Then they took away all the bowls and spoons: what good are bowls and spoons to a bear?

Now the landlord had no goods and wares left at all. He and the former soldier climbed up onto the sleeping bench for the night.

'What am I to do?' he asked.

'We can slip away into the forest tonight,' said the soldier. 'Bears aren't supposed to live in towns and settlements. It's not lawful – we'll be fined.'

Ivan woke during the night and ordered the landlord, 'Come on, bear! Jump! It's time we were off to the forest. You run first and I'll follow. We don't want you to get left behind.'

The landlord collected himself, jumped off the sleeping bench, and fell belly first onto the floor. He lay there for a while until he came to. Then he saw what had happened – nothing was left in his tavern, the guests had eaten their way for free through all his wares, there was no sign of that former soldier, and he himself was not a bear but a landlord again, though a good deal worse off than he had been before.

The landlord wanted to take the former Ivan to court. But where would he find him now that Ivan had walked free? And anyway, everyone always welcomes a soldier. Who was going to give him away into punishment?

The landlord made a complaint to Tsar Agey. The tsar summoned the landlord and asked, 'What wrong has the old soldier done you?'

'What do you mean, your Highness?' said the landlord. 'He turned me into a bear. I was a fool and believed him, and your soldier gave away all my goods and wares. He gave all my food and drink away to guests, and he ate all he could himself.'

Tsar Agey laughed at the landlord. 'Be off with you!' he said. 'Get yourself some more goods! There's no law against wit, and no profit in being stupid.'

After this, the tsar wanted to hear a tale himself: let the old soldier present a tale to him! Let him present what never had been and never would be as if it were really happening. 'He can't be smarter than I am,' he said to himself. 'I'm the tsar. The old soldier won't pull the wool over my eyes. I'll just have a good laugh at him.'

Tsar Agey ordered former soldier Ivan to be found, wherever he might be, wherever he was up to no good.

Ivan heard the tsar's call, and he appeared at once. 'Here I am, your Highness. What do you want?'

The tsar had the samovar put on the table and ordered Ivan to drink some tea. Ivan poured some tea into a silver mug, then poured a little out into the saucer. He almost sat down again on the carved chair, but he sat on a stool instead.

'You're a smart fellow, Ivan,' said the tsar. 'I hear you turned a landlord into a bear. Can you present a story like that to me? Can you pull the wool over my eyes too?'

'I could, your Highness. I'm accustomed to that kind of thing. But I'd be afraid.'

'Don't be afraid, soldier. I love a good yarn.'

'I know you do,' said Ivan. 'But this time it'll be me spinning the yarn, not you. But what time is it, your Highness?'

'The time – what's the time got to do with it? By now it must be after midday.'

'It'll start any minute!' said the former soldier. And then he called out all of a sudden, 'Water! Water, your Majesty! High water's sweeping down on your palace! Quick! We must swim for it! I'll tell you a story later, somewhere dry.'

The tsar couldn't see any flood, and there was no water anywhere. But he could see that the former soldier was drowning. He was choking, his mouth snatching at the air above him.

'What's up, soldier?' shouted the tsar. 'Come to your senses!'

Suddenly there's nothing for the tsar to breathe either. His chest's full of water. Now his stomach's full of water too. And now it's swirling into his guts.

'Save me, soldier!'

Soldier Ivan grabs hold of the tsar.

'Hey, Agey, swim this way!'

Tsar Agey swims for all he's worth. Ahead of him is a fish. The fish turns round towards him.

'Don't be afraid, Agey,' says the fish. 'It's me, Agey – your soldier for many a day!'

The tsar looks at himself: now he's become a fish too. 'We won't drown now!' he says joyfully.

'We certainly won't!' answers Ivan-fish. 'We'll live!'

They swim on further. Out of the palace they swim, into free water. All of a sudden Ivan-fish is no longer there. Ivan-fish has vanished. There's only the soldier's voice, calling from somewhere off to the right: 'Hey, Agey! Turn tail! Catch your fins in that net and you'll be gutted and scaled!'

The tsar hears, but there's no time to think. He swims straight into a fisherman's net. Ivan-fish is there too.

'What are we going to do now, soldier?' asks the tsar.

'We're going to die, your Highness.'

But the tsar wishes to live. He struggles and struggles. He wants to leap free, but it's a strong net.

The fishermen drag the net in. Agey sees one of them grab

Ivan-fish. The fisherman scrapes Ivan's scales off with a knife and throws him into the pot. 'No!' thinks the tsar. 'No one's going to scrape the scales off Tsar Agey!'

The fisherman grabs the tsar-fish and beheads it. He tosses that head away, then throws the carcass into the pot. Just then the tsar hears the voice of the former soldier: 'But your Highness, old fellow – where's your head?'

The tsar wants to retort, 'Well, where's your skin? They've scraped all your scales off! Why didn't you save me, you devil?' – but he can't. The tsar can't speak at all – he remembers he's lost his head.

The tsar clasped his head in his hands. Then he came back to his senses. He looked around: he was in his palace the same as always; he was sitting in an armchair and Ivan the retired soldier was sitting opposite him on a stool, drinking tea from a saucer.

'Ivan, was it you who was a fish just now?'

'Yes, your Highness, who else could it have been?'

'And who was thinking when I lost my head?'

'Me again. There wasn't anyone else.'

'Leave my tsardom at once!' the tsar yelled at Ivan. 'Let there be neither sight nor sound of you ever again. May you be forgotten by all my people and never remembered!'

The former soldier left the tsar's presence – and all he'd had to drink was half a saucer of tea. As for the tsar, he straight away made a proclamation throughout all his tsardom: let no one dare take into their home Ivan the retired soldier!

Off Ivan wandered. But wherever he went, people closed their doors to him. All they would say was, 'The tsar has forbidden us to take you in.'

At first, Ivan had no luck at all. He went as far as his own kinfolk – and they didn't want to know him either. They just said, 'The tsar has forbidden us to take you in.' Ivan walked on further. What would he find there?

He came to a hut and asked to stay the night: 'Let me in, good man!'

'I would, but it's forbidden,' the man answered. 'Still, I might let you stay if you tell me a tale. You really can tell tales, can you?'

Ivan thought for a moment.

'Yes, I suppose I can.'

The peasant let him in for the night.

Ivan began to tell a tale. At first his host listened with only half an ear, thinking, 'He'll just tell a pack of lies and then ask for a bowl of kasha.' Halfway through the tale he smiled. Then he began to listen more deeply. Towards the end of the tale he quite forgot who he was. He was no longer a peasant, but a bandit. Or he was Tsar of the Ocean. Or not just one of the poor but a very wise wanderer – or perhaps a fool. But really nothing was happening at all. There was only an old soldier – sitting close by, twitching his lips and muttering away. Coming back to his senses, Ivan's host asked for another tale. The soldier began again. Soon it was growing light outside and they still hadn't lain down to sleep. Soldier Ivan was telling his hundredth tale and his host was sitting opposite him, crying tears of joy.

'That'll do,' said Ivan. 'All I've done is make up a tale. Why waste tears?'

'Because of the tale you've told,' the host replied with a sigh. 'It's a joy to the heart and food for thought.'

'But Tsar Agey just got angry with me,' said Ivan. 'He said I must leave his tsardom and go where my eyes look.'

'That's the way of the world,' said the host. 'The people's meat is the tsar's poison.'

Ivan got up and began to say goodbye to his host.

'Take anything you like from in here,' said the host. 'Nothing of mine matters to me any longer – and there must be something you'll need for the road.'

'I've got everything I want already. There isn't anything I need. But thank you!'

'Whatever you own, it's not to be seen!'

The old soldier grinned. 'So there's nothing I can call my own, yet you'll give me anything of yours that I like? Don't you think I must have something to give in return?'

'You win!' answered the host. 'Well, goodbye! Come again – you'll always be welcome!'

After that, Ivan wandered from village to village, from the

home of one stranger to the home of another stranger. Wherever he went, he had only to promise to tell a story and people would take him in for the night: a story, it appears, is stronger than a tsar. There was just one thing: if he began telling stories before they had eaten, the people listening to him never felt hungry and supper time never came. So the former soldier always asked for a bowl of cabbage soup first.

It was better like that. After all, you can't live on stories alone, without any food.

Appendix

BABA YAGA: THE WILD WITCH OF THE EAST

Who is this wild witch, and why is she riding in a *mortar*?

Though only a few of the tales say it in so many words, most Russians would agree that Baba Yaga is a witch. The Russian word for witch is *ved'ma*. The word root *ved-* means 'to know,' and related words in Modern Russian mean 'news' (as in the title of *Pravda*'s one-time competitor, the Soviet newspaper *Izvestiya*), as well as information or consultation, and the particle *ved'* means 'indeed' (as if commanding one's listener 'know this!'). The word *witch* has a similar linguistic history: the root of the word is *wit*. This verb still shows up in 'to wit', 'unwitting', the old-fashioned 'God wot', and of course in keeping one's *wits* about one. Feminists and Wiccans have worked to reclaim the word witch in its sense of 'wise woman' or 'woman who knows', but in both Russian and English the words as commonly used suggest age and ugliness first, power second.

What does Baba Yaga's name mean? The first half is easy: *baba* in traditional Russian culture meant a married peasant woman, one at least old enough to have children. (In Russian now, *baba* is an insulting word for a woman: it suggests low class, slovenliness, lack of emotional restraint, or sexual availability of an aging or unattractive kind.) When Russians build a snowman, they call it not a man, but a snow *baba*. Suffixes bring out different shades of the basic meanings of Russian nouns: *babka* is a midwife (usually an older woman with experience around pregnancy and childbirth); *babushka* is an affectionate term for 'grandmother' (and, in the West, the headscarf old women in Russia traditionally wore); and a *babochka* is a butterfly, or else the visually similar bow tie. This last word is linked to an ancient belief that, when a person died, the soul left the body in the form of a bird or a butterfly (compare the Greek *psyche*, which meant both 'soul' and 'butterfly'). If a butterfly fluttered by, it was the soul of a little grandmother, presumably en route to a better place. Thus, *baba* can mean 'woman' or 'old woman' – though age is described in Russian folktales in a way that might surprise us. The 'old man' and 'old woman' in a tale are old enough to have children of marriageable age, but often only just – they might be in their late thirties. Baba Yaga is far older than that.

The second part of her name, *yaga*, is harder to define. One school of thought relates the word to verbs for riding – and it does sound rather like the Russian verb *yekhat'* (to ride), or the German word *Jaeger* (huntsman). Another theory is that *yaga* originally meant 'horrible', 'horrifying', and should be compared to the words *jeza* (shiver) or *jezivo* (chilling, horrifying) in South Slavic languages. If Baba Yaga originally played a role in a secret corpus of myths or initiation rituals, the taboo on such material might have discouraged people from saying her name in other contexts. Maks Fasmer's monumental *Etymological Dictionary of the Russian Language* has a longish entry for 'yaga', pointing out cognate words in other Slavic languages and arguing against several theories of the word's origin. The amount of space Fasmer devotes to all this suggests that we will never know the word's true origins. Baba Yaga is well known in Ukrainian and Belarussian tales, and figures very much like her appear in Czech and Polish tales.

In Russian, Baba Yaga's name is often not capitalized. Indeed, it is not a name at all, but a description – 'old lady yaga' or perhaps 'dreadful old woman'. There is often more than one Baba Yaga in a tale, and thus we should really say 'a baba yaga', 'the baba yaga'. We do so when a tale would otherwise be confusing. Otherwise, we have continued the western tradition of capitalizing Baba Yaga. There is no graceful way to put the name in the plural in English, and in Russian tales multiple iterations of Baba Yaga never appear at the same time, only in sequence: Baba Yaga sisters or cousins talk about one another, or send travellers along to one another, but they do not live together. In some tales our witch is called only 'Yaga'. A few tales refer to her as 'Yagishna', a patronymic form suggesting that she is Yaga's daughter rather than Yaga herself. (That in turn suggests that Baba Yaga reproduces parthenogenetically.) The frequent lack of capitalization in Russian publications also hints at Baba Yaga's status as a type rather than an individual, a paradigmatic mean or frightening old woman. This also suggests that Baba Yaga may be a euphemism for another name or term, too holy or frightening to be spoken, and therefore long forgotten.

Other names in the tales

Many Russian personal names are recognizable in English, since they are related to familiar Biblical or western names. Marya is the folk form of Maria, though it is pronounced 'MAR-ya'. The second part of Marya Morevna's name is a patronymic, formed from her father's name. It means 'Daughter of the Sea'; like Baba Yaga, she evidently comes from a distant past. Vasily and Vasilisa are forms of the name Basil (which does not produce a woman's name in English). Ivan is the most common name for a Russian fairy-tale hero, whether he starts as a prince or as a fool. Ivan is the same name as John; the relationship is easier to see if one compares the medieval Russian form, Ioann, to the German form of John, Johannes. Hans (short for Johannes) is the most common name for the hero of German folktales, while Jack (a nickname for John) is the hero of many British and American folktales.

One other important character whose name needs explanation is *Koshchey* or *Kashchey bessmertny*, 'Koshchey the Deathless'. His first name probably comes from the old Slavic *Koshchnoye* (Kingdom of the Dead), but it also suggests the word *kost'* ('bone') and Koshchey is often portrayed as a skeletal old man. Unlike Baba Yaga, Koshchey is always a villain, though he does possess a certain sense of honour: in 'Marya Morevna', he spares the life of Prince Ivan three times because Ivan once (unintentionally) set him free, restoring his monstrous strength with three bucket-sized drinks of water. It turns out, of course, that the epithet 'deathless' does not mean that he cannot be killed, only that his death lies somewhere outside him: it is the tip of a needle in an egg, in a duck, in a hare, in a trunk, etc., all located across the sea or in a distant forest. If I can tell you this, then the hero can find this out, too. The hero journeys to the tree, unearths or unpacks the alienated death, and then slays Koshchey to release the maiden. With Koshchey as well as Baba Yaga, the references to bones are ambiguous. Bones are the leftovers of a body after death, but they are also a repository of life force, a link between two incarnations. The Frog Princess hides leftover swan bones in her sleeve, then brings the swans to life. In at least one version of 'Marya Morevna', Koshchey must be burned after Ivan kills him, and his ashes scattered to all the winds to ensure he will never come back. Baba Yaga's epithet 'bony leg' may mean that one of her legs consists entirely of bone – or just that she is old and skinny in a culture that valued plumpness. Her fence of human bones, topped with skulls, shows another link with

Koshchey, and in some tales he has a *bogatyr* (giant warrior) horse he won from her: they are allies in villainy.

Besides names, many of the characters are identified by fixed epithets: 'fair maiden', 'fine' or 'goodly' young man. The tales often say no more than this, leaving the listener (or reader) to fill in whatever standard image of beauty or goodliness we prefer. The *bogatyr* is a traditional Russian warrior-hero, featured in epic songs but sometimes making a kind of guest appearance in folktales as well. In some tales we even meet *bogatyr* animals.

The objects around Baba Yaga

In most tales, Baba Yaga lives in an unusual house: it stands on chicken legs, or sometimes on just one chicken leg. Some scholars suggest that this underlines her connections with birds, though the geese, swans and eagles that are often her servants are much more impressive than a chicken, that most domesticated of fowls. At the same time, chicken legs might suggest that her dwelling, alive and mobile, cannot fly and probably does not move too fast or too far. One of our students recently returned from studying in Sweden, where she visited a swamp with houses built on top of tree stumps standing in the water. With their gnarled roots, she said, the stumps looked surprisingly like chicken feet. Some of the tales specify instead that Baba Yaga's house stands on spindle heels. Given the importance of the spindle in women's traditional crafts, and in other parts of the tales (Prince Ivan may have to snap a spindle to free and recover his princess), this, too, seems to come from the deep past. Often Baba Yaga's house turns around, as if in imitation of the spinning of the earth. The word 'time' in Russian, *vremya*, comes from the same *vr-* root of turning and returning as the word for spindle, *vereteno*. A spindle holding up a rotating house where a frightening old woman tests her visitors and dispenses wisdom suggests truly archaic rituals.

In Russian, Baba Yaga's home is most often called an *izba*. The *izba* is a house made of hewn logs, a kind of construction common all over northern Russia and Scandinavia. (Immigrants brought it to the United States in the form of that most American Presidential birthplace, the log cabin.) The word *izba* is often translated as 'hut', but it does not signify a shoddy piece of housing or even necessarily a small one. What does it tell us that Baba Yaga's house is an *izba*? It is a traditional peasant house, a house in the country (not a city), made of wood, and most often situated near a forest. When the hut or house is turning around, the hero or heroine must order it, in rhyme, to stop turning. Intriguingly, everyone in the tales knows what to say to make the house stop turning – even the first sisters or servant girls in tales like 'The Brother', who fail to retrieve the baby Baba Yaga has kidnapped. In 'The Frog Princess', the prince says, 'Stay as your mother made you. Stay with your back towards the sea and your door towards me.' Baba Yaga's house can be in the forest, in an empty field, or on the seashore; it is always on the border of another world.

When Baba Yaga goes out, she often rides in a mortar, rowing or punting herself along with a pestle, perhaps sweeping away her tracks with a broom. Her power lets her travel by means of these everyday housekeeping implements, much as western Europeans believed that witches rode on broomsticks. Her mortar and pestle may themselves be magic objects like the fairy-tale flying carpets and invisibility hats, but she never gives or even loans them to other characters. For many centuries the mortar and pestle were crucial parts of a woman's tool kit, used to prepare herbs for cooking or medicine, or to break grain for porridge or baking. Old photographs of Russian peasant households show large, deep mortars that could have held a substantial measure of grain, though they could hardly have accommodated an adult. Ivan Bilibin's famous picture of Baba Yaga in flight is in harmony with the old photographs: the mortar is a tall, relatively narrow tube, not bowl-shaped. As the food-related mortar and pestle hint, Baba Yaga's house is stuffed with edible riches – the golden apples a child plays with until his rescuer finds him, or the stocks of grain, meat and drink listed in 'Vasilisa the Beautiful', nourishing raw materials to transform into the good things of Russian peasant life: linen, wheat, poppy seed.

Baba Yaga's house may be surrounded with a fence of bones, perhaps topped with skulls (or with one pole still untopped, waiting for the hero's head), but even an ordinary fence and gate can play important roles in the story. While Baba Yaga is sharpening her teeth in preparation to eat the heroine, the girl pours oil on the hinges of the gate and manages to escape. Baba Yaga scolds the gate for letting the girl out, and the gate answers her back. Baba Yaga is also associated with the bathhouse, which in Russia resembles a sauna. In some tales she asks the heroine to stoke the bathhouse fire (sometimes with bones for fuel), to bathe her children (frogs, reptiles and other vermin), or to bathe Baba Yaga herself. Many of the tales mention Baba Yaga's stove. The traditional Russian stove is a large construction of brick and plaster (in a fancier house, it would be covered with ornamental tiles), the size of a small room and certainly the dominant object in any room it occupies. Some stoves were built so that they heated, and took up parts of, two separate rooms. The stove would incorporate shelves, ovens and hobs, nooks or hooks for storing cookware. Such a stove would hold the fire's heat, gently diffusing it into the house. This made it a favorite place for sleeping. The upper shelves, high above the fire and safely distant from vermin or cold drafts, would stay warm through the night. The stove is also associated with the womb, and not only in Russian: the English expression 'one in the oven' connects baking with the rising belly of a pregnant woman. Joanna Hubbs writes that the stove is also a repository of dead souls, the ancestors.[1] Even more than an ordinary peasant stove, Baba Yaga's is a conduit from death to rebirth.

To escape from Baba Yaga, characters in the tales may themselves employ very ordinary objects – sometimes stolen from Yaga's own house – and these, too, recur from tale to tale. Thrown behind as a character flees, a comb or brush turns into a thick forest, as if the wood from which they were carved were coming back to life. A mirror, already magical in its ability to show the gazer his or her own face, turns into a wide, deep sea. Throwing a kerchief or towel will create an impassable river, often a river of fire. Embroidered handkerchiefs or towels may create or turn into bridges over impassable waters, or they may convey secret messages. Towels in the Russian village bore beautiful ritual embroidery and were used in traditional ceremonies (such as welcoming a guest with bread and salt). To find the house of Baba Yaga, the hero or heroine may receive a ball of thread (once known as a *clue* in English), like the one that took Theseus in to the Minotaur. Baba Yaga lives (or, every baba yaga lives) in the heart of the labyrinth, and the hero or heroine enters this labyrinth to face his or her worst fears and vanquish them.

One final traditional element in the tales deserves explanation. Several tales mention searching for lice, or just 'searching' in a character's hair. This must have been a useful grooming practice, since lice are itchy and unpleasant; also, it feels good to have someone riffle through one's hair and touch one's scalp – especially if the hair is worn in long shaggy braids, like Baba Yaga's. Lice were surely common in old Russia, as they were in Western Europe at the time, but the reader should remember that 'searching for lice' can also mean playing with someone's hair in a pleasant, affectionate way.

Baba Yaga in the Russian pantheon

How is Baba Yaga related to other figures in Russian lore? The female figures best known today are *rusalki*, sometimes translated as 'mermaids' though they do not live in the sea. They are said to be the spirits of girls who committed suicide out of disappointed love, or the spirits of babies who died unbaptised (victims of infanticide?), and they are described lolling in the branches of trees or beside streams, combing their long hair, which is often said to be green. They tempt men off the path, intending to drown them, or they may torment children. *Rusalki* are most often represented as young and lovely (though the green hair recalls waterweeds, suggesting their connection with nature). At the same time, their activities are not so different from Baba Yaga's: they are younger, lovelier dangerous females, tickling children to death instead of eating them. If we see Baba Yaga as the crone face of the triune goddess (maiden, mother, crone), as Joanna Hubbs suggests in *Mother Russia*, then *rusalki* embody the maiden face. In many ways the *rusalka* resembles the South Slavic *vila*; some western readers may already know of *vilas*, since they play a role in the Harry Potter novels.

Thanks to a list of the Kievan pagan pantheon recorded in the historical chronicles of old Rus' (the East Slavic land that was ruled, before the Mongol invasion, from Kiev or Kyïv), the name of one goddess has come down to us from the East Slavic past: *Mokosh*. Her name suggests wetness – in Russian the root *mok-* means 'wet' or 'soak' – and she may be linked with Moist (or Raw) Mother Earth, *Mat' syra zemlya*, mentioned in songs and proverbs about planting or burial. This image of the earth invokes both the damp, chilly soil that is planted in the spring, and the earth as a mother's body to which the dead return – a cold, clammy body, unlike the body of the human mother. The Slavic pagan underworld was called *preispodnya*, 'close-under-place'. That suggests a world or afterworld in the near underground, close to the surface. Though Baba Yaga is most often found in the forest, her role in the mysteries of death and rebirth also links her to the harvest and the space underground where grain 'dies' in order to be reborn.

Mokosh is also connected to the Christian Saint Paraskeva, whom Russian peasants called *Paraskeva-Pyatnitsa*, or 'Paraskeva-Friday'. Friday was traditionally the day of the goddess. English *Friday* is named after Frigg or Freya, the Anglo-Scandinavian goddess of love, just as the French *Vendredi* is named after Venus. Paraskeva in Russian folk religious belief was a patron of women. She protected them in childbirth, but she also demanded that they respect her by refraining from 'women's tasks', especially spinning, on Fridays. Paraskeva's day was celebrated on October 28, according to the Julian calendar. Her day is close to Halloween and the Day of the Dead, the old cross-quarter day of November 1 that marked the beginning of winter; this suggests that Paraskeva, like Mokosh and Baba Yaga, is a queen of both harvest and death, a guardian of the mysteries of winter, of the unprepossessing dry seeds that hold life until the following spring. As Moist Mother Earth 'eats' the bodies of the dead, so Baba Yaga eats human beings. Paraskeva's role of guarding women in childbirth also ties into some of Baba Yaga's concerns. Images of Paraskeva on Russian icons may show her holding a spindle – the device that sometimes supports Baba Yaga's hut. Folk narratives about Paraskeva mention that women who spin on Fridays make her dirty, and the 'dirty' saint's tangled hair recalls Baba Yaga's grey braids.

Another, more occulted possibility is that Baba Yaga is 'the devil's grandmother', who shows up in a Russian saying approximately equivalent to 'go to hell': *Idi k chertovoy babushke*, 'Go to the devil's grandmother'. This suggests an interesting cosmogony.

Many of the tales involve a single Baba Yaga (especially those where she tests a daughter sent away by her stepmother, or where she or her avian minions kidnap children), but many others include three Baba Yagas, usually sisters or cousins,[2] whose houses serve as way stations for a hero or heroine in quest of a lost or distant beloved. Baba Yaga's trinity is not a Mozartian threeness, where hearing a motif twice lulls listeners into expecting the same result a third time, only to surprise them with something different. Baba Yaga's threeness is an exact, folkloric trebling, with ritual answers that are repeated the same way each time. Her threeness also suggests a connection with the three Fates.

Deeper meanings of Baba Yaga

Baba Yaga is a wonderfully rich figure: some of her appearances in the tales are specific, and we do not wish to blur her outlines by generalizing too much. As Andreas Johns points out, in his valuable *Baba Yaga: The Ambiguous Mother and Witch of the Russian Folktale*, 'Baba Yaga's particular combination of traits and functions makes her unique among witches and witch-like characters in world folklore' (p. 2). Like the Indian goddess Kali, Baba Yaga is terrifying because of her relationship to death. She mediates the boundary of death so that living human beings may cross it and return, alive but in possession of new wisdom, or 'reborn' into a new status.

Like most folklore witches, Baba Yaga is striking in appearance. She is unusually tall (stretching diagonally across her room when she lies down); she has a huge nose that may stick up to the ceiling, a bony leg (or, occasionally, a golden or other unusual kind of leg), and some-times iron teeth that she sharpens in anticipation of a tasty human snack. In some tales the descriptions are disgusting – in one example, her tits are slung up over a rail. The amount of detail in these descrip-tions is atypical for a wonder tale, and their vividness has attracted many illustrators.

Often, Baba Yaga is a tester and donor. She grudgingly hands over riches, a horse or a bird for transportation, or necessary weapons or tools, and she points out the path to the desired goal; sometimes she gives advice about how to recover the missing partner. She is both a cannibal and a kind of innkeeper, a woman who threatens but also often rewards. She is a goddess of death, but she also gives access to maturity and fertility. She dwells not in Rus' but at the border of the other realm. Sometimes she helps the hero or heroine evade pursuit, while at other times she is the pursuer. Sometimes she sneaks into Rus'; other times she is unable to cross the border and must let the fleeing hero or heroine go. In a few tales she gives the hero and hero-ine a 'self-flying carpet' to carry them back home from the thrice-tenth kingdom (i.e. the kingdom of death).

Baba Yaga was clearly not expected to be the same every time she appeared. Nevertheless, her various hypostases would have been pres-ent in the back of a listener's mind even if a tale stressed another of her roles. If she were being pleasant and helpful, a listener would still feel some tension: what if she suddenly starts to sharpen her teeth?

Sometimes Baba Yaga is a helpful if off-putting old woman, who lives in a peculiar house and, when someone arrives from Rus', com-ments on the smell with a 'Foo, foo, foo!' – resembling the western fairy-tale ogre's 'Fee, fie, fo, fum!' A male hero gets the best treatment if he interrupts her questions and demands to be fed, given a drink and put to bed – and only then begins to tell her his news. She often asks, 'Are you doing a deed or fleeing a deed?' and she may give the hero a ball of string that will lead him on his journey, perhaps to the home of her own sister, another Baba Yaga. In this benign form, a trio of Baba Yaga sisters may be replaced by ordinary old women, but their 'true identity' is clear. The shift from Baba Yaga to helpful old woman may be the result of Orthodox Christianity displacing or 'overwriting' elements from Russia's pagan past.

Sometimes Baba Yaga is a frightening witch who is nonetheless fair, a donor who rewards Vasilisa or the good (step)daughter, while pun-ishing the evil stepmother and/or stepdaughter. She may give the good daughter dresses and other kinds of wealth; she may simply let her go and 'reward' her by destroying her stepmother and/or stepsister(s).

Sometimes she is a frightening witch who is not a donor, or who is an inadvertent donor; in 'Marya Morevna', she plans to eat Prince Ivan even though he has fulfilled his part of the bargain to earn a wonderful horse. Lastly, she can be a thief of children and apparently also a cannibal. In one group of tales, her bird or birds steal a baby, who must be rescued by a servant or an older sister. In others, a boy she has stolen tricks her into eating her own children.

Often Baba Yaga's various roles blend into one another. There is always the threat that she will eat someone who fails her tests, and even when she is being fair or pleasant to a character, it is possible that she may change her mind. When she tears apart the bad stepsister, nothing remains but bones; the tale does not say where the flesh went, and perhaps it does not need to. At the same time, when we see her stealing babies (most often a little boy), the babies do not seem to be in immediate danger. The sister in 'Geese and Swans' discovers her brother playing with golden apples, which resonate with the apples of youth in other tales, and the brother in 'The Brother' is discovered sitting on a chair (not the cold, dirty floor) while the cat Yeremey tells him tales.

We see Baba Yaga travelling in her mortar, stealing children and wreaking havoc, but we also see her at the loom. Weaving, making the cloth for clothing, constitutes another link with the 'women's' saint Paraskeva (and her Friday prohibitions), as well as with images of the Fates as spinners or weavers. Baba Yaga is sometimes alone in her hut; in other tales she has a variety of helpers or companions, the three pairs of disembodied hands Vasilisa sees but wisely does not ask about. These recall the hands that wait on Beauty in the palace of the Beast. In 'Vasilisa the Beautiful', Baba Yaga also commands three riders: a white rider on a white horse, who represents dawn (the idea that dawn would be distinct from sunrise reflects an archaic worldview: the sun was the ruler but not the cause of the blue daytime sky: the sky grew pale long before the sun appeared and remained pale after the sun set, especially in northern latitudes, and in Northern Russia in winter the sun might not rise at all), a red rider on a red horse representing the sun (the Russian word for 'red', *krasny*, comes from the same root as the word for 'beautiful' – so the sun is both red and beautiful), and a black rider on a black horse, for night.

In some tales Baba Yaga has armies, and servants who magically create soldiers for these armies. Finally, she often has a daughter or daughters. (Baba Yaga never seems to have a son, though she may have a grandson ...) The daughters can vary considerably: sometimes they are stupid girls, who obediently follow Yaga's orders only to be baked in her oven and eaten by their own mother. Even a mean, stupid Baba Yaga never wants to eat her own children, and she becomes extremely angry after being tricked into doing this. In other tales, Baba Yaga has a single daughter, a great beauty, who aids the hero or heroine and is rewarded by being allowed to escape into the ordinary world and marry a hero or a prince. Helping the hero or heroine, of course, greatly endangers the daughter. None of these daughters appears to have a father; some of the negative ones are called *Yagishna*, 'daughter of Yaga,' using the Russian patronymic form that is customarily based on the *father's* name, never the mother's, except here.

In some tales, Baba Yaga seems to be involved because the mother is missing, even if the tale is about a stepmother. In 'Vasilisa the Beautiful', the heroine's doll, a deathbed gift from her mother, keeps her safe in Baba Yaga's house. Baba Yaga tests Vasilisa and other girls not only by requesting impossible tasks but also by making them show that they are proficient at the essential feminine tasks: cooking, washing, stoking the fires in stove and bathhouse. Even when she plans to eat the girl, Baba Yaga tells her to sit down and weave while she herself goes off to sharpen her teeth. All this reflects traditional realities: a peasant girl who did not know how to weave or cook or stoke the bathhouse would not bring good fortune to her family. Baba Yaga is often kinder, or at least more fair, than the stepmother who sends her unloved stepdaughter to the witch in hopes that she will be eaten or destroyed.

It has indeed been suggested that tales of Baba Yaga helped young people accept and understand their place in a traditional culture, after earlier initiation rituals had been abandoned. For young women, marriage meant entering a new household and adapting to new household organization, under the authority of the mother-in-law. More generally, everyone could learn from how the heroes and heroines of the tales handle Baba Yaga – when to tell the truth and when to lie, when to be meek and when to be demanding.

So Baba Yaga appears as an initiatrix, a vestigial goddess, a forest power and a mistress of birds or animals. In a hunting culture, like that of old Russia, all this made her a very important figure. Baba Yaga's link to death is less unsettling if we remember death's constant presence in the peasant world.

In many of the tales, Baba Yaga asks the new arrivals whether they have come of their own will or by compulsion. The question could very well be part of an initiation ritual, though the correct answer varies from tale to tale. Propp and others consider that tales about Baba Yaga are remnants of initiation rituals for adolescents. This helps to explain why so many of the stories end with marriage or with a separated couple being reunited. Marriage was a crucial moment in traditional society, marking the newlyweds as adults, producers of a new generation, and setting up or bolstering the economic unit of the family. Moreover, the tradition of wedding laments suggests that for a young woman marriage could be tantamount to death – even if many brides performed the ritual lamentation more as a way of keeping off the Evil Eye, to avoid tempting fate by seeming to be happy about the arrangements.

Given all this, it is perhaps no surprise that Jungian therapists still see Baba Yaga as an embodiment of occult knowledge, and her hut as a stage on a difficult path. One could argue that in the modern world people pass through many more roles and face many more tests than in the past. Modern encounters with Baba Yaga and what she represents still reaffirm our strength, cleverness and worthiness, teaching us how to win treasure or understanding out of loss, fear and pain.

Baba Yaga and childbirth

I would argue, though, that the tales also show another important traditional role for Baba Yaga. Recall that Paraskeva, the saint whose day is celebrated just before the end of the old traditional autumn, is a protector of women in childbirth. Her precursor Baba Yaga, in her role as a thief and presumably devourer of children, may serve to address fears of infant and child mortality. There is no record of anything like an initiation ceremony for a woman in childbirth, perhaps because the event was already hedged round with a huge number of superstitions, spells and careful practices intended to keep the child (and, to a lesser extent, the mother) from harm. Russian peasant women traditionally gave birth in the bathhouse – a sensible place, since it was warm, relatively clean and private, but also a place associated with Baba Yaga. In times of high infant and child mortality, the goddess of the borders of death would necessarily play a part here, too. Indeed, Baba Yaga's role in both types of tales, the 'testing' and the 'devouring', is formally similar. If adulthood meant the death of the child, and marriage meant the death of the maiden, then childbirth, too, carries an element of death – the death of the single human being and simultaneous birth of both child and mother.

In the stories where Baba Yaga kidnaps a child, the heroine passes through a series of ritual rebirths once she has recovered this child. In Khudyakov's version of 'The Brother', Baba Yaga's eagle notices that the stove protecting the maiden has become wider, and she asks the apple tree, 'Why have you, apple tree, become so curly, lowered your branches right down to the ground?' The tree answers: 'The time has come [. . .] I'm standing here all fluffy.' The wording, as well as the position of the girl and baby inside and beneath the lowered branches, suggests that the tree is pregnant, that its 'time has come'. Much as the testing tales lead into adulthood or marriage, the tales of girls who rescue babies stolen by Baba Yaga could serve to socialize young mothers in caring for new babies, and younger girls in caring for their own new younger siblings. The girl might be seen as representing the new generation of parents, while the mother of the stolen child is her own mother, an older woman nevertheless still young enough to have more children of her own, who knows how to keep a child alive in a dangerous world and now sends her daughter out to gain this know-ledge. The various 'pregnant' pauses in the narrative, where girl and baby hide from pursuit, show the girl emerging each time reborn as someone better fit to care for a child. The fact that the stolen child seems happy and safe with Baba Yaga – playing with golden apples, or listening to a cat telling a story – suggests that infant mortality causes little pain for the infant, more for the mother and other rela-tives who survive.

Forest, field and fire

Baba Yaga's birds – geese, swans, eagles – are not just hunting birds. They are psychopomps who bear a dead soul or a living person to the other world. No matter where Baba Yaga's house is located (forest, open field, seashore), it is always at the border of the other realm, over thrice-nine lands and near the thrice-tenth. The forest lies at the heart of Russian civilization, holding riches (the honey, wax and furs that early Slavs traded along routes from the Black Sea to Scandinavia) as well as terrors. The open field – or open steppe – appears in trad-itional Russian spells. These spells frequently begin with the words 'I rise up, saying a blessing. I go out, crossing myself, and I go to an open field'. An empty place where no one can see or hear what one says is the proper locus for working magic. Russia's traditional terri-tory has a seacoast only in the far north, on the White Sea – but many cultures have imagined the afterlife as located beyond the sea, in the land where the sun sets.

Baba Yaga is strongly associated with fire; Vasilisa comes to her house asking for a light, and Yaga sends her back home with a fiery-eyed skull that incinerates her stepmother and stepsisters. In some folktales, Baba Yaga herself is killed, baked in an oven (though sometimes she scratches her way out), or burned up after falling into a fiery river. But as Propp points out in *The Russian Folktale*, Baba Yaga is a recurring figure: if she burns up once, it only means that she no longer threatens the characters of *that* story. She will be back in the next one.

What other books say about Baba Yaga

One might say that Andreas Johns 'wrote *the* book' on Baba Yaga – *Baba Yaga: The Ambiguous Mother and Witch of the Russian Folktale*. Summarizing and synthesizing the results of hundreds of tales, he provides a range of information about the image of Baba Yaga and the many variants of tales about her. His readings of the tales are clear and well-founded, and not limited by any single theoretical perspective.

The prominent Soviet folklorist Vladimir Propp (1895–1970) mentions Baba Yaga in several of his works. Most interestingly, she appears at length in *The Historical Roots of the Wonder Tale*, of which only fragments have been translated into English. Propp's aim in this work is to trace each move of the wonder tale (or the magic tale, *volshebnaya skazka* in Russian) back to its origins in initiation rituals. He sees Baba Yaga as the guardian of the boundary between the world of the living and the world of the dead and sees her power over birds and animals as a trace of the primitive totemistic religion of a hunter/gatherer culture. Yaga is also, according to Propp, a link to the period in human society when the male role in reproduction was not understood – hence her daughters, or her many vermin-children, conceived with no man in sight.

Anthropologist Joanna Hubbs, in *Mother Russia: The Feminine Myth in Russian Culture*, draws on work by a variety of scholars. Hubbs's synthetic view of Baba Yaga connects her to other narratives or images of female divinity in Russian verbal and material culture, including the *rusalki*, the Goddess Mokosh, Moist Mother Earth, and the later female Christian figures, Mary the Mother of God and Saint Paraskeva. To Hubbs, Yaga is a figure of occulted female power connected to goddess worship, in which every mother was a priestess in her own house. Hubbs's work refers often to the work of archeologist Marija Gimbutas. Cherry Gilchrist's recent *Russian Magic: Living Folk Traditions of an Enchanted Landscape* (2009) gives a detailed and accessible introduction to the place of magic in Russia today.

There are many treatments of Baba Yaga tales for children. For adult readers, we recommend not only Russian and North American books on Baba Yaga. Dubravka Ugrešić *Baba Yaga Laid an Egg* (2008) is great fun and also intellectually rewarding. Before her international literary success, Ugrešić was a prominent specialist in Russian literature and culture. *Baba Yaga Laid an Egg* touches on a number of Yagian issues: the relationship between daughters and their aging mothers, the relationship between writers and their admirers, and the relationship between biographical experience and artistic invention. In the book's final section, Baba Yaga anagrams into a Bulgarian folklorist, and then . . . Well! We suggest that you read it.

Sibelan Forrester
Swarthmore, Pennsylvania, 2010

Bibliography

1. Russian folktales in English translation

Afanasyev, Aleksandr, *Russian Fairy Tales* (Pantheon, 1984); *Russian Secret Tales* (Clearfield, 1998)

Balina, Marina, Helena Goscilo and Mark Lipovetsky, *Politicizing Magic: An Anthology of Russian and Soviet Fairy Tales* (Northwestern University Press, 2004)

Bazhov, Pavel, *Malachite Casket: Tales from the Urals* (Fredonia Books, 2002)

Forrester, Sibelan, Helena Goscilo and Martin Skoro, *Baba Yaga: The Wild Witch of the East in Russian Folklore* (University Press of Mississippi, 2013)

Haney, Jack, *The Complete Russian Folktale* (M. E. Sharpe, 1998–2005; 7 volumes, published individually); *An Anthology of Russian Folktales* (M. E. Sharpe, 2009). This distillation of *The Complete Russian Folktale* is essential reading.

Ransome, Arthur, *Old Peter's Russian Tales* (Jane Nissen Books, 2003); *The War of the Birds and the Beasts* (Puffin, 1986)

Tsvetaeva, Marina, *The Ratcatcher*, tr. Angela Livingstone (Angel Books, 1999), a superb translation of Tsvetaeva's version of the Pied Piper legend.

2. Scholarship in English

Bailey, James and Tatyana Ivanova, *An Anthology of Russian Folk Epics* (M. E. Sharpe, 1998)

Balina, Marina and Larissa Rudova, *Russian Children's Literature and Culture* (Routledge, 2008)

Balzer, Marjorie Mandelstam and Ronald Radzai, ed., *Russian Traditional Culture* (M. E. Sharpe, 1992)

Bettelheim, Bruno, *The Uses of Enchantment: The Meaning and Importance of Fairy Tales* (Random House, 1998)

Degh, Linda, *Folktales and Society* (Indiana University Press, 1969)

Emerson, Caryl, *The Cambridge Introduction to Russian Literature* (Cambridge University Press, 2008)

Haney, Jack, *An Introduction to the Russian Folktale* (M. E. Sharpe, 1999). This introduction to *The Complete Russian Folktale*, published on its own as a small paperback, is also essential reading.

Hilton, Alison, *Russian Folk Art* (Indiana University Press, 1995)

Hubbs, Joanna, *Mother Russia: The Feminine Myth in Russian Culture* (Indiana University Press, 1993)

Ivanits, Linda, *Russian Folk Belief* (M. E. Sharpe, 1992)

Johns, Andreas, *Baba Yaga: The Ambiguous Mother and Witch of the Russian Folktale* (Peter Lang, 2004)

Kononenko, Natalie, *Slavic Folklore: A Handbook* (Greenwood Press, 2007)

Lüthi, Max, *The European Folktale: Form and Nature* (Indiana University Press, 1986)

Propp, Vladimir, *Morphology of the Folktale* (University of Texas Press, 1968); *The Russian Folktale*, tr. Sibelan Forrester (Wayne State University Press, 2012); *Theory and History of Folklore* (Minneapolis: University of Minnesota Press, 1984)

Sinyavsky, Andrei, *Ivan the Fool: Russian Folk Belief*, tr. Joanne Turnbull (Glas, 2007)

Tatar, Maria, *The Annotated Classic Fairy Tales* (Norton, 2003)

von Franz, Marie-Louise, *Shadow and Evil in Fairy Tales* (Shambhala Publications, 1995)

Warner, Elizabeth, *Russian Myths* (British Museum Press, 2002)

Warner, Marina, *From the Beast to the Blonde: On Fairy Tales and Their Tellers* (Vintage, 1995)

Zipes, Jack, *The Oxford Companion to Fairy Tales* (Oxford: OUP, 2000)

3. Individual collections of folktales in Russian

Afanasyev, A. N., *Narodnye russkie skazki* (Moscow: Al'fa Kniga, 2008); *Narodnye russkie legendy* (Novosibirsk: Nauka, 1990)

Balashov, D. M., *Skazki Terskogo berega Belogo morya* (Leningrad: Nauka, 1970)

Bardin, A. V., *Fol'klor Chkalovskoy oblasti* (Chkalov, 1940)

Karnaukhova, I. V., *Skazki i predaniya severnogo kraya* (Moscow: OGI, 2009)

Khudyakov, I. A., *Velikorusskie skazki* (St Petersburg: Tropa troianova, 2001)

Onchukov, N. E., *Severnye skazki* (St Petersburg: Mir, 2008); *Zavetnye skazki* (Moscow: Ladomir, 1996)

Ozarovskaya, O. E., *Pyatirechiye* (St Petersburg: Tropa troianova, 2000)

Pomerantseva, E. V., *Russkie narodnye skazki* (Moscow: 1957)

Tumilevich, F. V., *Skazki i predaniya kazakov-nekrasovtsev* (Rostov on Don: 1958)

Zelenin, D. K., *Velikorusskiye skazki Permskoy gubernii* (St Petersburg: Russian Academy of Sciences, 1997); *Velikorusskiye skazki Vyatskoy gubernii* (St Petersburg: Tropa troianova, 2002)

4. Anthologies of folktales in Russian

Azadovsky, Mark, *Russkaya skazka: Izbrannye mastera* (Leningrad: Akademiya, 1932)

Korepova, K. E., *Russkaya volshebnaya skazka* (Moscow: Vysshaya shkola, 1992)

Kruglov, Yu. G., *Russkie narodnye skazki (Biblioteka russkogo fol'klora)* (Moscow: Sovietskaya Rossiya, 1988)

5. Books by individual writers in Russian

Bazhov, Pavel: *Malakhitovaya shkatul'ka*. Available in, literally, hundreds of editions. The collection *Ural'skie skazy i byli* (Moscow: Novy klyuch, 2009) contains valuable extracts from letters and memoirs

Platonov, Andrey: *Volshebnoye kol'tso* has been republished many times, but many editions are incomplete. All Platonov's *skazki* and other children's stories are included in *Sukhoy khleb* (vol. 6 of the *Sobraniye* published by *Vremya*, 2009–11)

Pushkin, Aleksandr: There are countless editions of his *Skazki*. Both for its illustrations (variations on Pushkin's own drawings) and for the accompanying article, I recommend Pushkin, *Skazki*, ed. V. S. Nepomnyashchy (Moscow: Planeta, 2008)

Teffi, *Sobranie sochinenii v pyati tomakh* (Moscow: Terra, 2008)

6. Scholarly books and articles in Russian

Malakhovskaya, Natalya, *Nasledie Baby Yagi* (St Petersburg: 2007)

Mikheyev, Mikhail, *V mir Platonova cherez ego yazyk* (Moscow: Izdatel'stvo Moskovskogo universiteta, 2003)

Mineyev, V. N., 'O skazkakh Andreya Platonova', in *Russkaya rech'*, no. 3 (Moscow, 2007), pp. 113–17; 'Skazka A. P. Platonova Ivan-Chudo' (unpublished); ' "Volshebnoe kol'tso" A. Platonova: Literaturnaya skazka ili kontaminatsiya', in *Znanie. Ponimanie. Umenie*, no. 2 (Moscow: 2007), pp. 112–17

Propp, V. Ya., *Fol'klor i deistvitel'nost'* (Leningrad: 1976)

Sokolov, Yury, *Russky fol'klor* (Moscow: Uchpedgiz, 1938)

7. Fiction

Dubravka Ugrešić, *Baba Yaga Laid an Egg*, tr. Ellen Elias-Bursać, Celia Hawkesworth and Mark Thompson (Canongate Books, 2010)

8. Music

Much of what passes for recordings or performances of Russian folk song is saccharine. The ensemble *Polynushka*, however, is superb. Their research is scrupulous, the singers are true musicians and their performances are full of life. See: www.proutskova.de and www.polynushka.de

Acknowledgements

Earlier versions of some of these translations were included in: Robert Chandler, *The Magic Ring* (Faber & Faber, 1979); Ivan Bilibin and Robert Chandler, *Russian Folk Tales* (Shambhala, 1980); *The Portable Platonov* (Glas, 1999); *The Redstone Diary 2010* (The Redstone Press, 2009). 'A Tale of a Fisherman and a Fish' was first published in *Cardinal Points*, nos. 12–13 (New York: Stosvet Press, 2011). 'A Tale about a Priest and his Servant Balda' was first published in *The Long Poem Magazine* (London, 2012). A longer version of the appendix by Sibelan Forrester serves as an introduction to a forthcoming collection of tales about Baba Yaga, together with a selection of the finest nineteenth- and twentieth-century illustrations: Sibelan Forrester, Helena Goscilo and Martin Skoro, *Baba Yaga: The Wild Witch of the East in Russian Folklore* (University Press of Mississippi).

Except for the two Khudyakov tales, translated by Sibelan Forrester, and the four Bazhov tales, translated by Anna Gunin, all these translations are by myself and my wife. I am, however, a firm believer in the value of collaboration and I thank all the following for their help:

Kristin Bidoshi, Sergei Bunaev, Inna Caron, Peter Carson, Olive Classe, Jane Costlow, Nina Demurova, Boris Dralyuk, Edward Dumanis, Caryl Emerson, Peter France, Rose France, Yelena Francis, Melissa Frazier, Konstantin Goloviznin, Gasan Gusejnov, Edythe Haber, Jack Haney, Jeffrey D. Holdeman, Katia Hryharuk, Alvard Jivanyan, Masha Karp, Valeria Kolosova, Natalie Kononenko, Mark Leiderman, Sophie Lubensky, Bonnie Marshall, Irina Mashinski, Nancy Mattson, Olga Meerson, Vladimir Mineyev, Yelena Minyonok, Anna Muza, Elena Ostrovskaya, Natasha Perova, Anna Pilkington, Donald Rayfield, Margo Rosen, Jeanmarie Rouhier-Willoughby, Will

Ryan, Andreas Schonle, Alexandra Smith, Lydia Strong, Faith Wigzell, Antony Wood, Aleksey Yudin, Olga Zaslavsky. I also thank my students at Queen Mary, University of London, and members of the Pushkin Club (London) and the SEELANGS email group.

Notes

PART ONE

ALEKSANDR PUSHKIN

1. J. Thomas Shaw, *The Letters of Alexander Pushkin* (Indiana University Press, 1963), vol. 1, p. 189.
2. Haney, *Intro.*, p. 27.
3. A. S. Pushkin, *Skazki*, ed. V. S. Nepomnyashchy, p. 189.
4. Nearly all these thoughts about Catherine the Great are Professor Olga Meerson's, shared with me in private correspondence.
5. A. S. Pushkin, *Polnoye sobraniye sochinenii v desyati tomakh* (Moscow: Nauka, 1964), p. 172.

A Tale about a Priest and his Servant Balda

A-T 1001; Haney 661 and Af. 151 and 152 include many of the same motifs. The tale Pushkin recorded from Arina Rodionovna contains two more episodes. In one, the priest sends Balda to fetch a bear from the forest; in the other, Balda heals a tsar's demonically possessed daughter.

Pushkin's focus on the priest's 'business dealings' with a band of devils made this poem unpublishable. Vasily Zhukovsky published a bowdlerized version in 1840, four years after Pushkin's death. Pushkin's complete text was first published in 1882.

In 1933 Mikhail Tsekhanovsky invited Dmitry Shostakovich to collaborate on a cartoon film based on this poem. The film was never completed, and the incomplete footage was lost during the Siege of Leningrad. Shostakovich did, however, create the Concert Suite 'The Priest and his Servant Balda', and, nearly seventy years later, his pupil Vadim Bibergan revised and completed the film-score version; a recording was released in 2006.

Shostakovich himself wrote, 'the screenplay . . . has succeeded in retaining satirical sharpness and the entire palette of Pushkin's brilliant tale . . . The film is sustained at the level of a folk-farce. In it there is a mass of sharp, hyperbolic situations and grotesque characters . . . The tale sparkles with fervour, lightness and cheerfulness. And to compose music for it was likewise an easy and cheerful task.' (http://www.deutschegrammophon.com/special/?ID=shostakovich-balda)

1. I have followed the many Russian illustrators who have depicted Balda as *whirling* a rope, but it is possible that Pushkin intended Balda to be twisting material together in order to *make* a rope. In Haney 661 (a version probably influenced by Pushkin's) Balda says, 'I'm weaving this rope out of sand and then I'm going to catch all the devils in the lake.' (Haney, *Complete*, vol. 7, p. 7) The lines 'where the sea, / only a moment before, / had been / flat, calm and on the level' are largely my own addition. I needed a rhyme to prepare for the devil's appearance – and the only word that came to mind was 'level'. My hope is that Pushkin would have enjoyed the irony of the devil being, as it were, summoned by the phrase 'on the level'.

2. Pushkin's final version is *Vyshiblo um u starika* ('Knocked out the old man's mind'). What I have translated here – simply because I could make it work better in English – is Pushkin's earlier, manuscript version: '*Bryznul mozg do potolka* ('His brain showered up to the ceiling').

    Afanasyev sees Balda as related to Thor and Perun (the Slavic thunder god): 'The terrible power of his fingers can be understood in relation to the mythical understanding of lightning as a divine hand, the hand with which the thunder god kills the celestial bulls and tears off their cloud-hides.' (*The Poetic Outlook of the Slavs on Nature* [Moscow: 1994], vol. 2, pp. 746–53) In the penultimate episode of the similar Af. 151, the devillet challenges Shabarsha to throw the old devil's iron club up into the clouds. The devillet then asks Shabarsha why he is waiting. Shabarsha replies, 'I'm waiting for that storm cloud to draw near – then I'll throw the club up onto it. My brother the blacksmith's sitting up there, and some more iron's just what he needs.'

A Tale about a Fisherman and a Fish

A-T 555; see also Af. 75. Pushkin follows a version recorded by the Brothers Grimm. His draft includes one more episode: tired of being a tsaritsa, the old woman becomes a 'Roman pope'.

PART TWO
THE FIRST FOLKTALE COLLECTIONS

ALEKSANDR AFANASYEV

1. Haney, *Intro.*, p. 26.
2. My knowledge of Afanasyev's life is drawn mainly from Haney, *Intro.* and from Lise Gruel-Apert's introduction to her French translation of his folktales (Afanassiev, *Contes populaires russes* [Paris: Imago, 2009]).
3. http://www.swarog-fond.ru/article/articles/afanasiev.htm

The Crane and the Heron

A-T 244A; Af. 72. Folklorists classify this not as a 'magic tale' but as an 'animal tale'. Strictly speaking, it does not belong in this collection. We have included it because it is so perfectly told, and as a reminder that the magic tale is not the only genre of folktale. The animal tale is older and at least as widespread. The Sanskrit collection of animal fables known as the *Panchatantra*, probably composed in the third century BCE, derives from far older oral traditions.

The Little Brown Cow

A-T 511 + 403; Af. 101 (Haney 290). The earliest written version of this tale-type is in the *Mahabharata*.

1. A tsar (the word is derived from 'Caesar') is the Russian equivalent of an emperor. A tsar's wife is a tsaritsa; their son is a tsarevich; their daughter is a tsarevna.
2. The name Yagishna sounds like a patronymic. This new wife may well be a daughter of Baba Yaga. See Appendix.
3. Haney makes the interesting suggestion that the wicked stepmother of so many magic tales may stand in for the mother-in-law:

> There is little doubt that well into the nineteenth century the bride's mother-in-law played a dominant and dominating role in her life. [...] the bride was expected to join her husband's mother's household. Here she would be treated as a very junior member of the kitchen staff, abused by her mother-in-law in far too many instances,

and by her sisters-in-law as well. That was not her only concern. She had constantly to be alert for the predatory advances of her father-in-law, brothers-in-law and uncles. This is attested to by many folktales and folksongs. (*Complete*, vol. 3, p. xliv)

4. Ivan is the most common Russian name and Ivan Tsarevich is the archetypal hero of Russian folktales.

Vasilisa the Fair

A-T 480B*; Af. 104; see also Haney 270. Evidently a somewhat literary version, this is one of the seven tales republished in 1899–1902 with illustrations by Ivan Bilibin.

1. A common drink, lightly alcoholic, made from old bread.

Marya Morevna

A-T 552A + 400$_1$ + 554 + 302$_2$; Af. 159 (Haney 161). Another of the tales illustrated by Bilibin.

The Little White Duck

A-T 403; Af. 265. Another tale illustrated by Bilibin; also a somewhat literary version.

1. It was believed that thieves often took the hand of a corpse with them. As they went about their business, they would touch sleeping people with it. The sleeper would then remain in a 'dead sleep'.

The Frog Princess

A-T 402 + 400$_1$; Af. 269 (Haney 221). The slightly different version illustrated by Bilibin incorporates details from Af. 267. We have included a few of these – e.g. the account of the father's reaction to the loaves and carpets brought by the elder brothers' wives. This is the only time we have combined different variants of a tale.

1. Propp writes that the frog princess

is an animal, but at her wedding she dances. We can easily recognize the ritual dance of the times of totemism. She is the creator, the designer of the forest and waters. This is a very ancient, still totemic hunting stage of the princess. It is at this stage that the world is created through dance. Later the forest and the dance will disappear. The princess becomes the giver of water, sometimes she herself is water: 'And he noticed that wherever the princess went, wherever her horses stepped, springs appeared, and [the hero] followed her by the trail of springs she had left.' (Af. 271, variant) (Propp, *Theory and History*, p. 143)

2.   These details are omitted from the version published with Bilibin's illustrations.

Pig Skin

A-T 510B; Af. 290. In a version recorded by Karnaukhova (no. 15), the daughter is scheming and seductive. It is she, not her father, who makes the advances. Having aroused her father's interest, she says she will marry him if he buys her a dress with stars on it. Then she asks for a dress with the moon on it, then for a dress with the sun on it. Having secured the dresses, she makes her escape.

The Tsarevna in an Underground Tsardom

A-T 313E; Af. 294.

The Tsarevna who would not Laugh

A-T 559; Af. 297; Haney 314. The earliest written version is in the Norse Eddas. See Introduction, p. xii.

Misery

A-T 735A; Af. 303; see also Haney 392–7.

The Wise Girl

A-T 875E; Af. 328; see also Haney 529. Marina Warner remembers Angela Carter saying that this was her favourite among all the tales she chose for her *Virago Book of Fairy Tales*. Warner goes on to say that 'Angela liked it because it was as satisfying as "The Emperor's New Clothes", but "no one was humiliated and everybody gets the prizes" [. . .] its heroine is an essential Carter figure, never abashed, nothing daunted, sharp-eared as a vixen and possessed of dry good sense. It's entirely characteristic of Angela's spirit that she should delight in the tsar's confounding, and yet not want him to be humiliated' (Introduction to Angela Carter, *The Second Virago Book of Fairy Tales* [London: Virago, 1992], p. xi).

IVAN KHUDYAKOV

1. http://www.livelib.ru/author/8576
2. *Velikorusskie skazki v zapisyakh I. A. Khudyakova* (Moscow/ Leningrad: Nauka, 1964), p. 48. Milman Parry and Albert Lord drew similar conclusions, in the twentieth century, from comparing Homeric and southern Slav epics.

The Brother

A-T 480A*; Khudyakov, *op. cit.*, no. 53 (in 2001 edition); see also Af. 103, 113.

The Stepdaughter and the Stepmother's Daughter

A-T 480; Khudyakov, *op. cit.*, no. 14; see also Af. 95–7 and 99.

PART THREE
EARLY TWENTIETH-CENTURY COLLECTIONS

1. N. E. Onchukov, *Severnye skazki*, p. 14.

The Tsar Maiden

A-T 551; *Zhivaya starina*, 1897, vii, pp. 113–20; see also Af. 171–8 (also: A-T 400$_2$ and Af. 232–3). Many versions of this have been recorded; Afanasyev includes eight under the title 'The Bold Knight, the Apples of Youth and the Water of Life'. Often the tsar's reason for sending his three sons on their quests is stated more explicitly. In Af. 171, the old, blind tsar hears of a garden with apples that restore youth and 'water of life' that restores sight; Af. 172 begins, 'Once upon a time there was a tsar with three sons. He sent out his sons to search for his youth.' The little-known version we have translated is remarkable for its inclusion both of archaic elements – e.g. the forth-right words with which Ivan Tsarevich addresses the three baba yaga figures – and of such modernisms as the offers of 'coffee and tea'.

1.   Compare:

> The folktale horse is a hybrid creature, combining a horse and a bird. He is winged. The cult role of the bird passed on to the horse when the horse was domesticated. Now it is no longer a bird that carries the souls of the dead, but a horse. But it must have wings in order to fly in the air. Along with that, its nature is fiery: smoke pours from its ears, sparks scatter from its nostrils, etc. It also reveals traits of a chthonic nature. Before it begins to serve, it is under the ground. It has a link with the world after death. There are tales in which the hero received the horse from his dead father. The horse's functions are fairly various. The first is carrying the hero through the air, over thrice-nine lands, to another kingdom. Later he helps the hero vanquish a dragon. He is wise, prescient; he is the hero's true friend and advisor. (Propp, *The Russian Folktale*, chapter 7)

2.   In a version of this tale first published by the Sokolov brothers in 1915, the image of the horse and well is treated differently. When the hero is in the maiden's chamber, the hero 'watered his horse in her well, but he did not cover up the well. He left some cloth-ing behind.' The maiden then rides after the hero, catches up with him and says, 'Please return. I am not sorry that you watered your horse. What is precious to me is that you did not cover the well' (Mark Azadovsky, *Russkaya skazka*, p. 194).

Ivan Mareson

A-T 303 and A-T 301A; *Zhivaya starina*, 1912, II–IV, pp. 357–65; republished in Azadovsky, *Russkaya skazka*, vol. 1, pp. 224–36; see also Af. 155 and Haney 158. Recorded in 1896 by A. A. Makarenko from Yefim Maksimovich Kokorin, a Siberian peasant who lived on the bank of the Angara, 750 kilometres from its confluence with the Yenisey. Makarenko describes Kokorin – 'Chima the Blind' – as

> An elderly peasant from a family who had settled there long ago. From the first years of his married life he had been entirely blind and had been supported by the labours of his wife and son. [. . .]

He was a friendly and good-natured man, and his precise ability to remember the days of the calendar was a help to the people around him. He also had a rich store of sayings, riddles, songs, folktales and rhymes with which to introduce a tale (*priskazki*). Above all, he was endowed with a vivid imagination, an ardent fantasy and an unusual fluency of speech that enabled him to carry his listeners away.

Makarenko continues:

On a little shelf nailed into the wall stood a tiny oil lamp with no glass; there was barely any flame at all from its wick. Its feeble light was almost obscured by the blue-grey waves of *makhorka* smoke, the steam from all the human bodies and the soot from the lamp itself. Adults and children alike were crowded into the little hut. Sitting there in their clothes, in the warmth given off by the iron stove, and packed closely together, they were all sweating profusely. Some had dozed off. Others were listening with avid curiosity and extraordinary attentiveness.

Makarenko goes on to praise Chima's skilful use of pauses and different tones of voice, and his fine understanding of his listeners' psychology. I would add that this tale is remarkable not only for its emotional intensity but also for its scope. Not only does Chima include vivid details from Tungus everyday life but he also evokes both a sense of horizontal space – as the characters wander through the forest – and a sense of vertical space – as the hero battles with the fiery cloud above and the serpent below.

1.   Now usually known as Evenks, the Tungus are one of the native peoples of the far north of Siberia and China.
2.   The association between snakes and lightning is almost universal; a snake is often seen as an earthly embodiment of lightning.
3.   Literally: 'our way back to the upper tail'. Some indigenous peoples of Siberia referred to the upper layer of the universe as 'the upper tail'. Though told in Russian, this *skazka* incorporates much non-Russian material.
4.   Azadovsky writes, 'Usually, in tales of this type, the wife or betrothed of the deceived and abandoned warrior gives in when threatened. [. . .] Chima completely breaks with this tradition and has his Siberian heroine remain faithful to her man, despite being brutally abused.' Azadovsky considers the final recognition

scene to be 'among the finest pages of Russian folktale poetry' (*op. cit.*, pp. 221–2).

IVAN BILIBIN

1. 'Out of Their Minds', in Patty Wageman, *Russian Legends* (Groningen: Groninger Museum, 2007), p. 45.

Ivan Tsarevich, the Grey Wolf and the Firebird

A-T 550; see also Af. 168 and Haney 305.

1. Both this version and Afanasyev's are based on an eighteenth-century chapbook. Propp considers this version exceptionally fine. But he notes that, at this point, 'The hero reasons quite rationally, not at all in fairytale style. [. . .] This tale-teller, an eighteenth-century rationalist, ascribes his own views to the hero. A true hero always takes the road to death, meets mortal danger and overcomes it. In the given case the hero is thinking of his own life.' Propp then cites another variant of the words on the pillar: "Whoever rides to the right will find happiness, whoever rides to the left will find two happinesses, but whoever rides straight ahead will find unhappiness.' The youngest brother takes the road of unhappiness – which eventually, of course, leads him to happiness. Propp sees this treatment of the motif as canonical (*The Russian Folk Tale*, chapter 3).
2. This custom is still observed at Russian weddings. The guests shout, 'Bitter!', as if complaining that the wine is too bitter. In response, the bride and groom must kiss, as if the sweetness of their kiss will sweeten the bitter wine.
3. In a version collected by Khudyakov, the firebird, dulled by the lies of Ivan's brothers, turns into a crow. But when Ivan at last returns to his father's palace, the firebird once again becomes itself.

NIKOLAY ONCHUKOV

1. N. E. Onchukov, *Severnye skazki*, p. 70.
2. N. E. Onchukov, *Zavetnye skazki*, p. 14.
3. *ibid.*, p. 31.

The Black Magician Tsar

A-T 329; Onchukov 2 (Haney 197); see also Af. 236–7. Told to Onchukov by Aleksey Chuprov, aged seventy and blind. He was equally gifted as a storyteller and as a singer of *byliny*.

1. In the original, this is a pun. The Russian *buravchik* means both 'gimlet' and 'pizzle' (the penis of a bull or boar). A boar's pizzle is threaded like a gimlet. From this comes the idea of 'screwing' a woman.
2. The Magovey bird is mysterious, though she appears in a few other magic tales and *byliny*. Often the hero has to feed her a part of his own body. There are many variants of her name.
3. According to Marie-Louise von Franz, the hero succeeds because, instead of continuing to fight Evil on its own terms, he gives himself over to the Feminine. He receives help from three feminine figures – the tsarevna, the maid and the bird. Only when he entirely abandons himself to the bird does he escape the tsar (*Shadow and Evil in Fairy Tales*, pp. 236–53).

Bronze Brow

A-T 566; Onchukov 249 (150 in first edition); Haney 325. One of seventeen stories in Onchukov's collection recorded by the schoolteacher D. Georgievsky.

OLGA OZAROVSKAYA

1. O. E. Ozarovskaya, *Pyatirechiye*, p. 6.
2. *ibid*., p. 20.

The Luck of a Tsarevna

A-T 737B*; Ozarovskaya, *Pyatirechiye*, 27 (Haney 400). Recorded in 1925 from Tatyana Osipovna Kobeleva, who was seventy years old and blind. Ozarovskaya – who knew that she too was going blind – wrote, 'I was struck by the astonishing joyfulness that emanated from everything she said, and I saw her as an instructive example, since I knew that I would have to endure a similar old age' (*op. cit*., p. 20).

1. The brackets are in the original; they indicate a comment made by the teller.

DMITRY ZELENIN

1. Viktor Berdinskikh, 'D. K. Zelenin' in *Novy Mir*, 1995, no. 3: http://magazines.russ.ru/novyi_mi/1995/3/abook01.html
   See also: http://pagan.ru/forum/index.php?showtopic=613

By the Pike's Command

A-T 675; Zelenin, *Vyat.* 23; see also Af. 165–7 and Haney 368. Most oral versions of this widespread tale are similar; even illiterate tellers were evidently influenced by the many chapbook texts. Many versions begin with the fool (usually called Yemelya) being promised fine clothes. In Zelenin, *Vyat.* 138, Yemelya's sisters-in-law bribe him to perform various necessary tasks (fetching water, gathering firewood, etc.) by promising that his father will bring him red mittens and red felt boots when he comes back from the city. In Af. 166 a similar promise makes Yemelya agree to go and see the tsar.

The editor of one of the chapbook versions (Af. 165, Haney 368), tries to excuse Yemelya's brutality: 'But he didn't know that he ought to shout out some warning so that people wouldn't be crushed by his sleigh; he rode along without shouting anything and so he crushed a whole lot of people.' In Af. 166, however, Yemelya shows no qualms at all. Seized by an angry mob as he passes through the town a second time, he just says, 'By the pike's command, by my own request, go, stick, and sort out this mob for me!'

This story was told to Zelenin by Afanasy Timofeyevich Krayev, a senile seventy-five-year-old. Zelenin writes, 'I know only that he is illiterate, a drunkard and a lazybones, that he has no trade and that he has survived in recent years almost entirely through begging.' After saying how often Krayev left out important passages or jumped from one tale to another, Zelenin expresses regret that he did not meet Krayev ten years earlier: 'Krayev is one of the very few *specialist* storytellers I met in the province of Vyatka. Storytelling is, one could say, his profession. A great lover of drink, Krayev appears at every wedding in the district. In places where he, a semi-beggar, would never normally be treated to vodka, he is given a generous liquid reward for his merry tales. [. . .] I have no doubt at all that Krayev was once the bearer of a rich and splendid storytelling tradition' (Zelenin, *Vyat.*, p. 114).

1. Zelenin recorded this tale from Krayev twice; the two versions differ, though only slightly. In both versions, Omelyanushko replies to the soldiers in rhyme. In the other version he says, 'I'm lying on the stove, I'm nibbling turds' (*'Na pechke lezhu, komy glozhu'*).

PART FOUR
NADEZHDA TEFFI

When the Crayfish Whistled: a Christmas Horror

From *Humorous Stories, Book 2* (1911).

A Little Fairy Tale

From *Lynx* (1920).

1. The forest spirit, less dangerous than the water spirit but more dangerous than the house spirit.
2. From 1917 to 1946 the Soviet agency in charge of education and cultural matters was known as *Narkompros* or The People's Commissariat of Enlightenment. A *leshy* or forest spirit is associated with darkness. His role is to confuse people and lead them astray – certainly not to enlighten them.
3. 'The Humpbacked Horse', published in 1834 by Pyotr Yershov – though possibly, in fact, written by Aleksandr Pushkin – is one of the most famous of Russian verse fairy tales. A wily but honest peasant boy captures a flying horse. In exchange for his freedom, this horse gives the boy two beautiful black horses and a little humpbacked pony. The first two horses are his to sell or give away; the little pony is to remain his companion. Throughout his subsequent adventures the boy follows this pony's advice.
4. The Council of People's Commissars was elected at the Second All-Russian Congress of Soviets in late 1917. Its role was to be responsible for the 'general administration of the affairs of the state' while the Congress of the Soviets was not in session. It soon became the highest government authority of executive power. Lenin was the Council's first Chairman.

5. Zmey Gorynych is a green dragon with three heads who appears in one of the most famous *byliny*. He walks on his two back paws, and he spits fire.

6. The original name for the Soviet security service was the 'Extraordinary Committee' or *Cherezvychainy komitet*; this was usually shortened to *Cherezvychaika* or *Cheka*. Later acronyms were the OGPU, the NKVD and the KGB. The Russian security service is currently known as the FSB.

7. A female house spirit in Slavic mythology, sometimes considered the wife of the more important male house spirit. Usually she lives behind the stove or in the cellar, though she can also be found in swamps and forests. She is notably ugly; 'to look like a kikimora' means 'to look a fright'.

Baba Yaga
(1932 picture book)

A-T 480A* + 313H. First published as a large-format illustrated children's book in 1932. Teffi follows Af. 103 (Haney 103).

The Dog

From *Witch* (1936).

1. Vanya is referring to the old Russian saying that a person in love will oversalt their dishes when cooking.

2. In the late nineteenth and early twentieth centuries Hermann Friedrich Eilers supplied flowers to the court and owned a large florists opposite the Kazan Cathedral.

3. 'The Stray Dog' was a café in Petersburg, a famous meeting place for writers and poets. Between 1911 and 1915 nearly all the main poets of the time – regardless of their political or artistic affiliations – gave readings there.

4. Mikhail Kuzmin (1872–1936), a homosexual, was known as 'the Russian Wilde'. A composer as well as a poet, he sang his own songs at 'The Stray Dog', accompanying himself on the piano. As a young man, he was a close friend of Georgy Chicherin, who later became the first Bolshevik Commissar for Foreign Affairs.

5. Oscar Wilde used to wear a green carnation in his buttonhole. Wilde owed his fame in early twentieth-century Russia mainly to his trial and imprisonment, but many of the leading poets of the

time – Konstantin Balmont, Valery Bryusov, Nikolay Gumilyov, Mikhail Kuzmin and Fyodor Sologub – translated his work.

6. 'Waves of the Danube' is a famous waltz composed in 1880 by Iosif Ivanovici, a Romanian. In the United States it has become known as 'The Anniversary Song'.

7. i.e. officers of the 'Cheka' – the first of the many titles given to the Soviet security service. See p. 452, note 6.

Baba Yaga
(1947 article)

From *Earthly Rainbow* (New York, 1952).

1. Andrey Sinyavsky has written about the place accorded to cats in folktales:

> Like the cat, the folktale is attached to home, to warmth, to the stove by which tales were usually told in the evenings. But sitting at home, the folktale gazes out at the forest, longing for faraway lands and dreaming of miracles. In this respect, the folktale resembles the cat, which, for all its domesticity, is regarded as a wild and wily breed. [. . .] The cat is a barometer, a secret guardian, a good demon, a funny and peaceable hobgoblin, without which the house is unstable and seemingly empty. In short, the cat in the folktales makes for an invisible connection between forest and stove, between foreign lands and home, between the animal and human kingdoms, demonic spells and daily life. (*Ivan the Fool*, pp. 51–2)

2. One of the ancient Slavic gods, probably a god of wind and storm.

PART FIVE
PAVEL BAZHOV

1. In his preface to a collection of Sveshnikov's drawings, the art critic Igor Golomstock writes:

> To speak of 'free creativity' in Stalin's camps may well sound like the height of irony. In fact it is an expression of the logic of the

absurd that governed the entire epoch. The camp authorities –
unlike the authorities in the world outside – had no interest in the
inner world of their wards. They looked on them as men sentenced
to death and it was of no importance whether they died in the camp
itself or whether – less probably – they were released to live out
their final days as broken men; in either case any thoughts or ideas
they might have would die with them. Sveshnikov himself looked
on the fruit of his labours as an illegitimate child, a child whose
birth had not been registered and who had no right to exist. He
drew simply because he was no more able not to draw than he was
able not to breathe or not to think. In this sense his work is an
example of a pure creativity – free from both internal and external
monitoring, without any admixture of pride, ambition, material
interest or pragmatic calculation – such as is rarely found among
people living in freedom. (Boris Sveshnikov, *The Camp Drawings*
[Moscow: Obshchestvo Memorial, 2000], p. 10)

2. Danilushko also, no doubt, represents Bazhov's son Alyosha,
    a gifted poet and musician who died in 1935, at the age of
    nineteen.
3. Mark Lipovetsky, 'Pavel Bazhov's *Skazy*', in Marina Balina and
    Larissa Rudova, *Russian Children's Literature and Culture*,
    pp. 281–2. I have drawn a great deal both on this article and on
    personal correspondence with Lipovetsky.
4. See p. 452, note 6. The date of Bazhov's summons is unclear. His
    grandson Yegor Gaidar (Russia's Acting Prime Minister during
    the second half of 1992) gives it as 1938, but all other sources
    point to 1937.

The Mistress of the Copper Mountain

First published in 1936. Bazhov's wife Valentina Aleksandrovna
(whom he married in 1911) has written, 'I remember how on the day
of our silver wedding, beneath a linden tree in our garden, Pavel
Petrovich read aloud the tale, "The Mistress of the Copper Mountain". We were the first to listen to it and evaluate it. Each new tale
was read, first of all, in the family circle' (Pavel Bazhov, *Ural'skie
skazy i byli*, p. 374).

1. By the altar in St Isaac's Cathedral, there are columns of malachite
    thirty feet high.

The Stone Flower

First published in May 1938.

1.   An important traditional midsummer holiday. It was thought
     that the eve of Ivan Kupala was the only day in the year when
     ferns bloomed.
2.   On 25 September all the snakes in a given area were thought to
     gather together in one place. Another day associated with snakes
     was 22 June; snakes held their weddings then and their poison
     was especially active.

The Mountain Master

First newspaper and journal publication in 1939, the year that also
saw the publication of the first edition of *The Malachite Casket* in
book form.

Golden Hair

First published in 1939. One of Bazhov's few tales derived from Bashkir
rather than Russian folklore. Bazhov was deeply interested in the
folklore of other nations – especially that of the Tatars, Bashkir and
Kirghiz, many of whom lived in Sverdlovsk (now Yekaterinburg) and
the surrounding area. But he himself wrote, 'I understand that, without details from everyday life, nothing comes alive – whether it is
realistic or fantastical. Somewhere, for example, I have some material
from Bashkir folklore, but I am not doing anything with it, because I
do not feel competent enough with regard to relevant details from
everyday life' (Bazhov, *op. cit.*, p. 351).

1.   It is the custom among the Bashkirs for the bridegroom to pay a
     bride price, or *kalym*, to the bride's parents.

PART SIX

FOLKTALE COLLECTIONS FROM
THE SOVIET PERIOD

1.   Felix J. Oinas, 'Folklore and Politics in the Soviet Union' (*Slavic
     Review*, vol. 32, no. 1 [March 1973], p. 47). Much of the previ-
     ous paragraph is also drawn from this article.

2.   Both Propp and Miller – the leading members of the Formalist and Finnish Schools – were called upon to renounce their previous views at a meeting of the Academy of Sciences in 1936. Members of the Historical School were called upon to recant soon afterwards. During the late 1940s, Propp and other scholars were attacked again. His *Historical Roots of the Wonder Tale*, which draws widely on Western scholarship, was compared in *Novy Mir* to the pages of a London or Berlin telephone directory.

ERNA POMERANTSEVA

The Cat with the Golden Tail

A-T 311 + 431; Pomerantseva 1957, 24 (Haney 243). Recorded in 1948, in the Bashkir Republic, from E. I. Kononova. The narrator makes occasional slips, but the verve and charm of her narration more than compensates for this. This tale is known throughout Europe, but the only similar version recorded in Russia is Zelenin, *Vyat.*, 16. In Zelenin's version the sisters find three cauldrons in the third barn. One contains boiling gold, another boiling silver and the third boiling pitch. The first two sisters each burn a finger – as the bear discovers when he asks them to check his head for lice. Starting from the bandaged finger, the bear eats the sisters. Zelenin's version ends: *Medvedya ubilo, i skazku vsyu ubilo* (literally: 'It [i.e. the falling pestle] killed the bear, and it killed the whole story too'). Given the vast distance between Vyatka and the Bashkir Republic and the apparent absence of any common written source, the similarity between the endings of the two versions is remarkable.

1.   The Russian original is a feat of virtuoso rhyming. What the bear says to himself is *'S'est' by na penyok, s'est' by pirozhok!'* (literally: 'It would be good to sit on a tree stump, it would be good to eat a little pie!').

IRINA KARNAUKHOVA

Mishka the Bear and Myshka the Mouse

A-T 480*C; Karnaukhova 27 (Haney 275). Recorded in 1926 from Pelagiya Nikiforovna Korennaya, aged sixty-four. It was in her hut that Karnaukhova and her colleagues lodged during their stay in the village. Karnaukhova describes Pelagiya as 'tall, lively and very young for her age'. She no longer worked in the fields, but she worked hard managing the household and looking after her grandsons. One of her sons was a respected village schoolteacher. She herself,

probably in part thanks to the influence of her son [. . .] has a great love of magic tales, sees herself as a custodian of them and is always glad to tell them. She is [. . .] a true mistress of her art. Her tales are vivid and poetic, and her northern speech [. . .] makes them still more expressive. Lively and merry, always occupied with her housework and obliged at the same time to entertain a child, she tells her tales without standing or sitting still for even a moment. I had to write them down while she lit the stove, got the samovar going, gutted fish, swaddled babies and was generally and indefatigably busy. Her small grandchildren were a constantly present audience. She spoke quickly, expressively and emotionally. She sometimes even acted the main figures, putting her hands to the crown of her head to imitate the movements of a hare's ears, and so on. She spoke the dialogue in different voices. Her bear talks slowly, in a deep bass voice, hesitantly. Her fox babbles away very sweetly. Her hare stammers. Although she speaks quickly, she slightly draws out the vowels and so her voice is rich, clear and, in a way of its own, singing. Her general musicality and her love of song constantly make themselves felt. She tells nearly all her tales in a strongly rhythmic language and with considerable use of rhyme. Many of her tales even include little songs. (*op. cit.*, p. 445)

Jack Frost

A-T 480; Karnaukhova 28; see also Af. 95 and 96. Another tale told by Korennaya. Around forty different Russian versions of this have been found, but it is best known in the two versions collected by Afanasyev. In Af. 95, the woman has not one but two daughters of her own. After the stepdaughter's unexpected return, she sends both her daughters out into the frost together. As they sit there, the girls quarrel: if only one bridegroom should appear, which of them will he take? The words spoken by the good daughter to Jack Frost also vary a great deal. In Af. 95, the girl politely insists that she is not feeling in the least cold, even though she is so frozen that she can barely get the words out. In Af. 96, she welcomes Jack Frost with the words, 'No doubt God has sent you to fetch my sinful soul.'

Snake-Man

A-T 425M; Karnaukhova 59; see also Haney 237. This tale was told to Karnaukhova by Nastya Gribanova, aged twelve, whose grandfather was a well-known storyteller. Karnaukhova comments on the simplicity with which Nastya tells the story, the scrupulousness with which she observes the threefold repetitions and the realism of the details. She adds that Nastya had spoken earlier about people being transformed into other beings; for Nastya, this tale confirmed that such transformations really do happen (*op. cit.*, p. 396). This tale-type has been recorded most often in the south Baltic countries. In other Russian versions, the girl lives in the lake with her snake husband and claims to have a good life there. The bird into which she is transformed is nearly always a cuckoo, but her children are transformed into different birds in different versions. Erlenvein 2 (published 1863), ends with the bereaved young wife turning her daughter into a goldcrest and her son into a nightingale. 'The Beetle-Husband from the Lake' (Balashov 42) ends with the young wife turning her daughter into a goldcrest and her son into a dove; it is because she is an eternal widow – the narrator explains – that the cuckoo is unable to build a nest of her own. Magic tales usually end with the restoration to human form of all the positive characters. This particular tale-type is unusual in that it ends tragically. Though classified as a magic tale, it should really be seen as a myth of origin. This distinction, however, was certainly not drawn by the peasants who told these tales.

1.   In the original text, the snake emerges not from a lake but from a stream. We have changed the stream to a lake because the rhyme with snake makes it possible to reproduce at least something of the laconic power of the words through which the girl summons the snake: '*Vyd', moy lyubezny, gadom, stan' parnem.*' Most other versions of the story, in any case, describe the snake as living at the bottom of a lake.

The Herder of Hares

A-T 570; Karnaukhova 75 (Haney 328). This was told by Agrafena Efimovna Chernousova, a woman of fifty-five whom Karnaukhova describes as a fine storyteller with a repertoire of at least forty tales – as well as many jokes and anecdotes. Nearly all her repertoire, however, was obscene, and Karnaukhova felt unable to record more than a fraction of it. Karnaukhova heard Chernousova tell this tale twice: 'The first time was in the company of other women of her own age. This version was very witty but impossible to reproduce in print. Then she told the story in the presence of her young niece – and this version was entirely respectable.' What Karnaukhova recorded is, of course, the second version. All we know of the first version is that the birthmark, irrelevant in the recorded version, plays a more important role in it (as in Zelenin, *Vyat.* 12 and other versions). By threatening to divulge what he has seen, the herder compels the landlord to give him his daughter in marriage.

1. Though uncommon in most of Russia, this tale-type has been recorded several times in the far north. Onchukov 103 has a witty and complex ending. The landlord tells the herder he must tell a whole sackful of stories – only when he has filled the sack will he receive his pay. The herder tells his wife and his daughters (in this version there are three daughters) to hold the sack by the corners while the landlord pushes the stories further down, to make room for more. The herder then recounts his meetings with each member of the family. One daughter after another runs out of the room, complaining that the sack is too heavy. When the herder gets to his meeting with the wife, she says, 'That's enough now – the sack's full.' But the herder continues. As he recounts his meeting with the landlord, the landlord says, 'That's enough now, that's enough now – tie up the sack!' The landlord tries to escape. Not realizing that the herder is clinging to the bottom of the carriage, he drives off with his family. At the first post station, the herder demands, and at last receives, his payment.

A Cock and Bull Story

Karnaukhova 145; A-T 1920H (also 1885, 1889K, 1889P and 1900). Both parts of this tale are common in Russia. Many of the motifs probably derive from creation myths or shamanic rituals; the hero of the inserted story appears first to climb the world tree to the upper world, then to descend to the lower world. The tale was recorded from Irinya Aleksandrovna Sharygina, who was seventy-five years old and blind. Karnaukhova writes:

She looks after her two little grandsons. [. . .] When asked to tell a tale, she refused point blank. Her daughter called me when she began telling tales to her grandson, and I was extremely careful about how I listened and noted down her tales. In spite of this, the old woman realized what we had done and she began shouting out that we had put her to shame and not pitied her in her blindness. We had to convince her that no one in the village would know what had happened. 'I must die soon, and I have been led into sin,' she kept saying.

Karnaukhova says nothing about why Sharygina might have felt so guilty and ashamed. It seems likely that she believed she had infringed one of the many taboos around the telling of tales.

Karnaukhova adds that Sharygina began telling this story after her youngest granddaughter demanded that they light the stove. Sharygina told her that they had run out of matches and then – to calm her – said, 'Sit down – and I'll tell you how well Ivan did for himself without any matches at all.' (*op. cit.*, p. 508)

1.   Compare:

> In ancient times, evidently, there existed a strict law concerning the continuity of the folktale. The language of the folktale was sacred, and to disrupt it was forbidden. In Old Russia … the narrator would warn his listeners: 'Mind you don't interrupt the tale, because if you do, a snake will take you by the throat'. […] Also significant is another old aphorism: 'A tale begins at the beginning, and is told to the end, without a break from then until then.' The custom of not interrupting the folktale goes back, of course, to those distant times when folktales were meant not only for people, but for spirits, and the telling of tales was akin to magic. […] In antiquity the process of telling a tale was connected with the movements and processes in the mystical world around man. This is why the tale had to be continuous. […] Man surrounds himself with the folktale's continuousness, as with a fence, and keeps out misfortune. […] The folktale is like a sleepwalker who is afraid of falling down and hurting himself should someone wake him at the wrong moment. The folktale seems to sense that we are not alone, that someone important is coming as the speech proceeds, going through mountains, through walls, building bridges across chasms and crossing them thanks to the thread that the storyteller is pulling and knitting – to help himself and to save us. Interrupt him and he will fall down or get stuck, and something important in our life will collapse or come undone. But let him finish and everything will come out all right. (Andrey Sinyavsky, *Ivan the Fool*, pp. 84–5 and 98)

2.   Literally: 'the size of a cubit, with a nose like a large chest.' But what matters is the rhyme: *sam s kolotok, a nos s korobok.*

A Marvellous Wonder

A-T 571; Karnaukhova 148; see also Af. 256. Karnaukhova heard this from Nikon Demyanovich Chelakov, who was fifty-one years old and whom she describes as, 'a merry fellow who liked to tell jokes and indecent stories'. She continues, 'I managed to record stories from him while he was working on the road. He stopped me as I went by. Without any preamble, leaning on his spade, he began. A crowd of peasants quickly gathered around him. They clearly expected something amusing from him and were smiling already.' Karnaukhova knows no other variant in which the goose is given this name, and she is sure it is Chelakov's invention. She adds that the image of a magic creature (in northern versions, often a silkworm) to which a whole string of people become stuck is to be found in many variants of 'The Tsarevna who would not Laugh'. See p. 70.

FYODOR TUMILEVICH

The Snake and the Fisherman

A-T 507C*; Tumilevich, 1958, no. 6 (Haney 284). 'Old Hospitality is Soon Forgotten' (Af. 27) has a similar moral.

A. V. BARDIN

1. http://kraeved.opck.org/biblioteka/enciklopedii/obe/b.php and
    http://www.nivestnik.ru/2002_1/23.shtml

The Everlasting Piece

A-T 613D*; Bardin 208 (Haney 338).

DMITRY BALASHOV

How a Man Pinched a Girl's Breast

A-T 449*B; Balashov 50 (Haney 249). Collected in 1957 from Yeliza-veta Ivanovna Sidorova, born 1887, from the coast of the White Sea. Balashov describes how he used to visit her in the day, while her son and daughter-in-law were out at work: 'After telling several tales, she would say, "Well, that's enough for today. I'm tired. Show me how much paper you've covered!" And a smile would appear on her kind, wrinkled face. "Well, come back again tomorrow. I'll remember something else for you"' (*Skazki Terskogo berega Belogo morya*, p. 13).

PART SEVEN
ANDREY PLATONOV

1. In a letter of 20 November 1947, Platonov wrote to Sholokhov, 'I have several questions for you. [. . .] One – the most important – is the matter of bringing about the publication of Russia's epos. You understand yourself how important this is. We can't get this done without you, but with your help it will be easy.' (*Strana filosofov*, vol. 5 [Moscow: IMLI RAN, 2003], p. 965)

2. Aleksey Tolstoy's versions, though competent, cannot be compared with Pushkin's or Platonov's. Platonov may have genuinely overvalued them – or he may simply have wanted to invoke a prestigious authority.

3. *Masterskaya* (Moscow: Sovetskaya Rossiya, 1977), p. 80.

4. A famous and beautifully produced émigré art periodical, published in Berlin and Paris between 1921 and 1926, was titled *The Firebird* (*Zhar-Ptitsa*). As well as stories and poems by nearly all the leading émigré writers, it included reproductions of work by – among others – Leon Bakst, Ivan Bilibin, Marc Chagall, Natalya Goncharova, Konstantin Somov and Boris Kustodyev.

Finist the Bright Falcon

A-T 432; see also Haney 244. Platonov's version – the first of his versions of Russian *skazki* – is drawn mainly from Afanasyev 234 (and 235) and from a version published in 1941 by the Voronezh storyteller Anna Korolkova.

1. This motif occurs in nearly all Russian variants of this tale. According to Propp, 'It reflects some features of the ancient funeral rite. It was supposed that the deceased would make his way on foot into the other world. Therefore he was given a staff, to lean on, sound footwear, which with the advent of the Iron Age becomes iron, and finally he would be given bread to take along.' (*The Russian Folk Tale*, chapter 3)

2.   The motif of Finist's marriage is enigmatic. After admitting to some uncertainty, Propp writes,

> In the clan system both young men and young women were supposed to have two marriages. Married life began [...] in a distant sacred place, where the girl became as it were the wife of a god. Such is the pre-form of the fairytale palace where a girl lived with a monster, a creature of divine order and a human creature at one and the same time. It is as if she receives a marriage consecration. Once she returns home, she may enter into an ongoing marriage and begin a family. But with the development of the paired family such an order collided with its interests, which allowed no form of mutual life other than the married one. So a plot arises in which the beast-husband or god-husband is not replaced by a man, but becomes one, turns into the heroine's ongoing husband. (*The Russian Folk Tale*, chapter 3)

Ivan the Giftless and Yelena the Wise

A-T 401$_1$. Af. 237 (Haney 220) was certainly one of Platonov's sources. This version ends with the maid successfully hiding Ivan *behind* the mirror. When Yelena smashes the mirror in frustration, Ivan at last appears to her.

1.   The little old man seems to be an unusual incarnation of the *leshy* or forest spirit. The *leshy* – also referred to as the *lesnoy khozyain* or 'master of the forest' – is sometimes described, as on the first page of this tale, as 'moss-covered'. He appears only seldom in oral *skazki*. Haney has suggested (personal correspondence) that this is because peasants – at least until the early twentieth century – really believed in him and that there was a taboo on pronouncing his name. With characteristic subtlety, Platonov simultaneously observes and infringes this taboo.

The Magic Ring

A-T 560; Platonov's version draws, above all, on Af. 191 (Haney 315).

1.   In Russian folk belief, Skarapeya was a snake with power over all other snakes. Her name often appears in magic spells.

2. A monstrous snake with multi-coloured wings that shone like precious stones.

Ivan the Wonder

Some motifs from this can be found in 'Ivan Medvedevich' (A-T 302C*; Korguev 14 and Haney 262) and 'Fear-Bogatyr' (A-T 510B + 315A; Haney, *Anthology*, 112); both these stories end with the hero killing, rather than forgiving, his mother. 'The Milk of Wild Beasts' (A-T 314A* + 315; Af. 201–205 and Haney 182) includes the motifs of wolf's milk, bear's milk, lion's milk and the eggs of the firebird. Af. 206, 'Feigned Illness', is probably Platonov's most important source. 'Ivan the Wonder' is the least 'magical' and most 'psychological' of Platonov's *skazki*; no traditional teller would so emphasize Ivan's emotional maturation and his eventual willingness to pardon his mother. See V. N. Mineyev's unpublished 'Skazka A. P. Platonova Ivan-Chudo'.

1. In November 1935 Stalin had declared that 'Life has become better, life has become merrier.' These words became the most important slogan of the time – repeated on banners and posters, in radio programmes and newspaper articles, and in speeches at May Day parades and other public events. Platonov's allusion to this slogan is provocative.

No-Arms

A-T 706. This tale-type is common throughout Europe, and most of the main collections of Russian folktales include a version; Afanasyev includes several (279–82). Platonov's version, however, differs so greatly from all the recorded versions that it is hard to be certain which he knew and which he did not know.

1. This detail is one of Platonov's additions.
2. The old man's death is a detail added by Platonov. And in most traditional versions the old man's wife is still alive. Platonov accentuates both the old man's loneliness and the suffering he brings upon himself by obeying what he supposes to be his son's request.
3. The image of 'the commander' is complex. There is something of Stalin in him; in some respects he seems aloof. He watches the battle 'from a distance', and he appears slow to send reinforcements to fight beside his wife and son. On the other hand,

through the commander's words about 'the people being a father to all fathers', Platonov is obliquely criticizing Stalin, who liked to speak of himself as 'the father of nations/peoples' (*otets narodov*). In a speech at a victory reception in the Kremlin on 24 May 1945, two weeks after VE Day, Stalin praised the Russian people for its 'intelligence, steadfastness and patience' and its 'trust in the Soviet government' (Edward Acton and Tom Stableford, *The Soviet Union: A Documentary History* [Exeter: University of Exeter Press, 2007], vol. 2, p. 154). The humility of Platonov's commander's 'I am less than they' is in striking contrast to this.

4. This whole section – the son going to serve as a soldier, No-Arms fighting beside him, and the final recognition scene – is Platonov's addition. Platonov's is also the only version in which the heroine's arms reappear three times; in all the traditional versions her arms reappear only once, in order to save her son from the well, and then remain with her. The twin themes of mutilation and orphanhood are central throughout Platonov's work. Only in 'No-Arms', however, is a crippled hero or heroine restored to wholeness.

5. In most versions it is only the wife who is put to death. Onchukov's 'The Nine Brothers' is probably the only version in which the brother dies too. There are no versions, other than Platonov's, in which the brother first confesses, then dies at his own hand (Mikhail Mikheyev, *V mir Platonova cherez ego yazyk*, p. 353).

Wool over the Eyes

A-T 664B. Platonov's version follows Af. 375–7.

APPENDIX

Baba Yaga: The Wild Witch of the East

1. Hubbs, *Mother Russia*, p. 46.
2. The length of the Russian term for a female cousin, *Dvoyurodnaya sestra*, encourages speakers to abbreviate it to its second half, *sestra*, which means just 'sister'. Sometimes it is hard to know whether a Russian is referring to a sibling or to a cousin.

PENGUIN CLASSICS

THE HOUSE OF THE DEAD
FYODOR DOSTOYEVSKY

'Here was the house of the living dead, a life like none other upon earth'

In January 1850 Dostoyevsky was sent to a remote Siberian prison camp for his part in a political conspiracy. The four years he spent there, startlingly re-created in *The House of the Dead*, were the most agonizing of his life. In this fictionalized account he recounts his soul-destroying incarceration through the cool, detached tones of his narrator, Aleksandr Petrovich Goryanchikov: the daily battle for survival, the wooden plank beds, the cabbage soup swimming with cockroaches, his strange 'family' of boastful, ugly, cruel convicts. Yet *The House of the Dead* is far more than a work of documentary realism: it is also a powerful novel of redemption, describing one man's spiritual and moral death and the miracle of his gradual reawakening.

This edition includes an introduction and notes by David McDuff discussing the circumstances of Dostoyevsky's imprisonment, the origins of the novel in his prison writings and the character of Aleksandr Petrovich.

Translated with an introduction and notes by David McDuff

PENGUIN CLASSICS

THE IDIOT
FYODOR DOSTOYEVSKY

> 'He's simple-minded, but he has all his wits about him,
> in the most noble sense of the word, of course'

Returning to St Petersburg from a Swiss sanatorium, the gentle and naive Prince
Myshkin – known as 'the idiot' – pays a visit to his distant relative General
Yepanchin and proceeds to charm the General, his wife and his three daughters.
But his life is thrown into turmoil when he chances on a photograph of the
beautiful Nastasya Filippovna. Utterly infatuated with her, he soon finds himself
caught up in a love triangle and drawn into a web of blackmail, betrayal and,
finally, murder. In Prince Myshkin, Dosteyevsky set out to portray the purity of 'a
truly beautiful soul' and to explore the perils that innocence and goodness face in a
corrupt world.

David McDuff's major new translation brilliantly captures the novel's idiosyncratic
and dream-like language and the nervous, elliptic flow of the narrative. This
edition also includes an introduction by William Mills Todd III, further reading,
a chronology of Dostoyevsky's life and work, a note on the translation and
explanatory notes.

Translated by David McDuff with an introduction by William Mills Todd III

PENGUIN CLASSICS

NOTES FROM UNDERGROUND *AND* **THE DOUBLE**
FYODOR DOSTOYEVSKY

> 'It is best to do nothing! The best thing is conscious inertia!
> So long live the underground!'

Alienated from society and paralysed by a sense of his own insignificance, the anonymous narrator of Dostoyevsky's groundbreaking *Notes from Underground* tells the story of his tortured life. With bitter sarcasm, he describes his refusal to become a worker in the 'ant-hill' of society and his gradual withdrawal to an existence 'underground'. The seemingly ordinary world of St Petersburg takes on a nightmarish quality in *The Double* when a government clerk encounters a man who exactly resembles him – his double perhaps, or possibly the darker side of his own personality. Like *Notes from Underground*, this is a masterly study of human consciousness.

Jessie Coulson's introduction discusses the critical reception of the stories and the themes they share with Dostoyevksy's great novels.

'*Notes from Underground*, with its mood of intellectual irony and alienation, can be seen as the first modern novel … That sense of the meaningless of existence that runs through much of twentieth-century writing – from Conrad and Kafka, to Beckett and beyond – starts in Dostoyevsky's work' Malcolm Bradbury

Translated with an introduction by Jessie Coulson

PENGUIN CLASSICS

DEAD SOULS
NIKOLAI GOGOL

> 'It's not a question of the living. I've nothing to do with them.
> I'm asking for the dead'

Chichikov, a mysterious stranger, arrives in the provincial town of 'N', visiting a succession of landowners and making each a strange offer. He proposes to buy the names of dead serfs still registered on the census, saving their owners from paying tax on them, and to use these 'souls' as collateral to re-invent himself as a gentleman. In this ebullient masterpiece, Gogol created a grotesque gallery of human types, from the bear-like Sobakevich to the insubstantial fool Manilov, and, above all, the devilish conman Chichikov. *Dead Souls*, Russia's first major novel, is one of the most unusual works of nineteenth-century fiction and a devastating satire on social hypocrisy.

David Magarshack's introduction discusses Gogol's plan for a novel in three parts, tracing Chichikov's progress from sin to redemption, and tells how Gogol destroyed part of the manuscript in the grip of madness. The surviving sections, volume one and a fragment of volume two, are translated here.

'Gogol was a strange creature, but then genius is always strange'
Vladimir Nabokov

Translated with an introduction by David Magarshack

PENGUIN CLASSICS

THE DEATH OF IVAN ILYICH AND OTHER STORIES
LEO TOLSTOY

> 'Every moment he felt that ... he was drawing nearer and nearer
> to what terrified him'

Three of Tolstoy's most powerful and moving shorter works are brought together in this volume. *The Death of Ivan Ilyich* is a masterly meditation on life and death, recounting the physical decline and spiritual awakening of a worldly, successful man who is faced with his own mortality. Only in his last agonizing moments does Ivan Ilyich finally confront his true nature, and gain the forgiveness of his wife and son for his cruelty towards them. *Happy Ever After*, inspired by one of Tolstoy's own romantic entanglements, tells the story of a seventeen-year-old girl who marries her guardian twice her age. And *The Cossacks*, the tale of a disenchanted young nobleman who seeks fulfilment amid the wild beauty of the Caucasus, was hailed by Turgenev as the 'finest and most perfect production of Russian literature'.

Rosemary Edmonds's classic translation fully captures the subtle nuances of Tolstoy's writing, and includes an introduction discussing the influences of the stories and contemporary reactions towards them.

Translated with an introduction by Rosemary Edmonds

PENGUIN CLASSICS

FAIRY TALES
HANS CHRISTIAN ANDERSEN

Blending Danish folklore with magical storytelling, Hans Christian Andersen's unique fairy tales describe a world of beautiful princesses and sinister queens, rewarded virtue and unresolved desire. Rich with popular tales such as *The Ugly Duckling*, *The Emperor's New Clothes* and the darkly enchanting *The Snow Queen*, this revelatory new collection also contains many lesser-known but intriguing stories, such as the sinister *The Shadow*, in which a shadow slyly takes over the life of the man to whom it is bound.

'Truly scrumptious, a proper treasury ... Read on with eyes as big as teacups'
Guardian

'With J. K. Rowling and Lemony Snicket bringing black magic to the top of today's children's literature, the moment seems ripe for a return to the original'
Newsweek

'Tiina Nunnally's wonderful new translations of Andersen are an invitation to open-ended, mind-engaging reading' Rachel Cusk

Translated by Tiina Nunnally

Edited by Jackie Wullschlager

THE STORY OF PENGUIN CLASSICS

Before 1946 ... 'Classics' are mainly the domain of academics and students; readable editions for everyone else are almost unheard of. This all changes when a little-known classicist, E. V. Rieu, presents Penguin founder Allen Lane with the translation of Homer's *Odyssey* that he has been working on in his spare time.

1946 Penguin Classics debuts with *The Odyssey*, which promptly sells three million copies. Suddenly, classics are no longer for the privileged few.

1950s Rieu, now series editor, turns to professional writers for the best modern, readable translations, including Dorothy L. Sayers's *Inferno* and Robert Graves's unexpurgated *Twelve Caesars*.

1960s The Classics are given the distinctive black covers that have remained a constant throughout the life of the series. Rieu retires in 1964, hailing the Penguin Classics list as 'the greatest educative force of the twentieth century.'

1970s A new generation of translators swells the Penguin Classics ranks, introducing readers of English to classics of world literature from more than twenty languages. The list grows to encompass more history, philosophy, science, religion and politics.

1980s The Penguin American Library launches with titles such as *Uncle Tom's Cabin*, and joins forces with Penguin Classics to provide the most comprehensive library of world literature available from any paperback publisher.

1990s The launch of Penguin Audiobooks brings the classics to a listening audience for the first time, and in 1999 the worldwide launch of the Penguin Classics website extends their reach to the global online community.

The 21st Century Penguin Classics are completely redesigned for the first time in nearly twenty years. This world-famous series now consists of more than 1300 titles, making the widest range of the best books ever written available to millions – and constantly redefining what makes a 'classic'.

The Odyssey continues ...

The best books ever written

P E N G U I N 🐧 C L A S S I C S

SINCE 1946

Find out more at www.penguinclassics.com